Praise for the novels of Joey W. Hill

"Sweet yet erotic . . . will linger in your heart long after the story is over."
—*Sensual Romance*

"One of the finest, most erotic love stories I've ever read. Reading this book was a physical experience because it pushes through every other plane until you feel it in your marrow."
—Shelby Reed, author of *Seraphim*

"The perfect blend of suspense and romance." —*The Road to Romance*

"Wonderful . . . The sex is hot, very HOT, [and] more than a little kinky . . . erotic romance that touches the heart and mind as well as the libido."
—*Scribes World*

"A beautifully told story of true love, magic and strength . . . a wondrous tale . . . a must-read."
—*Romance Junkies*

"A passionate, poignant tale . . . The sex was emotional and charged with meaning . . . yet another must-read story from the ever-talented Joey Hill."
—*Just Erotic Romance Reviews*

"This is not only a keeper, but one you will want to run out and tell your friends about."
—*Fallen Angel Reviews*

"Not for the closed minded. And it's definitely not for those who like their erotica soft."
—*A Romance Review*

"All the right touches of emotion, sex and a wonderful plot that you would usually find in a much longer tale." —*Romance Reviews Today*

Berkley Heat titles by Joey W. Hill

THE VAMPIRE QUEEN'S SERVANT
THE MARK OF THE VAMPIRE QUEEN

THE
MARK OF THE
VAMPIRE QUEEN

Joey W. Hill

HEAT
New York

THE BERKLEY PUBLISHING GROUP
Published by the Penguin Group
Penguin Group (USA) Inc.
375 Hudson Street, New York, New York 10014, USA
Penguin Group (Canada), 90 Eglinton Avenue East, Suite 700, Toronto, Ontario M4P 2Y3, Canada
(a division of Pearson Penguin Canada Inc.)
Penguin Books Ltd., 80 Strand, London WC2R 0RL, England
Penguin Group Ireland, 25 St. Stephen's Green, Dublin 2, Ireland (a division of Penguin Books Ltd.)
Penguin Group (Australia), 250 Camberwell Road, Camberwell, Victoria 3124, Australia
(a division of Pearson Australia Group Pty. Ltd.)
Penguin Books India Pvt. Ltd., 11 Community Centre, Panchsheel Park, New Delhi—110 017, India
Penguin Group (NZ), 67 Apollo Drive, Rosedale, North Shore 0632, New Zealand
(a division of Pearson New Zealand Ltd.)
Penguin Books (South Africa) (Pty.) Ltd., 24 Sturdee Avenue, Rosebank, Johannesburg 2196,
South Africa

Penguin Books Ltd., Registered Offices: 80 Strand, London WC2R 0RL, England

This is an original publication of The Berkley Publishing Group.

This is a work of fiction. Names, characters, places, and incidents either are the product of the author's imagination or are used fictitiously, and any resemblance to actual persons, living or dead, business establishments, events, or locales is entirely coincidental. The publisher does not have any control over and does not assume any responsibility for author or third-party websites or their content.

First edition: February 2008

Library of Congress Cataloging-in-Publication Data

Hill, Joey W.
    The mark of the vampire queen / Joey W. Hill.—1st ed.
        p. cm.
    ISBN-13: 978-0-425-21932-4
    1. Vampires—Fiction. I. Title.
    PS3608.I4343M37   2008
    813'.54—dc22
                                            2007043401

PRINTED IN THE UNITED STATES OF AMERICA

10   9   8   7   6   5   4   3   2   1

Acknowledgments

An author never gets to this point without tremendous help and enormous luck, so I would be remiss if I didn't offer thanks from the depths of my humble soul to all of you with whom I've had the pleasure and pain of sharing this journey: readers, critique partners, fellow authors, reviewers, editors, my agent, family, friends, the Muse and the publishers—current and past, large and small—who've given me a shot . . .

Thank you for helping me, guiding me, believing in me and having patience with me. My growth as an author will always be built on the foundation of your support—any stumbles will be from my own shortcomings.

In two previous lifetimes, Jacob has served you. Once as the samurai warrior who guarded you as a child. Once as the knight who saved your caravan from vampire hunter attack during the Crusades. Despite the fact it happened centuries ago and he was only with you a short time, you always remembered him so vividly . . .

I believe Jacob comes to you only when your life is truly, genuinely in danger.

—Brother Thomas, former human servant to Lady Lyssa, Vampire Queen of the Far East Clan

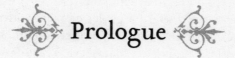

Prologue

Centuries Ago . . .

THE vampire hunters had been swift, their numbers considerable. Despite their foolish decision to launch their attack just before dusk, their commitment had bordered on fanatical, making them dangerous. The day might not have gone in Lady Lyssa's favor, but a knight had charged out of the golden desert sands still shimmering with the day's heat, his bloodcurdling battle cry reminding her of the wildness of the Irish moors. When the clash of weapons and the spilling of blood were over, he'd turned the tide against the attack.

"I wish to thank him," she commanded her retainers. "Bring him to me."

They'd obeyed her quickly, as they always did. The knight hadn't seen her at first when the lackey guided him just inside the flap of her tent. The first notes of his voice had curled pleasantly in her stomach like warm blood.

"I am not presentable for your Mistress. I should prepare myself first."

"But I desire the audience now."

He turned as she materialized out of the shadows. The servant retreated. She noted that the knight's tunic and mail still bore the blood of those he'd vanquished. So did the gauntlets he pulled off to reveal callused, capable hands. Sweat had dampened the hair on his head, but there were hints of true red in the brown. When he found her, those blue, blue eyes and the pale lashes with the same hint of auburn on the tips gave her steps a pause. The power of his gaze washed over her like a familiar embrace.

She'd thought she'd share a goblet of wine with him. Perhaps even hypnotize him into being her dinner tonight and then send him to a bed with several of her maidservants to reward him for his trouble on her behalf. Only two hundred years old, she nevertheless wasn't impetuous. But the idea of dismissing him melted away as she sent a mental compulsion to her staff to bring the precious bathwater to her tent instead of setting up a guest quarters.

He bowed. "My lady."

"Sir Knight." Composure reclaimed, she stepped to the carafe of wine and began to pour her best vintage into a goblet. "I find myself in your debt."

"The chance to rescue a lady of such fair countenance suggests just the opposite."

She turned, raised a brow. "A deft tongue. Far more appealing than my countenance." Particularly if he was equally deft with it in other ways.

Her gaze lingered, apparently communicating her thought well enough that the first hint of desire rose in his eyes. However, something else was in his expression as well. Speculative awareness.

"It was an odd attack, my lady. These men seemed to be seeking your death specifically. Not a ransom."

"Men fear what they do not understand." She finished pouring the wine. "I have enemies. That is my business, not yours. I'm simply grateful you were willing to put your sword into my service."

"Mmm." As he made the noncommittal noise, she offered the goblet, cupping the bowl with both hands. When he reached for it, she didn't relinquish it. He studied her, then put his hands over hers, lifting the goblet to his lips, allowing her to move two steps closer, the tips of her slippers just inside the span of his boots. As he drank deeply, she watched his throat work. He was not mannerless. While he thirsted, he showed restraint. He didn't spill it on himself or the rug beneath his feet. She almost wished for one red rivulet to run from the corner of his mouth down the side of his throat to give the lust in her belly more to stir it. Though in truth, watching him drink seemed to be enough. He paused, pressing his moistened lips together, distracting her.

"When the battle was over, I'd killed many. But not as many as were lying on the ground."

"My servants are not untrained," she said, wondering how he would taste if she lifted on her toes and pressed her lips over his wine-stained ones. "While they are not all warriors, I would have been ashamed if they hadn't been some assistance to you."

"They were. With pike and sword. Even your cook wields a pot well." A light smile touched his firm mouth, but didn't reach his eyes. "As stout of heart as they all were, I didn't see any of them who looked strong enough to break the neck of a full-grown warrior, or snap his back like a rotted branch."

When he lowered the goblet, she was aware his grip had tightened perceptibly on her hands, keeping them overlaid with his own. "One man . . . I pulled my sword out of his gut just as his comrade came upon my back. He would have run me through; I've no doubt of it. There was a wind like a passing spirit, on what has been a cursedly breezeless dusk. I felt a softness, much like the brush of a maiden's hair on my face." His gaze traveled to her raven tresses, tied loosely back on her shoulders with a twisted trio of ribbons. "The man spun away from me, so violently his feet left the ground. When he landed, his back was broken, his head wrenched back."

"I think you have been out in the sun far too long, Sir Knight."

"Perhaps you've never been in the sun at all, my lady. Your skin, like the palest cream," he murmured. "What manner of creature are you? Should I fear you as well?"

He looked more curious than apprehensive. Almost . . . amused. Disturbed, she drew her hands from beneath his and stepped away, reclaiming her haughty reserve. "*Do* you fear me?"

Her retainers slipped in, bearing a washtub and full water buckets.

Rather than answering, he noted them, his brow raised. "You are preparing to bathe, my lady. I should leave you your privacy."

"I am preparing to bathe *you*, Sir Knight." At his surprised look, she tilted her head. "A traditional courtesy, is it not? The lady of the house attending to her guest's bath?"

She saw the significance of that flash through his expression and wondered if he could imagine it in as great detail as she could. His muscular, naked body glistening with water, the beads of it tempting her to suck on his tanned, sun-soaked skin. He shifted, swallowing.

"My lady . . ."

"Do you intend to insult my hospitality, Sir Knight?"

She could almost hear the snick of the trap, and from the charming amusement in his gaze, she knew he could as well. "No, my lady."

"Then please remove your weapons and clothing and I will have my servants see to their cleaning."

That gave him pause for different reasons. She stepped toward him. "You may certainly keep the weapons with you here, if it reassures you. Or perhaps it's just that you've been wearing them for so long you've forgotten how to remove them."

Another step, and she was right in front of him again. The way those piercing blue eyes seemed to be contemplating her mystery roused things in her. It seemed as if he understood her fully, even as she played with him in this way. She reached out and fingered the trailing end of his sword belt, beginning to work it out of its loop, very conscious of what other delights waited under the skirt of the tunic.

While he didn't move, his expression maintained an intriguing blend of curiosity, desire warring with caution. He was obviously no fool.

Since he held the goblet, only one hand was free, but she suspected he was capable of putting up a good defense to stop her if he wished to do so. When she freed the weapon, she stepped closer to pull the belt away and bring it around to one hand, letting the tunic fall loose at his waist. She handed the sword, dagger and belt to a retainer. "Please see that the blade is properly cleaned and sharpened, and the scabbard well-oiled."

Heaven knew, her scabbard was getting well-oiled, just from this brief touch. He stank of blood and sweat, the heavy musk of days of travel, and yet she wanted nothing more than to be the hands that scrubbed all that off his skin, as if unwrapping a gift for herself.

She took the goblet from his hands then. "If you'll remove the rest and step into the tub, we shall attend to your bath."

Making herself turn away and cross the tent, she heard him shift, rustle, telling her he was removing the tunic and undergarments, untying the mail and handing it to the outstretched hands of her servants. She wondered at his willingness to give up his weapons, but then she realized the tent was well decorated with her own armaments. He could outfit himself if needed, and if she was telling the truth, she was saving him the time of preparing his weapons for his next battle. Even so, she suspected he was not a man who easily trusted another to do that, and that uncomfortably suggested he might be feeling some of the same strong pull toward her she was feeling toward him.

Setting aside the goblet, she heard him step into the tub and her servants quietly depart, leaving her alone with her prey. Her dinner. Her pleasure. She turned.

Holy God . . . And she meant it in the most reverent sense.

Even crusted with blood and grime, it was obvious his body was God's creation. Muscled haunches, broad back, long arms, wide chest and a cock already semierect, giving her a mouthwatering idea of its size and thickness when fully aroused. It had already lengthened at her regard, even as he obviously tried to look anywhere but at her. Perhaps he was thinking he shouldn't presume she was trying to seduce him, since she'd yet to make any direct overtures that way. But oh, that was fully her intent. She was hungry on two very vital levels.

She'd sent her marked human servant ahead to make arrangements for their stay, but there was something about this man that told her even if she'd had a meal readily at her fingertips she'd have sent it from her presence in favor of this one. She wanted to bid him stand still as she poured the water over him, watch it sluice over hard muscle, taking away the dust and making his skin gleam in the candlelight.

As she approached, she cast her eyes down, ostensibly a modest maiden, but really to get a better view of that impressive organ. Despite his best efforts to be chivalrous it was still rising, particularly when she took her time raising her gaze, letting it linger on all the terrain from thigh to throat. She was close enough to reach out to graze his flat abdomen with her fingers and she did, her nails scraping him.

"My lady." He caught her wrists. She was surprised to look up into a face that, while avid with a man's desire, was also filled with male laughter. "You are teasing me."

She smiled. "I am. I find myself ravenous, my knight. As you have suggested, my hungers are rather unusual. I wouldn't presume upon you to fill those hungers, because you have saved my life and the lives of many of my people tonight. But I admit I tend to be a selfish creature."

Studying her, he lifted a hand to cup her face. The sheer impact of that touch made her go still. Her eyes closed of their own accord, her mind wondering at her trembling response as he stroked along her temple. When his thumb passed over her lips, she drew it into her mouth and bit.

He started a little, but didn't draw back. She wasn't using any compulsion at all, and yet she felt him just watching her curiously, tightening his grasp on her other wrist.

"My mind tells me what you are," he whispered. "It tells me I should have helped them end you. But my heart tells me I would give the last drop of my blood to protect you. Is it a spell? Are you using your beauty to cloud my eyes to truth?"

She kept her gaze lowered, lashes fanning her cheeks, and sampled his blood. Finding it to her liking, she drew his thumb in farther, licking the welling drops away, suckling at him in a manner suggesting how she would like to suckle other parts of him. She heard him mutter a curse. When her eyes rose at last, he was still watching her draw the tiny trickle of sustenance from him. After she let him go, he looked at his thumb, bemused, before lowering the hand to her hip, drawing her closer to him, her shins pressing against the edge of the standing tub.

"You are a mystery, my lady. I ask myself why I'm not running from the temptation of you, so great that fighting in a dozen Crusades wouldn't eradicate the sin from my soul."

"You never answered my question. Do you fear me, Sir Knight?"

He smiled, and this time the response reached his eyes, lighting them like sapphires in the firelight. It astonished her. He sensed what she might be, and yet he truly did not fear her.

"I will die in these lands, but not by your fair hand. Though I think it would be a far better death to die with my head in your lap."

It cast a shadow over the moment. Imagining such a thing bothered her more than it should for this man she'd just met. "I forbid you to speak of such nonsense. We'll wash such thoughts away."

When she bent to pick up the first bucket, he touched her elbow, stopping her. "That's far too heavy, my lady. Please, let me."

She could lift him on the flat of her palm, but the gesture sent a wave of pleasure through her. He tipped the bucket over himself, wetting his hair and letting the flow run over his body, though sparingly. Enough to dampen him, but not wasting anything. A man who'd obviously been in the desert lands awhile, if the bronzed cast of his face hadn't told her that already.

When he set the bucket down and straightened to use the sponge to spread the water over himself for the soap, it was she who stopped him. Instead of allowing him to slick back his wet hair from his head, she did it for him. Rising on her toes, she let her fingertips follow the lines of his eyelids, feathering over his lashes to collect the water so he could open his eyes again. When she drew her hands back, her thumbs caressed his lips, his throat. His clear blue eyes stared at her now, an obvious struggle going on in their depths.

"My lady . . . I . . . You know you owe me nothing, yes? I demand nothing from you, even your hospitality."

"Deny hospitality to a traveler in the desert? Something rarely done to a mortal enemy, let alone a person who saved my retainers' lives and possibly my own?"

"It was a service I'd gladly perform a hundred times, so your beauty would grace the world another day."

"Or night," she murmured.

"A lady such as you," he continued doggedly, "surely has a husband waiting. I'll not bring dishonor to you. You owe me nothing."

She had to bite back a smile at his persistence, even as she felt his heat rising at her sultry teasing. "I do not have a husband, Sir Knight. I am a very wealthy, very independent creature and I do as I please. Right now, bathing you is what pleases me." She bade him turn then with her lathered hands. "If I wish to compensate you for your time, that's my business and none of yours. You may find I've asked far too much of you as it is."

She ran the soap across the wide, muscular area between his shoulders. She wished she was home where she could have bathed him in a tub large enough for them both, but that was a pointless wish since he hardly would have been called to rescue her in her fortress. Flattening her hands on the small of his back, she fanned out her fingers and ran them over the curves of his buttocks, making sure she dipped in between, rubbing him intimately and lower.

"Be still," she said quietly as he started. "Or I'll restrain you with ribbons from my hair to allow me time to please myself." Her touch moved between his parted muscular thighs and gripped his testicles, lathering the heavy sac, and then down the length of the leg to where it met the water just below his knee. She did it to the other leg, taking another opportunity to fondle his balls, tease the crease of his backside.

"Turn." When he did, she dwelled appreciatively on his erect member before she began to lather it as well. He rocked toward her, closing his eyes, but he clenched his hands at his sides and did not touch her as she ran her hands up his belly, over his nipples and back to his neck.

"You show restraint, Sir Knight. I like that. Your cock says it wants me, but your mind stays in control of your lust."

"My lady has not indicated whether she wants me to touch her." He opened eyes of blue fire, like the flames that licked through her blood at his words.

But she merely nodded to the next bucket. He raised it to rinse himself and she helped, spreading the flow of water over him, running her hands back through those delicious crevices under his genitals and between his buttocks, bringing herself close enough that the water splashed down her arms and wet her front before she withdrew enough to fan her hands across his chest.

Though she knew his desire was high, it had become a game by his own unintentional voicing of it. He would not touch her until she commanded it, and she would delight in teasing him to raging before she gave him that command. But beneath his lust there was something else, in the way he watched her, something that kept her alert to the shifts in his mood, as well as to her own unusually strong reaction to him.

"You're a sorceress," he said huskily. "A beautiful sorceress, determined to lead me to damnation."

She didn't respond to that, just moved close enough to step into the tub, her wet feet on top of his, her dress floating in the small space of the basin. As she lifted up on her toes to reach his lips, his hands circled her waist, her clad body against his naked, aroused one, his cock pushing into her belly and lower as he raised her. His wet hair tangled in her fingers as she let her lust rise as well. Her grip tightened on the edge of bruising, her breath in the kiss becoming a low growl.

"Like a lion cub," he whispered against her. He surprised her by lifting her in his arms. Stepping out of the tub, he took her to the tumble of cushions that was her bed. He squatted beside her, casually immodest as a soldier was. As she lay back, she watched him toy with the front lacing of the corset she wore over her dress. His jaw was set in an attractive line, rigid with desire like the rest of him. Every muscle hard, his erection damp with viscous fluid at the tip.

"It has been a while, my lady. I wish to be gentle."

"Don't be. I will not be gentle with you. I promise I will make you serve me over and over tonight, drain you well before dawn." Because she could resist no longer, she grasped his cock, hot steel covered in silk, the pulse of it seeming to match the pulse in her womb.

He exhaled sharply at her touch, his hand gripping the pillow by her head as she stroked him, her nail scraping the underside, her fingertips teasing his balls. Gods, but he was a finely equipped man.

His hand moved to her thigh, and he began to raise her skirt, gathering it slowly, gauging whether she was pleased or not. The touch of his fingers through the fabric burned. She wanted his hands fully on her. When the skirt was bunched under his large palms and he let his fingertips graze her thigh, she arched up as if he'd slid into her. His expression became more intent, and his attention shifted down to the slick lips of her cunt, already glistening for him.

She didn't want to be patient. Restless and almost on the verge of anger, she abruptly wanted to attack him for the way he made her feel. Longing for things . . . for this mere human.

She levered herself up and had him on his back before he could resist, though she noted he caught her arm a split second before she did it, as if anticipating her move, even if he couldn't counter her strength or see the speed of her movements. She straddled him on the floor of the tent, hands pinioning his wrists, her thighs gripping his torso securely and toes planted inside his knees, locking his legs down. However, her skirt was caught between them, denying her the full contact of his cock against the aching emptiness between her legs.

"So you still do not fear me?"

He put some serious effort into lifting his arms, subsiding a few moments later as she gazed down at him, expressionless. Except when she curled back her lip to let him see her fangs elongating.

His eyes widened, but then he shifted to her face, studied something there she suspected was different from what she intended him to see.

"No, my lady," he said at last. "But I sense there is something you fear about me. Let my hands go, lass. Let me touch you and give you pleasure. I won't abuse your trust." His voice became thicker, deeper. "You're wet enough to slide right on my shaft, and I'm sizeable enough to take you deep and hard. Just let me take you."

Who was seducing whom?

She released him but rose. With a short gesture, she bid him stay still as she crossed the tent. He rose up on his elbows as she refilled and retrieved the wine goblet. When she came back she moved over his body, straddling his thighs, sitting on his knees so she had an un-impeded view of his aroused member. Lifting the goblet, she tilted it over him, watched the stream of crimson fluid run along the length of him. His stomach tightened at the stimulation, a pleasurable response, but her eyes lingered on the trail of wine covering him.

She bent, her breath hovering over him, and licked delicately at the underside, the broad head of his cock. His hands fisted in the pil-lows on either side of him, giving her delicious visions of what it would be like to restrain and torment him like this for hours. Slowly she covered him with her mouth and went all the way down, taking the taste of his skin and seed with the fermented grape. She savored it, sucking on him as his thighs trembled, a powerful man restrain-ing himself to let her have her pleasure. Little did he know that if she desired it, he would have no choice. But she'd always preferred sub-mission like this, a willing choice in the end, though she couldn't deny the predator in her was equally provoked by the fight up to that point.

Releasing him, she raised the goblet again, trailing wine up his belly. Lapping it from his navel, she rubbed her breasts against his arousal. Spilled wine over his chest, over his throat. Licked at his nip-ples as he jerked in response. There she paused, inhaling him. She'd been tempted by the thigh, but somehow for this man, the throat, the flood of life pounding hard behind it like a waterfall, was more than she could resist.

He knocked the goblet from her hand and seized her by the waist, dragging her up his body with sheer animal strength. His ur-gency had a gentle power to it she found difficult to resist. When he touched his lips to the cleft of her breasts rising over the top of her neckline, the barest press of his mouth sent a shudder through her.

She watched, paralyzed by her own desire, as he opened the cor-set, untied the neckline of her dress and cupped her bare breasts in either hand. Sitting up with a ripple of stomach muscles to hold her straddled on his lap, he teased her with his cock, rubbing the cleft of her buttocks with the skirt in between while he captured a nipple, began to suckle.

"Oh . . . oh." Her body was moving of its own accord, grinding urgently against him, but he was of a mind to take his time, God bless him. Suckling with soft, moist noises. Something she would have thought coarse, but the sound of it made her hips move in sensual undulations, straining for more of the feel of that organ trapped behind her.

"What is it you want, my lady?" He said it against her flesh, his tongue stroking, curling. Her hand caught in his damp hair, found his nape. "Tell this knight what he must do to serve you best."

"Your cock," she whispered. "Inside me. I want to feel . . ." *Taken. Immersed. Impaled.*

He moved her skirt out of the way and obeyed, bringing himself into line with her, lifting her and then lowering her slowly, slowly onto him as she cried out with the stretching pleasure of it, the fiery sensation it burned to the core of her.

It had been far too long since she'd indulged herself in the pleasure of a man's body. A body like this. A man like this.

She grasped his jaw as he anchored her on him with his hands gripping her hips, fingers pressing into her buttocks. She didn't pause or ask permission. He was hers. She would do as she liked, not questioning why the need was so savage with this human who should be just a pleasant diversion. Dinner.

When she sank her fangs into his neck, he pushed her down even harder, growling as his hips jerked, pumped into her. She drew his essence into herself, the swirl of his blood on her tongue, a nourishment unlike anything she'd tasted before.

Except once . . . her samurai guard.

The memory interjected itself unbidden into this moment. Her stepfather, her mother's servant, had Lyssa bite each of her guards, not only to bind them to her, but so Lyssa would know how to bind a human and could practice locating them around the grounds. Jun had been first. She'd been nervous, but he'd put his arm around her, held her to reassure her she wasn't hurting him.

It had been a very different moment from this, but the sense of overwhelming acceptance and love was uncanny in its sameness, despite the fact Jun had been her childhood bodyguard and she'd just met this man. While intense circumstances could provoke a certain amount of intimacy, it couldn't explain a level this high.

Her body was gathering under the sensual assault of his. It had been a while since an orgasm had been more than just a release. This was magic. Powerful energy, almost a sorcery of its own, capable of altering her world. When they went over, it would be a little death in truth, where they would end up rising together as a new being. A phoenix created by two souls.

An odd thought for something she'd intended to be only physical. Coupling with her food was always a sensual experience, but solitary. She merely absorbed the reaction of her prey. But she felt linked with this man. He was riding the tide, holding her hand, being carried through the waves with her.

Banding his arms about her waist to cinch her closer, he kept his head to her bosom, suckling harder as he built to his own climax. Because her hips jerked more violently in reaction, she had to relinquish her hold on his throat as her own release crashed down on her. He brought his head up, palmed the back of her skull and kissed the blood from her lips, raw, hungry, as his seed jetted into her and he growled into her mouth.

It took her by surprise, the suddenness of it, the power, the sheer feel of it rippling over her, pleasure for pleasure's sake that shuddered outward and seemed to make everything else disappear, carrying her to another peak with him.

When at last she came down, she felt the stickiness of him between her thighs, warm and wet. She reveled in it, in his cock still inside her, hard and hot, while his eyes traveled her face, as if memorizing every part of her. He put her fingertips on the wound where she'd bitten him. Placing his hand over hers, he held her hand securely, obviously wanting her touch to staunch the blood.

They studied each other for some time. She didn't feel he was uncomfortable with the silence. Nor was she. In fact, the power of the past few moments eschewed any conversation. When at last he lay back on the pillows, giving her the wry smile that told her he was experiencing a man's typical reaction to an overwhelming climax, he moved her by drawing her down with him, curling her into his arms so she could lay her head on his chest, feel his heartbeat beneath her fingertips. She tilted her head to study his profile, the straight nose, firm, sensual lips that were perfectly shaped for a man. He had a tough chin, sloping cheekbones with facial hair that had stroked her so deliciously her skin still tingled with the memory of it.

Men did not typically think of her as someone to hold in their arms in this protective, sensually possessive manner. Most rightly realized they should maintain some distance, some wariness, an unconscious survival instinct warring with their lust. Or even that it was inappropriate to assume such intimate familiarity with her, no matter what carnal lusts they indulged at her behest.

She wouldn't have tolerated it herself, not from her usual dinner choice. But with him, she was content to lie there, smiling a little at the low rumble in his chest which told her he'd dropped into a postcoital, postbattle doze. Well, the man had been traveling on his own for some time, had fought a ferocious battle on her behalf and then pleasured her better than any man or vampire had for some time. She could forgive him a nap.

She did some of that herself, at ease with him until the dawn started closing in. As lightly as she slept, she was surprised to wake and find herself curled in the pillows alone, a light sheet tucked over her to protect her from the morning desert chill. He was already dressed, buckling on his sword, watching her coiled, naked form.

The impact of him leaving hit her on several levels, surprisingly intense. "What did you mean, you would die here?" She sat up, pushing her hair out of her face.

He shook his head, a slight smile crossing his face. Coming to kneel by her, he put a hand to her brow, her cheek. "You take care of yourself, my lady. I would suffer much to know any harm had befallen you."

"You could stay and see to that yourself."

She hadn't intended to say such a thing, but she knew suddenly, fiercely, it was what she wanted. What she would command. He was not going to leave her. If he tried, she would compel him to stay.

He shook his head again, a look of regret there. "My heart wants to stay more than anything. Nay, even down to my soul." A look of wonder crossed his face at the startling realization of it, a mirror of her own amazement, she was sure. "To protect you. To lie with you. To find out what makes you laugh." He reached out again to trace her lips, putting some slight pressure on one corner as if to make her smile. Miraculously he was successful, even as she swatted his touch away. Catching her hand, he lifted it to his lips. "But I made a promise, my lady. I promised a friend I would come to his aid, help with this battle he prepares to wage. No matter how senseless I believe it to be."

But you are mine. Sworn to my service. Where such a preposterous thought came from, she didn't know, but it baffled her. What made no sense had a tendency to irritate her. "Very well." She withdrew her hand from his touch. "Go play your silly war games. I certainly do not need to beg a man to stay with me."

It wasn't so much the stinging of her ego that hurt as what she saw moving in his eyes. She wanted to lash out at it. She had many commitments, much to do, but he'd fallen into her lap overnight, a treasure she sensed was beyond measure. One that wouldn't come again, perhaps for a very long time. Perhaps never. She wanted to squelch the absurd romance of such a thought. "Are you still here? Go and serve your foolish honor." She curled away from him, turning her face into the pillows.

"If I've offended you, my lady, it wasn't my intention." She was startled when his lips touched her rigid shoulder, lingered as she lay there stiffly. He even arranged the sheet back over her body before he rose. She heard him rise and move away toward the opening of her tent, a tent that, without windows, had seemed a sanctuary from the whole world for the past few hours.

With her speed she was able to wrap the sheet around her upper torso and make it to the opening of the tent before he took more than one stride outside of it. She reached past the flap and caught his arm.

The dawn sun struck her shoulder and the length of her arm. The full strength of it hit the top of her hand, but she held on as he turned, something much worse than the sun's light searing her inside. "Sir Knight," she said, "take care of yourself as well. If . . . if you can come to me at another time, I would be pleased to see your face."

"I doubt it will be in this lifetime," he said, real regret in his voice. With an oath, he abruptly surged forward, crowding her back into the safety of the tent. "By the Blood of the Cross, woman. I no more than tell you to take care of yourself . . ." He cradled the scorched hand in his, his gaze covering the lesser burns on her arm, but she impatiently grasped the collar of his mail with the other hand.

"Why not this lifetime? Why are you so sure you will die?"

He pulled his attention from the damage and looked at her in that intent way that made her want to stand still as if he were touching her with his fingers. "I've dreamed of my death in this campaign, and sometimes I know what will happen." Now he did touch her, tracing an eyebrow. "I do hope we might meet again, some other place. But no matter what happens, I could not have imagined such a treasured gift for my last day on earth than you. They shall have to send me to Hell, because nothing in Heaven can match you."

"Your blood is within me," she said abruptly, desperately. "I'll know where you are, always." *I'll know when you die.*

"I like that idea," he said, with a thoughtful nod. "Perhaps you'll come visit my dreams in this wasteland one more time or two. Give me a breath of coolness, the green of your eyes."

He brushed his lips across her hand then, studying the flesh that was starting to heal on her arm. Then his eyes were back on her face, so focused she couldn't think beyond the powerful hold of them. Her lips parted, for some reason tears gathering in her eyes. She, who never cried.

With an oath, he yanked her to him fully for another kiss, holding her as a man would hold a woman he loved, as she'd seen it done but never experienced for herself. She had one blink of time in God and the Devil's universe to savor the feel of his body, his mouth, the brush of his hair, and then he was gone. Out of the tent, striding into the sun-seared world where she could not hold him without turning herself to ash.

She'd never even asked him his name. Three days later, she knew he was dead.

1

Present Day

L YSSA opened her eyes, not surprised to find them wet with tears as she surfaced from her memory of the knight.

Though she had held Thomas in high regard, she wasn't sure she could allow herself to believe as the monk did, that the man who was her current human servant, Jacob, had been part of her over-one-thousand-year-old life span almost from the beginning. But the way Jacob made her feel, so much like that knight, certainly made her wonder . . .

Regardless, whether the knight had carried Jacob's soul or not, her subconscious welcomed the memories as a way to spend more time with Jacob without revealing her growing need for his company.

If she'd been a different type of woman, she would have seized on them as reassurance that the recent decision she had made—to give Jacob the third mark, essentially a death sentence—was pre-destined. Jacob himself had tried to comfort her, reminding her he'd insisted she do it. But Lady Elyssa Amaterasu Yamato Wentworth, the last vampire queen of the Far East Clan, did not capitulate to the will of a human. The responsibility was all hers.

Besides which, reassurance and tender comfort weren't what she sought as she moved restlessly in the solitude of her wide bed in the dwindling hours before dusk. She lifted her hand. Though it was very faint, she still had a mark from the day it was burned, reaching out of the tent to hold her knight. Just as the impression of Jacob's bite on her throat from the recent blood exchange of the third mark still remained, when the punctures should have disappeared within less than a day.

The images of the past and present mixed in her mind. Last night, after she'd marked him, Jacob had bathed her in the Jacuzzi tub. She'd used her fingertips to collect the water from his eyes so he could open them. Just the way she'd collected the water from the knight's eyes so he could raise his pale, auburn-tipped lashes. Like Jacob's lashes.

Jacob had asked her several times now what made her change her mind about giving him the third mark. She hadn't told him about Thomas's posthumous letter.

I know the prejudices of your world, certainly. You know I do. But hear me as I tell you that Jacob is the other part of your soul . . . He will not survive being parted from you again. Let him make his own choice, before you try to make it for him . . .

If Thomas had been right, Jacob had followed her through time, through her life. Fought to become her full servant, despite what that meant now.

She ached for a way to deserve the devotion Jacob gave her, despite how harshly she often treated him. She couldn't change who she was, but he didn't seem to want her to do so. His alpha nature resisted her dominance even as he was aroused by it. Just thinking of that made a response tighten in her vitals.

He was approaching his thirtieth birthday. Several weeks ago, she'd proceeded to make arrangements for a special gift. She hadn't really examined why she was going to the trouble for a servant she'd had for such a short time. But he'd made many things so much easier for her already, and a wise queen was always generous. Now, the significance of what she'd chosen, something she'd initially considered a jest based on the nickname she'd given him—Sir Vagabond—nearly made her want to call it off. But she wouldn't.

For one thing, she had more pressing concerns. She had to go get him out of jail.

2

As soon as he was certain Lyssa had retired for the day, Jacob headed out with a list of errands. When he was done, he dropped the Mercedes off at the garage for a transmission repair beyond his skill to do and got a lift downtown from the mechanic. On the way, he called Mr. Ingram. The limo driver Lyssa had hired to periodically drive her around while she was staying at her Atlanta home agreed to swing by the stores to pick up the items he'd purchased and then pick up Jacob in a couple of hours.

She was indifferent to how domestic tasks were performed unless they were done inefficiently. God have mercy on him if that were the case, for her tongue certainly wouldn't. He had to suppress a smile. His Mistress, so aware of everything else, yet so unaware of her royal hauteur. Also unaware—at least for the moment—about this particular self-imposed last errand.

Tomorrow the vampire scientist Lord Brian and his servant Debra would be leaving Atlanta for Tuscaloosa. They'd been waiting for a shipment, the carefully preserved cadaver of the Russian vampire Brian hoped would lead them to myriad developments regarding the only disease known to affect their species. The Delilah virus.

While Lyssa could certainly find out what he was about to do if she looked in the right corner of his mind or asked the right question,

Jacob was practicing the useful skill of not focusing on things he didn't want her to know so they didn't catch her eye when she was taking a stroll through his head.

And to hell with it if she found out. He'd rather ask forgiveness instead of permission on this one. His lady had the virus, though the two of them were the only ones who knew it.

By carrying the third mark, he'd willingly accepted the fact that the end of her life would be the end of his. The mark linked their physical flesh irrevocably. Some felt it even linked them spiritually, such that whatever the vampire's destiny in the afterlife, the servant followed. That was the way he wanted it to be, because she wasn't going anywhere without him. Her desire to protect those in her Region and the society she'd helped build was now her primary concern, and he'd sworn to make it his as well. He just didn't mention he was going to have two first priorities, one of them being to see if there was a way to save her life.

Jacob purchased coffee and a couple of donuts to compensate for his late night with his Mistress while waiting outside Debra and Brian's hotel. He didn't have long to wait. Debra headed out around nine o'clock and walked seven blocks to the library, carrying a stack of books. Jacob followed at a distance, wanting to approach her when she was inside the building.

He found her curled up in a comfortable chair in a secluded corner. While an open scientific journal and notebook with scribbled calculations were open on her lap like a security blanket spread across her legs, he was bemused to see she was reading a romance novel. As he took a seat in the chair across from hers, pulling it close enough for a discreet conversation, she closed the paperback, eyeing him warily.

From the color in her cheeks, he was sure she was remembering the dinner party where they'd recently met. Servants provided sexual entertainment for their vampire Masters and Mistresses at such gatherings, so at one point he'd had his hand deep inside of Debra, her pussy clutching his fingers as she screamed out her climax. While Brian, her Master, suckled the taut points of her breasts, Jacob's Mistress had watched it all, drawing in the energy like blood.

Such was a human servant's life. Dry cleaning, home repair, gardening. Arranging a table centerpiece and then replacing that centerpiece to perform as a sex slave in front of dinner guests. All in a day's work.

"Are you doing well?" Seeing the trepidation in her face, his reassuring tone was instinctive.

Some of her apprehension appeared to recede. "Yes. Thank you. I . . . What are you doing here? Is Lady Lyssa displeased with my Master? Or is there something we may do for her? We leave tomorrow for Alabama, but I'm sure he'll be happy to—"

Jacob shook his head. "I'm not here in an official capacity. I'm here for myself. Servant to servant. I was wondering if you could answer some questions I have." He leaned forward, clasping his hands loosely between his splayed knees. "I hope I didn't hurt you the other night. I'm new to this, and . . ."

"I've been Brian's servant for four years," she admitted, dropping her gaze to worry the corner of the book with a short nail. "That was the first time . . . I'd heard of it, of course. It's considered standard practice to use human servants for that . . . but . . . I was Brian's lab assistant before I became his servant and he . . . I guess for the most part it's just the two of us and the research. Of course, he has . . ." The color deepened in her cheeks. "But nothing like that. I guess I'd rationalized it. You know, two lab partners blowing off stress at the end of a long research session, but of course, when it happens, it's nothing like that. I mean, he's utterly brilliant, but when that part of him rises, I mean, the vampire part . . ."

Now she did flush all the way to her roots. Jacob bit back a grin. Beneath the pretty exterior, she was a stammering science geek. "He becomes something out of . . . well . . ." She raised the romance novel. Registering his amusement, she shook her head. "I'm quite the unworldly fool, aren't I? My apologies. I wouldn't usually talk about this, but . . . well, you're the first servant I've met that's newer to this than me. Most are so sophisticated and calm, they just look at me with this infuriating patronizing pity. Like Liam and Seanna," she added, referring to the other two servants who had been at the party, servants of Lord Richard and Lady Tara, the Alabama territory overlords. Jacob had been challenged—and commanded—to bring Seanna and Debra to climax at the same time. He'd succeeded, but like Debra it had been his first exercise in sating vampire lust in a group setting.

Taking a deep breath, she laid the book flat on top of the notebook and folded her hands, smiling a little. "Of course I'll be happy to answer your questions, Jacob. Though I doubt I can answer anything that deals with vampire politics. As you can tell, I don't get out of the lab that much."

"It's your experience in the lab I'm seeking," he assured her. Taking his own deep breath, albeit a mental one so he didn't betray the urgent need he felt for answers, he met her gaze. "My lady won't tell me much about this Delilah virus, and I want to know more."

"If she's made a conscious decision to withhold the information from you, it's not my place to offer it." Debra's direct answer told Jacob she was back on solid ground, but she tempered it with a quick touch on his arm. "Lady Lyssa is very powerful, and her patronage is vital to Brian. I can't do anything to offend her that might risk that." Her eyes widened in sudden alarm. "Perhaps even this conversation is inappropriate, if she doesn't know you're here. She doesn't, does she?"

"Hear me out. Please." Jacob quelled the compulsion to try and block her way as she made to rise. While he couldn't appear desperate or overly determined, he wasn't leaving here without answers. "Lady Lyssa finds it amusing, my desire to protect her to the best of my ability. But I do consider that part of my responsibilities. I suppose most of us servants do, no matter how laughable our Masters and Mistresses find the idea."

That apparently hit a chord with her. She sank back down, her eyes intent behind her wire-framed glasses. At the dinner party, Brian had taken them carefully off her face and set them aside. But after that tender gesture, he'd returned to his chair, demonstrating his ruthless support of Lord Richard's command that she strip in front of the assembled guests and allow Jacob, a total stranger, to intimately fondle her body and bring her to climax before them all.

He'd become part of a strange world. Innocence and dark carnality intertwined like a yin and yang DNA strand, creating an alternate reality with endlessly unpredictable twists and turns.

"I want to know how to protect her blood sources. The more I know about the virus, the more likely it is I can do that, right?" He kept his expression neutral, twisting the truth he had to safeguard. He was treading a very dangerous line. From his conversation with Lyssa last night, he knew if even a hint got out that the queen of the Far East Clan had the disease, all her work to protect her Region could topple. There could be other repercussions as well. Those who opposed the "civilized" structure of the current vampire society could erupt into bloody conflict with those who supported it, viewing her imminent demise as a possibly correct sign that the Council had been severely weakened.

"I give you my word, if Lyssa has any displeasure with our conversation, she'll take it out on my hide." *In spades.* "Not yours or Lord Brian's. I wouldn't speak to you, not another word, if I thought I was going to jeopardize your lord's standing with her."

That intent look again, telling him that while he was dealing with a woman with awkward social graces, her IQ was off the charts. "You have an honest face," she said at last. "Very open. Most servants lose that quickly. You'd do well to do the same. Other vampires pick up cues from the expressions of servants, and they can use that against your Mistress."

Jacob inclined his head, despite the clutch of worry the admonition created inside him. In the past, his lady had intimated almost the same thing about the ability to read his face. "I'll work on it, believe me. Tell me about the virus. How do I protect my lady from it?"

"I find it hard to believe that Lady Lyssa needs any assistance in protecting herself," she responded dubiously. She paused, then let out a sigh. "But I'll tell you what I can."

Taking her advice to heart, Jacob managed not to let out a victory yell of relief. Though he wanted to shout out questions that would tell him how best to help his Mistress's specific symptoms, he held his tongue.

"The Delilah virus gets its name from Samson and Delilah,"

Debra explained. "Delilah cutting off Samson's hair, a mortal taking away a superhero's power, his immortality so to speak. That's the key to it. In a normal human it's a dormant condition, no more harmful than any other part of them. But if they have it and a vampire bites them, there's a strong likelihood the vampire will contract the disease. Our research indicates that the dormant condition is becoming more common in humans, which makes safeguarding your Mistress's blood sources even more important."

"Why is it becoming more common?"

She shrugged. "That's the type of thing that's hard to prove, making it easy to jump to conclusions. There are so many things we don't know about adaptation and evolution. I know the news reports more and more mysterious deaths where the victims have been bitten, their blood drained. Humans of course typically assign that to human psychotics, killers with illusions that they're vampires. But we know it's evidence of vampires ignoring Council laws and taking more human kills to test their authority. So perhaps the virus is a defense mechanism developing in the human DNA. It would be a rapid adaptation, but we have proven to be a remarkably resilient species."

Debra's expression hardened. "Everything we're seeing in the lab tells us if vampires don't heed the warning signs, they'll have an epidemic. That's why Brian is in such a rush to meet with the Tuscaloosa facility. He wants to be ready with as much data as he can to present at the Council Gathering. Our only blessing so far is that the virus is a limited, one-way street. It can only be passed from a human to a vampire. The vampire isn't contagious to another vampire and can't pass it to a human. Perhaps because once it's in a vampire's system it attacks the brain more than the blood, as far as we can tell." Her face clouded. "However, with a human servant it's different."

"What do you mean?"

She considered the notebook spread out in her lap this time, her brow furrowed. "Jacob, some of this isn't validated. So please . . ."

"This conversation remains between us. Please. I couldn't bear to lose my Mistress like this." Just in time, he managed to bite back the word *can't*. The hitch in his voice caused her gaze to flick back up.

From the softening of her expression, she seemed to take it as an emotional reaction.

"Once contracted from a 'normal' human, we think a vampire has about ten years before he or she succumbs to it. However, there's a far more virulent strain. We've only discovered it recently. In the Russian vampire. Ironically, Brian's excited about it because he said that difference could provide vital clues to a cure." A brief hesitation, then she said through stiff lips, "Lord Andrev got the Delilah virus from his servant, Helina. She'd been his servant for eighty-six years."

"How . . . ?" Jacob's brow furrowed. "If they have the condition dormant in their blood, then wouldn't he have contracted it almost immediately, the first time he drank from her?"

Debra nodded, her eyes somber, her tone telling him how revolted she was by the information she was imparting. "There's research on this disease going on elsewhere. In the labs of vampire hunters. We believe they figured out a way to inject the dormant condition into a human. Lord Andrev was not a very compassionate man. Helina could have just killed herself to escape him, but apparently she . . ." Debra shook her head. "I love my Master, Jacob. I could never countenance such an idea, but I also know there are servants who are taken unwillingly into service. They come to accept the idea over time. But when Masters are like Andrev . . . Helina apparently was brave enough to decide she wasn't going to let anyone else be brutalized by him."

"She had to be extremely clever as well. Focused." Jacob considered the effort it took him to misdirect his thoughts from his Mistress's notice, even knowing he didn't have a chance in hell of doing it when she was paying attention.

"That's an understatement. Apparently, she did it by having thoughts of revenge and retribution constantly. Like staking him in his sleep, or setting vampire hunters on him, but she never followed through on the thoughts. A very deliberate 'Peter and the Wolf' strategy. Her vindictiveness and apparent cowardice amused him. He used it to taunt and torment her further."

"Why didn't he just kill her?"

"Andrev took joy in her misery and suffering," she said sadly. "He got off on punishing her for her wayward, disloyal thoughts. He didn't take her seriously, overestimated his ability to read her should she actually try to do something to him."

"Did she tell you all this?"

"No." Debra clasped her hands together, fingers pressing white circles into her flesh. "When he started having the first effects, she told him what she'd done in front of a gathering of his territory overlords, like our dinner the other night. Laughed in his face. Spit on him right there." She shook her head. "She had a knife with her Master's blood—God knows how she got that—and was going to plunge it into her heart, one sure way to kill a full servant, but unfortunately they stopped her. He had her tortured to death. Because of our resilience to wounds, it was a good two months before she died. And when she did, she wasn't recognizable as human. Some of the researchers were allowed to visit her, question her . . ." Debra swallowed. "I'm glad I wasn't one of them, as cowardly as that sounds."

Jacob closed his eyes. *Remember how savage we are . . .* His Mistress's own words, when he was learning his role in her household.

"In the end, he went to extra lengths to help us understand the disease, even at the expense of his own comfort. I never knew if it was revenge on her, to make sure another servant couldn't have this power over her Master again, or if he was trying to make amends, as people facing their own end sometimes do. It doesn't matter now, regardless. Except to the two of them.

"Based on the tests those researchers did, we know that a human servant injected with the dormant condition will get what we call the Delilah-B virus. The symptoms are somewhat different, but from the samples of her blood they took, they estimated she would have died in less than two years. Unlike a human carrying the natural gene, who isn't affected by it at all."

Thomas had died in less than two years. Jacob forced himself not to react to the thought. Fortunately, Debra was focusing on the information sifting in her mind. "It also accelerates the Delilah virus in a vampire. They don't have ten years. Lord Andrev was dead within two years as well. If he'd had a full servant at that point, it's possible he might have lived longer without showing signs of the disease, for as you probably know, a vampire can draw off the energy of a full servant."

He didn't want to ask the question, but he did. "How does the disease progress, symptom-wise?" It was the most perilous question, and he knew he'd moved into those waters by the speculative look she gave him. He kept a quizzical expression, as if he asked purely for curiosity's sake.

"It starts with a need to sleep longer. The vampire is more sensitive to the daylight and affected even when screened from it. As it advances, there are sudden spells of weakness that can cause fainting, vomiting of blood. You'll remember Lord Richard talked about that with his friend Antonio."

She sighed. "They start to lose the ability to control and guard their thoughts from a human servant. Andrev marked a volunteer human test subject so Brian could monitor the rate at which his ability to block his thoughts degraded. A vampire typically is a vacuum-packed can. Nothing will escape his mind if he doesn't wish it. But a sick vampire will start to slip, revealing thoughts to those connected to his mind. Often he doesn't realize he's revealing them. As we know, in a healthy vampire, even if he's upset about something, shutting down the path is as easy as closing a book for you and me." She demonstrated with the novel in her lap.

Cold dread gathered in his lower belly as Jacob remembered the night Lyssa's mind had projected an image of Rex, her late husband, torturing her. It was an image she'd obviously not intended Jacob to see. She'd reacted violently when she'd discovered him in her mind uninvited. His forearm still occasionally ached from the break she'd inflicted, despite the healing powers that came with the second and third marks.

"Because the attacks are so severe and abrupt in the first stages," Debra continued, "it's remarkable how completely an affected vampire regains strength and self-possession between them, as if nothing at all is wrong. Then suddenly the vampire doesn't recover the same way anymore. At that point, he'll start failing drastically. The time between the episodes will be harder to predict. They can happen daily, sometimes even more frequently. We call that Stage Three. Mood swings will be so sharp they can occur midsentence."

Given his lady's personality, Jacob reflected with grim amusement, it might take some effort to detect an abnormal mood swing.

"When the physical attacks come quickly on the heels of the emotional, the vampire has entered the final stage. It will be more rapid than any of the previous stages. In the fourth, impaired judgment will become significantly noticeable. There will be hallucinations, distorted reality, paranoia. Even bouts with suicidal thoughts, melancholy. Extreme emotional dependency. Neediness," she clarified.

"Wouldn't that be normal for someone dying? Needing to feel a connection to someone, to feel they're not facing death all alone?"

She raised a shoulder. "Yes, but it's unusual for vampires, even under great stress. Being predators, they don't gracefully depend on others."

They also typically didn't face the overwhelming emotional drain and fear that could come with the inexorable progress of a terminal disease. However, considering he needed Debra's help, he held that layman's thought to himself.

"Stages Three and Four are so close together and the symptoms can overlap so much, depending on the vampire, we debated whether to separate them. When the vampire starts losing control of the mind, there will be cycles of intense aggression, anger, followed by a total lassitude. Some have no interest in blood. They'd essentially starve themselves, but at that point they're very close to the end. One symptom unique to Stage Four is some kind of flesh-eating reaction which starts burning away their skin. It eats its way inward until there's nothing left to hold in the organs, the blood. It's as if they're turning to dust in slow motion, until the heart collapses, a self staking, so to speak. Then it's over. Stage Four can occur and be over in less than a couple days. Sometimes hours."

When Jacob spoke, he considered his even tone a major accomplishment, based on the visual overlay Debra had just put on his lady's body. Her lovely face. "How close do you think you are to a cure?"

"That's the million-dollar question for any disease, isn't it?" She pushed her hair back from her forehead. "It could be today, tomorrow, twenty years from now. We're more likely to find ways to prevent it, slow it, treat it, before we find a way to eradicate it. Like cancer. Though I'll say Brian's very excited about the connection between the servant and master. What they know in Tuscaloosa will be critical, how it meshes with his research."

"*Have* you found ways to slow it down, treat it?"

Regret crossed her face. "So far, no. Just the basic techniques of pain management we use on humans, which have some limited success with vampires. As I said, having a full servant can help prolong the life of the infected vampire. While taking the one annual kill all vampires need in a timely manner helps, increasing the number of full kills in a year doesn't seem to have any appreciable effect. That's a good thing, of course, because you know some of the vampires would have used it as an excuse to up the annual quota, like a preventive vitamin supplement." She managed a grim smile.

"And unfortunately, we haven't figured out a way to test humans for the dormant virus. We don't even know how vampire hunters isolated it, or if they even have. It's more likely they found the blood source of an infected vampire and are using that human's blood as a host to make up their vials. If they do, they could conceivably wipe out a significant number of vampires. Some of our best trackers are looking to find that research subject."

"No wonder you're concerned," Jacob murmured.

"Yes. It's one thing if the disease is contracted by an incautious vampire. Entirely different if the hunters choose to pursue a far more insidious and subtle method of hunting our Masters and Mistresses. That's why finding a cure is more important in this instance than prevention, though limiting blood donors to one's own servant and a carefully picked annual kill is the safest bet for the latter. We've had some reports that it's only an isolated cell of hunters trying this out right now. The majority of them still seem to have a fortunate aversion to it because of its similarity to a biological weapon. We all know how those can backfire."

Reaching out, she touched his hand. "The best thing you can do is to be very careful with your extracurricular bedsport, Jacob. You never have any idea who is watching Lady Lyssa, and she's very powerful. Someone could drug you, inject you . . ."

"I won't be with any other women." Then, because the exception to the rule sat before him now, he added uncomfortably, "Unless she commands it."

"Oh. So your Mistress requires fidelity. That's interesting, considering how old she is."

"No, she hasn't commanded it. Not specifically."

Debra cocked her head, considered him.

"You're giving me that pitying look you just said you get from older servants," Jacob observed darkly. "You're right. It's very patronizing. And annoying."

"Do you know why I'm reading this?" With a faint smile, she lifted the romance novel. "Part of it is escapism. Part of it is to remind me what my relationship with my Master *isn't*. The bond between servant and vampire is unique. Not family, not spouses, not lovers. The excess sex drive vampires have can force us into a deceptive intimacy. We convince ourselves we're lovers, probably because the reality is beyond our ken and we don't know how to classify it. Since we can't reconcile the feeling with the reality, we use sex to Band-Aid it."

She tapped the top of the book again. "If you allow yourself to believe it's something different from what it is, you've fooled yourself in a way that will only bring you heartbreak. In the worst cases it'll result in bitterness. They'll drive that lesson home again and again, twisting the knife."

At his speculative look, she nodded. "The first time I assumed more about our relationship than there was, Brian invited a vampire home from the lab and took her to his bed. He commanded me to prepare them a meal. Made me stand there holding the tray while he put whipped cream on her breasts and licked it off." She glanced away, obviously embarrassed by the revealing picture. "Later that same day . . . he took me. He hadn't even cleaned himself, so I could smell her. It was a lesson to show me the two acts had no relation to one another. Mind to mind, a vampire feels a closer bond to his or her servant than with anyone else. I can deny him nothing. Even that day I didn't, knowing he'd been with another woman."

"I would have pureed a full box of laxatives into the whipped cream."

It startled a laugh out of her. She put her fingers over her lips, glancing around in apology at any readers close enough to have been disturbed. "You're incorrigible."

But then she sobered. "We're toys in the beginning. Something new to play with. At first, even they indulge in the pleasure of mutual infatuation. They like our besotted reaction and get caught up in it for a while. But we're tools. Very important tools."

Hearing too much of his lady's words in what Debra was saying, Jacob still wanted to deny it. "You've made it sound like a terrible fate."

"Then I've spoken of it wrongly." She shook her head. "I'm doing research I would never achieve on my own in the human world. Brian has opened my eyes to impossible things . . . experiences I never would have had. But in order to fully embrace and appreciate those things your Mistress can give you, don't get bogged down in what she can't."

"You know what I think?" He covered her hand. "Maybe you should think about this as a scientist. Why did your Master go to such great lengths to convince you of your place? If he's not an Andrev, who gets off on manipulating his servant's emotions—"

"He's not." Debra's response was quick.

Jacob inclined his head. "Then why did he feel it necessary to drive it home so cruelly? You're bound to him forever. Why does he care what you think your relationship is, as long as you're serving him? Maybe because he has to remind *himself* of it, and that pisses him off. So he's cruel about it."

She pulled free abruptly. "I need to go." Putting the materials on her lap on the table between them, she rose and gathered her tote bag to slide the notebook and journal into it.

Jacob rose in automatic courtesy. He wanted to argue with her, but wryly he realized it was his Mistress he wanted to convince, not Debra.

"I think your desire to care for your Mistress is commendable. But just to prove the point . . ." She hesitated, then cupped his chin and kissed him briefly, her lips quiet and pleasurable against his before she pulled away. "That would offend neither my Master nor your Mistress. Now, in an attempt to grasp at some level of sophistication that would make Seanna and Liam proud of me, I thank you for the other night. We may not be on equal footing with our Masters and Mistresses, but we can be with each other."

She shouldered the tote bag. "You'll be treated with high regard, high value, because of who you serve, Jacob. But always as property." She gave him an even look. "Don't forget that."

"Thank you for the information," he ventured. "All of it." As she turned away with a nod, he caught her elbow. "You forgot this."

He'd picked up the romance novel she'd left on the table. Debra shook her head. "I think it's time I leave that for someone else. Someone who can afford the indulgence."

Before he could offer anything in response, she'd turned on her heel and strode away, hurrying for the door.

Jacob sat back down. Despite his resistance to Debra's words, he couldn't completely erase the doubts they'd created. Could any evidence that Lyssa felt more for him than what a vampire was expected to feel for her servant be a symptom of the disease? *Impaired judgment . . . hallucinations, distorted reality. Extreme dependency . . .*

"Bullshit," he muttered viciously. There had been no distorted reality the other night, after his lady gave him the third mark on the meadow floor of her forest preserve. But he was disturbed enough to take the time now to close his eyes, give himself back every detail of that precious memory, hoping he was trying to embrace reality, not escape it.

3

THEY'D walked through the forest together, naked like a gothic Adam and Eve. Jacob's arm had rested across her shoulders, his hand tangled in her hair so he could hold her close. The night had seemed heavy with the presence of supernatural creatures, the most powerful one being the vampire queen walking with him. A low-level hum in all his senses created a tingling in his vitals, a simmering in his blood he was sure were effects of his new third mark. Her slim arm was around his waist, her palm on his bare hip. Periodically, she lifted her touch to his back to trace the visible evidence of the mark, a scar that looked like the prehistoric fossil of a serpent, twisting from the nape of his neck to the base of his spine.

A reminder of her claim on him. A reminder of what he'd willingly surrendered.

The first mark had given her the ability to track him geographically. The second mark had allowed her access to his mind whenever she desired it. With the third mark, he'd given her his soul. He was bound to his vampire Mistress on every level now, a full human servant.

Getting there had been a rough road, despite the fact he'd come into her service only a short handful of weeks ago. Before that, he'd trained to be her servant, tutored under the hand of her dying servant, Thomas. Because that had been done without her knowledge or consent, she'd resisted Jacob's introduction at first. In the end, with nothing but Thomas's sealed recommendation, Jacob's own determination and something perhaps a lot bigger than any one of them, they'd reached this point.

When she stumbled, he realized shapeshifting from her Fey form back to vampire, a unique ability only known to him, had overtaxed the body that was more fragile than it should be. With barely a pause in stride, he lifted her. Accepting it, she linked her arms around his neck and laid her cheek on his chest, her face nestled under his jaw. Her nose tilted up to rub against the smooth trim of his beard.

"I want a bath, Jacob. I want you to bathe me. Prepare the water the way you did that first night you came. With the rose and lavender petals. The candles."

Bringing her lips to his throat, she scraped a sharp fang over him as he automatically lifted his chin, giving her access. The muscles in his stomach contracted at the surge of arousal. Not only did her lightest touch stimulate his now heightened senses, she'd opened her mind to his. Since he'd received the second mark he'd been able to hide little from her, but she could shield her thoughts from him at will. So her willingness to be open to him, at least for tonight, added fuel to the fire between them. He saw the provocative images in her mind, the twining of limbs, parted lips, flesh straining against flesh.

He also saw in the erotic swirl of her thoughts that she liked the way he offered his throat without hesitation to her, that it never failed to arouse her. When he gave her back a few images of his own, she covered his lips with her mouth, her tongue sweeping in to meet the demanding pressure of his. As she drew back, her lashes fell over her eyes in a half-lidded expression he knew signaled a mood to torment him. "You're going to wash me as a good servant would. Pretend to be a eunuch who cares only that his Mistress is clean and well cosseted, her sore muscles massaged, her skin perfumed and moisturized. In case she decides to entertain a lover tonight. And of course, you'll stand in the corner and watch."

"Your hair brushed until it's like silk," he agreed mildly. *My hands threading through it to caress your neck, your shoulders. I'll rub oil into your breasts and slick it down your stomach, massaging it into the lips of your cunt for that lover you anticipate taking to your bed. He'll ease into you like butter.*

He kept his pace toward the house casual, sauntering, playing her game instead of breaking into a sprint. She'd appreciate his restraint, even as she'd try to make him lose it, just to say she'd won. His lady was not a gracious loser.

Loser? He stifled a grin at the miffed thought.

"Like butter?" She spoke the words now, arching a brow. "Oh, I don't think there's enough lubricant for that. My lover has a very big cock. Long and thick. When it pushes into me, there's always pain with the pleasure of taking it." Her voice became a sultry purr, amusement swallowed by the unrestrained lust in her glittering green eyes. "The way I like it."

When she freed one hand from his neck to reach down between them, Jacob stifled a curse as she found him. Closing her hand over his steel length, she let her thumb pass over the still damp tip. "Just remember, Sir Vagabond. You're my faithful eunuch until I say otherwise."

As he emerged from the forest preserve into the more landscaped area of the backyard, they found the dogs waiting for them. Her pack of Irish wolfhounds lay in the grass or sat, eyes shining in the night, the moon gleaming off teeth revealed by their panting. Bran stood just ahead of the pack, the lead wolfhound's pale body a ghost in the moonlight. "They've had quite a run tonight."

"We all have." She tightened her arms on his shoulders and he returned the gesture, raising her, her soft curves pressing into his hard ones.

Once in her bedroom, he laid her on the bed before he moved into the bathroom to prepare the bath according to her specifications. He kept a discreet eye on her as he performed the tasks. Despite her seductive flirting, she closed her eyes, her face turning to the pillow as she let some of her weariness have her. Because of that, when he had the bath prepared, he came back to carry her to the tub. She lifted her arms, no argument again. He made a conscious effort to keep his mind away from the question of whether she would've had the energy to walk back to the house on her own. This night was not going to be about that. She'd given him the third mark. He'd be her legs, her arms, whatever she needed him to be forever. No matter what, she'd never be alone.

When he put her in the tub where she could sit propped up in the corner and stepped in to begin her bath, she ran her hand up his hard thigh, tracing the musculature there. Obedient to her wishes, he didn't interfere with her casual fondling, though his cock jumped in response. Reaching for the shower sprayer, he switched the water flow to wet her hair. She closed her eyes as he went to one knee before her. His hand moved over her scalp, the heated water running over her face. She tilted her chin, and he adjusted the spray appropriately to avoid getting it into her nose. Thanks to Thomas, her previous servant, he was well trained in the domestic arts. Thanks to the gods, he somehow managed to please her as a lover.

He shampooed her hair and then, still kneeling, he used the pitcher on the side of the tub to rinse her. The silken strands of her hair floated in the water around her arms. They gathered around the curves of her breasts. When he pressed a hand towel to her face, he combed her hair back with his fingers, allowing her to open her eyes at length without having to blink a drop away from her long lashes.

She retrieved the soap from his hands and washed his chest, the curves of his pectorals, pinching his nipples. Running her palms over the wide expanse of his shoulders, she followed the line of silken chest hair down over his sectioned stomach muscles, watching his cock rise high enough to brush his belly in response to her caress.

He knew that touching him this way, knowing what he was thinking as well as seeing his physical response, intensified her reaction. She could see the things he wanted to do to her. She scraped him with her nails, a little shudder running through her own mus-cles. *Not the thoughts of a eunuch, Sir Vagabond.*

A dead man would have such thoughts, my lady, if given the privi-lege of bathing with you.

As he well knew, the ability to chastise him for not playing her game exactly as she ordered only sharpened the edge of her lust. She gave him some of her fantasies of punishment even now, his arms and legs restrained while she taunted him with her mouth, punc-tured him with her fangs. Used a whip to mark his flesh and then soothed it with her fingertips, the press of her lips.

Two could play it this way. He guided her to her feet to wash the parts he'd been unable to do under the waterline. Standing up be-hind her, he cupped her breasts, rubbing the nipples between his fingers so she arched into his touch while he pressed against her, his very non-eunuch cock prodding her buttocks. With the soap sliding into that channel, it was easy for him to rub himself there, and in his mind he showed her his desire to grasp her cheeks in both hands and bring himself to climax just doing that.

But instead he turned her so he could kneel and run soap-slicked hands under the curves of her breasts, over her belly, down to her thighs and calves. Picking up the pitcher, she poured water over his head, then let the pitcher float away as she ran her hands over his skull, threaded her fingers through his hair. When he lifted his face at her insistent touch, she followed the almond curve of his eyes, sluicing away the water so he could raise his lashes.

It is odd, Jacob. I feel as if I've done this before . . . like déjà vu. She did it again, more slowly, but apparently the image was too elusive and the desire to simply touch him washed the other concern out of her gaze.

So he continued his ministrations, one arm around her hips as he gently put his hand between her legs to wash her pussy. Opening her stance in response, she bit her lip as he cleaned and stimulated at once, massaging her clit with clever fingers.

With her mind open to him, he could see how tired she was, yet her body was in a pleasant yearning mode. Caught between wanting some kind of release and wanting to stay like this, touched and teased by him forever. Her servant. Three marks. Forever hers. She wanted a nap. But she also wanted to be fucked by him. She usually thought of it in a different way, but the primeval urges of the forest were still too close. She swayed.

"Here, my lady." Standing, he put his hands on her shoulders to urge her to lie down in the tub again. This time he stretched out behind her so she was lying in the cradle of his body, her upper torso propped on his chest, head relaxed on his shoulder. He captured the pitcher and poured water over her breasts, using the interference of his hand to slow the stream, make it trickle over her. Water ran over her small curves, then rejoined the swirls of soapy foam and flecks of lavender and rose petals floating in the tub and clinging to her. He had one knee propped up, allowing her to lean her body into that side of him. When she plucked a rose petal off his thigh, she turned enough to mold it to his bottom lip. He went quiet under her touch, his attention dwelling on her face, her mouth, her chin. He let her hear every murmured desire of his body that came into his mind.

For her part, she let him know how beautiful she thought he was, inside and out. How for the first time in so long, she didn't feel alone. That she trusted him.

It suffused him with emotion, but he kept up the pouring, letting the water flow even more slowly over her breasts, concentrating on the nipple areas so she began to anticipate, her body lifting to the stimulation. Reaching over, he turned the jets of the Jacuzzi on, working from his current position to angle them for her comfort, along her rib cage, the outer muscles of her thighs. When he turned her in his arms, he put her onto his lap and lifted her legs so her calves rested on the slick surface of the wall built around the tub. As he eased her toward the side of the tub, he could tell from the desire that flashed through her expression she understood his plan a moment before he positioned her in front of one of the underwater jets.

Let your eunuch make sure you're slick and ready for that lover of yours, my lady.

A dead-center hit, right on the clit already engorged by his soapy fingers. As she bucked up with a gasp, he held her, giving her an anchor with an arm over her chest, his forearm pressing down on the tops of her breasts, increasing their sensitivity to the water that lapped across them from her convulsive movements. He clasped her upper arm, holding her in position while he reached under her with the other hand and palmed her ass, lifting her up to an angle where she was even more vulnerable to the spray.

"Oh, gods . . ." Her hand gripped his thigh, using more of her strength. He responded to the pain by easing his fingers between her buttocks, playing with her rim as he worked her against the jets, letting the punishing flow of water drive her. Her breasts, just the tips, were out of the water, jutting hard and erect from the instant, almost punishing level of arousal.

Go over, my lady. Let it go. Let me see you come.

It shuddered through her exhausted body the way surf would wash over her if she lay on a beach within the tide line. He wanted the climax to ripple over every exposed nerve, one nerve at a time. She made soft, keening noises of pleasure, pressing the side of her face into his shoulder and nipping at him, holding on. As she undulated, his cock pressed into her hip, eager to serve her, and he could tell that spurred her even higher. The power of denial, mingled with the knowledge she could have him whenever she wished.

She was still shuddering with all of it when he let her sink back into the cradle of his lap, removing his fingers.

"My lady . . ." He whispered it huskily, holding her close, almost as close as the interlocking pieces of their minds.

He prayed to whatever god would listen that he would never fail her, the woman who was the answer to a lifetime of questions and needs. In her mind, there were images of dark and light, wonder and happiness, violence and pain. His lady had led the proverbial interesting life. She was his destiny. He'd known it from the first time he'd seen her. Whenever, whatever lifetime that was. All lifetimes.

At length, she slid down against him, curling against his upper chest, stretching out her legs so they intertwined with his. She fell asleep that way, unconcerned about his arousal pinioned under the soft flesh of her right buttock. Or rather, highly cognizant of it and indulging a Mistress's pleasure in making him wait. However, he found himself oddly content to stay in this position, be her bed and hold her above the water. Though she had no danger of drowning, he didn't want her sleep disturbed.

While he didn't know the mood she'd be in when she surfaced, since she was capricious in that regard, he had no illusion tonight's magical connection would continue forever. The night a servant received his third mark was a honeymoon period. Even if his lady's mood prevailed, because of the illness she suffered and the challenges they faced, this honeymoon would be far shorter than either of them would wish.

~

Returning to the present and far less pleasant matters, Jacob focused on what Debra had told him. When Lyssa had resisted giving him the third mark, he'd thought it had been grief and stubborn guilt. She'd lost her husband, Rex, and her servant, Thomas, within the past two years. While she still hadn't shared the full story with him, Jacob knew Rex was the reason Thomas had gotten the fatal disease that somehow infected Lyssa. Debra had given him a horrific idea of how Rex had accomplished it.

Lyssa had killed her husband herself when she found out he was responsible for Thomas's death. She'd then had to make the vampire world believe the honorable and always loyal Thomas had poisoned and staked Rex and she'd killed the servant as punishment.

Despite her Machiavellian nature, she was also a woman. It was a web of lies and deceptions that would have broken any woman's heart. In the end, Jacob realized she didn't want to give him the third mark because he would die with her. She'd been protecting him. So he'd bullied, coaxed, nagged, cajoled. In what he knew she still considered a weak moment on her part, he'd convinced her. His choice. He wasn't afraid of death. He was afraid of being where he couldn't protect *her*. Love her. And with the third mark, she could draw from his energy to help prolong her own life and give her more of the precious time she needed.

If only Brian and his fellow vampire science geeks had known about Thomas, been able to study him until his death. Andrev was a born vampire, from human and vampire parents. Lyssa was born vampire and Fey, the oldest living vampire with powers no other vampire had . . . Perhaps it would go differently for her. If only they didn't have to hide it.

But vampires like Carnal were trying to undermine everything she'd built. Carnal, the vampire who'd been made by Lyssa's late husband, Rex. Carnal preferred a world where humans would be cattle for the bloodthirsty whims of the vampires.

As the number of born vampires had decreased, the Vampire Council had allowed more vampires to be made, against her advice. A growing number of these made vampires, whose impulse control and bloodlust were not as well controlled as their older, born brethren, were impatient with the many Council rules.

Closing his eyes again, Jacob pressed on the bridge of his nose, relieving the tension building in his head with his thoughts. The vampire world existed in prosperous harmony in the shadows of the human-dominated world primarily because of her efforts over the past several centuries to establish the current Vampire Council structure. The elaborate ritual courtesies and rules had created a balance between vampire bloodlust and blood need. In vampire terms, that form of governance was young. It had only been in existence for the past couple of centuries, following some bloody territory wars to enforce it, of which she'd been a terrifying part.

She was the Council's muscle. The last direct descendant of royalty among the vampires, she didn't sit on the Council but was considered an important advisory member of it. Over a thousand years old, the limits of her strength and actual age unknown, she was all too aware that when she died, the Council would have to manage on its own against those like Carnal.

She had over fifty vampire fugitives she'd granted asylum in her territory. The upcoming Vampire Council Gathering was the vital turning point. At the event that occurred every five years, she would petition for permanent asylum for them, as well as reinforce the strength of the Council in any way possible with her presence as their queen.

If she got through the Council Gathering without suspicion, even if she died soon thereafter—and his mind shied from that thought— the illusion that she was still around would be in place long enough for her vampires to position themselves accordingly. It was not unusual for a vampire of her stature to go into seclusion for extended periods, communicating with other vampires only through her servant or other trusted agents. She could conceivably be gone five years before the truth was known.

He was helping her put all the pieces in place for that illusion if needed, and she would consolidate it with the contacts she would make at the Gathering, confirming who her allies might be. Places her fugitives and even her legitimate territory vampires might go if they had to flee her Region.

She was finally trusting him to be her ally, to guard her back, while he wanted nothing more than to focus fully on what would cure her of this damn disease, keep her alive and vibrant forever.

"You do realize I could have slit your throat three times while you've been sitting here daydreaming?"

~

Jacob's eyes snapped open. The man sitting in the chair across from him didn't complement his surroundings the way Debra had. He wore a pair of worn jeans, a dark T-shirt and a bomber jacket Jacob was certain hid an array of weaponry. Probably a nine millimeter and loaded wrist gauntlets. There'd be a knife scabbard on his left calf, another down the back. He hadn't had his hair cut in a while, and the shave looked a couple of days old. Still, the glittering blue eyes of his brother were as vibrant as his own, though Gideon's face held far more lines and his hair was threaded with white. The result of lifestyle, not age. Only a handspan of years separated them. That and a whole hell of a lot of other things.

"Gideon."

"I thought about shooting you right here, but I was curious. I wanted to know why you've lost your fucking mind." He ignored the startled and offended looks of nearby patrons. Rising, he jerked his thumb toward the door. "Get your ass up and we'll go somewhere and talk where we can get a late breakfast. You're buying."

He strode toward the door with apparently no doubt Jacob would follow.

Jacob reflected darkly that there appeared to be far too many people in his life who thought they could order him about.

This day was just getting better and better.

4

On principle, Jacob made Gideon wait, paging through Debra's romance novel. He found a scene or two that engaged his prurient male interest, with at least one interesting idea to try out on his sensual lady. When he finally departed the library, he found Gideon as well as Elijah Ingram waiting in the parking area. Elijah sat in the driver's side of his limo, while Gideon leaned against the side of his own car close by, thumbs through the belt loops of his jeans.

Standing, Gideon looked even more like the mean son of a bitch he was. A couple of inches taller and broader than Jacob, he'd inherited their father's dark hair rather than their mother's auburn brown mix as Jacob had. They shared the blue eyes, and though Gideon shaved, the dark shadow along his jaw never fully went away. He was pure muscle. There were no soft spots anywhere on Gideon, unless one counted the mush behind the rock-solid skull.

He and Elijah were eyeing one another. Since each possessed the skill to take the measure of the other within three blinks, they'd settled down like a couple of yard dogs determined not to fight, ignoring each other while not missing a single twitch.

"This man says he's your brother," the limo driver offered as Jacob approached.

"Funny. Last time I saw him he said the exact opposite."

"Mmm." Elijah squinted through the open window. "You still need a ride? I don't have anywhere to be until late this afternoon."

"I guess not." Jacob cut a look at his silent sibling. "If you can run the things you picked up by the house and just leave them in the lockbox behind the column at the security gate, that'll be good. Be sure and send me a bill for your time and gas. Gideon'll give me a ride after he says his peace. If not, this is a college area. I've still got a working thumb."

"Don't let no cute college girl pick you up. Might do something you'll regret. Get the other arm broke."

"Or he might realize the smart thing is to go home with her and not look back. But he's never been all that smart. If you can't be smart, be pretty." Gideon straightened.

"If you think that, seems to me you got the cuter ass," Ingram observed, deadpan. Jacob stifled a chuckle as Gideon's lips twitched.

"Seems you've been making friends without me," his brother said.

"They're easier to make and keep without you around," Jacob said without rancor. "You don't tend to approve of my choices in friends."

The humor disappeared. "Lady Lyssa isn't your friend, Jacob. Whatever else you think she is, fine. But I can promise you, she's not your friend."

It was uncomfortably close to what Debra had just told him. Jacob wasn't in the mood for it. "If that's going to be the tone of this conversation, I'll just ride home with Elijah here."

Gideon scowled. "Oh, pull the railroad spike out of your ass and get in the damn car."

"There's that brotherly affection I know and love." Jacob nodded to Mr. Ingram. The driver turned over the ignition.

"You have my number, son."

"He's a little protective of you," Gideon noted as the limo pulled out of the parking lot. "When did you break your arm?"

"Your spies are falling down on the job. A while ago."

As Gideon turned to open the car door, Jacob noted his brother had a new scar at his temple, disappearing into the hairline. It looked like an impact wound, possibly from having his head smashed against a brick wall. He wondered what their parents would think of them now. The parents they'd last seen alive on an idyllic day at the beach, when the only vampires were in movies and the imaginations of young boys. Even there they hadn't dwelled long, for a child's mind was a crowded merry-go-round of graphic possibilities.

As if he were following the direction of his thoughts, Gideon's expression altered from hard purpose to grudging affection. "There's a good diner around the corner. Let's go there and talk."

~

The brunch offering was good. As if they both were aware of the potential for disruption if they tried to talk before satisfying their appetites, they ordered and consumed the special in silence. The portions were sizeable, catering to the construction workers who came in from their work on new office buildings to refuel on the higher calorie count they needed. The exception was one table near the two men, where a pair of elderly women shared a postbreakfast pot of coffee.

Since the construction workers were similarly indisposed to talking while eating, the diner was relatively quiet except for the comforting chatter of the two women.

Gideon flipped up the top of the ketchup, pushing it and salt toward Jacob's left side just as he thought about needing it. While Lyssa would call it more evidence of the psychic intuition she suspected ran through his family, Jacob knew it more likely was long familiarity. Gideon had always been good at taking care of his younger brother. He thought he knew Jacob through and through, and in a way, he did. Gideon just preferred to pretend certain things didn't exist.

As they both slowed down and came up for air, Jacob laid down his fork. *Here goes nothing.* "How long have you been in town?" he asked.

"A couple weeks. When Carnal left his territory, we thought we might have a shot at catching him vulnerable. No such luck, though."

"You're hunting Carnal?" The day might be looking up.

"He likes to think he's a badass. He takes out his full Council-sanctioned quota of humans every year. We suspect he's gotten cockier and is taking more, though he's good at covering his tracks. Most of his victims in the past two years have been violent criminals. Unless you count his servants."

Draining a person infected with evil spurred the natural aggressiveness of a vampire to a higher level, increasing the problem of uncontrolled bloodlust that would encourage unwelcome attention from human society. Jacob knew Carnal didn't need any encouragement in that direction. A vampire needed blood to live, but actually only needed to fully drain one human annually to maintain their full strength and faculties. Lyssa had argued strongly for limiting the number of human lives taken by a vampire to one kill per year as a result. The Vampire Council had compromised with a higher number to placate those like Carnal who were strongly opposed to any limits at all.

"Lately he's been in the mood for sweeter meat. Seven women, all young. He's found a loophole. There's no limit on the number of servants a vamp is allowed to kill in the course of a year. We figure he's going to pay Lyssa a visit while he's here, etiquette and all, and because he's always had such an obsession with her. So we thought—"

"Don't, Gideon." Jacob held up a hand. "I can't hear any of your plans."

"Are you listening to me? Seven women. Young girls he seduces, then traps into being his servant for a while so they don't 'count' toward the quota."

"You're not telling me anything I don't know." Jacob struggled to keep it easy, friendly. "Let's not talk shop. What's going on with you, other than staking vampires?"

Gideon stared at him. "You don't want to hear anything about a guy murdering innocent girls? Even if you're in a position to help? We're trying to—"

"Gideon," Jacob said sharply, "shut up. I'm carrying a third mark."

His brother went stock-still, his fork frozen in midgesture. His hand shot forward, fork still in it, forgotten so that when Jacob intercepted, slamming his brother's wrist to the table between them, the silverware clanged. Water glasses and plates jumped, drawing startled glances. "You don't have to see it," Jacob said evenly.

Gideon jerked back. "I knew you'd lost your fucking mind. Your moronic pacifist ideas about vampires—"

"Not pacifist. I just don't believe being a vampire should be a death sentence."

"No, of course not. Just because they kill humans, it doesn't make them all bad."

"Contrary to popular myth, you know vampires only have one food source," Jacob retorted. "Human blood, taken fresh. They have the right to survive. They're predators, Gideon. Like wolves or lions. They're not automatically minions of evil."

Gideon blew out a ferocious breath. "Yeah, Carnal's just your basic trying-to-survive guy. Tell that to the sixteen-year-old homeless runaway corpse he drained. But hey, guess we can consider it charity, since it interrupted the burgeoning kiddie porn career her pimp boyfriend planned for her."

Jacob shook his head. "I'm not saying Carnal isn't scum. I'd stake him myself given the chance. I'm saying they aren't all like that."

"But Lady Lyssa isn't like you, Jacob. Don't make the mistake of thinking she is." Gideon enunciated each syllable between clenched teeth. When Jacob pointedly picked up his juice, took a swig, he blew out another exasperated breath. "I completely lose touch with you for months except for the occasional postcard, and then you resurface right under my nose as some vampire bitch queen's lackey. Did you even think about what's involved? She seduced you, is that it?"

"Gideon." Jacob put down the glass carefully. "I'm not twelve. I need you to listen to me."

His brother brightened. "That's it, isn't it? She compelled you, whatever you want to call it. You can break out of it, Jacob. Shit, she's queen of all of them. She can screw with any man's head. It doesn't matter if you did it in the heat of the moment. That's their talent, seduction. Even this bastard Carnal, when he turns on the charm, no woman can say no to him."

"Gideon—"

"We could trick her. Get her into a coffin, bury her underground or put her in the center of a concrete slab. She couldn't do anything to control you—"

"You even think about hurting her, I'll kill you."

While most of their conversation had been pitched low enough that the remarkable parts of it were lost in the women's chatter and the sounds of utensils and waitstaff, the cold statement hit a pocket of dead air.

Jacob paid no attention to the turning heads, furtive glances. He kept his gaze locked on Gideon's. In his most dangerous moment, he'd never thought himself as intimidating as his brother. However, the startled look that flashed across Gideon's face made him suspect he might have grown in that regard since Gideon had seen him last. Perhaps because he finally had something he'd defend with everything he was. No matter what she did to him.

"I'm sorry." Jacob wiped his mouth, set aside his napkin. "I didn't mean to throw it down like that, but you don't listen. I trained to be her servant for almost a year. I have lash scars on my back, my fealty oath." Thomas had given him those fifty lashes on the cold stone floor of the monastery before he'd ever come and offered himself to her. Now those marks were overlaid by the serpentine scarring of the third mark, and Jacob felt their presence at all times, like her physical and mental touches. "I've committed myself to her. She's the woman I'm meant to be with. To protect."

My lady. He would have said it, but he didn't want Gideon to mock him. Truth was, he hadn't wanted to say any of it, knowing how Gideon would react. But Gideon was his only family, his only constant in life except the restless desire that had driven him to find his lady. For that reason alone he had to say the simple truth.

Maybe it would have been better if they'd fought before the meal. He'd still be hungry, but hunger was better than having the breakfast roiling in his stomach and this leaden weight in his chest.

"She dies, you die. You understand that? You stupid, fucking idiot." Gideon shook his head, ignoring the sharp looks from the women across the aisle from them. "I don't get this at all. Does this have something to do with us? With our parents? What?"

"It's a choice I made, and it has nothing to do with you. I don't agree with everything you do, but I've helped you kill vampires that crossed the lines." Jacob inclined his head. "There's a balance in nature, and vampires are part of it."

"They threaten our survival—"

"How?" Jacob demanded. "Billions of us, less than five thousand of them. Their offspring are rare, while we breed like rabbits."

"What if the Council is overruled and more made vampires are allowed? What if those like Carnal get the upper hand? What then?" Gideon's eyes narrowed. "Yeah, I'm not as dumb as you think I am. We do have our spies. We know the political climate is changing. The first imperative is human survival, Jacob."

"The first imperative is honor. Integrity."

"Oh, Jesus." Gideon sat back in the booth, scrubbing his hand over his unshaven face. "The chivalry bullshit—"

"Yeah, that bullshit," Jacob interrupted him, his own annoyance kicking up. "You used to remember it. Believe in it. It's why you started doing what you do, and that's why I followed you, at first. But there's a difference between killing for a just cause and murdering to satisfy the emptiness in your own soul. You need love to remember that, Gideon. To balance it."

His brother stopped pressing at his temple and stared at him. "I love you. Look how well that's turned out."

"Cheap shot," Jacob said. "She's been alive for centuries. You've never hunted her. Why is that? You could have taken her out the first night I saw her, when I was with you. When her husband broke her arm and she was off by herself."

Gideon picked up his iced tea and took a swallow as if he tasted something bad. "She keeps the bigger monsters in line. The Council she created serves that purpose."

"No, that wouldn't be enough. It's more personal, Gideon. Why isn't she a target?"

"She saved my life. Once." He swiped at his mouth with a napkin.

"Got knocked out in a fight with a vamp. Nasty one that was killing anything that moved. Apparently one of her and Rex's territory vamps. Woke up in an alley with her sitting next to me and the vamp dead. She nodded to me, walked away. Well"—he shrugged irritably—"after she told me I was an idiot and that I'd have a longer life as a Christian missionary in the Sudan."

"That sounds like Lady Lyssa."

Gideon ignored that. "But the debt's even now. She saved my life but stole my brother. Even if she's one of those who only take out one human a year, those are healthy, decent human beings who don't deserve to die."

"I'm not saying the situation doesn't suck." Jacob spread open his arms, linked his fingers behind his head and tapped at the base of his skull, his muscles tense. "It's a Hobson's choice. But say you've got a decent vamp who takes their one kill a year to stay alive and in control of their powers. And you have a decent human who has to die. A one-to-one relationship. How do you make that judgment? One vamp or one human? You don't see the deer herd going off and killing all the wolves when they come and take down one of their number. It's a balance, Gid. Not fair, not kind, not even close to compassionate in many ways. A balance. A vamp is going to choose a human and that human will fight. He *should* fight. Defend himself whatever way he can. Maybe he'll get away; maybe he won't. Maybe he'll kill the vampire."

"You're saying that it's okay for a vamp to kill humans."

"I'm saying that we're the only species that doesn't accept that being prey may be a part of Nature's cycle for us." Jacob blew out his breath, brought his hands slapping down on the table surface. The waitress who'd been approaching with more coffee backed off, went to another table. "We're expected to try and stay alive. Whatever the Powers That Be, I don't think they intended us to exterminate an entire species to make us a hundred percent safe."

Gideon's eyes narrowed. "What are *you* going to do, little brother, when she orders you to help her take down her annual kill? Tarnish that armor of yours? Lure to his death someone like your Mr. Ingram, a guy who thinks he has a purpose for living beyond being dinner to a vampire? Hell, I know you. You're not comfortable with that. You're not a killer."

"I was a killer when I helped you." Jacob pushed his plate to the side. "A killer takes someone's life intentionally, against their will, whether justly or unjustly. I haven't got all the answers. I just know I'm where I'm supposed to be."

"I don't understand you at all."

"Yes, you do." Jacob met his gaze. "You just don't want to. The first girl you ever loved died at a vampire's hand."

A muscle flexed in Gideon's jaw. "According to your logic, I should have said 'that's Nature' and walked away."

"No. Actions have consequences. Vampires know that as well as we do. But Gideon, you were eighteen and Laura was sixteen. You're getting more bitter, year by year. Would she have wanted this—"

"Stop crawling around in my head." Gideon jabbed a finger at him. "I don't care about their motives. If I can kill every last one of them, I will."

So no man will ever again have to grieve until his heart cannibalizes itself. Jacob remembered Laura. He'd thought she was too fragile for his brother's strong personality, but she had a sweetness no man could resist wanting to protect. So the man who chose to love her would have felt doubly responsible when he couldn't keep her from getting killed. Particularly a man who had lost his parents when he was only twelve, left with the self-imposed responsibility of looking after his eight-year-old brother.

His brother would keep driving himself with hate and blood until he was dead. The signs had been there for a while. Like any person with a family member addicted to a destructive path, Jacob had tried everything, even joining him. In the end the only thing he could do was walk away, refusing to support the self-destruction anymore. With a sinking heart, he realized that it appeared only to have made his brother more committed to his violent path. It was now Gideon against the whole world and all it had done to hurt him, manifested in the form of shadowy creatures of the night with gleaming fangs.

"Why, Jacob? Just . . . why?" *Why have you done this to me? To us?* It was as clear as if Gideon had spoken the thought.

Because he couldn't harden himself against the anguish in Gideon's voice, Jacob took one more stab at honesty. "She was in my dreams long before I even met her, Gid. You know how I've always felt like I was searching for something? That night we saw her, suddenly there was this huge relief inside me. *There you are.* Boom. The monk that trained me believed I've served her before. In previous lifetimes."

Seeing Gideon's lip curling up in a sneer, he continued stubbornly, "I don't know whether I believe that, and it's not relevant, regardless. Now's the important thing. You remember how you felt about Laura? Barely even met her, and you couldn't imagine life without her from then on."

Gideon's gaze frosted over, chilling the air between them. In a blink, any progress Jacob thought he'd been making evaporated. "She's nothing like Laura. Don't you ever put her and one of those bloodthirsty cunts in the same category."

"Young man." The lady across the aisle spoke sharply, even as her friend reached out a quelling hand to her. "That's enough."

Gideon glanced toward her. "Mind your own business, bitch. Stick your head back in the sand with all the rest of them, my stupid fucking brother included."

"Gideon," Jacob snapped. He nodded apologetically to the two women and noted the hostile looks from the construction workers seated behind them. Leveling a warning look at his brother, he spoke quietly. "I don't even know who you are anymore, Gideon."

"Same goes on that score, little brother."

Biting back a response, Jacob laid a twenty on the table. "I think we're done here. I'll cover this."

"With her money? I don't think so."

"It's my money, Gideon." Jacob stood, studying him. The large hands curled in helpless fury on the tabletop, the blue eyes glaring, the jaw so rigid it looked like it would crack under the strain. "As long as you're like this, there's nothing we have to say to each other."

"Don't think I won't hesitate to kill you if you get in my way."

Once, two boys had run through the surf, sunlight flashing on the water they kicked up, making it sparkle. Laughter had bounced between them like a tossed ball. He'd tried to grab Gideon, knock him into the water, but Gideon caught him in a headlock and they both tumbled in. Jacob tried to grasp at that image to block the pain of the icily delivered threat, but he couldn't hold on to it.

"You sick son of a bitch." He pitched his voice low, picked up the money Gideon had swept onto the floor and laid it deliberately back on the table, under his coffee cup. "Fuck you."

He turned away, wanting nothing more than to go off somewhere and get a shot of the strongest proof alcohol he could find. He wondered what Lyssa would think if he came home with his blood overloaded with sugar, caffeine *and* alcohol.

It was the gasp from the women, followed by a call of warning from one of the workers, that alerted him. He spun just as Gideon surged up from the table with a clatter of tableware to ram him midbody. They hit the edge of the ladies' table and toppled it along with its crockery as they tumbled to the floor.

Gideon landed one eardrum-shattering punch high on the jaw before Jacob rallied, rolled, broke the hold.

"You're coming with me. You're not going back to her."

Jacob swung, a hard uppercut that sent Gideon staggering back several steps and bought him the time to scramble to his own feet. "No, I'm not. You stupid, thickheaded—"

With a roar, Gideon came back at him. This time he managed to take them both over the dividing wall between two rows of booths. It tangled them with its occupants, a group of workers who reacted far more belligerently than the elderly women.

A rough shove and a few blows took him and Gideon back to the floor, baptized by spilled food and drinks, and even more colorful curses that would have the ladies' ears burning. Jacob blocked another punch, Gideon's he thought, then caught his brother's thrown fist and turned the both of them, wrestling, trying to pin him. Gideon was strong, seasoned, but Jacob was faster, and they were both armed with Irish temper. It had always taken longer to rouse in Jacob, but once unleashed it was no less violent. Gideon ducked under the next blow and rammed his fist into Jacob's stomach. Jacob reacted with another punch to his face, hitting his lip and winning first blood.

The restaurant was clearing, people were shouting. Jacob was vaguely aware a couple of the less sensible workers had jumped into the fray, trying to pull them apart. In the end, they had to give up and stand back to avoid being casualties, for the two brothers were too skilled at fighting to countenance interruption and the workers just kept being tossed to the outside.

Jacob maneuvered them to the corner, caught Gideon by the scruff and slung him against the emergency exit. The alarm detonated when the crash bar gave way under Gideon's weight, but by then they were in the alley and out of the area involving innocent bystanders or destruction of property Jacob knew he didn't have the funds to replace.

He charged Gideon with a yell, tumbling them into a collection of garbage cans that scattered like bowling pins as they landed among them. In some distant part of his mind, Jacob knew they were riding the rage, letting it drown out the memories of loss that had bonded them so closely as well as driven them apart.

It drowned out everything, including the police sirens.

5

BECAUSE Gideon tried to trip Jacob on their way into the police station and Jacob responded by using his shoulder to ram him into the wall, the officer who'd brought them in had recommended to the guard on duty that they be cuffed to the bars on opposite sides of the communal cell. He'd also threatened them with an officer assault charge because they sandwiched him in the middle of the scuffle. Gideon's private arsenal had not helped matters. While the cops had been partially mollified by his concealed carry permit for the guns, Jacob was sure they were running every background check on him possible, including searching the data banks for international terrorists.

Perhaps because Jacob had been a little more polite to the cops and wasn't carrying twenty pounds of weapons like an action movie star, he'd been cuffed where he could sit on a bench, whereas Gideon's choice was standing or taking a seat on the questionable cesspool of the floor.

The guard on duty was posted at a desk near the cell. He kept an indifferent eye on them and the other occupants, ignoring any wisecracks as he worked on paperwork. Their cellmates were mostly drunks sleeping it off, a few petty criminals, a scared-looking white-collar kid who'd probably been pulled with pot in the car and was thrown in the tank to put the fear of God into him. He was keeping his head down, his hands twisting around each other as he tried not to look toward several of the more hardened offenders who were sharing sullen company in the corner.

Jacob felt the ache of the fight in every muscle. His eye and jaw were swelling and there was bruising in his ribs, but he didn't think he'd cracked any. Gideon sported a similarly damaged face. Despite that, Jacob wished they weren't cuffed. Beating on each other was preferable to staring at one another across thirty feet of space, everything said and unsaid vibrating in the air between them, making his headache worse.

"You look like shit," he said.

Gideon's head lifted. "You're not looking so pretty yourself."

"No. I mean you look like shit, Gid. This is beating you down."

"Shut up." Gideon turned his face away. "You don't get to talk to me as if you're my brother. After we leave here, I'm not looking back. You're one of them now. My brother's dead. You hear me?" He spun around abruptly, making the cuffs clank against the bars and earning a sharp glance from the guard. "Dead."

"So love's all about meeting your terms, is it?" *Idiot, stubborn, hardheaded jackass. You used to sing to me when I had nightmares. You used to smile.*

Gideon turned away farther, hunching a shoulder, but to Jacob's surprise, he responded, his voice low and gruff. "I'm past loving anyone, Jacob. I just can't handle it anymore. This is probably just the way it's meant to be."

The desolation in Gideon's tone was as cold as death, and Jacob wondered if the analogy was uneasily close to the reality of his brother's life.

"That's fortunate."

Jacob's attention swung to the rear of the cell. On first glance, the man looked like a well-heeled middle-aged businessman, a hooker's John or a DUI. But he was neither of those things. His eyes glittered in the shadows, and his smile revealed the hint of a sharpened tooth.

Jacob cursed his focus on his brother, which had kept him from more carefully noting all the cell occupants. The vampire had been blending into the shadows, screened by the restless movements of the others. Of course, if he'd been deliberately avoiding notice until now, Jacob might have missed him regardless. It didn't make their situation any less fucked. Gideon had gone on alert as well, straightening from the bars, his eyes narrowing. "Kyle Miller," he said flatly, telling Jacob they were in trouble, if he didn't have the small handful of brain cells required to recognize that already. "Tends to like to take his full quota. Just another of your happy, fuzzy vamps trying to live," he added, a cutting edge to his tone that made Jacob shoot him a narrow look.

"It's like dinner theater," the vampire observed, remaining seated in the deceptively casual pose, his hands linked around his knees, idly fingering the expensive fabric of his slacks. "So many interesting dramas play out here. I could have used the sewers to head home an hour ago, but watching you two has been so stimulating. Oh, no worries"—when he nodded toward the boy, Jacob noted the vacant confusion in the kid's eyes, the lingering aftermath of vampire compulsion instead of alcohol or drugs as he first thought—"I've already supped well. I'm not interested in blood. However, I think I'll be killing him." He indicated Gideon. "As you can tell, he's known to me and my kind. His luck runs out tonight."

Jacob surged to his feet, the cuff bringing him up short. He could yell for the guard, but the guard would not only end up dead, he wouldn't even get the door unlocked before the vampire struck at Gideon. He wouldn't even know what had happened. At the moment, their conversation wasn't even being tracked, everyone else involved in their own miserable circumstances and the guard tuning out anything that wasn't life threatening.

In the meantime, Gideon hadn't moved at all. His brother met the vamp's gaze as if he wasn't hampered by a lack of weapons and limited mobility.

With a jolt, Jacob realized Gideon had perhaps had other reasons for wanting to meet with him today. Looking for hope from the only reason to live he had anymore—his brother—Gideon would have seen Jacob's betrayal as the last straw. Now he just didn't give a shit at all, which made him hazardous on a lot of levels, mostly to himself.

For the first time in his life, Gideon needed Jacob more than Jacob needed him. He might be past asking for help or wanting it, but that was too bad. Jacob wasn't going to let his stubborn brother's ass get wasted by some midlevel vamp.

"This isn't going to happen," Jacob declared. Kyle's gaze shifted to him.

"You're brothers. You're the prettier of the two."

"Told you," Gideon said, though he didn't shift his gaze.

"Asshole," Jacob responded mildly. He kept a matching deadly focus on their enemy, forming a triangle of tension that finally caught the guard's attention. Now the other inmates were stiffening, muttering. While they hadn't followed the exchange, they certainly could sense some violent entertainment brewing.

"Knock it off in there."

The vamp's gaze flickered over Jacob, lingered in areas less than comfortable. "Perhaps when I'm done, I'll take some dessert, after all. I can make you hard as I drink, human," he whispered. "Increase your pleasure and your prudish embarrassment. I bet your brother hasn't seen you jack off since you were young enough to share a room."

"You're not touching my brother," Jacob said. "Or me." He could hear the guard starting to move, the chair scraping back. If he came into the cell, he was dead.

"I'm not seeing you in a position to stop me."

"Perhaps not." Jacob inclined his head with cold courtesy. "But my Mistress can blow you away like dust."

In a blink, the vamp stood by Jacob, his face close enough for a kiss, his fangs exposed. He had a hand on the back of Jacob's neck, fingers snarled in his hair. Jacob steeled himself not to move. Gideon surged forward, metal clanking. The guard called out, telling Miller to move his ass back, his hand on his radio, a breath away from calling for backup.

It was all white noise as far as Jacob was concerned. He kept his focus on the man in front of him, all his energy devoted to maintaining a cool reserve, showing no fear or doubt even against the vampire's heavy wave of compulsion. It was like a sickly sweet cough syrup infiltrating his nose and lungs, but it was neutralized when attempted on a human already claimed as a servant.

The only good thing was it appeared to have confused the guard, who was rocking on the balls of his feet, torn between heading toward the cell, punching his radio and going back to his desk.

Kyle's nostrils flared, telling Jacob he'd detected his Mistress's marks, and not just the ones she'd administered with her fangs. Sexual emissions could be detected by vampires long after they'd occurred, even after bathing. On the first night she'd brought him to her home, Lyssa had rubbed her slippery response on his limbs, his cock, his chest . . . It had been a sensual experience he remembered vividly, and she'd told him it was one of the ways she would mark him as hers to other vamps. Since then, she'd done it several more times. "Who is your Mistress, mortal?" Kyle hissed it between his teeth, obviously warring between bloodlust and self-preservation.

"Lady Elyssa Amaterasu Yamato Wentworth."

The vamp tensed, but didn't retreat. "You lie."

"You know the marks are there, even if you're not powerful enough to detect who made them. Are you willing to risk her wrath if I speak true? Does she even know you're in her territory? My brother is under my protection. Hence, under hers."

"Don't need your goddamn protection," Gideon snapped. "Get away from him, Miller. Deal with me if you've got the balls."

"Lady Wentworth's servant wouldn't be in a jail cell like a barroom brawler. In the company of a vampire killer." Kyle surveyed Jacob scornfully. "Nothing about you says servant to me. Whoever's service you are in, you have not been in it long. He or she won't miss you overmuch. Killing you both is starting to look more appealing to me." His face got closer. Another millimeter and his lips would be meeting Jacob's, an idea so repugnant Jacob thought he might prefer to get his throat torn out.

Kyle was going to call his bluff, and he and Gideon were going to die. Even if he and Gideon had been armed and free, a vamp had a better-than-average chance of killing them. Cuffed to the cell bars, they were sheep staked out in a wolf's den.

"I think you need to remove your hands from my servant, Kyle. And every other part of your presence."

Kyle's gaze snapped to the cell door. Lyssa stood next to the guard, a calming hand resting on his shoulder, watching the exchange impassively.

Despite her stillness, Kyle reacted as if she'd swooped down upon him like a bird of prey. He backed away with none of his earlier grace, knocking into the cluster of smoking inmates. They shoved him aside, too interested in the appearance of a woman with Lyssa's striking features to react to the insult.

Kyle's use of compulsion had been like scattering marbles across the floor, causing imbalance, confusion, a loud mental clatter. Lyssa's was like the movement of water, simply taking away resistance and thought. The inmates did not make vulgar quips, just stared at her openmouthed, lust in their gazes. His eyes unfocused, the guard moved to the wall and pressed the buzzer to open the cell door. It slid open, but no one moved. It was as if time had stopped, and the only sound was the distant noise of the police station offices upstairs.

When Jacob glanced over at his brother, he found Gideon was as calm and riveted as any of them. If anything, his expression was even more blank and unaware.

"Don't do that to him," Jacob said. "My lady, please."

"He's seen much wear since I saw him last," she observed, not without a trace of compassion in her cool tone. "Don't worry about him. His weary mind needs the rest. We'll take him home and give him some cosseting, you and me." Her gaze shifted to Jacob, the jeweled beauty of her green eyes striking him low in the gut.

I was woken from my sleep to find you were in danger, a danger you were oblivious to until too late because of your preoccupation with your brother. As a result, I had to get here without adequate time to do my makeup or hair. When I get you home, you're going to pay for that.

Her emotions were a dark, shifting mass he couldn't penetrate. He'd known she might withdraw from him like this for a little while. He'd wanted the third mark, fought her will for it and won. But now she was shutting him out. He wanted to touch her even as he had a strange impulse to run away from her *and* his brother, from the conflict in his heart they represented. He wanted to tell her he was sorry, though he knew he wasn't. He wanted to cross the distance between them, kiss the hem of her dress, wait for her touch on his head like a benediction.

Despite the circumstances, he couldn't help his response to her. The emotional impact of his brother's current state made him crave her on every level. He'd just tried to convince Gideon what it was about her, and here it was, active, thrumming in the air. The third mark had made it almost unbearably powerful, the connection they had. He was torn between wanting to do anything she asked and needing to resist her, to perversely prove his love was more than just a magical compulsion to an otherworldly creature.

Flatterer. Her voice was a whisper in his mind, unable to be resisted. *I know that, Jacob. I also know what you've been doing today. All of it. I think it's best you don't defy me anymore. After all, you did say he was under my protection, correct?* "Do I have your obedience?"

"To the best of my ability, my lady."

" 'Yes, my lady,' will do."

"I don't wish to lie—"

"Oh, for the love of God, your honesty is fair killing me." The snap of her voice reverberated through the room like a shock wave. Kyle flattened himself against the wall. Jacob thought if Kyle could have dissipated and materialized beyond the bars, he would have done it. However, despite the popular movies, that was not a power vampires had. The only way out of the cell was through that door, past Lyssa. Kyle wasn't that brave. He stayed where he was.

At her snarl, the others had shifted, her menace disturbing the calm she'd imposed upon them.

Even children know a parent sometimes prefers to hear a lie. I know your soul, Jacob. Just say "yes, my lady," so I can have the fleeting pleasure of pretending it's true.

"Yes, my lady." He couldn't help the smile her impatient words almost coaxed from him. He did his best to control it, but from her narrow gaze he doubted he was successful.

A fleeting breeze and a quick impression were the only evidence she'd moved. She slammed Kyle to his knees with one hand, holding his skull to the filthy concrete wall at the back of the cell. With minimal pressure she could crush it. Jacob was sure Kyle was all too aware of that. He'd survive it, but he'd wake up in a hospital under human hands in the bright light of day.

"You *ever* touch what belongs to me again and there will be nowhere you can hide. So that you remember . . ."

Kyle let out a cry and held the side of his face, blood surging from between his fingers at his ear.

Lyssa flicked away the piece she'd taken, the diamond stud earring still in it. Thinking of it getting lost in the debris and trash that littered the floor of the cell, Jacob felt a bit nauseous. Dirt from shoes, gum . . . body parts. Some inmate would be willing to loosen the backing and filch the diamond stud for his own ear.

"My apologies, my lady," Kyle said. Though she let go, he stayed bent over, trying to convey obsequiousness and hold on to his ear, protecting himself as best he could. "If I'd truly believed—"

A howl, and he was holding the other ear. A bigger piece tossed away this time. Jacob watched it roll and stop behind the Nike-covered heel of the mesmerized kid, Kyle's earlier meal.

"Don't lie," Lyssa said. "Go home, Kyle. You've done enough for tonight. Don't let me catch you on my bad side again. You won't survive it."

He nodded, backing away from her, bumping Jacob and splattering blood on his shoulder before he spun toward the door. The guard still held it open. Looking around the room, Jacob saw she held fifteen men in a hypnotic state with no visible effort at all, his brother included. He didn't care for the way the men looked at her, under her control or not, but he supposed Lady Lyssa couldn't help but mesmerize any man's senses, with or without persuasion.

"Now you go for the charm," she responded to his thoughts. "Maybe you should have tried more of that on your brother. You wouldn't have landed up here."

"I didn't have much time to use it. Even if I'd wanted to."

She arched a brow. "Are you telling Mommy he started it?"

He shot her an annoyed look and this time she was the one who suppressed a smile, but it was a tight, controlled gesture. Drawing closer, she rested her hand on the joining point of his shoulder to his neck, ran a proprietary hand over his chest, the sore ribs. "You're in pain."

"It's not bad, my lady. Nothing a couple aspirin won't cure."

"Mmm." Now she raised her attention to his face, took his chin and made him shift his face left and right, displaying the swelling and bruising. "I wasn't talking about your body. The third mark will have that healed by morning, if not sooner." Her gaze shifted to Gideon. Something deadly in her expression warned Jacob. Quickly he twined his fingers with hers on the cuffed side, drawing her attention to him.

"He was trying to protect me, make decisions that are mine to make." *Much as it was my decision to accept the third mark.*

She withdrew her touch. "Release them both," she ordered the entranced cop. "We're going home."

"But bail—"

"The diner owner isn't pressing charges." She looked between him and Gideon. "Since the two of you aren't charging one another for assault—I assume—there's nothing to hold you for. That's what the police will remember after we've left."

"Why would the diner owner—"

"I paid him enough to convince him."

The cop unlocked the cuff on his wrist, went over to Gideon

and did the same. Jacob rubbed his arm, eyed her as she studied him.

Why didn't you just let me rot in here a day or so?

Perhaps I didn't care to spend the evening without my servant.

Before he could reply to that, she'd turned away. "Follow me."

6

SHE kept Gideon under her compulsion, guiding him into the limo and ordering Mr. Ingram to take them home. Jacob didn't like it. He'd wanted her to lift it as soon as they'd left the cell. Gideon's capitulation disturbed him, the lackluster look in his eyes too close to a different version of what he'd displayed when he thought Kyle was going to kill them. But Lyssa had given Jacob a quelling look as soon as he had the thought. Since she was trying to control the minds of a building filled with armed police officers, he managed to suppress his reaction until they were safely in the limo and driving off.

"Gideon's not weak. He's got a strong will. He's got to be fighting you like a son of a bitch."

"Compulsion imposed by a vampire of my strength does not allow that level of consciousness, Jacob." She curled her legs up under her in the seat facing the two of them. She wore a simple, short black dress that clung to her curves and stopped at midthigh. Sexy, classy. Even though she'd pulled her hair in a quick twist and hadn't put on any makeup or jewelry as she'd informed him, she didn't need any. It reminded him, however, how quickly she'd come to their aid, and diluted some of his irritation.

She wasn't likely in the mood to be pushed. Which might or

might not make him hold his tongue, depending on the mood he himself was in.

"It's like anesthesia," she continued, even as her eyes challenged him, acknowledging his thought. "You start counting down from a hundred and have just enough time for the worry, 'What if I don't go to sleep before they start cutting?' and then you're waking up in your hospital bed, the procedure done." Her gaze shifted between him and Gideon again, lingering, comparing them in a way that disturbed Jacob. It made him wonder what she was thinking. What she was up to. "You're right, though," she added quietly. "He does have a very strong will. He's just very, very tired right now. Sick to his soul. Let him have the rest. It's not painful, I promise. It's like he's asleep, in a dream."

"He'll hate knowing you did it to him. The longer you hold it, the worse it will be. Please, my lady. I know him."

She sighed, gave him a searing look. However, as she turned her eyes to the window, Jacob sensed a change in the charged air in the limo.

Gideon blinked. Straightened. His gaze darted to Jacob, then back to Lyssa. "How—" His eyes narrowed, pinned on Jacob with ominous intent. "You let her put her frigging mind control on me. You—"

"And I will do it again if you two start pummeling one another like you're in the back of your parents' station wagon. Jacob didn't *let* me do anything, Gideon. He's my servant. I am not his."

Gideon glared at her. "You can let me off at the next corner."

"I could, but I won't." Straightening out her legs, she crossed them, folded her hands over her lap and stared back at him. "You need a shower." Her delicate nose wrinkled. "Food. A good night's sleep. I'd offer the same to a stray dog. While the dog would be far more deserving and definitely more grateful, you also need some time with your brother."

"I have no brother."

She laughed, startling them both because the sound of it was so easy and relaxed. It rippled through the tension in the car, disrupting and confusing it. "Of course you have a brother. Your anger doesn't change that. Had Kyle done anything to Jacob, you'd have broken all the bones of your hand to slip the handcuffs and try to kill him. I've lived a long time, Gideon. Families have fights; they go their separate ways, sometimes for years. But you and Jacob are bonded. You love him. Your bafflement at the choices he's made, feeling betrayed and angered, perhaps even jealous, doesn't change the fact."

"I'm not jealous—"

"Not of his choice. Of how he feels about me. The commitment he's made to me, instead of to you."

The knife of the truth twisted inside of Jacob. She was right. In Gideon's mind, he'd not only left his brother to fight his adversaries alone, but had made the choice to join the other side.

Sometimes a person goes down the wrong path and the only way to help him back to the right one is to leave him alone to find it.

While he appreciated his lady offering virtually the same thought he'd had right before their fight, it didn't help the aching sense of guilt. He looked at Gideon, at the haggard lines of his face. Felt the anger and hatred emanating from him as he stubbornly crossed his arms and refused to say anything further.

You didn't leave Rex, Jacob thought.

No. I killed him. He might have been better off if I had left him.

Though she didn't say it, he heard it echo in the pregnant silence that followed the thought. *Thomas certainly would have been.*

And Jacob never would have gotten to be this close to her, because she wouldn't have needed a new human servant. Right or wrong, the thought was in his mind. From the shadowing of her expression, he could tell she heard it.

When they reached the house, Jacob expected Gideon to balk at going in, but his brother had apparently decided to go along with Lady Lyssa's intent. He got out of the car without comment and stared at the fortresslike structure while Lyssa spoke to Mr. Ingram.

He thinks he can scope out your home for attack advantage, my lady. I wouldn't advise letting him in like this.

I know, Jacob. Don't worry about it.

~

Jacob set a record for a fast shower, pulled on just a pair of jeans and was somewhat mollified to find Bran lying outside Gideon's door, along with a stack of extra towels. The wolfhound padded away happily as Jacob relieved him of his post and picked up the towels, giving only a cursory knock before he entered.

Gideon had apparently found a small towel in the bathroom. He held it around his hips, water still dotting his body as he surveyed the room with careful precision.

"Looking for vulnerabilities?" Jacob asked. "Ways to come in and stake her in her sleep? You might as well sign your own death warrant. She knows when a new squirrel enters her property."

"Vampires aren't always on guard, little brother." Gideon turned, held out his hand to take the towel that Jacob offered.

"No, they aren't. That's why they have human servants to pick up the slack." Jacob watched him swap out the smaller swatch of terry cloth for the larger one, tucking it in at his hip. At some point, a blade had left an impressive crescent-shaped scar over his kidney area. He wouldn't have been surprised if the intent of the attacker had been to cut out the vital organ. "But if you try to take her on her own ground, on any ground, she'll cut you down before you even glance her way. You've never dealt with a vampire with her kind of power."

"Is that what gets you going? All that power in that fuck-me-eight-ways-to-Sunday body?"

While Jacob refused to let his temper be tripped by such an obvious ploy, he did experience a strong urge to ram his brother's hard head into the dresser. It was good, sturdy oak. It might withstand the blow.

"I'm here by my own choice, Gideon. For my own reasons."

Gideon rubbed his hands over his face, the massive muscles in his arms bunching, turning scars into pale silver snakes rippling over his skin. "Just please don't tell me you're with her because you think she loves you."

"No." Jacob put down the rest of the towels. "I'm with her because I know I love *her*."

Gideon made a derisive hissing between his teeth.

"Boys."

The two men turned. Normally Jacob sensed when his lady was

near, a feather brush of something insubstantial along his neck like a light kiss, but this time she'd disguised her approach.

She'd taken down her hair and brushed it out, the task she usually preferred him to do. The long strands wove down the smooth cream skin of her arms. Her lips had been touched by red. The dress she wore now was a black formfitting satin, her breasts high and clefted deep from whatever creative underwear she wore beneath it. As she leaned against the wall next to the open door, her hands were folded behind her back, the position tilting her breasts upward. As she watched them, she rocked one foot back and forth on a stiletto heel, riding the skirt up, showing a hint of garter.

Pure sex. Any man would have been stirred by the sight.

Don't do this. But it was a weak whisper against the desire being conjured in him against his will. For once, she was using compulsion on him to override his defiance. His cock could care less about right and wrong. In fact, wrong was looking damn appealing.

"What are you—" Gideon had backed up a couple of steps, was shaking his head, trying to shake off the magic. Lyssa moved forward. When she did, her approach was like a wave of heat.

Gideon planted his feet, his expression defiant. She kept coming. Closing her fingers over the towel, she tugged it away and let it drop as her eyes lowered with blatant appreciation. He was already powerfully aroused. When her fingers closed around him, her nails teasing his testicles, he closed his eyes, a growl emitting from between his lips.

"So full of anger and pain," she whispered. "Your body is starved for a woman's touch. But you don't trust yourself anymore. You're afraid you'll want her so much, you'll hurt her."

Gideon's hands had closed into fists, his muscles taut, resisting whatever it was she was stirring to life inside him.

"You don't want her to give you her body. You want to take it. Feel her surrender to you, open her heart, but you're terrified of what you'll do to that fragile thing . . .

"And so tired," she murmured even more softly, now so close her leg brushed his, the hem of the snug dress touching his bare thigh, her stiletto planted between his braced feet. "You can't hurt me,

Gideon. I know the kind of loss you're feeling. Like you, it has made me into the creature I am now."

"What if . . . I want it to hurt?"

"I can make it hurt." Her lips curved, wet sin, as she twisted his meaning. But Jacob wasn't sure she hadn't answered his brother exactly the way he needed her to. "I can give you a night of true rest. The kind of rest a man gets after he's fucked a woman past the point of thought. When the body is so exhausted he has no energy left to hold on to anything."

"No . . . no biting." He opened his eyes, triumphant with the effort of making the demand. Darker things dwelled in his gaze. He almost looked demonic, a handsome, ravaged man willing to do whatever things Heaven or Hell demanded of him just to have something to distract him from his own emptiness.

"No biting." She nodded. "You're safe from that. You're safe from everything here tonight. I'm going to take care of you. So is Jacob."

Come to me, Jacob. I need to feel your touch.

He wanted to turn her over his knee and spank her, but he moved forward, a whirl of thoughts in his mind. He noted Gideon's body, hard and lean, crisscrossed with scars, a man who could never be mistaken for anything but a warrior. A man who'd been fighting all his adult life. A man who'd been trying to get himself killed since he was barely grown because he wasn't the one who'd died in an alley, like the girl he'd loved. Or on a beach, like the parents he'd needed.

Angry. Resentful of always having to fight. Protect.

Jacob paused. *He resents me.*

Of course. Her thought was matter-of-fact, almost a sigh of impatience. *The older brother, required by his honor to protect you. Of course he was angry that they left him. That he alone was charged with worrying about you. That he found love, something of his own, and it was taken away. That he was left by the brother to whom he'd given so much. None of that has to be here tonight, though. Not between any of us. There is only need.*

Despite his resistance, his anger at her manipulation of the situation, he was now standing just behind her. Leaning in, he buried his nose in her hair. The ache in his gut from looking at his brother's suffering lessened. With her free hand, she found his arm, guided it so his hand gripped her hip. Which inspired him to do the same with the other hand, sliding them both around her waist. It brought his body against hers, his hardening cock pressing against the cleft of her ass, so accessible in the soft satin. She rubbed against him, a slow, sinuous circle, even as her hand turned, her knuckles feathering up Gideon's hard belly, his broad chest. Her other hand was still wrapped around his brother's thick cock, her thumb teasing the head so he was already shuddering.

Jacob brought his hands under her breasts, lifting them, squeezing, drawing his brother's gaze there as she arched in aroused response. Savage male instinct compelled Jacob to do what he did next.

Seizing the neckline of the dress in both hands, he tore it open, baring her breasts to Gideon, holding the fabric in tight fists so she was pinned against Jacob's chest, her body fully leaning against him, head settling into the curve between his shoulder and throat.

Gideon's gaze lingered on the ripe curves, held up so temptingly in the satin demi-cup bra. His brother had always been a breast man. While small, Lyssa's were superbly shaped, firm, full. Jacob slid his hand down the satin, over the hint of hard nipple. Catching the slender strap between the cups, he yanked the bra up, freeing her breasts with a rough wobble of motion that added intensity to his brother's dark blue eyes. Jacob pressed the heel of his hand against her throat, his thumb teasing her there, eliciting a soft mewl of desire as her breasts quivered. Gideon's hands came forward now, his fingers dusting the tops as Jacob gripped one beneath with his free hand and offered it up. Gideon hesitated, then bent and closed his mouth over the nipple. His other hand captured the free breast, taking possession. She undulated beneath their hands, her head arching back even farther as Gideon suckled, squeezed.

He couldn't know what Gideon was thinking. Jacob wasn't sure if that was a place he wanted to go anyhow. Something hard to define was pumping through his own blood. This was the woman he loved, that he considered his, even though he knew his possessiveness amused or irritated her by turns. Over the past few weeks, she'd offered his body to others. Commanded him to submit. Taught him that pleasure could be found in surrendering to her will. During those times, he'd found he needed her touch, her command, as a compass to find that pleasure. So now the tables were turned. She intended to seduce his brother, perhaps only for the reasons she'd stated. But to immerse them all in the flood, she needed Jacob's ability to arouse her. That admission, so simply offered with those words—*Come to me, Jacob. I need to feel your touch*—had him torn between an intense, emotional reaction to the revelation, and a close-to-the-edge, violent response at the thought she intended him to share her with another man. His own brother.

Occupied as they were, both men still noticed when she lowered her hands and began inching up her skirt. Up, up, showing the lace stockings, the garters, the point of her bare sex. No panties.

I want you inside me, Jacob. In me from behind, before your brother fucks me. I want you there.

Jacob dropped his hand down, moved over her thigh. He pressed his leg behind hers to hold her trapped between him there and Gideon's hip. When he pushed his fingers into her pussy, into a wetness that sucked him in, he saw Gideon's eyes glitter with lust. She writhed, drawing in an uneven breath, her fangs baring.

"Beg me, my lady." He could have thought it, but instead demanded it in a rough voice. He didn't know if his need to punish her for this was her influence, his own or the synergy of the moment. It didn't matter.

Gideon's attention flickered to him, then back to the woman between them. As if Jacob's demand had released any last inhibitions, he surrendered to his own desires with the snarl of a rabid animal. Seizing both breasts, Gideon pulled them up higher, arching her almost impossibly as he descended on the nipple again, his suckling ferocious as he brought teeth as well as tongue into it.

She turned her head into Jacob's throat, pricked him with her fangs, rubbing her delectable ass harder against his cock. As her eyes lifted to his, she raised an arm and looped it around his neck, her palm flat between his shoulder blades. Using the leverage, she raised her legs. Gideon, picking up his cue, slid his hands under her, wrapped her around him, his cock trapped between their bodies, close to the point of decision.

You'll let your brother fuck me without staking your claim first?

You're playing with me, my lady.

I'm commanding you. Begging you. I need you.

He caught the hem of her skirt.

I won't be gentle, my lady. You've pissed me off too much.

I know. That makes you even harder.

With a muttered curse, he opened his jeans, bunched the fabric of her garment in his fist against her lower back and drove into her. She'd apparently lubricated herself before this, for there was a slickness between her buttocks that took him in fast and deep. She cried out, part pain, part something else as Gideon drove into her in front. They were both big men, and their sizeable cocks filled her to the point that Jacob could feel the pressure of his brother in the channel of her pussy as he fucked her ass.

Raw, visceral need. Nothing soft and feminine about this moment. She was letting them be the base male animals they were. Encouraging it. Desiring it, even as Jacob sensed her genuine intent to give Gideon a female port in the storm he'd created of his life. It hadn't been a lie, he knew. She did understand his pain and sorrow, even if Gideon didn't believe she did. Whether it was a woman's intuition, her many years of life, her own experiences in losing her husband or whatever combination of vampire and Fey magic that made her what she was, she had that gift. She'd brought out responses and emotions in Jacob he hadn't even known he had. He couldn't deny that, whether she was still compelling this moment or not.

As she bucked up, the paleness of her throat was displayed, the bumps of her sternum, the slope of her breast over her heart. Though he knew her to be more than capable of defending herself, the melting of her body in his grasp and the vulnerable offering of her throat to both an active and a former vampire hunter told him she trusted him to keep her safe, to protect her.

Her orgasm built like the strum of piano keys, playing along his length. It drew out the notes of his own response, making everything tighten until he was sure when he exploded it would rip him apart. Gideon's shoulders were bunched into rolls of hard muscle, his fingers gripping her hips with bruising force. His forearms brushed Jacob's, his thrusts knocking her ass harder onto his cock, her buttocks pressed against the top of Jacob's thighs. Gideon's eyes fastened on her throat, and he worked his way up her sternum, his lips curling back.

"Sssh . . ." She caught his chin, even as her breath rasped out of her. "No . . . Gideon. No biting."

The smile was in her voice, but Jacob also heard the strain, for she was so close. He gave another powerful thrust, taking himself deep. Gideon's face contorted as he did the same in perfect sync, and Lyssa's orgasm shattered her. She convulsed against their powerful grips, her cries elevating to a scream. They held on, Jacob stretching her, feeling the tight clench of her muscles, the rhythmic movements. He had to hold her tightly, for Gideon was thrusting into her just as hard, neither of them granting her any mercy, only wanting to feel the same type of mind-altering pleasure.

Jacob closed his eyes and rode the release. Jetting hard, he bathed her inside with his seed as he heard his brother bellow in the grasp of a climax just as intense. Over all that, he reveled in Lyssa's cries, the rake of her nails that marked his neck. Her legs were wrapped around Gideon, Jacob buried so deeply into her that his feet were almost on top of his brother's. Air moved over his own balls each time his brother's testicles slapped the base of her cunt.

When they finally came to a stumbling halt and he opened his eyes, he saw she had marked Gideon's shoulder with the nails of her other hand. Gideon's forehead had fallen to her shoulder, his own shoulders rising and falling fast, his hands still clutched on her hips. As if they were melded on every level, Jacob lifted his own hand as Lyssa reached up. Their hands overlapped to rest on Gideon's head, giving reassurance and comfort, encouraging him to take slow breaths, for his breathing was too deep and shuddering to be only from physical exertion.

In the midst of the maelstrom of response, this moment was quiet, separate. The eye of the storm. Jacob wanted to reach back through the years to touch his brother as he did now, to give him peace, to let him know he'd done well, help him heal. To let him know that he loved him, no matter what. None of the rest mattered.

Jacob took some deep breaths of his own, feeling his lady's shoulder blades pressed into his chest, her hair soft against his jaw. When he touched her chin, needing her, she obliged, lifting her face for a meeting of mouths, the taste of her tongue, the scrape of a fang. He was still learning how to kiss her without damage to his own mouth.

Practice makes perfect, Sir Vagabond.

Smiling against her lips despite the intensity of the past few moments, he drew it out, exploring her mouth even further, tightening his grip on her throat. Through the third mark as well as lover's intuition, he felt her simmering and knew he would want her again soon, too. He was still hard. From the squeezing pressure he was experiencing in her ass, he suspected Gideon was also. He ruffled his brother's hair, tugged on it, not to make him raise his head, but to continue that sense of comfort. Nearness. As he thought about the words Gideon had said to him at the diner, words that had cut so carelessly and brutally, he knew they meant nothing. Hadn't Lyssa proven as much when she'd laughed at Gideon for saying he didn't have a brother?

While he might want to have a heart-to-heart with her about her methods, Lyssa had shown him the depths of his brother's despair and anger in a way separate from his own ego. So it was the most natural thing to say the words that came to his lips now.

"You took good care of me, Gid," he murmured. "You always did. And because you did such a good job, I don't need you to do it anymore. Do something for yourself for once. Give yourself happiness again so you can remember what's worth fighting for and what's not."

Gideon slowly raised his head. Lyssa's fingers were still tangled in his hair, and as he moved, her palm slid down his face to his neck, to a bare shoulder. As he blinked at her, Jacob could see the emotions warring in his face.

"You made me do that," Gideon said at last.

"I could lie to you and say yes," Lyssa responded, "but the only compulsion I used on you, either of you, was in the first five minutes. When I took your towel, it was your free will that let it go."

Gideon withdrew from her, though he did it with courtesy. Even so, Jacob's hands tightened on her protectively, uncertain of Gideon's mood now. As Jacob eased out of her, letting her feet touch the floor, his brother apparently caught the wariness of his stance, for a muscle ticked in his jaw.

"She's safe with me, Jacob. I . . ." He broke off, arched a brow. "Am I your guest or your prisoner, Lady Lyssa?"

She surveyed him with a leisurely bold approval that brought a flush to his cheeks and made his cock jump, such that he turned away and picked up the towel. Jacob felt a ripple of amusement go through her at his muttered curse.

"While I do like the connotations of the word *prisoner* when it refers to a handsome and powerful male, you are in fact my invited guest, Gideon."

Wrapping the towel around his waist, Gideon sat down on the edge of the bed, maintaining an upright stance with visible effort. "Then you have my word." His attention went back to his brother. "While I'm her guest, I won't do or try anything to cause her harm."

As if he could.

Yes, my lady. He could. Please, for my own peace of mind, don't underestimate Gideon.

There was a robe hanging on the armoire, one she'd apparently left in here when she brought the towels. Jacob retrieved it at her unspoken command as she shrugged out of her disheveled dress and undergarments. When she put her arms back, he slid it onto her shoulders, satin onto silk, while Gideon watched. She didn't belt the robe. Rolling off the sheer stockings, she stepped out of the heels she'd kept on during their violent encounter. It made Jacob wonder if Gideon had stiletto marks on his ass.

Despite that, as she padded away from him and toward his

brother, with her hair down and feet now bare, he thought she looked like an innocent girl. However, Jacob knew the view Gideon was getting was much different. Not just the sensual beauty of her naked body, shadowed temptingly under the movement of the folds of fabric, but her jade green eyes that held all the mystery of Woman since the beginning of time. He'd been pinned by that gaze often enough to know.

When she reached his brother, for a couple of breaths, she simply stood, looking at him. Jacob couldn't see Gideon's face, but whatever she saw in it pained her, for a sympathetic response rippled through her. When she reached out, his hand shot up, caught her wrist.

Jacob started forward, but Lyssa's sharp mental command stopped him. She was in control of the situation. She lifted the other hand. When Gideon caught that one, she used her body, pressing forward, one step, two steps, until she stood between his knees, him holding her hands so the robe fluttered out to either side like wings.

Abruptly, he let her go, dropping his head so his hair brushed her bare breasts. A tremor ran through his broad, scarred back. He whispered something Jacob didn't quite catch. Lyssa repeated it for him.

Just go away.

She wrapped her arms around him, laying her head over his. "I think you've had far too much of that in your life. Those who've left you, and those you've driven away. Now it's time to sleep," she said softly. "Just sleep. Because soon I'm going to want you. I'll use you again and again tonight, Gideon. I can't draw all the poison out, but I can draw out enough to help you remember what it was like to be whole."

"I can't. I don't want this."

Jacob silently left them to clean himself up in the bathroom. When he came back, she was turning down the bed, easing Gideon into it on his side, then herself behind him. When she reached a hand back, Jacob slid in behind her, spooning around her body.

"Jacob will protect us while we sleep. He'll protect us both."

"Who'll protect him . . . from you?" Gideon muttered sleepily.

Her hand paused, but then she resumed her stroking of his brother's dark hair, spreading it on his shoulders.

"Sssh . . . just sleep."

~

Jacob, I'm hungry.

Gideon's breath was even. Lyssa passed her hand over his bare flesh, drawing the covers up over him. Then she turned and nestled into Jacob's arms, her nose nuzzling, seeking his throat like a kitten.

Thank God the third mark gave him stamina far exceeding that of a regular man, for she'd lived up to her promise, or threat, depending on how a man looked at it. Gideon was sleeping deeply, the sleep of a man who'd been brought to orgasm multiple times in just the past hour and a half.

The last time, she'd laid her robe over Gideon's face to form a loose blindfold. She'd tangled his wrists in the sash without tying it, giving him the illusion but not the reality of restraint. Then she'd moved down his body and put her mouth over him, causing him to fist his hands in the iron bars of the bed and yank hard as he thrust himself into her mouth. She'd been on her knees, her hips high in the air, and Jacob had stood on his knees behind her, thrusting into her wet pussy this time, feeling as if he was coming home, pumping her slowly, stroking her the way she liked until he was rewarded by her cry of release against the flesh of his brother's erection, the heat of her breath pushing Gideon over as well. Just the recollection of her slick folds rippling over him was enough to get him hard again. Apparently the third mark conveyed some of the vampire's sexual appetite with it. Or maybe it was just her effect on him.

My blood is yours, my lady. As am I.

She put her temple against his jaw. *I know that.* She laid her hand on his forearm, the one she'd broken not so long ago, her fingers gentle. As always, he felt a shadow of regret from her. She'd apologized for doing it. Actually, the night she'd done it, she'd tried to kill herself, thinking she was becoming the monster her husband, Rex, had become. Rather than a woman dealing with a terminal illness who had lashed out at the loss of control she was beginning to experience from the symptoms.

He'll be gone tomorrow, won't he? Jacob thought the question.

We've broken open an infected wound. Drained off the pus. He'll have to decide if he'll let it heal or get it infected again.

He rolled her to her back and she let him, her legs opening to accept him and the teasing pressure of his cock. An arch and the head was seated in her opening, her eyes darkening. Jacob began to ease forward, pressing his knees into the bed, moving slowly, quiet. He wanted his brother to sleep, and not just because of his own desire for privacy at the moment. Her fingers curled around his neck, bringing his full weight down on her so she could nip at his throat, lick, make his cock harden further inside so that her own muscles spasmed in reaction. He buried a groan against her hair even as her teeth pierced him with searing pain, followed by the stroke of her tongue as she began to take in his blood, replenishing the strength the evening had taken from her.

Moments like this, he almost could forget what they faced. Could pretend they'd have years and years to explore one another. Years to be infuriated by her, amused by her. Besotted by her. She'd seemed invincible tonight, omnipotent. So beautiful and powerful, she was beyond the touch of death and sickness. But she needed his blood, his strength. As he'd predicted, the third mark was helping her maintain her strength in a way he hadn't been able to offer with just the second mark.

Are you saying I told you so, Sir Vagabond?

His lips curved against her temple even as his fingers curled into her hair, the other hand dropping below the covers. He slid down the nip of her waist and flare of hip to grip her thigh, press deeper at a better angle. It caused a hitch in her focus, both in her mind and in the gasp that caught in her throat even as she swallowed his blood.

Smugness is a rare luxury with you, my lady. I beg your leave to indulge it.

Clever tongue. I think I'd have it cut out of you if it weren't . . . so . . . clever.

He kept his movements torturously slow. As such, they were both without breath or words at the end as the climax rippled through them. She pressed her mouth over the now closed wound to muffle her cries, he doing the same with his face pressed between the pillow and her hair, his body drawn into a bow over her trembling one, arms and legs intertwined in a way he never wanted to untangle.

When he turned his head, he saw Gideon had rolled over, his eyes half-open though still full of drowsiness. It made Jacob wonder if his brother was truly awake or would think the moment was just a dream when he woke later. Then Gideon reached out, stroked a hand of gruff affection over his head, grunted and turned away again. He'd have pulled the covers off them if Jacob hadn't grabbed hold and tugged at the key moment, keeping the blankets equally distributed.

"He used to do that all the time when we shared a bed at my aunt and uncle's," Jacob muttered with a fraternal look of disgust at his brother's wide back. *One night, to tease him, I wrapped up in the covers like a burrito before he got into bed. He had to dump me on the floor to unroll me.*

"It wasn't easy for the two of you."

Surprised, he raised his head to look down into her face, illuminated by candles she'd had him light earlier. "No, it wasn't. But it could have been a lot worse. Our aunt and uncle were good to us, even though they had three other kids. That was okay." His gaze drifted back to Gideon. "We had each other. Always." A shadow crossed his mind, a familiar specter, one he'd always wrestled with, but now . . . The woman beneath him had lived for centuries. While there were many times he rebelled against her sense of superiority, he couldn't help but wonder at her thoughts.

You did what you had to do. You weren't helping him by staying with him any longer. As I said, there comes a time when a person has to find his way out of the quagmire of his own nightmares. You've made it clear you'll be there to grab hold when he finally reaches up out of it. Be easy on that.

Nevertheless, he laid a hand on Gideon's back, pressing his palm there as if he could convey the sentiment through touch, brand it on Gideon's heart like a map home.

It's there, Jacob. It's there.

"You don't give up, okay?" Jacob whispered to his brother's sleeping form. "I need you to be somewhere in the world, you dumb, heroic son of a bitch. Find a woman of your own. Laura would like that. And as much as I love you, I'm not too fond of sharing mine."

He ignored Lyssa's laughter in his mind and rolled over, keeping her in his arms so he could hold her close under his chin as he succumbed to sleep again.

7

"*S*HE'LL never view you as an equal. Watch your back. Serious plans in the works. Guard your lady well."

That was the note on the nightstand in an uneven scrawl when Jacob woke. His body hurt all over, and his brother was gone.

Reaching out with his mind, he found his lady had left her shields down enough to let him locate her, asleep in her underground bedchamber. She'd gotten so she always went there when dawn came, rarely using the upper chamber anymore. It was about ten in the morning. She'd also left him a note, on the opposite side of the bed.

"*I made sure your brother took some breakfast with him. He thanked me for my hospitality and said if I ever hurt you he'd stake me out in the sunlight and happily watch me burn. I kissed him goodbye until his toes curled and he couldn't walk without embarrassing himself. Maybe we should invite him to join us for Christmas.*"

Christ on a pogo stick. He laid his head back on the pillow and groaned. This day was not going to go well.

~

As if the gods were laughing at him, when she woke, she was in quite a mood. She made him oil every curve of her body to moisturize her skin. As a result, he had to handle every part of her intimately, without sexual intent. He was thorough, making damn sure when he finished she was as aroused as he was. But rather than sate their desire, she announced she wanted to work in her rose garden. She donned the dress she used for gardening and with smug amusement, commanded him to change into a pair of jeans. He was going to help her transplant rosebushes.

She didn't let him wear a shirt. Or any underwear. When her gaze lingered on his chest, he saw in her mind the image of her mouth covering his nipple where she'd given him the second mark. To bite him anew, to feel that rush of energy from his pain and pleasure both.

Pulling the zipper up was an excruciating, cautious exercise.

Insatiable. That was a word for vampire appetites. So insatiable that even when they were sated, they made sure the object of their lust would be primed and ready for them. His lady liked building sexual energy until it was explosive. Because she'd taught him it was worth the wait, he curbed the desire to try and leap on her like a dog. As he slid into his shabby loafers to join her, a smile passed through her eyes. She gave a soft "whuff" that made him chuckle and Bran's ears prick.

Once they got to the garden and started working on the rose-bushes, fortunately the lust settled to a slow simmer, a more quiet intimacy descending. Lyssa trimmed while he dug the holes for transplanting.

Though Jacob unearthed the delicate plants under her supervision, Lyssa knew he hardly needed it. He courteously followed her lead as she put the bushes in almost the same arrangement she knew he would have chosen.

She'd turned on music in the solar and opened the outside speakers so the soft, sultry tones of Jerri Adams floated through the air, singing about what her heart was telling her. The moon was high up in the sky now, a white, glowing pearl. In the corner of her eye, she saw Jacob light a couple of the tiki torches to add to their illumination as she examined the leaves of the rosebushes, checking for blemishes or parasites.

He didn't initiate conversation. He teased her in ways she

unexpectedly enjoyed, gave her conversation when she needed to hear another voice, companionable silence when she didn't. There were people who could pick up when a person didn't want to talk, but just ignored it, their inner need to express themselves overriding whatever else was happening. He wasn't one of them.

He was precognitive, but that kind of sensitivity came from intuition. Just like now. When she noted his gaze sliding over her breasts, down to her abdomen, the thought that went through his mind took her by surprise. But he kept on with what he was doing, giving her the option of ignoring it if she chose.

Perhaps because of his proximity to her, the way she felt about him, maybe even Thomas's damn nonsensical ideas about past lives, shadows rose in her subconscious. She blocked them. Not only did she not want Jacob privy to those memories, she didn't want to visit them either.

"I suspect I'm barren, Jacob," she said abruptly. "I've been alive all these centuries and I've lain with both vampires and humans. Very few vampire females are fertile. That's why born vampires are considered aristocracy. If they're conceived by two vampires, the rarest form of all, they're treasured."

"How are you considered, my lady?" He lifted his head. "Being of a vampire mother and your father a Fey lord?"

She trimmed off several leaves on one of the bushes and discovered a hybrid bloom, an unexpected combination of crimson and white. Funny, when all the others on the same branch were red. Full bloodred.

"I'm unique among the vampires, so I suppose they don't know what to consider me. Since my mother was not only royalty, but one of the rare children spawned of two vampires, I'm treated as full-blooded aristocracy. They simply choose to ignore my Fey blood, as long as it's evident only in ways that don't disturb their comfort zone." At his curious look, she raised a shoulder. "My exceptional longevity, even for a vampire. Some discreet evidence of powers I have that they don't. No one knows about my ability to transform to a winged Fey form, Jacob. Only you. Not even Rex or Thomas knew."

That surprised him, she could tell. As uncomfortable as it was to discuss this, she found it easier than discussing her fertility. She made the attempt out of deference to the type of night it was. Whereas yesterday or even tomorrow she might tell him to mind his own business.

"The Fey and vampire worlds have a long history of enmity. The Fey consider vampires beneath them, and vampires have a savagery that has resulted in . . . unfortunate incidents. Fey are also very private. Rarely seen in this world anymore, though we know they exist." She gazed at the roses. "My parents were the classic story of the Montagues and Capulets. When the Fey High Court found out about their love, my father was transformed into a rosebush and planted in the desert to die. So the story goes. I never met him. He was gone when I was born. My mother took refuge with the vampires and they defended her when the Fey made several assassination attempts before I was born. That's why I chose vampires as my dominant species. The vampires accepted her, probably because of her royal blood and the fact that she never spoke of my father, never denied or defended, probably to protect me. She made it easy for them to forget, to pretend the relationship didn't exist. When a truce on the issue was finally declared, she took a shogun lord as her human servant and married him for appearances. Thomas told you all of this, didn't he?"

"Some of it, my lady. What would happen if the Council saw you in your shapeshifted form?"

Jacob had found her Fey form wild and beautiful, like a winged, feminine gargoyle, gray skinned, slim and leanly muscled, fierce and dangerous.

She cupped the hybrid rose in her palm. "It would disturb them. At the very least. At the worst . . . they might drive me out of my Region. Make me an outcast. Or they might try to kill me."

He blinked at her matter-of-fact tone. She'd helped set up a "civilized" society for vampires and they'd prospered in ways they'd never enjoyed before. Despite that, she accepted without emotion that a difference in her physiology could cause her own to turn against her.

It struck him then, why having a human servant might be so

important to his lady. Vampires had to dissemble and use subterfuge to exist in the human world. They needed nimble minds to handle the vicious politics of their own kind. But she'd had to conceal far more than most. Particularly in the past couple of years.

"I never told Thomas," she went on, "probably because I've guarded the knowledge of it for so long it never even occurred to me that he needed to know. He didn't, not really. It's a form I can consciously take or not, as I wish. I just do it sometimes in the woods to remember my father, that he loved my mother. That he was willing to die for her. For us."

Jacob reached out a hand, brushed his fingers along her skirt, tugged. "I thank my lady for that trust." *For her love. Even if she's not comfortable calling it that.*

Lyssa saw in his blue eyes how much her words meant to him. It twisted in her own heart, reminding her how much he was willing to offer her. The most important things in life always seemed to boil down to just two—love and sacrifice.

He'd sat back on his heels. There was a smudge of dirt on his cheek and sweat glittered in the cinnamon threads of chest hair from his exertions in transplanting the bushes and setting posts to keep the dogs out of the area.

"Don't be stupid," she said abruptly. "Don't do anything to get yourself killed. It would upset me greatly."

It was an ironic thing to say, considering he'd bound the candle of his life to the diminishing flame of hers. But unlike him, she would live if he was killed. She wasn't sure if she'd have the strength to continue if that occurred. For good or bad, for the first time in her life she realized she was dependent on the strength of another to get her through.

She didn't know how much of that escaped the net of her mind to him, but as he studied her, he passed his forearm over his brow and managed to get more dirt on himself. The smile that tugged at her lips melted into her heart when he bent and kissed her leg, just above the anklet she wore.

"That's one rule of yours I'll try to obey, my lady. Just help me out by doing the same." When he nipped her, teasing her out of her mood, she reached down to caress his back, pass her fingers along the line of his spine, the abraded feel of the serpentine third mark.

He straightened after a time, hesitated before speaking. "We should talk about your annual kill. The one you've gone well over a year without."

"That's my business."

"The attacks you are having come closer and closer together. Like the third mark, the annual kill will help strengthen your resistance to the disease."

"Giving you that third mark has made you irritably patronizing. I simply need to get through the Council Gathering. The sacrifice you've made, taking the third mark, should help me do that."

"*Should.* But every bit of strength would help." He sat back on his heels again and looked up at her, his gaze troubled. "Believe me, my lady, I'd like nothing more than to agree that it's not needed. But I can feel the doubt in your mind. You don't think the third mark will be enough to make it through the Gathering."

She tossed an annoyed look at him. "Have you ever killed a man in cold blood, Jacob? A man who means you no harm, a man whose spirit is good and kind? I cannot take a human whose blood is infected with evil, so I will be murdering this person. You will be helping me. Be sure what you ask or demand."

"You've already picked him out. I saw your notes."

"That was five months ago. He's likely moved."

"He hasn't. I checked." Though his jaw was set, she could feel what he was blocking from himself but couldn't block from her. He was forcing himself to make this all about her. "You know Lord Brian is researching a cure. Every extra day you give yourself to fight this disease may give you time—"

"Have you ever wondered at the way humans say they're 'fighting a disease'? It's a force of nature, not a malicious combatant." She snapped off another leaf, ignored the prick of a thorn.

He pressed on. "You've told me before you shouldn't second-guess Fate. Why second-guess Her on this? Perhaps it's not your time to die. Your presence, your life, is far more significant than most."

"When you're dying, Jacob, one thing you realize very quickly is how insignificant you really are." She didn't like where this was going, and she turned away, conveying her dismissal of the subject. But of course he refused to let it lie.

"Illness skews your perspective. Maybe that's Nature's way of making it easier for you to let go when it's time. But you have other contributing factors."

"Don't go there, Jacob."

You lost your husband to madness, lived years with his increasing brutality, which ended in a savage act of betrayal. Rex murdered your human servant, then you had to kill Rex yourself.

Though she'd closed her eyes, his fingers closed over hers with a gentle power she was helpless to resist. "I'm begging you to consider that your willingness to accept your own death may in fact be part of the terrible weight of guilt you carry. In time, the grief will ease and you'll embrace life again. If you have the chance to do so. I'm just asking you to give yourself that chance."

She pressed her lips together. "You won't make me cry, Jacob Green. I don't want to think about these things. I shouldn't be allowing you to speak this way to me."

"You told me on our very first night vampires don't cry." He rose, turned her and took the tears away on his fingertips. "You know what I'm saying. It's logical. It makes sense."

It made sense. Perhaps it did still lay so heavily on her she preferred death to the struggle to get past it. But what lay at the heart of her resistance to the annual kill was not that. It was her fear of what such a thing would do to Jacob. To the pure essence of him she was beginning to need for her own sanity, to cleanse her own dark shadows when they rose in her.

"You honor me with your thoughts, my lady. But as I told *you* when we met, I'm far tougher than I look. And I *look* pretty damn tough."

She fought the smile he was trying to coax from her. *Idiot. Arrogant knight.*

Arrogant queen. "My lady . . ."

She suppressed a sigh. "Set it up. But I'll handle it alone. You won't go with me. I don't need your help."

"With respect, you said you would. That it was optimal to have the help of both a driver and a servant. You don't have a driver for this, so I'll be both." He brushed his knuckles against her cheek, gave a half smile that didn't reach his eyes.

I'm your human servant.

8

"DAMN adjustment," Jacob grumbled as his third arrow went off the mark, missing the twenty-foot-distant target. He glanced down at Bran. "You know, she could use a couple of Labrador retrievers. Unless I need a moose pulled down, you're pretty useless."

Bran gave him an unreadable expression. Jacob wondered if he'd learned his inscrutability from his Mistress.

He retrieved the arrow himself, checked the sheath again, rechecked the arrow to ensure the closely trimmed feathering was unmarred. As he suspected, it was the launch mechanism.

As he made another adjustment to it, Bran raised his head, gave a menacing growl. Before Jacob could turn and seek what was raising the dog's hackles, the radio on his belt beeped, telling him there was someone at the gate. The roof contractor wasn't expected today, but he supposed a miracle could have occurred and they'd arrived a day early. Of course, Bran typically didn't react in a hostile manner to service people. He acted intimidating while they were here, but Jacob harbored the suspicion that was purely an act for the dog's personal amusement. The wolfhound knew the difference between a threat to his Mistress and a visitor the way Jacob knew the difference between black and white. Which was why his brow creased now, noting the dog's rigid stance.

He pulled on his sweatshirt and unclipped the radio. "May I help you?"

A pause, long enough that he almost repeated the question. Before he could press the button, he heard a female voice speak hesitantly. "My lord Carnal wishes to pay his respects to Lady Lyssa."

Oh, bloody fucking hell. He'd forgotten entirely. Gideon's visit had disrupted the week's schedule. While there was nothing to be concerned about, for the house was well prepared for guests, he would have preferred some mental preparation to deal with Carnal.

The first night he'd met Carnal had been outside of the area mall. The man had been the sick playmate of Lyssa's late husband, Rex. Carnal had cleverly played on Rex's dementia until it culminated in a horrifying night where Rex had tortured Lyssa and allowed Carnal to sodomize her. According to Lyssa, it was all part of the political games vampires played, but her reaction to Carnal's appearance that night said her feelings about the situation ran much deeper. As extraordinary as his Mistress was, she had difficulty accepting she could feel violated and revolted as much as any rape victim. But then, *victim* would never be a label Lady Lyssa Wentworth would tolerate for herself.

Jacob now understood the reason for the pause on the radio. Carnal had expected Lyssa to answer and intended to speak to her directly. At the sound of Jacob's voice, the vampire had quickly changed tactics and made his servant respond, not deigning of course to speak to the hired help. Which meant Carnal had not been certain Jacob would make it as her servant. Well, he knew now.

"Hold on one moment and I'll see if my lady is taking visitors."

It was just before sunset. In another half hour it would be twilight. She might or might not be up. His lady was not necessarily a . . . *Morning person* was not the right term, but *early evening* just didn't have the same ring.

My lady? It was as easy as picturing her in his mind and thinking the words, but it still amazed him how clearly she came through, as if standing right beside him. The second mark had given him a hint of that clarity, but it was nothing in comparison to the third.

Yes.

He waited, knowing she would simply look into his mind and pick up the situation like a snapshot. The pause drew out. He wondered if she'd forgotten as well. Of course, sometimes she relied on Jacob to remind her of her schedule, and he'd been woefully off his game since Gideon's visit.

I'll look forward to punishing you for that.

He rolled his eyes, even as he felt his groin tighten at the sultry implication of her words. At this rate, that particular appendage of his was going to fall off.

His sense of humor didn't last long, however. Despite the teasing comment, she still hadn't given him an answer.

"Shall I send him away, my lady?" he ventured at last, though he knew he might get snapped at for interrupting her thoughts. Knowing how long a vampire could deliberate without it being considered rudeness, Carnal might even now be enjoying a sip from his servant, or mixing her blood with a cup of wine in his vehicle, anticipating at least a fifteen-minute wait. With someone of Lyssa's standing, it could be longer, though nothing about Carnal suggested he was the patient sort. In fact, Jacob had sensed from him that resentful undercurrent often emanating from the type of person who thought they were entitled to a corner office, even though they'd quit high school and barely put the time of day into their current low-end employment, thinking it beneath them. Power. Carnal wanted more power. He thought he could handle it better than anyone else, which made him a danger to those who actually did have more power, like his Mistress. Who might underestimate him, assuming if he didn't have the energy to prove and earn his worth, he would lack the energy or cleverness to steal the title from someone else.

Do not fret, Jacob. I never underestimate Carnal. Or anyone, for that matter. Show him to the main hallway.

There are no chairs there.

He will not be staying long. But we must observe the ritual courtesy and share a drink. He prefers brandy. I wish my current wine.

Yes, my lady. When he waited long enough to be satisfied no further communication was forthcoming, he clicked the radio again. "Please proceed to the main door."

Before he disengaged the driveway gate, he sprang onto one of the retaining walls, gaining a view through the screening of the crepe myrtle branches. The car was a Jaguar sedan with darkened windows of course, probably specially treated to filter out the UV rays. When the gate closed and the security field reengaged, Jacob dropped off the wall and headed for the front drive. He wasn't exactly a credit to his lady in his current dark jeans and Harvard sweatshirt, but it would have to do. He wasn't going to let this one out of his sight to primp.

Oh, Jacob?

Yes, my lady?

You'll need to lock Bran and his siblings in the garden shed. Bran is not fond of Carnal.

As he reached the curve of the driveway, his step quickened, as much from his lady's words as from the sound of Bran's thunderous, furious barking. Lyssa's mild comment was an understatement. As the rest of the pack milled restlessly, the dog was circling the car. No, not just circling it. Lunging up to slam his paws on the passenger window like human fists and snarling, saliva flecking the glass as he attempted to scrabble in and get at the occupant behind it. It at least told Jacob where Carnal was in the car. The girl was apparently driving.

"Bran. Bran!" When Jacob caught the dog's collar and hauled him off, he had to do a quick circle to keep the dog from turning on him. He snapped at him in Gaelic and Bran went to a sullen growl, showing his teeth, his eyes fierce, his concentration on the car unbroken. Jacob managed to lead him off, but the dog resisted every step, trying to get loose. The farther they got from the car, the more fiercely Bran struggled, until Jacob was strangling him. He paused, contemplating the dog's desperate need to protect. *My lady . . .*

Bran. Obey.

Her voice was sharp enough that it reverberated in Jacob's eardrum with a painful vibration. Bran subsided to a lower growl and allowed himself to be led off, even though his posture made it clear he was unhappy about the situation. Jacob wasn't too happy about it, either. The other dogs followed them to the garden shed. When he got them locked in, Bran stood at the dusty window staring at him, panting in distress. Jacob found it hard to turn his back on the animal.

When he returned to the car, he nodded, made the all-clear gesture. The door opened and Carnal stepped out, his expression irritated. "A servant who cannot control a simple mongrel doesn't seem much of a boon to my lady Lyssa."

Bran's bloodline was far purer than anything Carnal could ever hope to have, but Jacob curbed the barb. Not so much for diplomacy, but because he'd also known a lot of mixed-breed dogs with far more integrity and value than the piece of garbage fouling Lyssa's driveway with his presence.

"I didn't see you jumping out of the car to take him on, and last time I checked, you're an all-powerful vampire." Jacob locked gazes with the vamp, just as he'd done the night they'd first met, even when his Mistress had ordered him to lower his eyes. He'd earned her wrath for the defiance, but he hadn't regretted it, particularly later when he'd found out what Carnal had done to Lyssa.

Carnal's lips drew back. "You haven't learned manners yet. I shall speak to your Mistress about that."

Jacob ignored him, circled to the other side of the car and opened the driver's side door, finding he had to do so gently, for Carnal's servant had a death grip on the handle.

"It's okay; I put them up," he said reassuringly. When the girl looked up into his face, he bit back an oath, suddenly remembering Gideon's warning. She wasn't even eighteen years old. Perhaps barely past fifteen. Nevertheless, he offered her a hand out of the car, making it clear he had manners aplenty for those deserving of it.

"Melinda, stop being a sniveling coward and come here."

She withdrew her hand from Jacob's and went around the back of the car to walk obediently behind Carnal as Jacob led them to the door.

Seven girls . . . young women he seduces, then traps . . . sixteen-year-old runaway . . .

She was a beautiful creature with pale white-gold hair, green eyes and a body far too lush and tempting for a minor, all full breasts and curvy hips. Long legs. Wearing a pair of tight hip-hugger leatherlike pants and a snug silken shirt under which she wore no bra, she exuded sexual provocation, a heady mixture with her obvious innocence. A temptation to a man with a conscience, an open invitation to one without one.

That night at the mall, Carnal had referred to his "new" servant, which told Jacob she was just as young as she appeared. He was agreeing with Bran's assessment more and more, and feeling uncomfortable to boot with the inability to do anything for the girl.

If it wasn't her, it would be another. The Council set an age minimum of twelve on human servants, and even that was a struggle. There was a curious deadness to his lady's comment, injected into the boiling cauldron of his thoughts. *Bring them to the hallway, Jacob. I will deal with this and then we can be rid of them.*

He could think of more effective methods to be rid of at least one of them. However, keeping what he hoped was an impassive expression, he opened the door, gestured. Carnal strode past him with barely a glance. Melinda followed, her throat working nervously, lips pursed together as she attempted to saunter in a way Jacob was sure Carnal had taught her, trying to emulate the sexual confidence of a much older woman.

"My lady will meet with you in her main hall." He indicated the direction.

Carnal flicked a look at him. "Fine. I know the way. You can go back to your duties."

You wish, you prick. "My lady has requested my attendance." Not exactly true, but she'd indicated he should make sure brandy and wine were there, after all.

Carnal's eyes glittered, his lip curling. With a jerk he turned on his heel, headed for the hall. Apparently he wanted to make it clear he didn't care for being shepherded in like a supplicant, instead of being met by Lyssa herself as an honored guest would have been.

Lyssa's visitor had an inflated sense of his own importance. Lyssa had never encouraged it, Jacob was sure, so he knew it must have come from Rex. It was possible Thomas hadn't known all that had transpired to make Carnal so much more significant after Thomas's exile. During Jacob's training, Thomas had only mentioned in passing the tall, dark-haired vampire who strode ahead with such hostility emanating from him.

No. Not hostility. Meanness. Violence. Everything that compelled his brother to hunt vampires practically vibrated off Carnal. A barely restrained bloodlust, a low trigger point. Jacob knew the only thing that stopped Carnal from attacking him was the fact he was here for other reasons, and Jacob was under Lady Lyssa's protection. Vampires like Carnal were usually the easiest to kill, relatively speaking, because of their absolute conviction of their own superiority. It made them careless, easy to set up. *Get him, Gideon.*

Almost as soon as he had the thought, he withdrew it. He didn't want his brother near Carnal without him to watch his back. *Never underestimate Carnal . . .* His lady's advice echoed in his mind.

Melinda moved quietly behind him, but she glanced at Jacob several times. Giving him a shy smile, she pushed her hair over her shoulder, the move of a high school girl attracting a boy's attention. Her smile faltered as he drew closer, keeping pace with her, his size and obvious maturity apparently a little intimidating to her. Even so, she surprised him when she slid her hand into the crook of his elbow, her fingers tracing a light pattern on his biceps. He had to suppress the urge to remove her touch. Perhaps the kindness he'd shown her at the car was the first she'd experienced at someone's hands for a while. He didn't want to imagine the type of groups Carnal ran with. He certainly didn't want his head assaulted with such images that included Melinda. The fingers that held on to his arm had nails embellished with tiny flower stickers. He felt sick.

"You'll come to no harm in my lady's house." They'd reached the main hall, so he gave her hand a light pat before he extricated himself, not unkindly, to go to the wine rack and uncork Lyssa's favorite to breathe. He lifted the brandy snifter from the side bar. "My lord? A drink for you and your servant?"

"She requires nothing." Carnal watched his servant with a gleam in his dark eyes. Oddly, Melinda had followed Jacob and now stood as close as possible without hampering his elbow while Carnal stood across the hallway. She reached out again, her fingertips whispering against the side of Jacob's body, along the line of his hip. "Except perhaps you. She's an erotic little creature. She'll fuck any man if he stands still long enough. Very malleable. She can pretend to be even younger. Suck on your cock as if she's a babe with a thumb in her mouth."

Jacob set the brandy snifter down harder on the side bar than he'd intended. Melinda jumped, her fingers trembling, even as she struggled to maintain a come-hither expression. Trying to feign what could not be feigned. She managed only to look frightened when Jacob sent her a quelling look. However, she held her stance. Probably because she knew there was a greater threat to her in the room than Jacob's annoyance.

He had no idea what the hell was going on here. If Carnal thought he could get his child servant to distract him enough to leave him alone with his Mistress, the ploy was pitiful, transparent. And revolting.

"I'll pour my own brandy," Carnal said abruptly.

That was fine by Jacob, for he had no desire to wait on the creature. He moved away from the bar. Melinda thankfully stayed, waiting for her Master.

"She seems young to have such advanced appetites." Jacob paced off several feet and crossed his arms, keeping Carnal under close scrutiny as he examined the brandy choices.

Carnal cast Jacob a disparaging glance. "A teenager's sex drive is far closer to a vampire's appetite than an adult's. I can fuck a woman in her thirties to death in no time. While the innocence of the young is often tedious, it can also be very . . . intriguing. Teaching them about unnatural desires." He lifted a bottle, uncorked and opened it to sniff. "Their hormones are too strong to allow their morality or narrow upbringing to hold out against the craving for long. Melinda is special in those areas. You've not lived until you've watched her tears fall in delicious shame as she's writhing, her legs spread, her body on the brink of an orgasm I'll make her wait hours to have."

He was just going to have to kill him. It was as simple a thing as knowing that the dogs would need dinner in an hour. Kill visiting vampire, dispose of body—preferably by burning—then feed the dogs. Jacob stepped forward.

Carnal turned away, missing the menacing gesture, though from Melinda's indrawn breath, Jacob knew she didn't. The brief flare of hope in her eyes, quickly extinguished, nearly choked him.

"Lyss—Lady Lyssa." Carnal stumbled over the greeting, though Jacob suspected he clearly remembered she'd rescinded her husband's permission for Carnal to call her familiarly. "I thought I heard you come in. Though of course you're such a delicate, quiet creature you've probably been standing there for quite a while, listening to me educate your young servant on our ways."

Jacob turned. His lady stood at the end of the hall, framed by the ten-foot-high, arched, stained glass window there. St. Francis of Assisi raised his hands to offer food to over a hundred differently colored birds hovering in the sky around him. Bursts of sunlight in rose and gold glass outlined them and haloed her. While it was now dark, she had outside lights positioned to allow enjoyment of the stained glass even during the night. Wearing black slacks with a slim belt and gold blouse, her hair up, she looked tailored, self-contained. Even from here, though, Jacob could feel the latent energy pulsing around her. Restless. Dangerous.

An elegant diamond bracelet draped the thin bones of her wrist. Diamond studs adorned her double-pierced ears. A vampire had to pierce her body each time she chose to wear post jewelry, since once the posts were removed, the openings healed completely. Lyssa removed her earrings every morning. Female vanity had always been a remarkable thing to him, but his lady's devotion to it had brought him to a new level of admiration.

When she inclined her head to their visitor, it was a cold gesture. Jacob couldn't hear any thoughts from her. All her shields were tightly locked down, but his intuition sensed those currents of energy circling in the air of the room like the closeness of an impending thunderstorm.

Carnal had moved toward her. Vampire rules of courtesy required a distance of ten feet unless the higher-ranking vampire invited the other vampire within that personal space boundary. Jacob noted that Carnal stopped at the proper distance and then took one additional step, as if he were mocking the rule. Or her.

Lyssa did not remove her attention from his face. "What is your business in my territory?"

"As you know from our meeting at the mall, I am only passing through, my lady. A trip to the Midwest. Your husband was kind enough to acquaint me with many of the western territory overlords. I've been doing some fortunate trading of talent and resources over the past year."

She studied him in silence. The quiet of the hall began to have a weight to it that pressed in on Jacob, made him itch for a weapon. Carnal cocked his head. "While I am merely observing the ritual courtesies you demanded, I was hoping I might interest you in sharing dinner with me."

"I am otherwise engaged."

Carnal's back was to Jacob, so he saw the slight lift of the shoulder. When the vampire moved back to the side bar, his countenance was accepting, cordial. "Since you have no immediate need of my company, then, allow me to pour your wine and we'll complete the formality." He glanced at the bottle. "Your preferred vintage has changed. When Rex lived, you preferred muscatel. Port. This is barely more than grape juice."

"It's made with an exotic flower, only available in one place in Asia." As far as Jacob could tell, the only part of Lyssa's face moving was her lips, an eerie effect. "The blooms must be cut at the end of the spring season. Exactly one hundred bottles have been made in the three-hundred-year life of the tree. It grows in the memorial garden of a great teacher, Yang-Sun. I studied with him. He taught me much about patience. Inner silence. Balance."

Carnal paused. Jacob shifted so he could see the angle of focus between the two of them. As she reached the last sentence, Lyssa's pronunciation had become more exact. On the last word he saw the tips of her fangs. Her eyes glowed in the dim recesses of that end of the hall. While Jacob's section was modestly lit, she'd apparently purposely put herself in shadows.

"There is one pure note of silence within ourselves," she continued.

"So powerful that if we stepped inside it, we could blink our eyes and save the world from evil. Or destroy it utterly, like the soul of an unnatural creature never meant to exist. Watch it shatter and blow away as dust. Forgotten. Insignificant. Never to be remembered except with a child's mocking laughter."

Melinda had crept to Jacob's side again. He couldn't blame her for seeking comfort. The mood in the hall was deadly, and almost all of it was coming from his lady now. The young girl's fingers touched his hand at his side, linked with his fingers. Her breast was pressing against his arm, her hip bone against his buttock. Her breath was sweet and soft on his shoulder.

While her physical actions might support the inconceivable things Carnal was saying about her, nothing else did. Melinda had no natural sexual aggression. Either Carnal had her trained to act like a nymphomaniac for his own amusement or he thought Jacob stupid enough to fall for the obvious distraction. But it made no sense. For Carnal to attempt to harm Lyssa in her own home would be suicidal.

Carnal pricked his finger with his fang to put several drops of blood in Lyssa's glass. He reached for the bottle of wine as it drained into the bowl.

There. As Carnal picked up the wine bottle, the finger next to the pricked finger shifted a minuscule amount. Something wavered on the glass edge. Jacob narrowed his gaze. In the dim light of the hall, he knew the eyes could play tricks, but his intuition made him sure. Carnal splashed several swallows of wine efficiently into the glass.

"My lady." Jacob stepped forward, shrugging away from Melinda. "He put something in your wine."

Lyssa's gaze flickered to him, then back to Carnal.

"Your servant speaks out of turn, my lady. He has faulty eyesight." Carnal snapped his fingers as if summoning a pet. "Melinda, come here. We shall prove our intentions to Lady Lyssa. When they are proven to be honorable"—he gave Jacob a scathing look—"I hope you'll give me a guest's right to chastise him for the insult."

When Melinda came to him, moving without hesitation but somehow conveying rigid protest in the lines of her body, he curled his hand around her nape, tugging on her hair. "My little nymph. Sweet child. Try this exotic wine Lady Lyssa says holds the secrets of the universe. It will taste like the best candy. Just like you."

In a blink, his voice had become tender, seductive. Jacob knew vampire allure could disguise even a monster as evil as Carnal, but witnessing it was a jarring step into a different reality. As Gideon said, he easily could coax an impressionable girl to him, bind her before she knew what was happening to her.

Obediently she put her lips to the cup, tipping her head back when he exerted pressure on her chin with his thumb. She swallowed, then again more frantically as he gave it to her in one draught. It was not much more than a quarter cup, but still too much for the one swallow in which he forced her to consume the rest.

"It was a common Inquisition torture, forcing someone to drink too much." Carnal watched her struggle with the discomfort of the fluid ballooning down her throat into her stomach. Jacob realized Carnal was directing his words to him. An attempt to intimidate or threaten, he supposed. He remained silent and still, though everything in him wanted to pull the girl away from him.

My lady, your silence is getting damn irritating. Her preternatural stillness at the end of the hallway was just flat-out disturbing.

"The Church wasn't allowed to invade the body, cut it open with interrogation techniques," Carnal continued. "That entirely unspiritual practice was reserved to the secular authorities. Therefore, if the Church couldn't obtain a confession their way, they might turn the person over to the local law and see if it could be sliced out of them. But I find the Church's nonsurgical methods were most inventive."

Setting the glass aside, he turned his attention back to the lady of the house. "A waste of your beautiful and rare wine, Lady Lyssa. I hope you punish him severely for this." Reaching out, he collected the drops of wine that had escaped from the corner of Melinda's mouth. Well trained, she didn't jerk back, but her eyes were wide and mouth tight, anticipating pain. He jerked his head. "Go and stand next to her arrogant servant while I prepare my lady another cup."

Melinda turned and moved toward Jacob. Her eyes were watering from the strain of taking down the wine. It was a good thing the wine wasn't more potent. As thin as she was, Jacob doubted Carnal let her eat much, just enough steroid-laden meat to maintain her breast cup size.

Carnal placed two more drops of his blood in the cup and poured another splash of wine, this time in exaggerated, open movements. "So your servant doesn't have another attack of paranoia," he explained mockingly. "Perhaps he would behave better if you castrated him. You don't need an inferior human cock when I'd be happy to offer mine. A mortal can hardly be expected to have the stamina to please you."

Lyssa watched all of them as if they were part of a play she'd paid money to attend, a silent member of an audience cloaked in darkness.

Carnal took several steps forward again. Paused at the invisible ten-foot barrier and extended the cup. "My lady?"

The night she'd marked Lord Brian, the ritual had been far more intimate. She'd taken the blood directly from his throat, taunting Jacob as he stood silently behind her chair only a few steps away. But she'd needed more of Brian's blood because he was staying in her territory and was under her protection. For Carnal, all that was required were these few drops in a cup to allow her to monitor his movement through her territory. It was an act of surety, part of the whole manual on etiquette governing vampire interaction, a Book of Shadows embraced by each new Council. When Jacob reviewed it under Thomas's tutelage, there were times he understood why many of the younger vampires made fun of it. However, knowing how quickly vampires could revert to unthinkable brutality, he'd come to understand the uncanny genius of it. It had been surprisingly effective in helping vampires govern their bloodlust, for it imposed a detailed, Sun King–type aristocratic hauteur on their personal interactions that appealed to them.

This was a simple, standard ritual. In the mundane world, no different from someone paying a toll. Yet as she stared at that glass, Jacob sensed something rising in her, something as unstable as an atom exposed to forces that could cause it to split and become nuclear.

"My lady?" Carnal's brow was raised, a slight smile upon his lips. He took a step forward, then another. Coming into her space uninvited. Her gaze rose, her eyes dark pools holding the capability of destruction. Jacob couldn't tell if it was outgoing, where she might obliterate Carnal, or incoming, something attacking her vital organs, destructive to herself. If she wasn't so damn closed off he could tell. His gut wasn't helping him a bit.

Something was off. At her lack of response to Carnal, the way she studied him as if he were merely an uncomfortable thought, rather than a physical threat directly before her, it finally came to Jacob.

Even when she was shielding her thoughts from him, there was an essence to her that was accessible, touchable. But it was missing right now. A woman who had been violated shut down when confronted by her violator. Instinctively, all her defenses would be raised against anything male. Wagons pulling around in a circle, warding against attack from any side. While it hurt him to acknowledge that was what she was doing, Jacob knew it was a survival response.

"Don't," she said through stiff lips, raising a hand to stop Carnal's forward movement.

He wasn't sure if she was anticipating him or speaking to Carnal, but Jacob was already moving, sensing a threat his instincts assured him was there. Formalities be damned; she needed him at her side.

A cry split the air, interrupting whatever Lyssa had been about to say. Jacob spun in time to see Melinda drop to her knees and collapse on her side, her body convulsing, fingers clutching at the air, throat working. She bucked to her back, her head and heels the only parts of her touching the ground before she flung herself back on her side as if a monster were manipulating her limbs.

Jacob lunged to her, yanking the radio from his belt. But it was already too late. Before he could hit the emergency number, her body slowly eased back to the floor, death rattling in her throat, her eyes glazing over. Foam spittle gathered at her lips.

"Hemlock, mixed with some other special ingredients to hasten the process," Carnal remarked.

Jacob raised his head, torn between horror and fury as the vampire

studied his dead servant with indifference. "In a vampire, it pro-
duces the reputed paralysis, giving another vampire temporary
control of him or her." He glanced over his shoulder at Lyssa, who
remained motionless, her pupils wide and dark in the shadows.
"There's also an aphrodisiac mixed in, so it's a delightful concoc-
tion. Just enough pain to blend with the pleasure of arousing a
body restrained by its own muscle paralysis. I thought you might
find it enjoyable, as well as appreciate the devious nature of the
ploy. I doubt any of your other suitors have been as creative." He
lifted a shoulder, glanced contemptuously at Melinda. "Unfortunately, what is pleasurable for us is fatal to a human. But fascinat-
ingly painful, even if for a disappointingly short time. Melinda was
not a fighter."

He made a face abruptly. "God, the worst thing about human
death is the release of the bowels and bladder. However, her blood is
still warm and quite tasty, at least for the next few minutes. My gift to
you. As you know, young blood is quite sweet. Let me get you a taste."
His eyes glittered at the implication of Lyssa taking blood from his
fingers. When Lyssa's attention rose from the girl back to him in reaction, he smiled, a slow curve of his thin lips. He began to move toward
Melinda, giving Jacob a curt look. "Step aside, servant."

Jacob stood up. Lifting his arm, he fired the arrow from the wrist
sheath beneath his sleeve.

If he'd gotten the damn adjustment worked out, it would have
gone straight through the hellspawn's dark heart. As it was, it lodged
in his shoulder, two inches too high, but close enough to wipe that
smirk off his face. He had a blink to think another arrow might work
and then Carnal was on him, shoving him hard into the wall, a roar
of rage blazing hot on him, the vamp's hand on his neck.

In the same flash of time, Jacob fell to the floor. Carnal was now
on the opposite side of the room, his body plowed into the masonry
of the hallway wall. Sheetrock caved in an outline around his body,
dust rising around him. Lyssa had hit the side bar in the maneuver
and it crashed to the floor, making the thump of his body trivial in
comparison to the din of shattering glass on the wood floor next to
the carpet runner. Jacob scrambled to his feet.

"Stay where you are." Her voice was cool, authoritative. Whatever had held her frozen several moments ago was gone as if it had never existed. His lady was fully present, giving him a cursory look that told him she expected him to obey. She turned her green gaze on the vampire she held against the wall with one hand on his throat.

"He's dead, Lyssa," Carnal snarled, coughing against her grip. "I'll kill him where he stands."

"He is my servant, to reward or punish as I see fit. Marked by me and therefore my property. My slave." Her voice hardened as did her grip, for Carnal gagged against it. "You may seek what recompense the Council feels I owe you for the insult, but they'll laugh at you for your presumption. This is a failed courtship ploy only, and my young, inexperienced servant took it as a threat upon my life. Such loyalty is a boon. Jacob used to be a vampire hunter, Carnal. It is one of his many talents."

"I was nearly successful in my attempt," Carnal growled. When he reached over Lyssa's hold, she didn't interfere as he yanked out the arrow with a grunt, let it fall to the floor. Jacob wished he'd poisoned the tip. Carnal made a visible attempt to rein back his temper, despite the fact she continued to hold him pinned. "I knew whether your servant had perverse tastes or an overinflated sense of honor, the little creature could prove a useful distraction. His focus is considerable. Your choice is perhaps better than I first thought. But he's a guard dog, Lyssa, not submissive enough to be your servant. He's too young. Too alpha and temperamental."

"He's not the one in this room I consider inferior to his station." Her words dropped into the air like ice. Jacob felt the coldness to his marrow.

"Ten feet of space, elaborate rituals of courtesy to try to pretend we aren't what we are," Carnal hissed. "They're sheep for our slaughter. All of mankind should be our slaves. If we agree on nothing else, I do not fathom why we don't agree on that."

He had balls, Jacob gave him that. His lady's heat had turned the hallway into one of the lower regions of Hell. Watching her and Carnal closely, Jacob knelt by Melinda's still and lifeless body. Picking up one of her hands, he verified the lack of pulse.

"You were part of Rex's life that he forced into mine," Lyssa said to Carnal, her voice flat. "I have no desire to share a conversation with you, let alone anything else. You're not welcome here." She glanced at the broken glass on the carpet runner, the various spilled wines and liquors staining it, and shifted her attention to the young woman whose postmortem waste was doing the same. "You'll go back to your own territory, taking the shortest route out of mine. If you wish to get to the Midwest, you'll circle around to the west or fly. If you come in my territory again, I'll kill you."

She dropped him, took a step back.

My lady, watch out.

Jacob sprang up, lunging forward. But even with his ability to anticipate what Carnal was about to do, he was no match for a vampire's speed. With a roar, Carnal flung himself on her.

As he leaped, Lyssa ducked under him. Catching him midbody, she flipped him, spinning so he ended up on his belly on the carpet and wood. His face pressed against the shards of broken glass while she pinned his neck with one hand and held the arrow he'd dropped against his back.

"You think you have the power and strength to woo me, keep me?" She raked the arrow downward, tearing his shirt and finding skin. Kept going, moving over the hump of his ass until the lethal point pressed against a lower, far more vulnerable area. "Perhaps I should fuck you with this until you bleed on yourself, over and over. Bind you in a stock *you* couldn't escape and watch for my pleasure. Would you like that? *Would you?*" Her voice ratcheted up into a snarl, startling in its abrupt jerk from silky murmur to abrasive threat. Carnal flinched as she tore the back seam of his trousers with the tip.

"No. No, my lady. I . . . I'll leave. I concede. You are far above my station. I should not have presumed so much."

Jacob saw something ripple over her skin, something between disgust and desire. It startled him, for the menace of it crawled over his own skin and stoked the room's already uncomfortable heat. As she blinked and the wall sconces reflected crimson in her gaze, he realized what he was seeing was a war with her own bloodlust. Since she'd been alive for so many centuries, it rarely got a grip on her, but he saw it now. The desire to rip, destroy and wallow in the blood of her enemy. Carnal must have felt it, too, because at the end of his admission his voice had become unsteady. Jacob found himself fervently wishing his lady would lose her infamous control and tear him to pieces, even if she vanquished them all.

Carnal cried out in sudden fear as she jerked him up at a painful angle and sank her fangs into his neck. Took a scant swallow and then withdrew, wiping her mouth distastefully with the back of her hand.

"You thought I was weak," she hissed. "That night had nothing to do with you. You were never his equal, never more than his toy. You were his bitch, because I wouldn't be."

Carnal made a low sound of anger, but it was like the hiss of a frightened cat. It subsided entirely when Lyssa added her knee to the small of his back.

"If I hear that you so much as took a wrong turn to get out of my territory, I will hunt you down. I will chain you inside a coffin with a handful of nettles stuffed in your mouth, your nostrils"—she flicked them with the tip of the arrow, earning a flinch—"and in your ass. I'll tie them in knots around your cock. Then I won't release you until I can stomach the sight of you. Which may mean forever. Your screams for mercy will be music to my ears. But not as much as your silence, when you realize you're not important enough for anyone to interfere with my will on this."

The venom in her threat was overpowering, touching everything within distance of it. Her whisper echoed in the hallway, pricking even Jacob's bowels with fear. She meant every word, for her bloodlust was spilling into his mind, telling him how strong her desire was to do exactly as she'd said.

But in the time it took Jacob to move forward another step, though he was not sure what he was intending to do, she was standing back at the end of the hallway. Eerily in the same pose she'd held when they first saw her, haloed by the gentle St. Francis offering food to the birds.

Slowly Carnal rose to his knees, his frightened eyes and the streaks of blood caused by the glass the only color in his face. He got to his feet awkwardly. Gone was the mocking smugness. He kept his eyes down as he backed away, and there was a tremor in his hands. When he turned toward his dead servant, he came toe-to-toe with Jacob.

"No," Jacob said. "You won't touch her."

Submission to his lady apparently did not mean submission to a human servant's insult. Carnal backhanded him. Or at least Jacob assumed that was what had happened, for it felt like he was struck in the face by a battering ram he never saw coming. He landed hard on his back nearly twenty feet from Melinda's body. Rolled to his feet at the same time his lady uttered a sharp command. Perhaps his enraged mind wouldn't have registered it, but she blasted it into his brain the way she'd done with Bran.

On your knees, Jacob. Facing me.

"My lady—"

"Now. Obey me." Her attention flicked toward him. "Or you will regret it in ways you cannot even imagine."

His jaw flexing with the effort, he dropped to one knee and bowed his head, though confusion throbbed in its clash with the force of the rage welling in him.

"You will leave your servant with us. Her blood is mine." Her gaze remained tinged with red as she leveled it upon Carnal. "Get out. Now. I should have killed you the first time Rex brought you home."

With a snarl, Carnal spun on his heel and stalked toward the end of the hallway.

"And Carnal?" When she snapped it out, Jacob had the satisfaction of seeing him jump, though the expression he turned to her was sullen.

"My lady?"

"In two minutes, I will release the dogs. That gives you enough time to get in your car and drive it off my property. Just. Don't tarry."

As the vampire's footsteps quickened, signaling his departure from the hall, Jacob began to raise his head.

"Stay as you are. Stupid, foolish man." Her tone was scathing as he listened to her move in his direction. "Don't speak until I give you permission or I swear I'll break your neck. I'm out of patience with all of you."

In the corner of his eye, he saw her kneel at Melinda's side. She took the girl's lifeless hand and studied the nails, her own perfectly manicured woman's cuticles catching the dim sconce light as she passed her fingertips over the flowers preferred by the fancy of a child. He didn't know what he'd do if Lyssa did in fact choose to drink from Melinda, but instead she feathered a hand over the girl's forehead, closed her eyes. Wiped the spittle from the corners of her mouth with a handkerchief she had in the pocket of her slacks.

"Do you know John 14:27?"

Of all the things he'd expected her say, that wasn't one of them. When Jacob shook his head, she spoke the words softly. " 'Peace I leave with you, my peace I give to you; not as the world gives do I give you. Let not your heart be troubled, neither let it be afraid.' "

She raised her gaze, looked at him then. "There are several translations of the Bible in my library, as you well know. Take her deep into the forest preserve and bury her. Say that over her grave and whatever else you think she'll need for peace, though I think release from Carnal's service satisfies that adequately on its own."

He struggled to get his mind around what she was saying. "But . . . her family?"

"She has no family. Carnal likely bought her from them. There's an underground market for the young for vampires. Somehow, at some point, a favor was done, so there was a binding on a firstborn. It's an old vampire tradition to secure loyalty. Feudal. Taking a firstborn into service, utilizing the trade skills and resources of the family."

"No one will look for her." Jacob made it a flat statement, knowing better than to offer it as a question. His lady couldn't give him an answer he'd want to hear.

Humans were expendable in the vampire world. Hadn't Debra as much as suggested it? Hadn't his brother left him a note hammering it home this morning? *She will never view you as an equal.* Even his lady had emphasized it in myriad ways.

She'd just commanded him to bury a young woman like a stray cat they'd found on the side of the road. An act of compassion for certain, but all they would do. A human servant could be buried in an unmarked grave, the death challenged only if the Master or Mistress was offended by it.

"The grave does not need to be unmarked, Jacob. Mark it any way you wish." She picked up his thought, of course. At this moment, he could almost hate her.

"In your world, I have no value except as your slave. Your property."

As she studied him in her dispassionate way, he couldn't help but notice she kept her hand on the girl's cheek, stroking her temple. Perhaps Melinda's mother had done that. Imagined her daughter growing up to be married, a mother, someone with a successful career. Someone who won awards or traveled to amazing places.

"Yes, Jacob," Lyssa said at last. "And that truth just saved your life."

9

HE did what she instructed. Using a Coleman lantern to give him light, he dug the grave. He worked fast, using the exertion to help him block out the horror of what he was doing until he was just mindlessly slashing at the earth. Plunge, step on the edge of the shovel, lift, heave. Sweat poured off him. Perhaps there were tears there, too, for his nose was running when he was done and there was a tremor in his hands. He used the ladder he'd brought to get himself out, then took Melinda down into the grave. As he started shoveling dirt, he had to close his eyes. "Go and be at peace, lass," he said hoarsely to the weight of the darkness. "Don't stay here and look at this. Just go."

Because of the thought, in the end he didn't mark the grave. He didn't want the girl's spirit to come back and visit, seek any attachment to the place. She was much better off wherever she'd gone.

When he was done, the forest was quiet. He had a cowardly desire to avoid his lady's company tonight. Go out and get stupendously drunk. Instead, when he got back to the house, he cleaned up and took a shower, letting the hot water run over him though he knew nothing would clean this away. Donning jeans and T-shirt, he headed for the study.

She was there as he suspected. Reading, her head bowed over the large book in her lap. Bran lay on her feet. The fire was going. As he stepped in, she didn't lift her head.

"Did you know what he was about to do?" Jacob asked.

If the wrong answer came from her mouth, he would have to walk away. Rejoin his brother and let the same bitter rage deaden his soul so it wouldn't ache like this anymore. Maybe Gideon had it right.

Closing her eyes, she laid her head back on the chair, the flickering shadows from the fire guarding her expression. Her face, while sad and tired, was heartbreakingly beautiful as always. It made something twist in his gut. He didn't know if he wanted to throw up or fall to his knees and put his head in her lap.

"My world is a horrible and yet beautiful place, Jacob. Vampires are as deeply complex and unpredictable as humans. Carnal, however, is simply a monster. A monster of his own creation."

"But he suggested . . . it was a courtship act?" Jacob didn't bother to hide his disbelief.

Her lip curled distastefully. "Yes. As a vampire hunter and even under Thomas's tutelage, you weren't exposed to courtship strategies. Proving you can outmaneuver your object of interest is a way of gaining favor. I want you to burn that rug," she said, raising her head and opening her eyes. "I don't want his blood from that cup in my house."

"So to court you I would have to become a cross between Machiavelli and a serial killer."

"You don't court me, Jacob." She sat up, her expression becoming closed to him again. "You serve me. But you matter to me, if that gives you any comfort."

"Were you part of making those laws? The specific ones that apply to tonight?" *The one that allows the murder of an underage girl to go unpunished?*

Lyssa cocked her head. "Yes and no. You're familiar with the fact the original draft of the Declaration of Independence included language to abolish slavery?"

He blinked at the topic shift, but inclined his head.

"They had to remove it, else they would have lost the support of the southern states, and the whole concept of an independent country would have been lost to noble principle. Everything is timing. Getting vampires to agree to ritualized behavior, which would minimize body count, had to be propped on the foundation of their superiority. Even then, we still had to endure the territory wars to get everyone under the umbrella of the Council. And there remain many like Carnal who've not gained enough power to satisfy them. They must be watched. It will always be a problem." When her visage darkened, he realized he'd unwittingly reminded her that she could not help the Council do that for much longer.

"My lady—"

Her gaze snapped back to him. "Which comes back to another issue. Carnal could have killed you easily tonight."

"If my aim had been better—"

"If you had killed him, what then?" She rose, tossing the book on the side table with a flat slap of noise. Bran rose and resettled several feet away, his eyes shifting between them. "Do you know what's done to a servant who kills a vampire?"

"What the hell did you want me to do?" He pressed forward, almost nose to nose with her. "Let you drink it?"

"You have a mind link, Jacob. Why didn't you use it? No, be silent." She flung up her hands in irritation. "You'd only tell me the same lie you're telling yourself. It was just male ego. You wanted to call him out publicly, rather than letting me know so I could have dealt with it another way."

"So you're saying I killed her. I'm responsible for her death." His jaw was so rigid with anger he had trouble making his mouth move to say the hateful words.

Lyssa shrugged. "She wouldn't have lived long in his service. His servants never do."

"So that's a yes."

"I'm saying that you are my servant. Pride is not a luxury you have. Ego has no place in your service to me. If the moment calls for pride, it will be at my behest, not yours."

She moved away abruptly, leaving her light scent teasing his senses and the slender nape of her neck begging for a stranglehold.

"I'm done with this. Begone from me tonight. Don't forget about the rug."

It was the wrong moment for a dismissal. The thoughts in his mind came at her like depth charges exploding in an ocean of blackness. Lyssa almost flinched, but she faced the fireplace, ignoring him. Perhaps her timing was off, but he was expected to obey. That was all. She would have made concessions for his feelings after the terrible events of the night, but the defiance she felt rolling off him raised her own hackles. "Why can't you just learn to obey?"

"Because a human servant isn't a trained monkey," he snapped. "And because you keep wanting to draw a line between us you know doesn't belong there."

He'd stomped forward, back into her space, his blue eyes blazing, hands clenched. She had no concerns he would try to hurt her. That wasn't what the fury pumping off of him was about, but it had the ability to strike her just the same. Drawing herself up, she pivoted to square off with him fully, forcing a look of disdain on her face and securely locking her mind from him.

"Jacob, even if we were the same species, pedophilia doesn't even cover our age difference."

"Don't give me that," he said. "What about someone like Lord Brian? There's not much difference between us, about three or four decades."

"I do view Brian as a child, still a fledgling."

He rolled his eyes. "I'm a grown man and you're a grown woman. If Thomas's crazy theory is right, my soul is older than you because I was an adult guard when you were still in diapers."

She glared at him. "That's ridiculous, and it's not relevant. I demand your absolute obedience to my will, even when it conflicts with your bullheaded, outmoded ideas of chivalry. Thomas let it guide his actions, just once, and he ended up dead."

"It was his fault, then. For loving you too much? Just as it's my fault that girl is dead? It couldn't be because you vampires are totally fucked up. It's our fault for being idiot humans."

"No." It burst out as a shout, startling her. She couldn't remember the last time she'd shouted. Often she'd felt impotent fury at Rex's actions, but it had to be controlled. She let this loose, let it fill her, the whole useless mess that had been this evening. "It was my fault. For letting him believe he had the *right* to love me that much. For enjoying his friendship too much, for forgetting that you can only *serve* us. It doesn't matter what I wish or want. You cannot be one of us."

"Who would want that?" While Jacob knew it was a mistake, Irish temper was Irish temper, and it didn't often respond to his reins any better than he did to hers. "Cold, ruthless, soulless creatures who think they're so bloody fucking superior to us, when they can't even get along without adopting rigid territory rules as if they live in medieval Europe. Who are no better than any species that thinks it has the right to brutalize other ones because they can't fight you. Who consider us nothing . . ." The girl's dying gaze flashed through his mind. "Nothing," he repeated. "You consider me nothing, my lady."

A muscle twitched in her delicate jaw. He knew he should stop. Instead, he plowed onward.

"But there are times when it all slips away, doesn't it? Then you're just like any of the rest of us that live and breathe . . . need. Then I'm something to you, far more than you want me to be. Keep your mind closed like a bloody fucking trap all you want; I know it. I've felt it when you touch me, watch me when you don't think I know you're watching. And that cunt of yours that gets so wet for me doesn't mind stooping to take in the cock of a dumb animal, does it?"

The strike was fast, snapping his head back as she took him across the face with her knuckles, cutting him with the rings she wore. But it wasn't about strength. She could have punched him through two walls, but she chose the act of female contempt instead.

"I won't be spoken to like that." Lyssa bared her fangs. Blood was trickling from his lip. Despite her rage, she found she had to fight to keep her voice steady and push away the overwhelming desire to slam him to the carpet, tear into the wound and force him to understand just what a vampire's nature would stoop to doing. "Get out of my sight. Don't seek me until I bid you come to me."

"Gladly. After all, you don't need me around until you need your hair combed or your ass wiped. Things most of us *inferior* humans learn to do for ourselves before we reach kindergarten." Snarling, he turned on his heel, leaving the room. The kitchen door at the back of the house slammed hard enough to vibrate the walls.

She stood there, the fire crackling behind her, absorbing the anger in the room. It was as if the flames were swallowing the air as well, for now she was short of breath, her violent reaction draining away and leaving only the emotional pain she knew it had masked. She'd used it as a weapon, and her feelings for him had almost turned it against herself, with dire consequences for them both.

The truth was he'd scared her to death. Each time she thought of him shooting Carnal, she experienced the terror anew, when she'd thought she wouldn't intercept in time. She also remembered her dark pleasure at the way he'd hurt Carnal. That second of entirely personal and vengeful satisfaction could have cost Jacob his life.

The thought brought another disturbing, if far more distant, memory to her mind. Jun, her samurai guard, who had watched over her during her sleeping hours in the opulent nursery she had below-ground. Sometimes, she'd been able to coax him into taking his long dark hair out of its knot so she could press her face into it. Pretending she was behind a curtain, she'd hide from him until he flipped it away and revealed a ferocious warrior's face that made her giggle. He played a flute to help her sleep, rocking her on his thighs, letting her hold on to his hair and sway, as if in the cradle of a solid oak's branches.

The disturbing part came later, when his face was a mask of ferocity in truth, teeth bared, muscles bunched and running with sweat and blood as he took a spear through his abdomen and yet kept fighting. Holding on to the shaft, he'd cut down its bearer and snapped the end against a wall, pulling it free and charging forward, roaring at her maidservant to take her and run, run . . .

Lyssa shuddered, pulling herself back to the present. When Jacob stood facing her just now, she'd smelled the soap on his hands from washing off the soil of Melinda's grave, scrubbing it from beneath his nails. His eyes were sick with what he'd just done, and she'd wanted to comfort him. She'd made him bury her alone, just as she'd made Thomas die alone, and both of them had done nothing but serve her with complete loyalty.

She'd lost her objectivity. Every time she tried to reclaim it, she just ended up cutting him even more deeply. She was dissecting him in her attempt to understand herself. He'd been so angry at her, his fists clenching, eyes blazing, but all she'd been able to think about when she saw that trickle of blood on his lip was how much she *didn't* want to be arguing.

She found him standing by one of her fountains, the one with the center sculpture of Pan. The dancing satyr among the artful sprays of water formed the backdrop to her rose garden. For the first time since she'd met Jacob, she found herself hesitant to reach out and touch. She simply stood, a shadow in the night behind him.

It was foolish. By withholding her love she couldn't protect herself from loss. Denying herself love was a far greater loss in the long run. So, taking a breath, she laid a palm on his back. She drew comfort from the heat of him, selfish though it might be.

His shoulders lifted and fell in a sigh. "Did I tell you Thomas found the meaning of my name amusing?"

She shook her head. He glanced back at her, then looked up at the moon. "Supplanter," he said. "Otherwise meaning to take the place of something, the implication being that the something you're replacing is inferior, used up, no longer viable or relevant."

Lyssa arched a brow, uncertain of where he was going. "Thomas was a scholar," she observed. "One with a wicked sense of self-deprecation. There were times I thought of choking him."

Jacob gave a halfhearted snort. "Yeah, me, too. But that was actually better than the biblical relevance of the name. The one who took the birthright of his older brother through trickery. Genesis 25:23. 'The older shall serve the younger.' Jacob talked Esau out of his birthright by withholding food. He tricked their father, got the blessing meant for Esau. When his brother learned of his trickery, Jacob fled into exile from his brother's wrath."

It was not difficult to imagine him sitting by Melinda's grave, finding those Bible passages and attaching them to his own life. His brother believed Jacob had abandoned him. A young girl had died tonight while he could do nothing. He was servant to a dying vampire he loved, but he could not save her, either. She didn't have to read his mind to know the flow of his thoughts, that he was drowning in them.

What did what was appropriate matter anyway? There was just right now. His pain, and in truth, hers. Lyssa curled her arms around his waist and chest and went on her toes, holding him in her embrace. As he bowed his head, she brushed his shoulder with her lips. "Gods, today was awful," he muttered.

She felt gratified when his fingers closed over hers on his chest. Loosening her grip, she coaxed him to turn and face her. Reaching up, she framed his face in her hands, feeling the softness of his trimmed beard under her touch.

He shook his head. "I don't know how to get my mind around what happened tonight. All I feel is anger. I want to cry. I want to rage. I want to hurt something and I need . . . I don't want to have to think at all. I don't know how to be your servant right now. I'm . . ." He shook his head again. "I feel completely lost. I . . . I've been preparing myself for the annual kill, and that's been hard. Getting my mind around it, knowing it was going to happen. But this knocked my legs right out from under me."

He moved away from her touch, putting the fountain between them. Somehow his walking away now made her feel even more bereft than when he'd left her in anger. She didn't want to let him go, but she didn't know what to offer him. Her life was what it was, and he had committed himself to being a part of it.

"Jacob," she spoke, bringing him to a halt. As the silence stretched out and he turned, raising a brow, she was surprised at how difficult it was to say the words when it was something that happened so long ago. "I lied to you, in a way. I do believe I'm barren now, but I did conceive. Once. Things happened . . . I ran into some difficulties and she was born early. Too early. I buried her in Jerusalem."

The baby had come out deformed because of her mixed heritage, Lyssa had thought. Fey, vampire and human, an aberration that couldn't live.

At his shocked expression, seen through the wavering spray of water, she nodded. "It was the knight's child."

She firmed her chin, raised it. His eyes had become brilliant, fierce on her face. "He died soon after he left me, so I was never able to tell him. Sometimes I thought it was better that she went to be with him, because he could always protect her, would always put her first. His soul was pure, untainted by politics and evil things."

He came back around the fountain, stopped within five feet of her. "Why did you tell me that?"

"Remember I once said I could live ten thousand years and never understand some things, that none of us ever would? Like why someone like Melinda dies, or my . . . *our* child was born too early." She made herself say the words, though she couldn't meet his eyes. Swallowing, she pushed away the recollection of the tiny body swaddled in velvet and silk, being laid in the earth. "We shed our tears and have to go on. I just know . . . if I was Melinda's mother I'd be glad it was your hands that held her at the last, safeguarded her to the next life. Never doubt your heart, Jacob. It's the best I've ever known.

"The night of the third mark. I should have . . . I tried to let you go. But I couldn't. I just couldn't. I'm sorry." It flashed in her mind, the baring of his throat, the deep penetration of her fangs. The mark he bore on his back, his binding to her. No, she couldn't let him go.

He shifted, uncrossed his arms and turned away, this time obviously fighting with his own emotions. He needed her. But he didn't know how to arrange the ugly confusion of grief and anger battling inside him to approach her in an acceptable way. She could see it in his mind, not as clear thoughts, but a tumble of response rising in him like storm wind.

"Go—" She stopped herself. No, she wouldn't make this a command. "If you wish, go to bed in my room. I'll come to you soon. You can sleep in my arms, or bury yourself in me in whatever way will help. Be whatever you need to be to deal with this night or whatever is coming."

His hands closed into fists at his sides and yet she saw in his mind the image of those same hands closing over her flesh, holding her with brutal need.

She knew that life had a way of piling up horror upon horror, test upon test, on a soul. Like the weighting of stones on a witch's body until she was willing to say or do anything, sell her very soul for the crush to ease. The only way to get through it was to remember what you were. What you intended to be, who you intended to be.

He deserved that. He was not a supplanter, a pretender taking someone else's rightful place. Whether or not he was meant to be her servant, he was meant to serve her. Before her now she could see not only the present Jacob, but that knight. His large, capable hands and firm lips. Anticipation tightened in her lower belly as he turned, took a step toward her, then another.

He wouldn't go to her bed alone.

10

Jᴀᴄᴏʙ thought he'd be worn out and simply seek oblivion. Instead he took his Mistress again and again, using them both hard. The world might treat the idea with crass vulgarity, but in the darkness, with despair closing in, a man found sacred sanctuary in the wet heat of a woman's pussy. His woman's.

Exhaustion finally took some of the pain, leaving it vibrating discordantly off of the waves of the last orgasm, but it wasn't enough. He pulled out only to give him the ability to maneuver his mouth down her throat toward the sweet taste of her nipples, the valley between her breasts. When his hand slid between her thighs, she opened to him, let his fingers slide into the channel he'd already soaked with his fluids and her own. Her breath whispered out in a quiet sigh of pleasure.

Perhaps Carnal should not have spoken so hastily about inferior mortal stamina.

Her thoughts drifted through his mind, her pleasure with him spurring his efforts.

And do vampires value stamina in bed over other attributes? When he thrust his cock into her again, her tender tissues took him slowly, her hips tilting up as he slid his arm under her waist, his palm spreading out between her shoulder blades to bring her to his mouth, nip at her sternum. Tease the flesh of her breasts with his beard.

Like size, it's what they do with it that matters. For the man . . . or vampire . . . who doesn't know what he's doing, stamina can become never ending . . . torment. When she moaned, he relished the sound fiercely, deepening his penetration, knowing as her nails curled into his back and her cunt muscles tightened that he would make her come again. And again. Her climaxes, her screams, would drive the memories back, let him fall into a sleep where they could not follow and strangle him.

"What about the man who knows what he's doing *and* has stamina?" He nudged into her hair and bit her ear, moving to the tender skin below. Need pulsed like blood hunger beneath the thin veil of his teasing.

She drew his lips insistently back to hers.

"That man I might just have to keep forever."

He fell into exhausted sleep, still deep inside her. She'd had her arms twined around his shoulders as he rested in the cradle of her thighs, pressing her into the mattress. When he woke that way several hours later, she surprised him further by staving off her dawn slumber with creative use of his morning erection, bringing them both to peak again.

≈

She didn't shun his company for an indefinite time period as she often had in the past when he'd crossed the arbitrary boundary lines she set between them. It was as if suddenly she intended to give him a collection of pleasant vignettes, like a photo album of good memories shoved between the bad to break them up. It didn't make the pain of what had happened in her master hall bearable, or even better. Just a crucial step closer to what she had said. *We shed our tears and have to go on.*

The very next night, she invited him to join her in the study, reading while he channel surfed and watched her out of the corner of his eye. Finding nothing on, he switched to music and retrieved a couple of the X-Men comics he'd picked up on errands. Lying on the carpet on his stomach, he propped his chin on his knuckles and turned the pages, studying the graphics. As he stared at the colorful images, the simple concepts of good and evil playing out among the complexity of human emotion, he remembered Melinda's harsh death rattle. His lady's anger, the strike of Carnal's fist. The silence of the forest, as if every creature sat in judgment of him.

He tuned in to find he'd been staring at the same page for ten minutes. Thinking that looking at her would take his thoughts in a better direction, perhaps to the memories of the most recent night, he found his lady watching him. She pointed to the floor at her feet. Bemused, he scooted over, and she amused him by propping her feet on the small of his back. Kneading him with her toes absently, she continued to read, occasionally moving down to stroke his buttocks in the loose jeans he wore, dipping her toe beneath the waistband.

Before long, she set aside her novel and came down on the floor with him. He explained the comic book's characters as she lay back on his chest and he held the comic up over them. It was like they were studying the stars in the sky. The soft weight of her body held him to the earth when the lack of gravity threatened to send him spinning into space.

How many had told him she wasn't his lover or friend? Debra had said it was something unclassifiable, that *lover* was the closest frame of reference, a dangerously erroneous one.

Lyssa would set him back on his heels again; he knew it. It didn't matter. He wasn't going to stop serving her, protecting her. What was between them *was* a deeper relationship than lover or friend, because it encompassed both of those things and went to a far more intense level.

Debra was wrong. They knew what to call it. Mistress and servant. A "'til death do you part" no marriage ever envisioned . . .

$\sim$

"How on earth did you get up in there?" Jacob felt through the tools next to him and chose a different clamp, pulling aside a set of wires beneath the Mercedes. He'd been inspecting the car's undercarriage, specifically the brake line, when he'd noticed the car had a small, furry tenant. Feline. He'd thought he was on the verge of getting to the little creature, but now he was having a harder time seeing her or him, cloaked in shadows as the animal was.

Bran jarred his leg. In his lower vision, he saw the dog crouch down and hunch his shoulders with a hopeful look for his progress.

"Not . . . helping," he grunted, shoving the dog with his knee.

He always put fresh flowers in his lady's room at sunset with intriguing tokens of his sunlit day. This object might be a good one to leave for her. Depending on how coated with grease it was. And how long it took to extract it.

"Ah, damn it. You must be female." His target managed to shift into another, deeper crevice, into which it would have been impossible for even his lady's delicate fist to fit. "Keep it up. I'll get a corkscrew and pluck you out of there by your soft tissue."

"What are you doing under there?"

Speak of the devil. Or perhaps—at least for the moment—an angel. Tilting his head, Jacob saw a pair of pretty bare feet planted on either side of his left leg. At the same moment, his fingers brushed his goal. An unhappy mewl greeted his triumph.

"Come here, little mite. Sssh . . . it's okay." He managed to hold on to the squirming thing, only because it was too young to be strong, and the mouth too tiny to do any damage. "Can you tell Bran to go sit a few feet away, my lady?"

She bade the dog move back and he heard the dog chuff, pad away as Jacob wriggled out from beneath, holding the tiny kitten to his chest to keep it from streaking away.

"How on earth did that get here?"

"Without the dogs eating her, on top of that. She's not more than about eight weeks old. Mother probably got hit by a car and the kittens scattered."

As he came out, his lady changed her stance so she was straddling his waist, standing above him, her brow raised. She was holding her strappy high-heeled sandals in one hand and wore a tailored suit with a short skirt, suggesting she was heading out on one of her business errands.

Now she stepped to his side so she could squat beside him.

Now see, you little rat, if not for you I could have run my hands up those beautiful legs and . . .

"Think again. Not with that grease all over you." Reaching out, she touched the kitten with a finger. The animal was cowering under the cup of his hands, quivering so she appeared to be a faceless ball of matted, oily fur. "Oh, goodness, what are we going to do with you? The dogs won't tolerate you; that's for certain."

"I thought I could take her over to Elijah's. He's had to take his grandson in. Even if his son or the kid's mother comes back to get him, he could likely use some company."

Lyssa raised a brow. "You've been male bonding."

Jacob gave a mock shudder. "You make it sound so sordid."

Smiling, she came down to him, catching his lips in a kiss, stroking her fingers through his hair. "How do you know it's a she?"

He couldn't cover the thought that came into his mind quickly enough. With a smothered laugh, she gave him a sharp nip.

"Men tend to be pains in the ass, too, Jacob. Quite frequently. In fact, they're probably the main reason women don't always have a sweet disposition."

"I bow to your great wisdom, my lady."

"Only because you know I could stomp on your groin with my heel."

"There's that sweet disposition showing itself now."

He grunted as she drew blood this time, but the tip of her tongue flicked at it, took it off his lip, her green eyes meeting his, glowing with sensual intent. His body stirred. If he hadn't spent so much time retrieving the feline, he would have let her toddle back under the car and see if he couldn't coax his lady into getting dirty.

"Uh-uh." She smiled again, those wet lips curving. "You set up the appointment with the bank to sign the trust papers. Told me I had to be there on time, you bossy thing. It's your own fault." She turned her attention to the creature in his hands, stroking the fluffy back between the bars of his fingers. "Give her some scraps or milk before you take her. Poor thing feels like she's starving."

He watched appreciatively as she balanced herself against the car to put on one shoe and then the other. "Keep walking around barefoot on this asphalt and I'll have to give you another pedicure."

"An odious thought. I've had nightmares about the first one you gave me." Her wicked smile gilded the image she allowed to flash from her head into his. The way he'd knelt between her legs, his mouth on her dew-kissed flesh at the Eldar Salon, the soles of her feet pressed into his bare back.

She adjusted a strap. "I'm not coming back to the house tonight. I'll be back in two days. Keep Sunday night open. We're taking your motorcycle out."

Jacob frowned at the unexpected announcement. "Where are you going, my lady?"

"My business," she said, but rather than sounding impatient or imperious there was an anticipatory gleam to her eye. "And don't argue with me. I'll be fine and I'm going. I'll stay in touch, so don't worry like a shrewish wife."

His gaze narrowed. "Sunday, then. Any special preparations, a particular destination?"

"Somewhere special. A surprise."

"Where?"

"That's why it's called a surprise." She easily evaded his attempt to catch her calf between his feet. Moving nimbly out of his reach, she headed for the BMW. "You better not have reprogrammed my radio."

He hid his grin as she turned the ignition and AC/DC's "Back in Black" blasted out her windows. Sitting up, he eyed Bran, who gave the bundle still securely held in his grasp a calculating look. He parted his jaws to pant, showing a foam of saliva. The kitten squeaked.

"You're too much of a sportsman for this little mite. Let's go find a box and take her somewhere not populated by a legion of hellhounds."

Still, as he rose to do just that, his brow furrowed. Where was she going for the next two days? *And where the hell was she taking him Sunday?*

∽

At least she did stay in close mind communication. Just before dawn on day one, he'd woken with his mind flooded by an image of her in a hotel lounger, dressed in nothing but a black satin garter belt and stockings. Her hand covered herself, playing lazily with her pussy, which she kept frustratingly out of view with artful placement of her fingers. She'd nearly brought herself to orgasm before she cut the link, her playful laughter making him want to choke her even as she succeeded in reassuring him of her well-being.

After that, he wasn't able to tell where she was or what she was doing, but she regularly fired off demands for correspondence to be sent, phone calls and paperwork to be handled. There was a plethora of things she wanted done related to the Gathering in addition to his normal duties.

Despite her teasing and his full schedule, he worried about her. While she hadn't experienced any symptoms of the virus for the past few days, underscoring how the third mark had boosted her immune system, he knew it wouldn't last forever. He dreaded seeing symptoms reappear, because how soon they did would be a barometer of the disease's progress.

She needed that annual kill. He'd set all the details up, forcing himself to treat it as he did a domestic task. He'd communicated three possible dates based on the man's daily routine. She'd agreed to the date that was the furthest out, two weeks, and refused to consider anything closer. On one hand, it made sense. She was choosing the date closest to their departure to the Gathering so she'd make the most of the strength the kill would give her, while milking along the benefits of the third mark. Which also told him she suspected, no matter what measures they took, her time was short.

The idea of witnessing her annual kill and handling the disposal details was a hard ball in his stomach. But he knew that making it happen sooner was not likely to dissipate that ball. His conscience was starting to resemble a pitted battlefield.

It didn't matter. He had to push it out of his mind. Make her his primary focus, everything else just the details.

You think by learning how to clear your mind I can't read your face, your heart, Jacob? Your body? It had been just a whisper in his mind as she picked up on his thoughts, but he resolved to keep his mind off it anyhow. He knew his conflict over it bothered her, and he didn't want to give her an opening to deny him the right to be at her side when she did it. If her time was short, there were many reasons, both emotional and functional, that he needed to stay as close as possible.

When she came back on the second night, so close to dawn he met her at the car with a cape, she was pale. She didn't speak, but once they were inside she pushed him down into a chair, straddled him fully clothed and bit into his throat, seeking nourishment she seemed to need badly. She murmured her pleasure at the taste of his blood, the feel of his hands on her hips as she purposefully rubbed against him, arousing him to the point of bursting.

Because of his worry, his need for her had a sharp, emotional edge that made the physical craving even more acute. But she'd moved off of him and left him with a wicked though somewhat wan smile. *Until Sunday, my servant.*

~

She was a demon, he decided. It was now Sunday night and he stood in the driveway waiting on her. With mild concern, he wondered if it was possible for constant erections to cause permanent brain damage from blood loss.

I'm ready whenever you are, my lady.

He'd sent that mental communication to her about fifteen minutes ago. Since she was a woman, he'd expected and had the time to make a few more adjustments to the bike, as well as throw a stick to Bran's brother Fionn. Sunday night was blessed with a pleasant temperature and light breeze to keep off the mosquitoes. A sliver of moon was tilting in the early evening sky.

She came out wearing a lavender knit shirt, dark jeans, matching sandals and some simple jewelry. Except for the mall, he'd never seen her in jeans. The lines of the denim were straight and elegant, turning her ass into an upside-down heart where the garment nipped in to the waist. She had her hair clipped up loosely so tendrils fell around her oval face. No makeup, not that she needed any. All in all, she looked like she was ready for a picnic in the park. She'd told him to wear comfortable clothes, so he was in his normal garb of jeans and a T-shirt.

She handed him a flyer. "That's where we're going."

He glanced down. Started. "There's a Renaissance Faire at Langston Field?"

She nodded. "They set up outside of town several nights ago, and I thought you'd like to go."

Seeing the pen and ink depiction of the knight on the horse and the amply endowed wench offering food and drink brought back memories, most of them good. Though he tried to squelch one of them in particular, he felt her amusement sweep over him.

"Too late, Sir Vagabond. Now you're in trouble."

"She was just a friend. We were a bit drunk that night."

"Not too drunk to give her a good time, I see."

"If you're going to eavesdrop on my thoughts, you deserve what you get." When his thumb passed over the drawing of the knight and his steed, other memories came back. Sitting on the back of a powerful horse, charging forward side by side with other knights. Brief, poignant moments where he felt immersed in something that had always been more than a performance to him. But it hadn't been enough to hold him, keep him. Only the woman in front of him had been able to do that.

He raised his attention to Lyssa, knowing she was watching him closely, inside and out. "Why are you doing this, my lady? I'm not complaining; it's just these past few days . . . I guess I'm waiting for the other shoe to drop."

Stepping closer to him, Lyssa slid her hands up behind his neck and brought his head down for a kiss. They didn't often do it this way, where his greater height was particularly marked. Jacob lost the flow of his thoughts as she stretched up on her toes and pressed her body into his. Abandoning whatever the hell it was he'd asked her, he kissed her back, wrapping his arms around her. Softness, firmness, perfume, blissful *curves*. With the hand holding the flyer, he gripped her left buttock, the paper crackling as he molded it to the perfect shape.

"Don't ask questions. I just want to give you something. Something you'll like."

You're doing that now, my lady.

He brought both hands into play, grasping her tightly to lift her against him. She made a noise of pleasure, goading him further. He was raging for her, his cock enormous in a blink of time. He wanted, needed her now.

When she pushed away and backed up several steps until she was leaning against the bike, her gaze was one of wanton challenge.

It seems you've missed me. Am I teaching you to be insatiable?

The playful demeanor disappeared. Christ, even the dark mink sweep of her lashes could make him hard. She opened the top button of her shirt, teasing the cleavage with long-nailed fingers he'd painted himself.

I want you.

Which of them had thought it? And did it matter? He closed the gap between them and crowded her, trapping her between himself and the bike. As she put a palm on his chest, his hand closed over her deceptively delicate wrist, pulling it to the side and behind her, arching her body up into his.

Perhaps it was her own strength that made him act more savagely, more unleashed than he'd ever been with a woman. Her hair smelled like the exotic scent she used. It was something that if inhaled too deeply couldn't be detected, but it was there when one breathed normally, part of the lightness of the air. Capable of teasing a man to madness, like all of her, for she could deny him whenever she chose.

She watched him, the shadows in her eyes suggesting her internal struggle with her overwhelming desires and needs. Her lips parted as if there were things she wanted to say that she never would.

It was a struggle his sudden, sharp, male need cared little about.

Whatever it is, my lady, let it go. I just want you. It's that simple, every day, every moment. The beginning and the end of everything I need is here.

When he lifted her onto the motorcycle's seat, she relented, wrapping her legs around him as he growled his approval into her mouth. Pulling the clip free, he buried his hands in her abundant hair, deepened the kiss, invading her with ruthless determination as he intended to invade her elsewhere. His hands went under her knit shirt, his long fingers tunneling beneath the band of the bra and pushing it up so he could support her breasts with his own hands, earning a quiver of response from her as he captured her nipples in the creases between his thumbs and forefingers.

He knew she was wet for him already, knew it the way he knew he was ready to detonate. Putting his hand between them, he rubbed the heel of his palm against her mound and was rewarded by a convulsive tightening of her legs, her hips jerking up to meet him and increase the friction.

He pulled the shirt over her head and unfastened her jeans swiftly, backing off enough to strip them down her legs, taking her sandals off. Despite the urgency goading their actions, he had to take a moment to savor it. She sat on his bike in the driveway, under the spreading branches of a live oak dripping with Spanish moss. Wearing just her bra, a swatch of silky gold panties and all that glorious hair. The lawn rolled away behind her, verdant green painted with touches of fall color.

Her hands were on him, too, opening his jeans. She'd barely unzipped them before she gripped his bare buttocks and brought him back to her. Pulling aside the crotch of the panties, he thrust roughly into slick heat with a deep groan of relief she matched with a cry. He pumped into heaven, feeling the friction of the panties' elastic against the shaft of his cock even as he tightened his arm around her waist, keeping her close. Her buttocks rested just on the edge of the bike seat as she held her legs clamped high on his waist. When she leaned against his strength, her head dropped back as he held her with one arm and pushed her bra back up with the other. Holding it at her throat, he let his fingers apply pressure there. Her breasts trembled at his thrusts, his cock pushing in and sliding out of her pink lips, glistening and soaking the surrounding thin silk.

Fuck me, Jacob. Ah, God . . .

"I missed you," he muttered as she brought herself back up,

straightened and curled her arms around him so her head was tucked under his chin, her upper body pinned against his chest. Her fingers still dug into his buttocks, driving him, holding on to him. Perhaps because she was not looking at him, he could say what was rolling through him. While he knew she could hear it in his mind, he wanted her to hear him utter the words deliberately, as an oath instead of just a stream of consciousness. "I miss you every second I'm not inside you like this."

Letting her hold on to him, he slid his hands under her thighs, bringing her clit more in contact with his cock, which was hard as the chrome of his bike.

Her eyes widened and her body convulsed, giving him a surge of furious triumph as her nails bit into him. Her fangs glittered from the soft white light cast by the outdoor lanterns as her mouth opened on another cry. She spasmed inside as well, giving him no more choice in the matter than he'd just given her. He flooded her, feeling the two heats mixing together, wetting his ball sac. The inside of her thighs pressed against his hip bones. He kept pushing into her, staying right with her through each aftershock, wanting the impression of his cock filling and completing her, imprinting on her memory. So perhaps she wouldn't deny herself or him for such an interminably long time again.

One day, two days . . . the hours when she slept. All of it was too long.

Humor rippled through her, mixed with passion as she caught the thought. She held on to his shoulders, breathing shallow breaths as he held her close, pressing his head on top of hers.

"What is it you miss so much during my sleeping hours, my greedy servant? My smile? My eyes? Or this?" She contracted upon him, squeezing him with such artful skill he thrust against her in answer.

"All of you, my lady. Everything you give me when you do this. Your wet pussy, your panting breath, your nails digging into me, your heart and desire in your eyes, those soft whimpers in the back of your throat. It tears the heart out of me." *I never knew there was anything that I'd want for all eternity until I met you.*

Her nails pierced his skin, her forehead pressing against his chest so he couldn't see her face, but her emotional reaction to his words and thoughts flooded him like a wave.

Sometimes he forgot she'd lost her husband so recently. That such admissions could hurt her because the intensity was reminiscent of what she'd wanted but never had with Rex. When he felt her struggling to rein it in, he knew whatever she'd planned tonight, she didn't want to be drawn into her own shadows. Changing tactics, he raised her head with a nudge of his, brushed her lips with his mouth. Nipped sharply. "You got this out of your system? Ready to go now?"

She blinked back the tears he knew she didn't want him to notice and managed to toss him an arch look. "I think I might need to freshen up first."

"No. Don't." He gripped her with a sudden fierceness. "Wherever we're going, I want to know that my seed is sticky between your thighs. When you take your panties off just before dawn, I want you to smell me on your flesh and in the silk."

As her eyes darkened with desire, he knew he'd banished the shadows. Reaching up, she stroked her thumb over his lips, her touch lingering when he made the contact a kiss. "I won't be taking my own panties off, Sir Vagabond. I can almost guarantee you that."

~

The Faire was set up on acreage outside of town, a nature preserve set against the backdrop of Stone Mountain with its impressive carving of the trio of Confederate generals.

Nearly five acres of pavilion tents were interspersed with torchlight to distract attention from the large outdoor stage lighting that had been rented to further illuminate the area. A roar of cheers rising beyond the forest of tents told Jacob some type of competition was in process. The crowd of parents and children he saw milling among the tents suggested it was not a joust, however, which would typically draw most of the Faire attendees to the makeshift arena at the rear of the fairgrounds.

Other than a small scattering of cars, there were five school buses in the parking lot. "This is a school booking," he noted. "It might not be open to the public."

"It's not," she agreed. "They're holding a special nighttime performance for an inner-city school. It was made possible by a private benefactor who asked if she might attend herself to see the children enjoy the Faire. And bring a guest."

He digested that as she used his shoulder to brace herself and swung her leg over the bike. He'd redone her hair for her and she'd rearranged her clothes, but as he wished she'd not done anything else. To all outward appearances she was perfect.

"I suspect this benefactor is someone with more money than God."

"That's such a ridiculous saying. What use would God have for money? Hence, a pauper has more money than God."

"A pauper you are not, my lady."

Lyssa cocked her head. "These children don't have much of the good memories money *can* buy. Plus, it served my purpose. I was planning a birthday gift for someone very dear to me. Terry said you liked the nights the troupe entertained schoolchildren the best."

Jacob came to a halt. Eyes widening, he turned, taking a closer look at the cars and the pavilion tents in the distance. The colors. "This is my old troupe. They changed the flyer."

She nodded. "Happy thirtieth birthday, Jacob."

"This took some time to set up. When did you—"

"You think I just sit around every evening, waiting for you to do my hair and wipe my ass?"

He winced. "I'm never going to live that one down, am I?"

"I'm still offended by it." She sniffed. "I plan to bring it up as often as possible, because that's my right as your Mistress."

He snorted. "It has nothing to do with you being my Mistress and everything to do with being female."

However, he tugged her forward until she was standing toe-to-toe with him and he had his lips pressed to the tip of her nose.

"Thank you," he said.

～

The faces were new, but Jacob saw Terry hadn't lost his touch. The British owner and operator had been a well-known Shakespearean actor in his homeland. Everyone he hired understood their primary goal was to make the Faire goers believe they had stepped out of the world they knew, into a world based in history but gilded with the romance that fantasy and time could give it.

Will you feel like a knight in shining armor when you help her tear the throat out of an innocent? Gideon's voice, dubbed over his conscience.

His decision was made, damn it. Viciously, Jacob shoved the thoughts away, but not quickly enough.

You do not have to come with me, Jacob. I have told you that before.

Yes, I do. He blew out a breath. He didn't want to think about this now. He truly didn't. She'd gone to a lot of trouble. Just . . . *Does he feel any pain, or fear?*

Lyssa turned, her expression softening. Reaching out, she touched his arm. "No. For this, I use what you like to call pheromones, for lack of a better word. At least at the crucial moment. His last thoughts are that he is being most pleasurably seduced by a beautiful woman." Jacob frowned at that. Though her eyes flickered, she continued. *When I break the skin, there is usually surprise, but the chemicals balance it, increase his arousal. Before he can feel the panic that comes with the instinct his life is in danger, I break his neck. I can finish feeding on him postmortem as long as he is alive when I break the skin, and I drink what I need within the first fifteen minutes after his death.*

"I may not view humans as equals, Jacob," she said, low, "but they are too much a part of my life for me to simply cut a decent person down in the prime of his life and feel nothing. You are not alone in your feelings on this. It is just . . . I struggled with it many years ago." *I accepted it. Today shall belong to us. We will deal with the rest tomorrow. Agreed?*

Jacob managed a smile. "Agreed, my lady." *When have I ever been able to deny you anything?*

When she let her hand slide down his forearm to his wrist, her reassurance echoed in his mind. *You are not alone in this.*

"A kirtle, my lady, with a lovely corset?"

The gown a red-haired woman displayed at the opening of one of the pavilion tents was deep green velvet with wing sleeves and a touch of deftly done embroidery at the neckline. The corset to go over it was a tapestry of hunter green and gold, the lacing strings strung with copper beads, reminiscent of a medieval world with the elegant touches of the modern-day artisan's mind.

"This is lovely. Do you have something for him?" Lyssa nodded at Jacob.

The seamstress rummaged through her line of designs, hung up on a line tied between two wooden posts decorated with ribbons and clusters of dried flowers, like miniature versions of maypoles. She produced a green tunic edged in gold, brown hose and a pair of supple boots.

"Beautiful, but no." When Lyssa shook her head and stepped forward, she brushed shoulders with the woman. "Look at his eyes. Those eyes should never be wasted."

"You're quite right, my lady. There appear to be many parts of him that should not be wasted."

"They're not, good woman. I can promise you that."

While Jacob smiled at her relaxed banter with the seamstress, it made him wonder how many of her trips away from home recently had been to visit with Terry and his troupe. To arrange for his birthday, when she faced many important matters and an uncertain amount of time to accomplish them.

Haven't you heard, Jacob? I have a new human servant who is the epitome of efficiency. He handles so many things for me now I scarcely know what to do with my evenings.

Watching her going through the selections as if she were just any other woman enjoying her shopping, his heart tightened in his chest. It seemed there was no end to the things she was, the emotions she could pull from him. And that was the answer to his brother's voice in his head.

Yes, Gideon. I'll do anything for her. It's beyond what the world calls right and wrong. It's what I must do. It is what it is.

"Here." Lyssa pulled out a tunic in blue, embroidered in silver. When she turned to face him, her green eyes were intent. "I like the green dress very much, but do you have the same in blue, with a corset done in blue and silver? I would wear his colors, after all."

"Of course. I make all of the designs in pairs for that very reason."

Fifteen minutes later, with the aid of the curtained partition of the tent and an exchange of money, Jacob had left his bundle of street clothes in the woman's care and gone outside to make room for other browsers while his lady changed. When he felt her emerge, he turned.

He swallowed. Though the blue dress had simple lines designed to lie softly against the curves of a woman's body, the cinch of the corset enhanced them and lifted her small breasts. She was perfectly at ease in the garb, displaying aristocratic patience as the woman pinned a jeweled scarf on her hair. Whether in jeans, silk or velvet, every inch of her said royalty. A queen. It was her birthright.

Only a little while ago his mouth had been pressed against her lips to the point of bruising. She'd parted them, let him plunge into the soft moistness within, penetrate her body the way she could do to his heart with just a look.

You don't wear my colors, my lady. I'm wearing yours. When she stepped toward him and lifted a hand to his cheek, he looked away, pressing his jaw into her palm.

I've stood with kings who had not a tenth of your bravery, wise men who would be put to shame by your resourcefulness. Priests who would be blinded by the light of your integrity.

"Cease, my lady." He caught her hand. When he squeezed a little harder than he intended, he immediately loosened his grip, trying for a lighter tone. "You'll make me vain and then I'll be no use to you at all."

The way you look in that tunic makes me think of how you look without it. Like when you get out of my pool and water is rolling down your naked body, your nipples drawn up tight, begging for the scratch of my nails . . . your eyes so fiercely blue . . ." As she took another step closer, her thighs brushed his. She spoke in a whisper now, her lips close. "Would those tight hose bear the strain if I commanded your cock to rise for me? It's making me wet, the desire to take you inside me again. You know women of this time period didn't wear underwear."

Jacob swore softly, though his mouth couldn't help but tug into another smile. Daring to dip a hand beneath the fall of her hair adorned with the jeweled net, he curved his hand around the side of her throat. When he tipped her chin with his thumb, her lips parted, showing him a hint of fang.

"Don't worry, Jacob. I have my ways of whittling you down to size if you get too vain."

"You can cut any man's knees out from under him with nothing more than a sweep of your lovely lashes, my lady. I'll argue with you no more. At least for the moment."

She laughed then, and the throaty sound was enough to turn heads. "Just what I expected from my stubborn servant. A conditional surrender. Let's go see the games that knights like to play."

11

But in the way of women, she took her time about it. The noise of the distant crowd had died off, the increased traffic in the pavilion area alerting them that the current tournament was over. A mead seller informed them that the main jousting tournament would be in a half hour. So he wandered hand in hand with his lady, looking over articles of clothing, jewelry, weaponry, goblets. Jacob was watching her consider a set of beaten silver goblets when he heard his name called.

Turning, he saw Elijah Ingram coming their way, holding the hand of his six-year-old grandson.

"Happy birthday," Elijah offered as they approached. "Mrs. Wentworth was kind enough to invite us to join in the party tonight. Were you surprised?"

"Immensely." Jacob shook the man's hand. Dressed in jeans and a golf shirt, Ingram looked different. When he drove the limo, he always wore a dark suit and tie, and usually was armed. Even in the more casual clothes, the black man had an authoritative presence that suggested he wasn't to be trifled with. His grandson had no fear, however. He gripped two of the man's fingers in his small hand, his eyes full of Lyssa as she turned from making her selection.

"Pretty lady. Princess."

"Yes, she is," Mr. Ingram said. "This is Mrs. Wentworth, John. She invited us to the party tonight. What do you say?"

"Thank you," the boy said and then lifted the item he had in the other hand. "They made me a balloon dog. I'm going to take it home and let Whiskers pop it so she'll grow up to be tough. Won't be afraid of no dogs."

"Any dog," his grandfather corrected.

"Whiskers?" Lyssa smiled. "That must be our little grease monkey."

"Monkey is right. The cat is into everything." Ingram tried to return the smile, though Jacob noticed it didn't quite reach his eyes. There was a wariness to his posture even as he continued, his gaze shifting between Jacob and his Mistress. "Tough I don't know about. If she isn't sleeping in my armpit at night, she screams like there are ghosts in the house. I'd have been happy to drive you tonight, Mrs. Wentworth. And you are looking mighty pretty," he added, somewhat stiffly.

She waved a hand. "I'm becoming fond of the motorcycle."

"A regular biker chick," Jacob agreed. "Before you know it she's going to have the Harley T-shirt and fringed jacket."

The little boy giggled, and she winked at him, squatting down. When Elijah tensed, Jacob abruptly understood the man's reserve. Lyssa caught it as well. From the tightening of her facial features, he suspected she would have straightened and turned away, that haughty veneer falling into place to mask her reaction, but she was already down to John's level and he moved into her space without hesitation.

Elijah reached after him. Jacob put out a hand, drawing his attention and firmly stopping the gesture. Elijah's gaze snapped to him and Jacob met it with a level stare of his own, a slight shake of his head.

"I love Whiskers. Thank you for giving him to me. You smell good," John informed her as he reached out and touched her hair, checking out the jeweled hairpiece.

"You're very lucky to have such a wonderful grandfather," Lyssa told the boy. "He's as brave as any knight here. I'm going to go look at jewelry. You can go with me, ooorrr . . ."—she drew out the syllable as the boy wrinkled his nose at the idea of jewelry shopping—"you could go see that juggler over there. We just saw him pull a ball out of a boy's ear."

When she rose, she met Ingram's gaze. "As mistakes go, I think he may be your son's most beautiful," she said. She left them then, walking toward the jeweler's tent.

In her mind, Jacob caught a flash of a delicate ear, a misshapen cheek. A velvet cloth being pulled over a baby's face, then the curtain fell back over the thought. He didn't think his lady knew he'd seen it. Elijah's actions had struck a vulnerable point in her, enough that she hadn't guarded her thoughts as she usually did. At least that's what he told himself as he struggled to handle the images which hit him hard and low in the gut. The knight's daughter.

His daughter. Their daughter.

"I'm sorry," Ingram said, keeping one eye on John, now involved with the juggler. "I just . . . You know what she is, Jacob."

Jacob watched her study the rings and noted the jeweler stepping back to let her look, not yet engaging her in dialogue. She used that unapproachable air when she needed it. Like her seductive talents, it was even more effective than a vampire's compulsion at giving her space when she wanted it.

"She's many things," he said quietly. "But she'd stake herself before she'd harm a child. Human or otherwise. Don't hurt her like that again, Elijah. She invited you here because she knows we're friends, but she also invited you because she likes you. She might be pretty damn near invincible in our terms, but her heart can be bruised just like anyone else's."

He pressed a hand to the man's arm to let him know they were square, but then he left him to go to Lyssa's side, surprised at the protective anger swirling through him.

The rings were tied with ribbons and hung from the tent frame, which also served the purpose of having them catch the light of the trio of candles the jeweler kept on the counter. The candles rested in a tray of water and polished rock for aesthetic effect.

Jacob slid a hand to the small of her back and reinforced it with a touch from his mind, a wordless reassurance. She put her hand up on her hip, her fingers curling over his. No response in words or thought, but he felt her accept both offerings like a comforting embrace.

As she looked at the designs, he reached out to touch one he liked. A simple and delicate thing with a sapphire center stone. The stone rested in a fairy's lap, her tiny metal-etched hand resting atop it. She lay reclined in the clasp of her lover who appeared to be human. The sinuous intertwining of their bodies made up the top half of the band and the setting for the stone.

Lyssa pressed closer to his shoulder, examining it. "It's quite deft, isn't it?"

He nodded, glanced at the jeweler. "How much?"

To him, it was expensive. He knew to Lyssa it was a paltry sum. The night he'd met her she'd been wearing a necklace the equal of which he'd only seen on movie stars and fashion models. So he wasn't sure what made him nod and dig the money out of his pocket. It constituted about a week of the salary he accepted from Lyssa.

"For an admirer of yours?" she asked in a neutral tone. Jacob lifted his shoulder in an uncomfortable shrug. "A token, my lady. You may keep it or gift it, if it's not to your liking. I just . . ." He'd never given her a gift, and today he wanted to do so. "I thought it would please you."

She was giving him that arch look she did so well, and he wouldn't be baited. She'd never struck him as the type who wanted slavish devotion, preferring Bran's dignified and unquestionable loyalty to slobbering affection. But she knew full well how much Jacob felt when it came to her, so it would do no good to hide it. He couldn't bear her laughing at him, though. So he shrugged again and began to pocket the ring. "I'll give it to someone else, and not trouble you."

Clasping his wrist, she stopped him. Extended her left hand. "Let's see if it fits."

Nodding, he tried her middle finger first. The ring was too tight. "If you'd prefer the right hand, my lady, we can put it—"

"I prefer the left hand, Jacob."

He thought her dark green eyes could rearrange all the shadows of his soul into the shape of herself. "After all"—her voice was soft as their gazes held—"you did promise me forever, didn't you?"

She put his heart in his throat so easily he wondered she didn't just pull it out completely. If she didn't, he was sure he'd choke on it one day. When he slid the ring over her ring finger it fit perfectly, snugly at the base as it should. He gripped her hand for a moment, her fingers linked with his. Abruptly, she turned, drawing him onward.

"It's about time for the joust, isn't it?"

~

The knights were galloping across the field to the cheers of the assembled crowd as they arrived. Though the wooden bleachers were filling up quickly, there was a space in the center portion of the third row. Lyssa accepted Jacob's hand as she navigated to the cushioned seat, holding up the edge of her skirt to avoid tripping on it. When she sat, she spread it beneath her, folding a triangle of the excess fabric over her thigh and crossing her ankles, her back straight.

Though she could tell Jacob was pleased by his surroundings, there was a pensiveness to him, too. She could feel the swirling nuances of his mind. He wasn't caught up only in his Faire circuit memories.

"Jacob?" She touched him. "Are you all right?"

"Yes, my lady." Shaking his head, he ran a hand along the back of his neck. "God. It gets clearer and clearer, the longer we're together. I remember . . . it was dim, in that closed tent, and hot. I noticed you weren't even sweating. You . . . had me disrobe. You honored me by bathing me. I was embarrassed that I was so . . . aroused before you." A touch of color rose in his face, amusing her even as it made her heart clutch.

Even being bathed by that cool water, a treasure in the desert, couldn't cool my ardor. You dried my feet with your hair.

It was the knight's voice, his formal cadence of speech in her head, and the hair rose on her arms at the sound of it. "You fell asleep at one point with your head in my lap," she managed.

Turning his head to look at her, the breeze moved his hair on his shoulders, tangling against the gleam of his beard. "With the taste of your grapes in my mouth. Your sweet breath on my face . . ." His brow knit. "Why did I leave you?"

"You were joining a battle elsewhere. I wanted to keep you, but since you were a man of honor and had come to my aid, I quelled the urge to turn you from your path." An ironic smile touched her mouth. "It was a struggle. Then as now, I'm not your equal in honor. *Fair play* isn't always in my vocabulary."

"You have an honor and sense of duty that rivals that of the entire Round Table, my lady. But you'll not hear me argue about fair play." Catching her swatting hand with a laugh, he kissed it, then looked back at the field. "I loved doing the circuit, but probably the best times were after, when it was just us. The players. It felt the way it should. Real. Sometimes . . . well, a man's imagination gets away with him, then, doesn't it?"

I'm not Gideon, Sir Vagabond. I'm not going to laugh at you.

His jaw tightened. "If there is such a thing as reincarnation, and if they were who we'd like to believe they were, I wondered if you'd find Gawain and Lancelot, maybe even Arthur, someplace like this. So they could be as close as possible to the wistful dreams of lives gone before." A wry smile touched his lips. "With the conveniences of cable and microwave pizza within reach instead of drafty castles, invading hordes and winter food shortages."

"Perhaps. But I tend to think spirits of men that strong couldn't bear to live only in the shadow of what they once were. They would need a new quest, equally important." She glanced at him. "Isn't that why you left?"

The trumpeters lifted their instruments, forestalling a further reply as they heralded the beginning of the tournament. Elijah and John joined them, sitting in the row just below them.

Having both Jacob and Elijah close, seeing this plan for Jacob's birthday come to fruition, gripped Lyssa with a quiet contentment she hadn't experienced in some time. She turned her attention to the field, eager to see what would happen next.

A horse in trappings of red silk cantered onto the field. The other knights had cantered back out of the ring, into the large canopy tent set up next to the arena entrance. This knight was in gold and silver armor and bore the Faire pennant. As he came to a stop on the other side of the wall dividing the tournament field from the audience, the horse made a knee, bowing with his knight.

"My lords and ladies"—the knight turned his mount in a stylish circle and his baritone resounded through the air—"the hour grows late, and so it is time for a very special tale. I must ask you all to listen carefully, for this tale has never been told at our Faire before, and it never will be told again. You also will see something no one else will see again. So you must pass it on to your children and your children's children. That is how all legends endure."

Jacob's brow furrowed. While it had been some time since he'd been with the Faire, he knew Terry enough that if his player said the story had never been told before, it hadn't. He wouldn't take the risk of having someone attend his Faire twice, as many often did, and hear the "story that had never been told" twice.

"Once, a long, long time ago," the knight continued, "there was a horse of unparalleled beauty. Fate placed her into the hands of evil men. As many of us know, evil cannot accept the existence of something beautiful. They do their best to twist it, make it ugly. So they hurt her. Beat her." The volume of his voice swelled, carrying his dramatic but genuine tone of outrage to the corners of the field. "They tried to take away her spirit. When they couldn't, they were determined to destroy it utterly."

Unbidden, an image of Rex flashed into his head. The first night he'd seen Lyssa, when he'd been with Gideon. Watching at a distance as her husband broke her arm. Rex had done it just to see her reaction. Jacob curved his fingers protectively over his lady's delicate hand. Lyssa glanced at him curiously, telling him she'd been listening to the knight and not to his thoughts. He pushed the dark images away, not wanting to take her there.

"When they thought they'd broken her, she was sold. She was scarred, her beauty gone. Frightened and bitter, she fought the touch of man however she could. It was almost as if she wanted to be destroyed. When the heart is so painfully abused, it can no longer see the light of love, the warmth of hope. All it desires is escape from a world that seems to be only darkness and evil."

Lyssa's gaze shifted to young John, sitting on the far side of Elijah. The shape of the child's small skull, his ridiculously delicate neck. Leaning forward, she placed a hand on Elijah's shoulder. He turned as she moved, telling her he was staying well aware of her whereabouts, but he accepted the touch, met her gaze. She nodded, easing some tension in his shoulders as he received and understood her unspoken gesture. No, she didn't blame him at all for being overprotective.

"But she was bought by a knight," the man in the arena continued. "A knight with a true heart so pure, he was able to heal this noble steed with patience and love." The narrator paced the horse forward, deliberate, slow steps, stopping just a nose from the arena wall. He pitched his voice lower, but it still carried to all present. "For you see, this man didn't mark time the way we do. 'Do I have time to do this today? Can I get this done before I'm old and gray? Wouldn't I rather be doing something else?'"

She glanced surreptitiously at Jacob. He was leaning forward, his body language saying he obviously recognized the horse in the story, but she knew he didn't know all that was planned yet. Her intuitive knight, so clever at reading other people, so oblivious to things about himself.

"He measured deeds, not time. And so he healed her heart, a priceless gift to us all. Unfortunately, when one deed is done, it's time to move on to the next. So in time he left her in loving hands to undertake his next quest."

The knight backed the horse now, crabwalking her to a left-facing profile. The lights around the bleachers disappeared and the spotlights turned, focusing on the entrance to the large pavilion tent. The baritone voice reverberated out of the darkness.

"She has become the star of our show. Though she bears the scars of her trials, we feel she is more beautiful now than before. She brings light into our souls just by existing."

Two knights came out of the tent entrance, each one bearing a length of ribbon in their hands that threaded back through the closed curtain.

"My lady . . ."

Lyssa found Jacob's hand, squeezed it.

"Tonight, Boudiceaa's knight has come home. She will bear no man's hands on her while he is present, so her usual rider has stepped aside. You are all witness to a spectacular, once-in-a-lifetime experience. We call this knight from the stands to take his place among our ranks again."

One of the two men holding the ribbons pushed back his visor, showing a broad grinning face. "Aye, enough of this maudlin nonsense," he shouted out. "I, Sir George of Canterbury, want to see if he's grown soft. I intend to kick his arse."

The children burst out laughing, but quickly quieted as the narrator boomed out, "Boudiceaa, come find your master."

Tears pricked Lyssa's eyes at Jacob's expression, something she could detect even in the darkness. She'd never been able to surprise Rex with a gift like this. Jacob's speechless amazement made her feel a way she wasn't sure she'd ever felt before. She wasn't sure if she wanted to embrace him, or run off where he couldn't find her to compose herself.

In the end, she simply watched with the others as another damsel he'd saved erupted onto the field to the astonished cries of the audience. She was sure most of them had never seen such an overwhelming sight in their lives. An Andalusian galloping full tilt, mane flying, tail flowing. The ribbons George and the other knight held were attached to her light halter, so as she galloped past, they snapped free, fluttering back toward them.

Centuries of breeding had created the almost unreal beauty of the premedieval warhorse. Though the Andalusians eventually had been replaced with breeds more capable of carrying a knight in full armor, she was a treasure for the lighter garb of modern Faire knights.

To Jacob she was wholly beautiful, despite the scar she bore across her nose and that had taken her eye. There was also a long scar running down her back haunch, results of the cruelty that had brought her to auction. In teaching her to trust him, she'd broken his arm, left teeth marks in his shoulder, clipped his temple with a hoof. He'd made so many trips to the emergency room during her training that Terry had threatened to put a gun to her head and end her misery and hatred. But Jacob had prevailed.

Aching for his brother, confused by the emptiness in his heart he hadn't known how to fill until he'd met Lyssa, the mare had been priceless to Jacob. By giving him the chance to save her, she'd rescued him in return.

She unerringly headed in his direction as the lights were restored to the bleacher area. A performer and also female, she deliberately slowed down to maximize the effect of the fluid gait, crested arch and flowing tail. Murmurs of awe swept over the children and parents like a wave. But when she reached the wall she lifted her head, snorted, put up a hoof and banged the lower boards, causing squeals from those seated on the other side.

"You have to go to her," Lyssa murmured. "I would never stand between such a love."

Jacob turned, placed his forehead against hers.

You knew I needed this.

I love you. I wanted you to know what that means to me, no matter what happens between now and the end of it.

His eyes darkened with emotion. Cradling her face in both hands, he kissed her fair brow. When he rose, holding on to her hand as long as he could, the knights shouted their approval. It got the crowd started as well. Jacob noted many of the Faire players from the pavilions had come down and were now lining the arena wall to the left of the bleachers.

It was the easiest thing in the world to simply put a hand on the wall and vault stylishly over it. He was glad the boots he was no longer familiar with didn't trip him up and shame him. In a blink, Bou was on him. He embraced her, pressing his face into her muscular neck. When he lifted his head he found that Terry, the other knight holding a ribbon, had dismounted and was grinning at him from a foot away. He handed his reins to a squire who trotted his horse off the field.

"So I hear you've become a kept man these days." Terry raised his voice for the benefit of the audience. "I'll just go keep your fair lady company while you're impressing us—or not."

Jacob gave him a narrow look. "Behave yourself with her."

Terry laughed and stepped close enough to grip his shoulder. A fierce look crossed his countenance. "It's good to see you again, Jacob. Happy birthday."

Jacob glanced at Lyssa, sitting in her blue and silver colors among a sea of mostly brown faces. One or two children had moved close enough to finger her skirt. After assuring their chaperone or parent it was quite all right, she was touching the head of one little girl with an assortment of pigtails. His gracious lady. When it suited her.

Bou butted him in the chest, nearly knocking him down while the children giggled. His heart swelled at the bright, healthy look in her eye. Terry and his troupe had cared well for her, continued to nurture her spirit to even greater heights, as he knew they would.

~

When Terry came to sit by her, Lyssa made room for him with a welcoming nod.

"Look at some of my newbies." He nodded toward the squires and a couple of the knights leaning on the wall who weren't part of this tournament. "They're wondering who the hell this interloper is, taking Martin's regular ride. They've heard stories about him of course, but they'll expect him to be rusty, or not as familiar with the moves."

Terry wore his sandy brown hair in a Roman style, short at the nape, his face clean shaven. His hands were callused and gnarled from hundreds of camp breakdowns. In his twinkling hazel eyes, Lyssa saw a man who loved where he was and what he did. Who made no apologies for preferring the romanticized past to the jaded present. He grinned as the horse bent one knee to Jacob, inviting him to mount. Lyssa caught her breath as Jacob took hold of a handful of mane and swung up on her bare back in one lithe move, canting her into a pretty circle, his movements flowing easily into hers.

Not too long ago, she thought she'd like to see him on a horse. Her reaction to it, body, heart and soul, was as absurdly overwhelmed as she'd expected it to be.

"Martin rides her well, but you can see it's the difference between day and night. You should have seen her when she came here. The most foul-tempered and frightened bitch I'd ever met, of any species. No one could handle her. Only Jacob knew her soul was still underneath all that. Looking back, I think she knew she could trust him the minute he touched her. She just had to knock him around a bit to prove it was her idea."

Yes, Lyssa thought. *It's just that way.*

Jacob leaned forward, spoke in the mare's ear in a loud mock whisper, mindful of his audience, falling into the mannerisms of a natural performer as though he'd never left.

"See her? That's my lady." The horse's ear swept back. "Want to show off for her a bit, make me look impressive?"

Leaning back, he tossed Lyssa a grin before he uttered a command in Spanish. The horse began to perform a high prancing walk. When he changed the command she moved sideways at that gait, and then back again, forming a cross. The spotlight returned, zeroing in on Jacob and Bou.

The mare paused, all muscles quivering. Jacob let the anticipation build. Lyssa saw the children as well as their chaperones come to the edge of their seats.

He barked a one-syllable command. Boudiceaa leaped straight up in the air, kicking out her back and front hooves at once as the children cried out in reaction. When she landed gracefully, she turned in another circle, bowing her arched head, tossing her mane as if well pleased with herself and the applause.

"Do it again," several children called out, making Jacob laugh and comply twice more, earning a dramatic whinny from Boudiceaa on the last jump.

"That's a battle move," he explained to the amazed group. "Knights used it to help them fight in close quarters. The horse was a soldier, too."

Looking toward Terry, he called out, "Are you still doing open jousting, or have you become complete pussies, lugging around that tilt barrier everywhere?"

"I can't wait to see George knock you on your arse," Terry responded dryly as the children and parents responded with laughter and oohs. Glancing at Lyssa, he spoke loudly. "George hits like a battering ram, my lady. I'm afraid there will be nothing but pieces left. You should pick yourself out another knight."

The kids offered appropriate jeers to that remark as the floodlights came back on, displaying the full sandy arena again. George trotted his horse forward, impressing them with a half-rearing motion where his horse appeared to wave his front hooves mockingly in Bou's direction. "What say you, skinny Irishman? I think your gentle bones might break if I knock you off that pretty horse."

Jacob snorted, but couldn't help but grin at George's broad wink. When he turned Bou to accept a lance from one of the squires, he glanced over to see Lyssa smiling, leaning against Terry's arm as he whispered to her.

"My lord, I suggest you get your lips away from my lady's ear, or perhaps George will not be the only thing impaled today," he declared. Terry grinned, lifting a brow.

"My thoughts were running along those very lines. She's quite fair. I can't imagine you're anything but an annoyance to her. You think I'm afraid of your tiny lance?"

"No. I think you're afraid of your wife."

Laughter at that from the adults. Terry's wife, the charming and not-at-all-worried Beatrice, still managed to give him a threatening look from where she stood with the other members of the troupe, hands on her hips, a fetching pose in the tavern maid garb she wore. She shifted her attention to Jacob and gave him a smile, a welcoming and warm embrace itself. With lines along her attractive face and her auburn hair pulled back, she looked as maternal and lovely as he remembered her.

"Your lady has been telling me she is willing to give the jeweled net in her hair to the man who wins the joust today," Terry announced.

"My lady, you best tie the favor to my arm now, for I can tell you I'm the best of this sordid lot." This from George.

"George has been hit numerous times running the quintain," Jacob pointed out. "It explains why he has delusions of grandeur." Which of course led to the children, now actively part of the game, calling out for an explanation of the quintain.

While George was handling that, Lyssa saw a fifth man come onto the field. He was dressed more like a wild Pict than an English knight, for he wore only a pair of breeks and no shirt on his upper body, unless one counted the Celtic tattoos on his well-developed biceps. He brought his mount up to the rail, so close that the gelding's large head reached over and his velvety lips were in range of the children. They squealed and shrank back, but at a calming word from Beatrice, they reached out tentative hands to touch the soft nose.

"Warrick," Terry murmured to her. "God's gift to women. Too many of them don't disabuse him of the notion because of his fair looks."

Lyssa hid a smile. The narrator with the baritone, who Terry whispered was called Elliott, had picked up after the quintain explanation and was now on to another history lesson to entertain the audience while the field was being set. "Does anyone know how the giving of the favor came about?"

"I shall explain it," Warrick boldly asserted. Quite deliberately, he shifted his attention to Lyssa. She cocked a brow, amused as he began to speak as if he was talking to her alone. Jacob was a few paces away, and he and Bou had nearly matching expressions of disgust, entertaining the audience. She wondered how he'd trained the horse to do that.

"A knight could fight in honor of a nobleman's wife, perhaps even his liege lord's woman. If he won, he could treat her as his own wife . . . for one night."

"A sanctioned form of adultery," Lyssa noted in a low voice to Terry. Elijah shot her a glance over his shoulder, humor flitting through his dark gaze.

"Secularly at least." The Faire owner grinned. "The Church

frowned upon it. I suspect problems arose if the lady in question was more pleased with her 'night with a knight' than all her days with her husband."

When Warrick continued to boldly stare at her, Lyssa returned the favor. Gave him a slow and thorough appraisal, her green eyes darkening.

His skin shuddered, visibly. Whinnying, his horse began to back up. Jacob had sidled Bou closer and now pushed against Warrick's mount, breaking the eye contact. He shot Lyssa a deprecating look.

I told Terry to behave, my lady. I didn't think I'd have to tell you. He clapped a hand on Warrick's back, startling the man out of his sudden stupor. "Believe me, Warrick, she *will* eat you for breakfast. Stick to the tavern wenches."

"She can have me with bacon and eggs on the side," Terry quipped.

"Does she have as deft a tongue as face?" This from a knight in purple and white, filling in on the rowdy banter since Warrick seemed to be having trouble finding his own tongue. "I wonder—"

The crowd burst into laughter as he had to do a quick duck, for Jacob twirled the lance dexterously, nearly taking his head off with its reach.

Lyssa found herself delighted to watch them, a complement of well-conditioned men, circling one another and exchanging insults. It was obvious this ritual of genuine heckling had been a mainstay of their competitions with each other, which gave it the tension of a serious sport rather than the distracting sense of a performance.

They'd decided to give the children a taste of the rings first, so with those set up at the edge of the field, the trumpet sounded. Jacob did not even need to tap his heels. Boudiceaa was off and running.

Lyssa watched, her heart in her throat as much as anyone as five men charged down the field toward four hanging rings, Boudiceaa a full two lengths ahead.

"Speed is confidence, my lady," Terry explained. "A man not as sure of his aim will hold back. Look at him, riding her with nothing but his knees guiding her, and her going flat out. Not even a bridle."

They reached the end of the field. Jacob speared his ring with the lance, spun his steed and managed to cut and bump against George's, making the man drop his lance before Jacob left him behind. Bou galloped with spirited abandon back up the field.

"Holy Christ!" Terry laughed out loud. "Wouldn't have believed it if I hadn't seen it. That boy is unstoppable."

George roared for another lance as soon as they came up the field, making a great show about the insult done him. He faced the children, voicing his outrage as Jacob and Bou pranced behind him, mimicking his gestures and making them laugh. When George whirled, the pair immediately looked serious and repentant. Bou executed a little dip over her front leg, her forelock hanging down, and Jacob bowed from the waist. George glared at them, then spun to address the crowd again. Boudiceaa began to do a high step trot in place, moving left, one set of legs coming over the other as Jacob held one hand in her mane only.

When George whipped around, catching them this time, Bou froze in place, one hoof still in the air. Jacob made a show of looking around as if he was seeking what was upsetting George.

"He's very good," Lyssa said over her own laughter, as well as Elijah and John's.

"Oh, he's an outstanding player," Terry agreed. "You've given us all a gift, my lady. We're delighted to have him back, if only for a night. I don't think George has a chance, but it would be fun to see the young upstart knocked on his tight arse for once."

Jacob had been brought a breastplate, helmet and buckler. Once donned, he hefted his lance. Elliott summoned the trumpets and then, when the squire whipped the flag down, the men charged. Jacob surged forward on Boudiceaa with a bloodcurdling yell. George and his steed thundered toward them across the open field.

Lyssa remembered the actual medieval tournaments where jousts had been done with a tilt barrier, where the lances had to be held at an angle over the knight's body. It was impressive and a little frightening to now see it done the way it had been done before that, two men charging each other on powerful horses, the lances leveled straight for each other.

With three marks, Jacob was more protected than George. She

told herself there was no chance the lance was going through the breastplate, not with the tip guarded by a coronal.

The lances struck the bucklers, splintering the weapons and forcing both men back against their horses' haunches with the impact as they galloped by one another. Squires raced out with another lance for each man. With barely a pause for action they were charging one another again.

Halfway there, George's mount stumbled and he dropped his lance. He kept coming on with a roar, however. A few strides off, Jacob tossed his away. When the horses were abreast, he lunged out of his seat, his knee pressed up high on the seat to propel him across.

They fell with a resounding thud to the far side, clear of George's horse, tumbling in a tangle of arms and legs. Lyssa realized she'd come to her feet. Terry eased her back to her seat. "The first thing a player learns is how to fall, my lady. No worries."

"So this isn't . . ." *Real* was not the word she was seeking.

As if in agreement with that, Terry shrugged. "George and Jacob have a long history of competition. They tend to like to beat the pride out of each other before they call it quits. It makes for a good show; that's for certain."

As the two men separated, the squires ran out with long swords. The kids were having the time of their lives, on their feet, calling out for their favorite. John was likewise hollering and clapping, stamping. Elijah had a firm hold on his shirt so he wouldn't bounce between the planks of the seat and the floor of their row, though she noted their somber limo driver was shouting out his support for Jacob along with his grandson.

By the time the squires were there with the swords, both men had shed the armor and helmets. The clash of swords was loud in the brightly lit arena, clods of dirt and grass chipping up around them from the footwork. George spun and struck and Jacob retaliated, moving forward. Neither man seemed to get an advantage for too long, though there were a couple of near misses where Jacob ducked under a slice of the sword. Lyssa's heart jumped into her throat again.

The children gasped as Jacob was knocked to a knee, rolled away.

As George came after him, bringing the sword down, Jacob writhed around it, punched him in the jaw and followed it up with a shove from his foot. George toppled backward. In the blink of time he was on his back in the dirt, Jacob was up, his blade at his throat. Immediately, he backed off, bowed and awaited George's next move.

"I yield," George called out with a rueful smile. There were some cheers, some groans, depending on which knight the child had decided to champion.

Grinning, Jacob handed George up and the two men embraced. George said something that earned a quick laugh from Jacob. He rubbed his arm, as if indicating George's sword blow well could have turned the tide in his favor.

Then her servant turned, found her in the crowd. Seeking his lady's approval of his victory. Emotional and physical response flooded her in such a hard wave she drew in a breath as if she'd just felt a sharp pain. As he moved toward her, his eyes rested on her face with that potent absorption that made her have a craving to devour him alive, their impressionable audience notwithstanding. Trying to slow her rapid heartbeat, she let her attention move from his face to the broad shoulders and the sweat that dampened the front of the thin tunic. The capable way he still held the sword, as if it were an extension of his hand. The graceful power of his body as he walked toward her.

Looking at him was not doing a thing to slow her heart rate.

Bou was walking alongside without reins to guide her. When they reached the wall, the children were already pressing forward with the supervision of the Faire people. As Bou bent her head to allow herself to be touched, Jacob placed a hand on her neck.

"My lady," he spoke. "Have I won your favor? Am I deserving?"

More than you know. However, Lyssa rose, tossed her hair. "I know not. Perhaps it was as much luck as skill that won you the game, since the other man's horse stumbled, costing him the second lance."

There were jeers and boos. Jacob placed a hand over his heart as if he'd been struck, staggering back to laughter.

"What say all of you?" she called out. The children shouted out their opinions immediately, and Terry guided them on the predominant call of "Favor! Favor!" even as George scowled ferociously and yelled his disagreement, waving his arms in a gesture to silence them all.

Jacob raised a brow as they quieted at last. "It seems they have more faith in my abilities than my lady does."

I have too much faith in your abilities. It makes me fear for you.

Despite the dark thought she blocked from Jacob, she accepted Terry's hand to proceed down the bleachers until she stood just above him. Removing her scarflike net and kissing the jeweled fabric, she tied it on his arm, letting her hand linger on the sleeve of his tunic to feel the muscle beneath. As the audience cheered, she heard John hollering out his approval and Elijah's whistle. Jacob wound his fingers in a loose lock of her hair and tugged, giving her one of his smiles.

"Fortunate scarf, to get a taste of your lips." Those vivid blue eyes locked on her. "What must I do to win such an honor? Slay a dragon? Lead an army?"

Refuse to do anything, even in my service, that would make you turn away from me or love me less than you do today.

She covered his surprised mouth with hers before he could respond to the thought she'd given him as clearly as a spoken sentence. She knew how much of his heart was worrying over what he would help her do next week, knew there was nothing she could do to stop it. He was right. She had to have the blood. Perhaps, with the time being as short as it was, she should have been like Carnal and simply taken a criminal life. But as powerful as she was, and knowing what the disease could do to her emotional control in its later stages, she couldn't take the risk of being influenced by the blood of an evil carrier.

Nothing could make me love you any less, my lady. I love you more every day. How many times must I tell you that my life is yours to command?

Earlier, she'd told him she loved him. It was not the first time she'd said it, but now she knew she should never say the words again. How could it even come close to meaning what it meant when he said it? She was accepting the type of love from him she'd already given up the right to offer in return.

She knew the world was more than the two of them. During rational moments, she knew giving him the third mark had made sound sense. He'd as much as pointed that out. But during other moments she wondered if the stories and legends she'd always ignored had been right. If vampires were in fact evil, and she'd drawn a good man into Hell.

Because he wasn't just sacrificing his life for her. He was offering her everything, including the right to tarnish the integrity of his soul.

12

JACOB watched Carl Ronin step out of the upscale sushi bar and bid his friends good night. Turning up the collar of his jacket, he began to stride down the cobblestone street that marked the downtown art district. It reminded Jacob that not six blocks away was the Eldar Salon, where he'd convinced his lady to consider taking him as her servant. Tonight he faced the most difficult part of being one.

He would stand by, waiting as she took the life of a man who had done nothing to deserve his life being cut short. Then he would dispose of the body for her. Through his extensive research, he knew Carl worked for an ad agency. He was currently between girlfriends, though he'd been close to marrying the last one. If he had, it would have saved his life, for Lyssa didn't take married men as her annual kill. So thorough was his lady in her research, Jacob even knew that Carl had two dogs and he'd made provision in his will that they should be given to an old army buddy if he ever became unexpectedly deceased. He had a downtown apartment within walking distance of this bar that he visited twice a week.

He had no idea his life would end tonight.

His Mistress materialized so easily out of the shadows Jacob didn't even see from which direction she came. Wearing a black cocktail dress and a shawl, she looked as if she'd just come from a party. She asked Ronin for directions to a small bistro not far from his apartment, so it was natural for them to fall into step together, him offering to show her there. Her hand lightly moved to his arm, drawing his attention there. She was already releasing her vampire pheromones. She'd apparently decided to do it early, not taking any chances of things going wrong.

Carl's dick would be getting hard, making him believe he was feeling some type of instant attraction to her, a connection that would erode barriers typically held in place by commonsense suspicion.

When she laughed at something he said, she took a more secure grip on his biceps as she apparently made a misstep in her skinny heel. His hand naturally slid around her waist. As she looked up at him through her lashes, Jacob knew Carl was thinking he'd walked into his best luck of the evening, maybe his entire life.

When Gideon had taken him on his very first vampire hunt, Jacob had fought the anxiety and fear in all the usual ways. With denial, avoidance, acceptance, analysis. He hadn't realized how valuable the privacy of his own thoughts was for that process. Several times over the past couple of days, when he hadn't been able to mask his building reaction to what was coming, she'd reiterated that he didn't need to come with her, that she'd do this on her own. He'd finally asked her—begged her, actually—to just to stay out of his mind until it was over. He was her servant. He'd do what needed to be done. She wasn't going alone.

Gideon's visit had been too recent. What if he was still out there with a team to interfere, to catch her unawares? What if Carl was more resourceful than expected? As long as she was at full strength and awareness, no one could sneak up on her. But therein lay his concern, and one of the reasons he himself had pushed her to do what she'd put off for months.

The pheromones were doing their job, or maybe just her proximity alone, which Jacob knew could play havoc with a man's senses. When Carl's hand slid lower, to the top of her buttock, she pressed closer to him, giving him a view of her cleavage.

He should feel nothing but sympathy for the man, glad that he could take pleasure in a woman's body in his last moments of life. Instead Jacob tamped down a desire to break his fingers for touching his Mistress. Jesus, jealous of a soon-to-be-dead man who was responding to a chemical inducement, like a drug.

Compared to previous annual kills, she was hurrying it along. From Thomas he knew that in earlier years she'd enjoyed her prey, even spent most of the evening with him, taking her own carnal pleasure while giving him the sensual experience of his life. She hadn't used compulsion or pheromones to anesthetize him until the actual kill moment.

He knew enough about vampires, let alone his Mistress, to know that dallying with prey fulfilled a vampire's fetish for power and control. Holding a life in her hand before extinguishing it. The same way she might part her red, wet lips to blow out a flame and leave a room in darkness.

They're predators, not minions of evil. He remembered his words to Gideon and used them to balance him now. All predators, though having to kill to survive, took some pleasure in the kill, for lack of a better word. A predator's nature was one of dominance, power. Each kill confirmed that dominance, the fine line between predator and monster, murderer. He believed his lady when she said this one life was all she took for her survival each year, but she might be incapable of not deriving some pleasure from the act.

Jesus, what was the matter with him? She was taking a man's life in order to prolong her own, not for her own selfish reasons, but because she knew the lives of the vamps in her territory and the whole structure of vampire society might rest on how long she could maintain the illusion of her power and existence. He understood that. But could Carl please just remove his fucking hand from her ass?

You will never be comfortable with how I view your species . . .

He closed his eyes. He wished she'd get it over with so he could just act, do something other than sit here and think about what was about to happen. When she turned the corner, he eased the car off the side street. They would cut through the park. She would draw Carl into the shadows of the trees. At that point, he would want nothing more than to be inside her. And she'd bite him . . .

She'd opened her mind to him now so he could follow her. Carl made a joke, a fairly good one, about the type of things a lady might encounter in the park at night. He was still feeling lust, his mind alive with the things he wanted to do with her, but through his lady's eyes Jacob noticed Carl simultaneously kept a lookout around them. Protective. Protective of her, a woman he'd only met a few moments ago, because he'd been raised a gentleman. Chivalrous.

Jacob noticed she asked Carl nothing about himself. She kept the conversation on the present, the bar he was just at, the beauty of the night, how far his apartment was . . .

~

Reaching up, Lyssa caressed Carl Ronin's jaw with her fingers. "You are perhaps a little too good," she murmured.

He raised a brow. "Then tell me how I can be not so good."

She smiled. "Kiss me."

Lyssa brought his head down to her, stood on her toes as he framed her face, closed his eyes and brought their mouths together. He didn't rush it, demonstrating the prowess of a good, experienced lover. Leaning into him, she rubbed her abdomen against his aroused cock, signaling what she wanted. When he broke the kiss, lifting his head, she moved to his throat, licking him, nibbling. His arms tightened around her back, moving down to mold his palms over her ass and discover that stockings were all she wore.

"Jesus," he muttered. "You're a gift from Heaven."

"Or Hell," she said softly. When he smiled against her hair, Lyssa felt the pull of it against her temple. She sank her fangs, slow and easy, into his skin, increased the hold of her arm around his back and waist as he jumped, startled. She shot a full measure of pheromones into his bloodstream so the alarm was brief, vanishing as if it had never been.

He groaned, jerking against her touch, the flood pushing him to a hard, brutal orgasm, dampness spreading across his trousers. She massaged him through his clothes, giving him the full measure of satisfaction as she began to drink.

"I . . . Jesus, I'm sorry . . . Oh, God . . ."

"Sssh . . . there will be time for more. Let me just touch you . . ." Lyssa slid one hand to the side of his skull and cradled his jaw with the other, tilting his chin up. She rose on her toes, her fingers sliding into his hair to take a tighter hold.

~

Though he knew it didn't make sense, Jacob shut his eyes again, wishing he could shut out the image.

Pain. So excruciating he thought somehow he'd connected to the man's mind and was learning a snapped neck was not as painless as it had always been supposed. But this was not Carl Ronin's pain. It was Lyssa's. Blinding, rocketing through her head, so fast and brutal she'd been unable to close her shields, something she'd never let happen before. Jacob received it full force through his own temples, in his gut where it gnashed like one of those sharp-toothed parasites in a space movie, tearing through the lining, loosening his bowels. Lights flashing . . .

"Shields, my lady . . ." He was out of the car and trying to run, though he could barely see, staggering. "My lady . . . shields. So I can . . . help you . . ."

He gasped it, heard her cry out, a scream of agony. Adrenaline shot through him, diluting the hold of the pain. His will kicked in to carry him through the crimson mist, his mind telling him this was psychological. She was experiencing the pain, not him. Only when the end came would the pain be real, since he would die with her. And this was not that moment, damn it.

But his lady never cried out. No matter the pain he'd seen her suffer thus far, she kept quiet. The way a wild animal in pain kept silent, not wanting to draw the attention of another predator. One only cried out when one preferred a predator to end the pain instead of prolonging it.

Somehow though, she heard him. Suddenly the pain throbbed away like fading strobe light, the nausea pushing one last, lingering sick wave through his stomach before it, too, dissipated. He lengthened his strides, coming over the hill that overlooked the copse of trees in the park they'd specifically chosen for its isolation.

Lyssa was collapsed on the ground, trying to struggle to a sitting position. Her hair was disheveled, dress rucked up from her collapse. As she lifted her head, the moonlight shone on her elongated fangs and reflected the red of her eyes that came through most strongly when she fed. Even from his distance, anyone would know she wasn't human.

He saw Carl's hand was on his neck, fingers soaked with blood. He stared down at his shirt where drops had splattered. The flowing stream of it had turned his collar bright red. Slowly he raised his head, his eyes widening as he saw her fangs, the preternatural light in her eyes.

He backpedaled, stumbled, turned and began to run.

Jacob's gaze darted between him and his lady. Her head dropped, her body shuddering. Her strength apparently deserted her, for her arms went out from under her and she rolled to her side. Convulsions shuddered through her, but even amidst her fogged, pain-filled brain, her mind spoke to him.

Let him go. It doesn't matter.

The rejuvenating blood of an annual kill combined with the third mark would give her more time, widen the space between the episodes again. Give her more time to protect her territory. Maybe give her more time for something to change. Even a cure. Debra had said Brian thought they were close to something.

Something, *anything* that would give him more time with her. He could feel his soul hanging in the balance, but didn't know what decision would damn or absolve it. He'd made an oath to protect her with his life. An oath she'd just exonerated him from. But she'd also told him that no matter what, he had to put her desire to protect her territory, her people, first.

Let him go . . .

His attention went back to her, curled on the ground, suffering. His lady.

His feet were in motion before he even realized he was moving, and then he was running. A lean, strong man, skimming low over the grass of the tended park where children came to play and lovers to tryst, lying on picnic blankets and drinking wine. Where people brought a book to read. Where old women fed pigeons and business-men read their papers on their lunch hour.

Things that had nothing to do with now, when the park belonged to things of the night, beings with dark intentions.

He'd hoped Carl wouldn't see him coming, but the man's survival instinct had kicked into high gear. As Jacob came out of the trees less than twenty feet from him, Ronin cursed, increased his stride. Panic made him jerky but adrenaline gave him a speed he'd probably never realized before.

Jacob caught him anyway.

Lyssa rose on one shaky arm in time to see her servant take Carl Ronin down, like a wolf single-mindedly pulling a stag to his knees by the scruff of the neck. He knocked Carl face-first into the turf, planted his knee into his back. Before Carl could speak more than one muffled plea into the grass, Jacob had jerked his head up with both hands. In one violent, powerful move he twisted it, cracking the spine, severing the connection to the brain. Just time for that one short, desperate cry. Less than a second of time, but one that seemed to echo through the park like it was a canyon.

It was nothing Thomas could have done for her. Even if he had Jacob's strength or skills as a fighter, she wasn't sure he would have done it for her. Of the handful of servants she'd had throughout her life, she couldn't think of one that would have done this. Rex would have, but it would have meant no more to him than picking up meat at the market. Where the life of the creature it had once been was neatly hidden away by precise cuts and cellophane packaging.

Jacob rose to one knee, breathing hard, though she knew it wasn't physical exertion. Her head was pounding, making her too dizzy to read his thoughts, but she wondered if she would have had the courage to do so even if she could.

He lifted Carl in a fireman's carry and brought him swiftly. His hands were shaking as he deposited the body next to her, easing him to the grass, cradling the back of his head. He closed the staring eyes.

"My lady. You said you must drink within a few minutes of his death. So you must drink. It should help your pain as well."

But what will help yours?

She had no words for this moment. Not when he sat down on the grass and slid his thigh under the man's shoulder and head, holding Carl's neck at an easier angle for her to reach the important arteries. Lyssa lowered her head, fitted her fangs to the original bite mark and drew deep, filling her mouth with the warm, still vibrant blood. Despite the agony rolling through her, she made herself do it, knowing Jacob was right. She made herself shut everything else out to do what she had to do. As he had done.

I know you think our species is inferior . . . The words of Thomas's letter mocked her, made her want to spit out the blood and vomit into the grass. But she didn't.

At length, she felt Jacob's sweat-dampened palm, the hand that had just taken a man's life, touch her head. Stroke once, then grip, grip hard as she continued to draw blood into her body. His hand followed the movement of her skull as she drank. Wet, warm drops splashed against her cheek, her temple, and she felt him shudder with his silent strangling sobs. It moved Carl's body in slight, disturbingly lifelike twitches. She didn't stop or look up, knowing Jacob wouldn't want her to do so. After tonight, he wouldn't want to speak of it again. There was nothing to be said. It was what she had to do to live, and he had helped her do it because he had sworn to serve her.

She wouldn't forget it, while Jacob would always wish he could.

As if he were a male vampire competing for her favor, he'd proven his strength and power to take down her kill. Brought it to her as a mate would.

These were dangerous thoughts creeping into her mind, but this was her time, the dead of the night when she walked in full strength with fear of nothing. The crickets and frogs were silent. The smell of blood was in the air and a predator was close by. Her headache was gone as if it had never been, as if it had never knocked the strength from her so she could not finish the task she'd started. The nausea was gone as well. The vitality that came with an annual kill coursed hot and strong within her. Would it get her as far as she needed to go? It had to. Most importantly, it would get her through this moment.

Her servant had no coherent thoughts right now. Just a hurricane of rage, grief, desperate energy. A need to control something, balance his world that was spinning out of control. Like the night with Melinda, but even more strongly. Primeval impulses rode close to the surface, and the rush of energy surging through her responded to them with a savage eagerness. When death and life joined hands and death prevailed, mortals had an irresistible need to do something that defied it. Immortals in contrast would skirt as close as possible, absorbing its untouchable power.

Rising to her feet, she straightened her dress, unpinned her hair and shook it down. Threading her hands through it, she let it fall away from her face, down her back, arching her throat so she knew it caught the moonlight. She knew its paleness and the rise of her breasts over the scooped neckline had drawn his gaze, even as his hands remained clutched on the man in his arms.

"Jacob." She met his haunted gaze. Reached out a hand. "Come to me, dearest."

She backed a step away, then another, moving even deeper into the shadows of the trees as he rose. As he stared at her, his eyes were a brilliant color, glittering with so much life and conflict she thought he might possess an electric force field capable of delivering voltage. His hands opened and closed, his body tense, his rational mind arguing with what his body and the darkest part of his soul knew they needed. Hungered for.

Grounding. Connection.

"Because you brought my kill to me as a mate would do," she said softly, "tonight I offer you the rights of a mate. I submit to your desire. Your will."

He gave a harsh chuckle, ran a hand over his face. "You're a piece of work," he said thickly. "I can't . . . I need to take care of him." His eyes said something else entirely though, running with greedy desire over her body, conveying a consuming want that tingled over her skin like the electric brush of his mouth, the snap of his teeth.

"We will. Together. I'm not dishonoring his sacrifice, Jacob. But I need you. I want you. Now. This very second."

"Do you, then?" His voice altered, became abruptly soft and deadly, so that she felt the sharpness of his attention like the prick of fangs in her vitals. "You just said you owed me your submission. I'll make the demands."

She slid the straps of the dress off her shoulders and stood before him as it pooled around her ankles.

"Off. I want it all off. Even the jewels."

She complied, rolling one stocking off and then the other, peeling off the earbobs and necklace, dropping them on top of nylon carelessly, as if they didn't cost as much as they did. She knew that would inflame him further. Her hair fluttered over her shoulders, the tips of her breasts, tangling in her fingers.

His breathing quickened, a laboring as if he'd been running. When she trembled, his gaze darkened. "Are you afraid of me, my lady?"

He could overpower her with the force of his emotions where he couldn't with his strength. He could take her down and make her helpless to his mercy, though she knew he had no room for mercy in his current state of mind.

"Yes," she whispered.

"Good," he said, and closed the distance between them.

The kiss was hot and brutal. His hands closed on her breasts with no intent to be gentle, though his violence was enough to arouse her. He squeezed, bringing pain with the spearing pleasure of it. *Mine*, the rough touch said. His fingers pinched her nipple, and when he bent her back over his arm and fastened his mouth over the other one, he bit hard, eliciting a gasp from her.

He took her to the ground, dropping to one knee so he had her trapped between the one raised leg and the knee pressed to the grass. When she tried to rise and touch him, he seized her wrists and wrapped them in her stocking from elbow to wrists, knotting it between her clenched fingers. He pushed her arms over her head so he could thrust the fingers of his other hand into her cunt to tease her. She was soaked at his fierce possession, and he swore as she widened her trembling legs, opening to him. She understood in a way he didn't that something terrifying was roaring through him, something that could only be relieved by pummeling into her, a receptacle for all his sins. She would gladly take them.

He stripped off his jeans and shirt, becoming a pale, naked

animal like herself in the moonlight. Some of Carl's blood stained his neck at the collarbone. Another smudge over his pectoral showed that some had gotten down the shirt. Her pussy clenched, anticipating, but she should have known his anger was not assuaged. He straddled her head, thrust himself deep into her mouth. He braced himself with one hand on her wrists so she had no way of controlling his thrusts.

When he pushed deep against her gag reflex, she had to quickly relax her throat muscles to accommodate him. She'd chosen to put her mouth on him before, but never had she serviced him like this, and it was clear why he intended her to do so now. What wasn't so clear to her was her gushing response to the brutal taking, but nothing had to be rationalized. They were more animal than human or vampire at the moment, obeying some primal need to validate, bond. It was a war of Dominance and submission where she'd given him the reins, so effectively she didn't know if she'd really offered or he'd simply taken them.

Her pussy was wet, ready. She growled against him, scoring him with her fangs even as she licked, suckled, swirled her tongue over him to taste his salt. As she writhed, he reached back and gave her clit some light swats that made her buck up to his touch, mewl with need against him.

"Suck me well, my lady. I may come in your mouth, make you swallow every drop of me to earn the pleasure of being fucked."

Her cunt convulsed at the thought, and there was a savage part of her that wanted to fight him, wanted to rebel. But when she tried to lift her arms he shoved them back down, gave her a glaring, almost mean look that told her he would fight her if she crossed him. It only made the edge of her desire that much sharper. She didn't know if he was doing this to shred the edges of his soul or use it as fire to cauterize the wound the evening's events might have caused. She let go of the desire to care because she just needed him, the bloodlust and physical lust working so strongly together they were unable to be contained in her body. She was far past the bright edge of climax, on the knife edge of something far more powerful that might shatter them both.

His cock was pulsing in her mouth, his fingers clutching spasmodically on her arms, telling her he was close. She tried to push the issue by increasing the force of her suction, bringing her fangs into play to pierce his skin, just enough to make it difficult for him to pull out without pain, an effective cage as she worked against his length with her tongue.

He thrust his fingers into the corners of her mouth, his thumbs pressing on either side of her throat to hold her as he wrenched open her jaw and withdrew. Faint rivulets of his own blood marked him, his size only increased by the challenge. His thickness was extraordinary, even for him, though she knew that life-and-death situations often had such an effect on men.

Lifting her legs, he folded his own under him and tilted her hips up onto his lap. Straightening both of her legs against one of his broad shoulders, he banded his arm over them so they were held together. Lowering her with the power of that single arm, he guided his cock into her ass, bringing her down on it with ruthless determination, penetrating the area she'd never allowed him to penetrate except the night with Gideon. Even lubricated by her saliva and the juices of her pussy that had flowed into that area, he was a great deal to take, particularly in this state. She gasped at the invasion, the bruising fullness of him, a sound of distress in her throat. But desire was there, too, as her pussy spasmed, jealous of that channel, wanting him inside in a different place.

He spoke through clenched teeth, seating her on him even further. "No, my lady. It's your ass I'll fuck tonight, reminding you that you're my Mistress. Mine alone."

The darkness made his eyes almost black, his face sharply etched. He began to rock her up and down on his length, abrading her sensitive tissues. She'd be aware of his presence there for days to come, healing powers notwithstanding. She'd shudder from desire at the mere memory, even as the pain kept her focused on the message he wanted her to understand. He'd killed for her. Served her. He was hers. Somehow he'd committed to that so deeply with this night's actions that it had all become a wall of mirrors. She was as much his as he was hers.

"Tell me I'm hurting you and you love it, that you want me to make you come."

She arched her throat, her body undulating, a simultaneous struggle and yet involuntary response at once.

"You'll say the words. Call me what you never called him. Tonight . . . at least . . . I'll know it's true."

She trembled, shaking her head, fighting that even as her pussy convulsed. Despite the pain in her ass at the thrusting of his large cock, she was being provoked by his words toward the goal he was fiercely determined to achieve.

"I'll never stop serving you, my lady. But you'll give me this truth." He put his hand down and found her clit with his thumb, sliding all four other fingers into her.

She screamed, and still his devilish knowledge kept the climax out of her reach. Telling her he held everything at this moment.

"Please . . . please . . . Let me . . ."

"Say it, or you won't. I won't let you until you say it."

He was human. *Human.* Yet he had done what no man or vampire had ever done for her. Not just tonight, but in so many other ways.

"I can't . . ."

"You can." He was ruthless, as ruthless as she'd ever thought of being. He pinched her clit so briefly, but it sent a spasm as strong as an orgasm rocketing through her. "Say it, and goddamn it, you'll look at me when you do."

She opened her eyes, met his furious ones. The hard jaw, his hair falling wild about his shoulders, his broad chest and shoulders dominating her vision. Looming over her against a cloudy sky now devoid of stars, a sky showing only the smoky hint of the yellow moon. Her trembling legs pressed against his shoulder. The guttural sounds coming from her lips and his harsh breath were the only sounds in the night as he increased his thrusts in her ass, taking a full measure of satisfaction there while he held hers out of reach with those immobile fingers.

"Master." It was a bare whisper on her lips, torn from a place deep inside her, a place she'd locked away from Rex and everyone else. She'd never trusted anyone enough to hand them her soul.

He closed his eyes then, an emotion passing over his expression so strong it closed her throat, made her almost unable to speak. But she did, even as she clutched him with her internal muscles in a way that brought his eyes back open. "Master," she repeated. "Let me come for you. Serve you well, as you've served me. Always."

With a look that contained both fierce triumph and utter despair, he worked his thumb against her, began to thrust with his fingers.

It hit her like a tidal wave rising undetected by radar directly offshore until too late, striking her hard in her midsection and spreading out from there. Tremors of earthquakes shimmered through her, intensified when he came inside her at the same time, thrusting up into her so roughly she was sure he tore her delicate opening, but she didn't care. She would heal physically in moments, while the rift in her defenses he'd created would remain that way forever. From here forward, she'd only have him to stand between that opening and the rest of the world. The conqueror and invader would serve as her defender and protector.

As he always had.

13

THEY would travel to Miami to pick up their charter plane to get to the Council Gathering in South America. While they could have flown the entire distance, vampires hated to fly. He didn't know if it was the similarity to a large coffin, or the fact they were separated from the earth, but Jacob made arrangements for Mr. Ingram to drive them to southern Florida.

They left during daylight hours, so the limo with its darkened rear windows had been pulled up to the door and Lyssa had ducked into it, using a cape to go from the house to the car. Bran had stood at the gate, watching them leave. He'd chased them down the drive but reluctantly obeyed Lyssa's compulsion to stay as the gate closed.

As they pulled out, she turned and watched the dog out the back window, laying her hand on the glass as if she were touching his furry face and the faces of the other siblings who came to join him. Jacob reached out and covered her other hand with his, squeezing with reassurance. In truth though, her sudden apprehension worried him.

We've prepared as much as we can, my lady. We're ready. It will be all right.

She gave him that absent smile that told him he didn't know what the hell he was talking about, not having ever been to a Council

Gathering. He couldn't argue with her on that, of course. They'd be spending three days among over two hundred of the most powerful vampires in the world. Overlords and Region Masters most of them, though there were others, like Lord Brian, invited because of their status. The political positioning and volleys would be fierce. Among a host of other vital issues, she had to convince the Council to grant permanent residency status to her fugitives and get through the meeting without raising any suspicions about her health.

With such somber thoughts on her shoulders, it didn't seem possible to offer anything that could draw her mind away from it. So he rummaged in his knapsack and withdrew a small box. "Travel chess or 101 Games You Can Play on the Road?"

You're incorrigible.

But he did win another small smile.

She of course slept during the full daylight hours, waking late afternoon. They kept the screen between driver and passengers open and conversed as any travelers would. With her dry wit, Lyssa even got Mr. Ingram to laugh about the tragic foibles of his son. They listened to him talk proudly about how John had become his class's top speller and was making friends in the school he'd transferred to when he moved in with his grandfather. Ingram blamed Jacob for causing a business tax crisis in his house with Whiskers' propensity for shredding anything paper. Then he and Jacob exchanged ideas on home improvement when he mentioned he was building a workshop at his small house.

At dark Lyssa had them stop at a closed produce stand and take several oranges. She gave Jacob a hundred-dollar bill to leave tucked under the chicken wire with a note of thanks.

When they passed a group of bikers that included a large woman riding behind her boyfriend in only a thong and a leather fringe jacket, Jacob reminded Lyssa she still hadn't allowed him to order her some appropriate biker wear. He won a narrow glance and a death threat that made him grin and Elijah laugh.

Jacob reflected there was something quietly stirring about traveling on the highway with only the lights of other late-traveling motorists strobing across the paleness of her face, outlining the curves of her body and then plunging her into darkness again. She didn't say much, seeming to prefer to listen to them talk. The men both picked up on that, occasionally soliciting a comment from her out of politeness, but knowing she would speak if she desired to do so.

At length she curled up on the seat again, pillowing her head on Jacob's thigh. When she tucked her fingers beneath the column of it, he laid a hand naturally along her side, fingers on her hip.

It had been two and a half weeks since her annual kill. Her strength and vitality seemed to have improved with no further episodes, but in the last week he'd noticed her doing this, not only sleeping during daylight hours but taking a one- or two-hour nap in the middle of her "day." She'd explained she wanted to make sure she was as rested as possible for the grueling hours of the Council, but he knew the real reason. She was anticipating weakening again.

Like a terminal patient who'd waited too long to seek treatment so that the treatment was not as effective, the annual kill and third mark were not likely to carry her as far as they would have if she'd acquired them six months ago instead of a handful of weeks. He should have listened to Thomas, come to her side sooner.

Do not worry about what cannot be changed, Jacob. And the annual kill has helped a great deal. I am just conserving the energy it has given me. Never fear.

The brutal images of that night still haunted him. The way Carl Ronin had struggled against his hold, his eyes white. When he realized he had no chance of escape, the fear of death was in his eyes. With his prescience, Jacob could feel every nuance and change in the man's emotions like a roar in his head. The desire to live was the strongest of man's emotions, a primal instinct that rose to the forefront when it was challenged. It made Jacob wonder about the knight . . . him, when he was the knight. Had the internal screams of men dying around him been louder than the outer din of an army in full-pitched battle? He was glad not to have that memory.

He'd gone to church, lit a candle for Ronin, asked his forgiveness and then put it aside to take care of his lady. There'd been too many details he was handling on her behalf now, too many loose ends he was tying up for her. She needed his focus, and she'd have it. Time was too short for anything else.

As he raised his eyes to the mirror, he met Mr. Ingram's gaze and knew that the driver was as cognizant as he was of the significance of her nap. "You know," Elijah said after a bit, "my mother died of cancer. Some people, you just can't figure it, because they don't deserve that. They just don't deserve it."

That was nothing but the simple truth, though Jacob appreciated what it took for Mr. Ingram to say it. He knew the man still viewed Lyssa as something of a creature of darkness. He could hardly argue with that.

The men maintained a companionable silence for the next hour, letting her nap undisturbed. When she woke, she fished about and found one of the oranges. As she began to peel it, she kept her bare feet tucked under Jacob's thigh, her gaze considering him beneath her lashes as if she was still drowsy. Elijah began a discussion with Jacob on which nailer was best for laying a hardwood floor.

He answered, keeping his eyes on her, sensing the shift in her mood. Her fingers coaxed the skin from the flesh of the orange, her knuckles getting moist from the abundant juice of the homegrown fruit. Her hair was in a twist over one shoulder, the edge brushing the top of her thigh, outlined by the way her skirt lay upon it. Her toes curled, pressing into his thigh muscle. Moving his hand to her ankle, he stroked the delicate bones there.

When she raised a slice, she leaned forward, apparently wanting to feed him. As she caressed his lips, her fingers grew moist with his saliva as well as the juice of the fruit. He couldn't resist a nip that caught a finger. As he drew it deep in his mouth to suckle it, her eyes glowed like a cat's at him through the darkness.

"So, Mr. Ingram, why does it make a difference what kind of nailer you use to put down hardwood floors?" She said it with a smile in her voice, but she had an entirely different expression as she extended the next slice of orange to Jacob.

Take it from my fingers. I want to feel your mouth again. Did you know some vampires don't allow their servants to eat or drink except from their Master or Mistress's hand? Ever. To underscore their bond.

He met her gaze in the shadowed gloom of the backseat. That focused intensity she was so good at projecting washed over him with the same arousing effect of feeling a gush of warm, wet response between her legs spill over his fingers.

Do you think I need a reminder?

No. But I like making you dependent on my will.

He considered that. She'd worked one foot even deeper beneath his thigh, and the movement of her toes teased the flat base of his testicles constricted in his jeans.

It's a long trip, my lady.

It is at that. How long do you think you can stay hard for me?

When do I ever stop?

Though her mouth curved, she continued her peeling. Offered another slice. This time after he took it, he captured her wrist in his hand, held her there. They stared at each other in the darkness. Slowly, he moved his mouth to her palm, feeling her nails curve in, the points pressing against his eyelid and the soft, vulnerable tear duct as he suckled her pulse, let his thumb stroke the same territory, the network of highly sensitive nerve endings he knew were there.

He'd tried not to make the first move, but this maddening proximity to her was more than he could resist. Since that explosive coming together after Carl, she'd been withdrawn. The intensity of that night had been far over the top of what he'd ever been with a woman, and he'd realized it had broken new ground for his lady as well. When they next came together it would be there, this different level between them, and she apparently hadn't been ready to face that.

She'd kept him busy with preparations and the handling of her day-to-day affairs. That level of activity was all that kept the hunger for her at bay. He'd had the overwhelming desire several times to assuage it in the quiet darkness of his own room, usually in a half sleep when his hand moved to himself without conscious thought, dreaming of her body, her touch.

Oddly, it was worse when he was away from home. She'd sent him on a couple of out-of-town trips, for he was now accepted as her agent, her assistant to the highest level, and not just to the perception of her vampires. She trusted his judgment without requiring her consultation on most things, simply allowing his voice to become her own.

Now, with her pulse pounding beneath his hand, he wouldn't deny the savage need anymore unless she refused him. Fortunately, he sensed she was ready to embrace it as well, whatever form it would take between them.

I'm curious, Sir Vagabond. Did you . . . assuage often?

My mind is open to you, my lady. You know all.

He felt her there like her hair or lips, brushing him in light, provocative touches.

You didn't.

No, he hadn't. He'd pulled his hand away from himself, chosen a cold shower when he'd needed it. *You seem surprised.*

You've never demonstrated such . . . a submissive characteristic before. Waiting for your Mistress's permission.

It was that. But it was more than that. *I wanted only you, my lady. After experiencing the wet, hot silk of your pussy, my cock finds my rough hand a woeful substitute.*

"I do not find your hand that way at all." Lifting it, she pressed her face into his touch. Her left eye, most of her nose and half her lips disappeared behind the cover of his palm and fingertips.

He noticed then the screen was up, likely raised by a compulsion she had sent Mr. Ingram or just the man's perceptiveness.

"When our flight lands, it will be daylight and I'll sleep on the plane. But when we rise at sunset, I have to meet with the Council first thing. Without servants present." She cocked her head. "The Council and several other high-ranking vampires meet on the first night to discuss issues of more confidential concern to our kind. It's a courtesy, mostly an overview of the things we'll hear over the next three days and those things we won't, but will manifest themselves." A slight smile touched her lips. "A briefing, if you will."

"I remember, my lady."

He moved his touch to her calf, his fingers teasing under the hem of the skirt, finding her knee. Her gaze held his steadily, but he noted her lips parted at the provocative touch.

"When you go to our rooms to get us settled," she said, her voice throaty, "you will . . . assuage your need. I want to see you in my mind with your hand on your cock, stroking yourself to release."

Enough was enough. He was only human, after all. Ignoring her breathless laughter in his mind, he reached out and dragged her across the seat to him, clamping down on her mouth with his own. He knew that was what she wanted, though he didn't know if it was his psychic intuition, their mind link or just the bond between the two of them.

Soul mates. Those disturbing words again, planted by Thomas. He didn't know if it was true, but he couldn't deny it seemed like he knew her mind better than his own. Raising his head, he met her gaze. "My lady . . ."

"Sssh. Give me what I need, Jacob. It is just us here. Soon I shall have to be very different, very cold. I'll have to remind you that you belong to me in ways that are not comfortable to you. It is our way. But for now, take my woman's heart. Hold it for me so I'll be able to find it again after this is all over."

Dropping his hand to her waist, he curled his fingers under her shirt, felt the soft skin stretched over the smooth valleys between her ribs. Moving up to the satin of her bra cups, he brushed them with his thumbs. When he took the shirt over her head, he watched the way her clipped-back hair formed a twisting spiral as it funneled through the neckline and then fell back to her shoulder, down her now mostly bare back. Spanning her skin with his large hands, the tan skin against the pale unblemished, he put his lips on the top of one curve, his jaw brushing her.

Her breath held, her teeth biting down on her lips as a distracted smile of pleasure curved them. Her fingers rested on his shoulders. For once they didn't dig in, just held as if she were seeking an emotional anchor. Her skin was so sensitized that if he teased one small part of her with tiny touches of tongue and lip, he knew her body would begin to quiver, like ripples in a lake that expanded and became a wake on a shore from that one minute disturbance.

She knew how to draw an extraordinary level of sensual enjoyment from the simplest acts, and he'd been a good student. He could bring her to climax with this one contact because of how deeply she could focus on it.

But that wasn't what she needed now. He put his hand between them, freed himself from his jeans and found her beneath her skirt, bringing it up to her hips so he could slide his finger under the band of the silk panties she wore, move the crotch aside and test her wetness. She was slick and warm already. When he guided her onto him, she sank down on his length with a noise between an animal sound of acceptance and a murmur of contentment, completion. She tightened on him, inch by torturous inch. When he had her fully seated, he put his arms around her, pressing her against him, her head down to his shoulder. Her arms shifted to wrap around his shoulders, almost like a child being carried home in an adult's arms. Following instinct, he began to rock, slow, sliding strokes up inside her. Wrapping a complex dichotomy of desire and comfort tightly around their bodies, a lullaby of searing sensation. Her hips moved on his, circular desire, tightening, releasing, lifting, lowering. He nuzzled her neck as she moved her grip to his hair, his trimmed beard making friction across the top of her left breast, eliciting a soft, shuddering sigh.

He'd never wanted anything to go on forever so much, this magical journey through the night in the quiet solitude of a moving car, baptized by the lights of the passing vehicles. The soft sound of Ingram's preferred slow groove station came through the back speakers. Jacob's release built with hers on every stroke as they moved in perfect harmony on a star-kissed sea of their own world.

It was a sweet ride, holding her body close, feeling her move with him, her cheek pressed against his hair, her grip there alternately tightening and stroking. He was sure Mr. Ingram knew what was happening back here. Somehow, despite the fact he'd never formally taken Lyssa's offer of a job, Elijah had become part of the journey they were on, a journey Jacob was all too aware had an end. Mr. Ingram knew it, too, and maybe that was why he was with them still. Sometimes, despite all the reasons a man's mind told him he needed to avoid a situation with a woman, his heart overruled him. No matter the pain or danger, this was the course that called to him.

"Jacob." A soft murmur of sound, her voice breathless. He took her up high, down slow, stroking her with his full length, despite the fact he knew he was going to explode in no time from such exquisite slick torture. She liked to squeeze, liked to feel the ridge of him push through her muscles.

"Ah . . ." He kept it slow as her hands began to jerk in their hold on him, her body tightening, ready. He held her to his pace and she let him, didn't try to take the lead, smiling even through her strain, acknowledging the wonder of it. He wasn't even sure if he was in the lead or if they were in fact on a tide that was inexorably, rhythmically, pulling them both toward their destination.

A cry broke from her lips, but he kept pushing her down on him, again and again, until her whole body was quivering, rocketing with the intensity of the climax he was inflicting on them both at such a pace. When he began to come, he banded his arms even more tightly around her, burying his face in her neck, pressing his lips there as he surged strong and hard into her pussy, piercing her deep, giving her a taste of pain with the vibrating pleasure of her aftershocks. Her teeth scored his ear, responding. He smiled, closing his eyes as shudders racked through him.

He let himself be content to hold her then, knowing his lady never told him false. At the next moonrise, they'd be at the Gathering, where everything would be different. She'd given him this to remember. And just as she'd asked, he had her heart in his safekeeping, beating in his own chest. He was sure of it.

~

Jacob stretched his legs after they deplaned from the private jet on a narrow landing strip. They were somewhere in Chile or Argentina, but he knew little else about the location of the Vampire Gathering. The stronghold where they'd hold the annual Vampire Gathering was secluded, another hour's travel by off-road vehicle. Lyssa had said the private resort getaway was located on the coast and backed by the lush, temperate rain forest of this region.

She'd explained that the resort belonged to Lord Mason, a vampire Jacob knew was one of the older ones at over six hundred. He was rarely seen, choosing to live in seclusion in the Saudi desert. However, he loaned the property to the Vampire Council for their purposes, apparently having no desire of his own to visit it, but equally having no desire to relinquish it.

Mason and Lyssa had a history. Jacob had seen at least one correspondence from the vampire to her. Though he hadn't been privy to the contents, he knew it had somehow contributed to the events that led her to give him the third mark. Thomas had also told him something of Mason. Years ago, Lyssa had wanted Mason to be more involved in the Council formation, but Mason apparently was not a joiner. He wanted nothing more than seclusion and turned away from the notion of "civilized" vampires. Lyssa had been disappointed, perhaps even feeling a bit betrayed by the friend she'd hoped she could count on. Since that had been so long ago, she'd obviously gotten past it enough to exchange correspondence with him again, but that was all.

Jacob had tried not to be selfishly glad of that. Thomas had implied there'd once been something more between the two of them. If not for Mason's aversion to vampire society, it might have been Mason instead of Rex that Lyssa would have chosen for marriage.

You don't court me, Jacob. You serve me.

He pushed that memory away, knowing he needed to be steady and balanced as they stepped out onto the tarmac to meet a full complement of Council members. For the next three days he would be surrounded by creatures that saw him as food, a sex slave, an inferior being, a tool. For his lady's benefit, he would have to perform accordingly. Knowing his lady, that performance could take many forms. And most of them would make him nervous as hell if he dwelled on the possibilities at all.

Humans were expected to satiate vampire desires as sexual submissives on many different levels. At the Gathering, that aspect of a servant's role was turned to high volume. Until now, except for the dinner with Lord Tara, Lady Richard and Lord Brian, most—though not all—of his submission to his lady had been private. He suspected that would not be the case here.

While he didn't agree entirely with Debra's assessment of it, he knew on one important level she was right. His lady loved him and had told him she did, something unique to a vampire-human relationship. She also viewed him as her servant, expecting his obedience. While she trembled under his touch, she wouldn't hesitate to physically hurt him if he defied her to the point of blatant disrespect. And he understood that. Accepted it in a way that wouldn't make sense to Gideon or anyone else. Perhaps it only made sense to someone who had the mind-set to be a human servant.

Now he stood at her back, a deferential few feet behind while she exchanged greetings. A meeting of hands, a brush of the lips across the cheek. A contingent of humans stood back, waiting as well. From their appearance, he knew these were not the human servants attached to these Council vampires.

The overlords invited to the Gathering were not of equal rank. Therefore those of the lower ranks might have their servants pressed into all sorts of duties during the Gathering—cleaning, waitstaff, bellhop services. While he and Lyssa had discussed that, she had neglected to tell him how these servants would be garbed.

The group of men and women waiting for direction had extremely attractive bodies, noticeable because they wore little on them. Their individuality was denied them because they wore full head masks with nose and eye openings, but no mouth opening. From the stretched concave curve in that area, it appeared they wore ball gags beneath so speech was not possible. They could only receive and follow orders. Each wore a modified form of chastity belt where the genitals were visible but caged by a closely fitted wire mold. Other than those two items, they wore nothing else.

It made him terribly grateful he was attached to a high-ranking vampire. Never mind that their identities were safeguarded by the masks. He was sure it was not for their benefit, but a practical consideration for their Master or Mistress, so no one could identify their servant and try to manipulate them for political benefit.

He would not be commandeered for any services of which his lady did not approve. She'd also made it clear he was to follow only her direction and to never, ever let his guard down once they were off the plane.

As two of the humans were ordered to move and claim the

baggage of another vampire who had just arrived, he noticed something else. The men's cocks were hard and erect in the caged wires that pressed the engorged shafts against their bellies. The women's eyes were wide and flared, their bodies obviously being kept in a stimulated state, the wires over their pussies wet with their arousal. As they turned, bent, he saw the chastity belts were fitted with dildos inserted into all available openings, depending on gender. It was the type of discomfort that vampires enjoyed inflicting, allowing them to inhale the scent of human arousal to stoke their own desires.

He pulled his attention away from that back to his lady. Accustomed enough to the internal stratus of vampire society not to expect an introduction, he nevertheless was conscious of a penetrating assessment by each vampire who stepped forward and greeted his lady. They'd gone over each member of the Council thoroughly, so he had no problem recognizing each one. He'd also gotten impressions of them through his many communications with their servants over the past month on his lady's behalf. He noted names, body language, the shift of eyes, the level of deference exhibited and his lady's reaction to each.

The last one who stepped forward was Belizar, the head of the Council and obviously of Russian Cossack stock. With steel gray eyes and swept-back hair streaked with silver, he had an aura that said he had no problem removing the body parts of anyone who crossed him. He had a throbbing power hard to ignore. His gaze swept over Jacob, then again to Lyssa as he stepped back but retained her hand.

"Lady Lyssa, you do us great honor by being here. I'm pleased to see you've at last overcome your grief to take another servant. May it please you one day to feel the same about another mate."

From the grip he had on her hand, there was no doubt who Belizar felt that should be. And of course an allegiance between the head of the Vampire Council and the last Far Eastern vampire of royal blood would make logical sense to everyone present. No one would think it an inappropriate implication.

No one except Jacob, who knew the wound in her heart from Thomas's loss and Rex's betrayal was still deep. Not to mention the fact it had resulted in a death sentence hanging over her. From the ripple of feeling he picked up from her, he wondered if this was what she'd dreaded the most. Not the life-and-death politics and the worry that the disease would make itself known here, but the reminder of what she'd lost to reach this point. She'd had a lot to deal with since it had all happened, but when all was said and done, she was still a grieving widow, on several levels. He had to quell the urge to take a step closer behind her, to let her feel the reassurance of him at her back.

Lyssa drew her hand away with an easy, light smile that betrayed none of that ripple of reaction. "I've no plans in that direction right now, Belizar, but your kind wishes are much appreciated. It's lovely to be back at Mason's home again. Will we be honored by his presence?"

"With Mason, nothing is ever certain." This dry comment from one of the female Council members. Lady Carola from Germany. "Often we don't know if he's alive or dead."

"Break into his private wine stock and we'll know. I think he's injected a drop of his blood into each bottle so he'll know if it's disturbed." This from Lord Uthe, a tall, ascetic-looking denizen of the night with dark eyes that looked toward Lyssa with a friendly, reserved affection that did not raise Jacob's hackles the way that Belizar had. Uthe was the unofficial second in command of the Council, bringing a razor-sharp shrewdness to augment Belizar's charismatic, volatile style.

Belizar glanced toward Jacob. "Take your lady's things to her room. These servants will take you there."

Jacob executed a slight bow. "The offer of assistance is appreciated, but I take orders only from my Mistress, my lord."

Based on his experience with Carnal, he supposed he could have been more diplomatic about it, using his mind link with Lyssa to verify this was what she wanted him to do, but Jacob wanted no misunderstandings about whom he served.

Belizar's eyes flashed. In them Jacob saw he had the arrogance and sense of superiority possessed by vampires Jacob and Gideon had fought in the past. Only in his case, his superiority was likely justified, bolstered by experience. The experience of ripping off the arms of humans who'd annoyed him.

But Jacob had been sure to have nothing in his voice to suggest the comment was anything but obliging the directives of his Mistress. Belizar was picking up the subtle male undercurrent, but Jacob's tone was courteous enough to make him uncertain if he was being challenged by a mere human. That arrogance was working in Jacob's favor.

And you said I didn't know how to play politics, my lady.

While she didn't respond, he thought he felt a flicker of amusement from her. It certainly wasn't coming from Belizar. The head of the Council shifted his gaze back to Lyssa, a dismissive gesture.

"You are far more fortunate in the loyalty of this servant than that murderous traitor."

"In more ways than one," Carola murmured, giving Jacob a thorough appraisal that reminded him uncomfortably of old charcoal drawings of Jamaican slave auctions. If she reached out to check his teeth, she was going to pull back a stump. "There's entertainment and sport in the resort area until dawn, Lady Lyssa. Once he's settled your things, perhaps your servant could join in for the viewing pleasure of us all."

"After our meeting," Belizar reminded her. "We have quite a full agenda. I hate to rush you when you've only just arrived, Lady Lyssa, but I want you fully briefed on what we will be addressing over the next several days."

"Let us proceed to it now, then." Lyssa turned to Jacob. "Take my things to my room; get us settled in. I'll meet you in the resort area when we are done."

"If you wish your servant to participate in the games, Lady Lyssa, he will need to be suitably attired," Belizar said. "My servant, Malachi, is already there. As you'll recall, there's none that can match his skill. It's been a while since he's had a worthy new opponent. Would your servant be worth his time?"

Standing behind his lady, Jacob couldn't see her face, but he saw her shoulder lift in an indifferent shrug. "I think it far more likely that Malachi will not be worth Jacob's."

The Council members shifted, feral smiles showing their appreciation. Belizar's eyes sparked at the challenge.

Lyssa turned to Jacob again. "It should take you less than an hour to settle us in our rooms. After that, I expect you to strip off everything and go to the resort area, passing your time there until I join you."

~

Jacob put his hand on the door latch, took a deep breath. His mind told him to turn the bronze handle, but he decided to give himself the liberty of ten more seconds before he strode out into the palatial hallways of Mason's castle in nothing but his skin. Maybe another ten minutes. Would ten hours be pushing it?

An hour earlier, as he'd traveled to this room with his escort of masked servants, they'd passed a variety of vampires and higher-ranked human servants. Most of the humans were clothed. Though some were in fairly sensual and accessible garments, it was still clothing. The vampires of course were fully dressed.

He realized quickly the chastity belts were a protective rule of sorts for the domestic servants. They were apparently required to submit to the liberties any random vampire wished to take with them. He passed one outdoor lounge area by a pool where a masked servant was on her knees being made to stroke a standing male vampire to climax. At the same time the vampire suckled on the breasts of another servant who was straddling the shoulders of the one servicing his cock.

Jacob remembered Debra's admonition that some servants believed they were the same rank as their Master or Mistress, rather than just property to use as they wished. If a Master or Mistress, regardless of rank, wished to subject their own servant to a masked servant's status, they could. He supposed what he was seeing was a damn good reason for servants attached to higher-ranked vampires to toe the line, to avoid such a fate.

Even so, many vampires, male and female, gave him openly speculative looks as they passed, examining him as a piece of attractive flesh they might get the opportunity to sample. He forced himself not to flinch from the whispering touch of fingers along his hip, the curve of his buttock. Despite the body language protests of his trio of female porters, he'd insisted on taking two of the heaviest suitcases. Their bulk allowed him to innocently fend off some of the more adventurous vampire hands he encountered.

He realized again just how vital Lyssa's protection and name were to him as he saw a vampire casually catch hold of a porter's harness straps and jerk her around to tease her generous breasts to hard points for the amusement of another female vamp. The servant stood docilely, though he was sure she was a total stranger to both vampires.

Being around vampires in the human world could be perilous, certainly. But here where the turf was all theirs, their dominance as Masters was undeniable, the charged, barely leashed energy of their sexual cravings feeding the undercurrent of violence that was inseparable from a vampire's nature. It gave Jacob a heavily compressed sense of uneasiness in the vitals, despite the irony of the event's main purpose being to honor the Council, a symbolic bow to their success in creating a "civilized" vampire society.

At the same time, he couldn't help comparing the structure of the Vampire Council with that of business conferences held for human professions. Away from home and the typical settings of their day-to-day life, people tended to have lower inhibitions. Like those conventions, this one would conduct business, but play would occur as well. With human servants half-clad or pretty much unclad everywhere one looked, the play was bound to get pretty intense.

The palace itself stoked such imaginings. It was something out of *Arabian Nights*. Huge urns overflowing with flowers in passionate colors, fountains with erotic and often disturbing statuary. In an open courtyard, they'd passed one over eight feet tall. Demons raping a nymph, penetrating her with organs that appeared to be of a life-threatening size. Her hand pressed against the nearest one's fanged and deformed face, trying to stave off the inevitable. It was horrible, but having been around vampires long enough, he knew the idea of her resistance was what made it erotic to them. The water artfully trickled over her thighs, as if despite her repugnance and resistance, her body was lubricating itself for them. For surrender.

Given all that, could he be blamed for the fact that, once in the room, he'd dawdled? He had to set out his lady's toiletries, arranging them in accordance with her needs over the next several days. Freshen her clothes with the ridiculously mundane items of steamer and iron, sprinkling the lavender she liked into the fabric. Set out her makeup and brushes where he'd have them readily to hand.

He'd removed his clothes, but done a quick run through the shower, touched up his shave and beard and brushed his hair. Even though he'd rather smear himself with pig manure to keep all those strange hands as far from him as possible, he knew he had to be presentable to honor his Mistress. Now he stood at the door, his hand on the latch, and he wasn't sure if he could do it.

Jacob, you have not obeyed my will.

Her voice was a soft breath in his mind, the barest of whispers.

I'm just fortifying my courage, my lady. I find it a little more difficult to do this when you're absent. Humiliating to admit, but there it was. *Too many vampires appreciative of a tight ass around here.*

He sensed her smile, but an intensity of purpose, too. *I've never known your courage to falter. You shall conduct yourself well. However, I'm referring to what we discussed in the car. What I commanded you to do when you got to my room.*

Jacob withdrew his hand from the door. "Now, my lady?"

I am sitting in one of the most boring and self-pretentious gatherings you can imagine. Carnal, for all he is a monster, is at least interesting. It appears it will go on for at least another two hours. What do you think? Her voice turned to a purr and he suddenly, vividly, imagined her hands on his cock, her moist lips opening to take him in.

Stroke yourself for me, Jacob. Go back into the shower and turn on the water. I want to see it run over your muscles as they tense, as your very tight ass clenches and you pump yourself with your hand. I want to see the images in your mind, your fantasizing about me . . . A pause. *And I would suggest, at least for this, you do indeed fantasize about me.*

He grinned despite himself at her dry tone, and some of the tension lessened. "I would not dream of doing otherwise, my lady."

I like it when you speak aloud like that. You come through even more strongly. I can feel your voice vibrating through my body. Go to the shower, Jacob. I need to feel your desire.

He complied, moving through the large suite of rooms, past the canopy bed draped with velvet. With his cock already hardening, it was easy to imagine lying upon the mattress with her, rolling her under him, spreading her white legs, sinking into her as he wrapped his hands in her miles of hair.

Yes . . . When the shuddering sigh ran through her mind, it rippled across his skin. *I'd like that.*

The bathroom also had its share of sensual offerings. A large Jacuzzi tub big enough for three or four people, a double-headed shower and jets that came out of the walls. He adjusted the temperature and stepped in.

Get your hair wet.

In a chamber nearly a quarter mile away on the extensive palace's grounds, Lyssa sat at a twenty-foot-long ornately carved table that had once graced the hall of a Celtic king. The full Council and two other high-ranking guests, including her, listened as Belizar ran down the agenda of business that would be covered in more detail over the three-day Gathering. Since she was already well aware of most of the items, listening with only partial attention was not detrimental. However, as Jacob filled the screen of her mind, she hoped Belizar wouldn't stop to ask her any questions.

As the water poured over Jacob's skull, his hands rose, the automatic gesture to slick his hair back. She could see him in full, delicious detail, blocking out everything else. The long muscular body, the running water sculpting each muscle of his curved biceps and chest. The sectioned stomach muscles, the flex of his buttocks as he shifted. His cock was erect now from her soft persuasion and the vision of what she wanted him to do. She lingered over every detail of his body, down to the arches of his feet. The toes she'd curled her own around to warm her feet when she let him stay with her at night. Too few times.

For the past hundred years, perhaps two hundred, she'd never let her mind be distracted from a meeting such as this. There'd been too much at stake. Too many vampires testing the oligarchy of the Council. Too many battles, both political and physical, for her and Rex to fight. When those were past, there had been Rex himself to fight.

She'd heard the songs about living in the moment, living as if there were only one day to live. A lovely sentiment, but if everyone acted as if they were dying, chaos would result. Life was meant to be lived in all its frenetic activity.

But somehow a gift was given to the subconscious of someone whose days were truly numbered. For the first time in centuries, she had the overwhelming sense of having a free pass to slow down as the world kept speeding up around her. To open the senses, the mind and soul to all the things she hadn't had time to enjoy as fully as she wished. She hadn't indulged such thinking since the days when she was young and believed she would live forever.

Jacob, I want you to sleep with me. From here forward, whenever possible, when you complete your duties, you will come lie with me in the day and sleep.

His hands stilled, his head bowed, cocked slightly as if listening to her with his ears. "Whatever you wish, my lady. It would be my honor. You're all right?"

Yes. Warmth gripped her at his automatic reaction. To protect. To care. *Put your hand on yourself. Bring yourself to climax for me. But do it the way you would if you were alone, doing it without my command.*

Bracing a hand on the opposite wall of the shower caused the muscles along his back to ripple delightfully, drawing her gaze to the slope of his hip and the straight line of thigh. The ends of his hair were wet silk along the line of his shoulders. It had gotten a little longer this past month and often he'd kept it tied back, too busy to get it trimmed. She could have done it for him, she realized. Would have if she hadn't liked the look of it, blowing around his face when he worked the grounds, or when she threaded her hands through it as dawn approached, a way to soothe herself to sleep.

How easy it had been to get used to him in her life. To want him present in every moment. When she'd sent him away on the two-day trip to verify the condition of several safe houses, she'd wandered the grounds with Bran like a ghost, restless spirits needing his grounding presence.

She could admit it, as long as she was only admitting it to herself.

He took hold of himself, curling his hand around the thick length, and began to stroke. He'd put soap in his palm to give it lubrication, and also to goad the vision which filled her mind now. Driving into her slick heat, her pussy taking him deep and snug, a hot, wet fist, her hands reaching for his ass to pull him closer, her nails digging in.

She loved the way men thought about sex, rough and unromantic in their minds. Something so vulgar when shouted from a construction site could be so sexy when it was a husky, guttural demand heard in the female mind.

Another example of the dichotomous nature of women.

Thomas taught you that word. She hid a smile.

Not just the word, my lady. The whole sentence. It came up often during my training. I can't imagine why.

But the uninterrupted flow of his imaginings distracted her from his teasing. In his vision, her nails dug in hard enough to draw blood. He liked that, liked to feel her savagery. He had no fear of her strength. He trusted her.

Now he'd turned her, was holding her on her side and making rhythmic movements of his hips against her buttocks as he held her in the curve of his body. His palm lay flat on her abdomen, the tips of his fingers grazing her clit, making her strain for him even as he rocked her back into him so he would feel the give of her soft buttocks against his thighs as he thrust in and out of her cunt. His other hand gripped her breast, squeezed, felt the texture of her nipple stab into his palm as he pressed his mouth to the side of her throat, tasting her.

Vaguely she noted Belizar had moved down two agenda items. She had no idea what had been discussed. She hoped she was correct about her familiarity with them. Her thighs were quivering under the table, her panties soaked. While those in the room could detect arousal, there was so much of it running rampant throughout the castle they simply would think someone had indulged with their servant before coming to the meeting.

She wanted to be in the shower with him, letting him lift her up against the wet tile with his strength as if she weighed nothing. Sometimes she'd chosen an alpha male for her dinner for just that reason, that brief moment when his animal passion would take him over so that he'd lift her, slam her up against the wall of whatever dark place they might be. But now all she wanted was to imagine Jacob doing it, her legs wrapping around him so he could drive in, the tight, almost painful fit that felt so perfect, the exact blend of pleasure and pain to meet her desire for both. All of him inside her.

She realized when the same thought reflected back into her that she'd again let him see into her mind, had opened herself so he knew how aroused she was.

Are you where you can touch yourself, my lady?

No.

A pity. His thought was as ragged as she imagined his voice would be, and then she realized she could hear him so vibrantly because he *was* speaking, just as she'd requested. His hoarse voice echoed in the shower against the rush of the water. "I would have enjoyed feeling you come in my mind. Knowing you responded to me even as far away as you are. That with . . . one . . . soft . . . whisper . . . I could compel you to . . . come. Only by thinking . . . of fucking you."

Come for me, Jacob. She said it desperately, before he could do it to her. He was close, and she was flushed at the shuddering feel of him, goading the pre-orgasmic state of her body. He'd waited for her command to climax. Did he do it because he knew it spurred her own response exponentially, to the point she almost didn't care if she brought herself to climax in this company? Or because it was *his* "dichotomous" nature to serve her like this, the perfect submissive, even as he drove her to distraction with his stubborn willfulness and aroused her past the point of good sense with his physical and emotional alpha tendencies?

His hand curled into a fist high on the wall as he began to come, his lower body bucking hard, the way a man moved when not worried about exercising too much force on his more delicate partner. He'd never held back much with her, knowing her strength, but she knew he did hold back some, always testing her lead to make sure it was not too much, waiting until she spurred him with fangs or nails.

His head bowed down, a grunt of exertion coming from him as he pistoned into his hand. The milky fluid shot against the shower wall in front of him, ran down the tile. It felt as if it had jetted into her, her cunt convulsing sharply, once, twice, ready at the squeeze of her thighs to take it to completion. She wouldn't, couldn't . . .

No, my lady. An urgent clip to his thoughts, even as he physically gasped for air. *You can't. You are a screamer, you know.*

The sharp edge of regret was in the humorous thought that steadied her enough to pull her back from the dangerous ledge. When she surfaced from her erotic fog, he was leaning against the shower wall, breathing hard, his hand still holding himself. In her mind she rubbed her face against his knuckles there, smelled him. Shared that visual with him.

Go out among the others now, Jacob. Think of me and know no shame. Your body is my possession and I want to show it off, let others feel envy at what I possess.

Coveting is a sin, my lady.

So was gluttony. But apparently she never got enough when it came to her young servant.

It's the older woman, younger man thing. Midlife crisis. They've made movies about it . . .

I'm going to find a cock harness and leash and make you wear them for the next three days, tugging you behind me like a poodle.

She'd turned his mind back to the challenge of exposing himself to others but, as she'd hoped, he was feeling less anxious about it. When the muscles in her stomach loosened at the sound of his laughter, she realized he'd managed to relax her, too. Perhaps he'd known she needed it as much as he had. Like the quick action to pull her back from embarrassing herself, it reminded her that no matter what, he never forgot his duty to her.

Never forgot his duty . . . his honor . . . loyalty.

The thought disturbed her. An unexpected anxiety clutched

her low in her stomach, dissipating the lingering desire. When cold fingers walked across her spine, it tripped a physical wave of panic for Jacob's well-being. As she forced down the overwhelming urge to get up, leave the table, go and find him, protect him, a vision filled her mind. Taking over her senses, it blinded her to anything else as if she'd been picked up and dropped into another world.

Blood and sacrifice. Jacob on a . . . table . . . a cry of agony. An explosion . . .

The premonition was gone so abruptly she started, earning a quick glance from Belizar. When she steeled her expression to impassivity, he continued without pause. Inside, her thoughts scrambled like an animal in a trap.

She'd dreamed of her stepfather's death a week before it happened.

She'd dreamed she would lose her samurai guard . . . two days before it occurred.

She'd had one evening with her knight. Three days later, the news came to her that her nightmare of his death had been reality.

While she hadn't dreamed of Rex's death, perhaps that was because she'd killed him herself.

She told herself Jacob was fine. Near her. Within range of her thoughts. Reaching out, she found him without alerting him to her presence. He was in a courtyard, moving toward the side of the castle where the entertainments were taking place. Finely, beautifully naked, moving with lithe grace, his head up, every inch the servant of a vampire queen. He projected it so well that most of the vampires, while stopping for a second or third lingering look, didn't break the boundary of dignified reserve around him.

God, he is a treasure. My treasure. Please let no harm come to him.

He was fine. He was going to be fine. For Heaven's sake, when she died, he would die, so why should she be panicking over a vision of his death?

The night he'd killed Carl Ronin, he'd slowed the car down by a church. He'd studied the smooth sculpture of the Son of God, mounted on a pedestal to the right of the front double doors. The Virgin Mary had been on the left, her face wreathed in sorrow.

"It doesn't have anything to do with holy water or being burned by crosses, does it?" he said quietly. "Why vampires don't go into churches."

"No, it doesn't."

She'd wanted to take his hand, suffering for him, but knew there was nothing she could say for this, no comfort she could offer. She wondered if there was any comfort for the fear she now nursed in her breast, that something might be conspiring to take Jacob away from her. It had to be the disease, playing games with her mind. For the first time, the idea of a recurrence was reassuring. Nevertheless, she kept a part of her mind open to his movements and whereabouts even as she tuned back in to the meeting.

"Lady Lyssa, you indicated you had an important item for the Council's deliberation. You have the floor."

"My lords, my ladies." Her voice was imperious and strong as she rose. From their attentive and respectful expressions she was satisfied she hadn't cast any suspicions that she'd been dallying in areas far from this Council room. It *was* the disease, damn it. She shut the door firmly between her mind and Jacob's.

"I want to address the issue of permanent asylum for the fugitives in my territory."

14

Here he was, in a resort full of vampires, with no weapons. Not even clothes. Gideon would be laughing his ass off.

But as he remembered her words, her touch on his body and his mind, Jacob's back straightened, his head lifting. He was Lady Lyssa's human servant. The man granted the right to touch her, feed her. Given access to her heart, sometimes even her soul. And she wanted him seen.

This was her world, and to be everything she needed, he had to be a part of it fully.

It had been easy enough to find the resort area. It was on the southeast side of the palace where a huge lawn was sculpted with elaborate hedge gardens and open spaces for a variety of games. The panoramic ocean was the backdrop to a spectacular view of the surreal and fantastic. It was an Escher painting come to life in vivid color. A verandah of alabaster white railings and columns overlooked it all, following the line of this side of the castle. There were two exit points, marble staircases that made matching crescent shapes to the bottom, inviting guests into the gardens and play areas.

It appeared that over a hundred vampires of various ranks were there, sipping drinks and lounging at chairs and tables on the verandah, socializing and watching the entertainments going on below.

Before he could follow their gazes, the smell of burning flesh and a strangled cry drew his attention toward a pavilion at the base of the closest set of stairs. While a servant knelt at his Master's feet, another man, apparently a blacksmith, applied a brand to the servant's buttocks. When he removed the iron, the vampire considered the mark, amused as it began to fade. Except for the bitten back cry, the servant was motionless, awaiting his master's bidding.

Because of Lyssa, Jacob had gotten in the habit of assuming all vampire-servant pairings were opposite gender, but he realized quite obviously it would vary depending on the sexual preference of the vampire.

"A fun diversion," the vampire said. "Perhaps we will come back later and do other body parts if you do not please me."

There was no fear in the servant's expression as he rose and followed his Master, telling Jacob the man enjoyed suffering such pain at his Master's demand. Or that he'd learned to mask fear well.

No. His intuition had been deepened by his third mark connection with Lyssa, and he'd been able to sense the absence of fear in the submissive male. Plus, as he'd seen vividly with Melinda, a servant didn't last long in the service of his Mistress or Master if there was not some bond of trust between vampire and servant.

He found himself lingering over the memory of how the vampire had looked at the mark, bent to pass his fingers over it. The emotional tremor of the servant's body at the touch, the unguarded response in the vampire's eyes when he wasn't affecting the amused boredom.

When a hand brushed the bare skin over his ribs, Jacob managed to turn toward the touch with an expression of mild indifference, rather than jumping back like a cat in a room full of way too many fanged rocking chairs.

Seanna gave him a thorough look. Her Master, Lord Richard of the Alabama territory, was apparently pleased to have her garbed in a creation of black straps that left her breasts bare. The straps crisscrossed, lifting and binding the generous mounds. Her nipples were captured in silver clamps connected by a decorative chain. While the skirt of studded straps she wore fell below her knees, the straps parted when she moved, showing her shaved mound and generous ass. Since she wore the fetish wear as if she bore the trappings of an Amazon queen, Jacob couldn't deny the outfit looked damn good on her. Enough to cause an embarrassing stirring of his cock.

"Irishman."

"Seanna."

A smile curved her lush mouth. "So formal. Last time it was much more affectionate. 'Arrogant bitch,' wasn't it?"

The teasing light in her eyes dissipated the anxiety he expected at having to deal with her. Seanna was emanating the respect of a peer, underscoring that he'd won his spurs as Lyssa's servant. Since she had connections with the servants of many other high-ranking vampires, he knew that was a good thing, even as he maintained a healthy wariness.

"You made it difficult for me to walk that next morning," she accused him with mock gravity.

"I'm sorry if I hurt you," he said, seeking something safe to say. Her brows rose.

"It was all a pleasure, Irishman. A pleasure I'd be happy to repeat with you if you're otherwise unengaged while waiting for your Mistress. We could go to the statuary gardens, become some of the live entertainment."

She nodded in the direction of the hedge gardens, where the attention of most of the vampires on the verandah appeared to be resting. However, since an inordinate number of them now seemed to be studying him, he let Seanna take his hand and coax him down the stairs. As they got to the base and passed the blacksmith's pavilion, he realized what he'd thought were more statues in the hedge gardens were living humans.

When Seanna strolled toward them, he saw they had been placed in poses in the midst of circles of flowers and elegantly landscaped shrubs and ordered to remain motionless. One woman bent over, holding her ankles, her hair brushing the ground. Nine blond locks had been tied in knots and staked out in a fan shape on the ground with decorative wrought-iron wickets. A man stood behind her buried to the ball sac, his hands gripping her hips, his head back as if in the throes of climax. Both were slightly quivering, showing the tension of holding such a provocative pose.

"She'll come before long," Seanna confided. "See? Her Master has put a clitoral stimulator on her so she can't stop milking that slave with her pussy muscles. When she comes, her Master will punish her for everyone's enjoyment."

"And if he comes first?"

"Then the male servant will have the honor of the punishment." Seanna linked her arm in his, her hand whispering along his biceps as she guided him past the two. The same heightened senses which allowed him to detect emotions also brought him the smell of the girl's arousal. As they passed the copulating pair, Jacob could see the stretched pink lips of her pussy, the deep red flush of her nipples. Because he had no control of his cock, which had a mind of its own about such stimuli, he tried to ignore Seanna's appreciative gaze at it through her lashes.

It was only going to get worse, for the garden was full of such sights. Not all vampires were on the verandah. Many wandered through the gardens just as they did, glasses of wine or other chosen drinks in hand as they gazed at the posings and commented on them. Seanna used the pressure of her hand to guide Jacob off the path as a group of six vampires came toward them.

"Eyes down," she whispered.

Though it made him want to grind his teeth, he did it, because he knew the etiquette at this conference was even more stringent than when entertaining Lyssa's guests in her home. There was no purpose to insulting vampires Lyssa might need to secure the fate of her territory.

"That servant of Lord Richard has a pair of superior tits," one of the male vampires observed as they strolled past. "I'll have to see if he would be willing to let me borrow her and grease them up. It's been a while since I've had a nice titty fuck."

"Lawrence, you're such a crude thing," the woman chuckled. "Your alley street upbringing is showing."

"Shouldn't be a problem getting Lord Richard's permission," the other man with them put in. "He likes to watch almost more than he likes to fuck."

"Not me," the woman purred. "Why, Rodney, that's Lady Lyssa's new pet. Now he *does* look irresistibly fuckable, just as Lady Carola said. Look at the size of that cock."

Seanna's nails dug into his arm as the woman stepped to the edge of the sidewalk and gripped his privates as casually as she might have handled some of the landscaping to determine its origin.

"I could take him to the grass right here, ride him until he begged for mercy."

If she didn't take her hand off him, she was going to be the one begging for mercy. She had disturbingly clever fingers, however. Rubbing up and down his shaft, massaging the skin over the hard core.

"Ah, he likes that."

"Remember, Marta, he's not wearing a head mask. He can be briefly touched, but not taken. You'd need her permission for that."

Her hand withdrew reluctantly. "Idiot Council rules," she muttered under her breath. "What does it matter if I fuck him now and she fucks him later? His dick will still be the same."

"He's her property, dear Marta." This from the taller man, drawing her away. "That has nothing to do with the Council. I wouldn't suggest irritating Lady Lyssa for no cause."

Seanna loosened her fingers on Jacob's arm as they moved off, and gently reached down to pry open one clenched fist. "Easy, Jacob. That was pretty tame for this group."

Jacob nodded, a muscle flexing in his jaw. He could do this. He had to do this. Even so, instinctively he moved to Seanna's outside as they passed another group. She chuckled.

"Chickenshit. Just enjoy the feel of it," she said under her breath, smiling and giving a slight bow, a sweep of her lashes, as she passed a pair of vampire males. They gave her breasts a passing caress, one briefly catching hold of a strap of her skirt and letting it flow between his fingers to give them both an unencumbered view of her ass. She stopped, waiting, and when they released her, she kept walking.

Since he knew getting out of here as fast as he could wasn't an option, Jacob tried to tune in to what she was saying, knowing she was trying to help, to distract him. He wasn't proud. He'd try anything that might keep him from bolting.

"There are rules. Only brief touches and looks. Maybe five seconds at most, unless you're one of the servants marked as anyone's. One of the domestics, or those chosen as entertainment. As you probably know, those are most often servants of lower-ranked vampires. However, sometimes it's servants who are younger, newer, whose Masters and Mistresses want them to undergo more intense training at being a submissive. Sometimes it's a veteran servant being punished for a transgression. That's always fun to watch because the vamps are more outrageous with them. Those servants have a letter A painted on the forehead of their masks."

He moved on with her to another garden pose. This one involved five people in a chain of intertwined arms and legs. The first man bent over, his mouth pressed to the pussy of the woman lying on her back, legs up and spread. He had her lifted so the curve of her body and his formed a triangle. Behind the man, a woman with a strap-on had her hands braced on his back as she was embedded in him. Behind her, another man was buried in her pussy. A final man straddled the first girl's head, his cock filling her mouth as he reached up and kissed the woman who was fucking the man going down on her. The landscaped circle in which they were posed had an interior circle of rocks from which hidden fountains jetted arced streams of water, moistening their skin. Colored light worked with it to form patterns on their flesh.

"Astounding, isn't it?" Seanna observed. "Each year, one set of territories is responsible for arranging the artistic entertainment for the Gathering. I think they've outdone themselves. This year the

Latin American territories were responsible." She pressed her hand to her breast and fanned herself, winning a reluctant smile from Jacob despite himself. "Oh, my God. That hot Latin blood and imagination."

"So for most of the vampires, this isn't a business get-together."

"Oh, never think that. This is extremely serious. Yes, the main point of being here is to pay honor to the Council. The 'real' business is done on the third night, after the Ball. What they call the 'Court' session, where disputes and political matters are discussed." She sobered. "But the whole three days are highly ritualized. Everything, from Lady Lyssa choosing a partner for the first dance at the Vampire Ball, to strolling in this garden . . ." She bowed her head as they passed another vampire pair and squeezed Jacob's arm to remind him to do the same as they passed. He was glad to keep moving even as he complied.

"The Ball choice is just a formality."

She gave him a glance. "Formality has great significance to the vampires. During the time she was married, she always chose Rex, except when she was paying honor to a certain vampire's contribution for that year, a platonic honor. But the year she married Rex, he was the one she chose, and it was significant exactly for that reason. Since she's no longer married, there's speculation that who she chooses this time might be her next consort, if not a marriage partner. Of course, she might choose Brian for his scientific work."

Lyssa had told him it likely would be Brian for just that reason. "Is he here?"

"Yes. I saw Debra briefly. She's even skinnier than when we last saw her, and far more intense looking. Her face is going to crack if she keeps holding that serious expression all the time." Seanna's voice dropped as if sharing juicy gossip with a girlfriend, amusing Jacob. "Another rumor going around is he's made some remarkable finds he'll be presenting at Court. He's set up a temporary lab here to finalize some of his notes."

"Did he say what about?"

"No. Not even a hint." Her lush lips formed a very distracting pout. "I don't think he intended to let Debra out of his lab to have any fun, but Lord Belizar put an end to that. He made Lord Brian put her into the pool of servants available for entertainment. They're one step above those being used for domestic help, but Brian is too low ranked to get away with keeping her by his side the whole time."

Jacob thought of Debra subjected to the humiliations of the female servants in the corridor and rage flooded him. "She's not seasoned enough for this. That dinner was her first experience in this kind of thing. And this is . . ." He let his gaze course over the garden. "You'd have to do this for at least ten years before you could face it without sweaty palms."

"It's your first time and you're holding your own," she pointed out with a chuckle. "It's all in the attitude. How do you think any of us learn? Don't worry. On this at least, the Council and the overlords know what they're doing. Vampires get terribly aroused seeing a servant deal with all this for the first time. If she sheds pretty tears of humiliation, she'll earn a spanking and become everyone's particular favorite."

At his expression of revulsion, her tone softened and she put out a hand. "I'm sorry. I'm teasing you too much. I forget you don't really understand our ways yet. For a person who has chosen this life, the system works, Jacob. It really does. She may find it difficult, but by the time she leaves here, she'll have been brought to climax so many times, she'll start internalizing the intense pleasure of being a submissive. Even though your Mistress is highly ranked enough to keep you out of all that, it's obvious she's cognizant of the value of the process, to a certain extent." Her gaze coursed over his naked body. "Aren't there things you'd have never thought would bring you pleasure that get you aroused now? The idea of her restraining you . . . the touch of a whip on your skin . . . fucking your ass with her fingers . . ."

Jacob shifted under her knowing look, and she let out a sultry laugh. "It irritates you, but it also makes you hot."

Jacob ran a hand over the back of his neck, kneading the tension there. "I feel like you're my guide on an erotic tour of Wonderland."

She gave a mocking curtsy, affecting the smooth tones of a tour bus coordinator. "Why, perhaps we can interest Mr. Green in joining in our festivities today, after all. You'll find Castle Mason is an absolute playground for the games our Masters and Mistresses like to play. And you have your choice of a wide variety of partners."

"You look forward to all of this."

"Very much so." She dropped her chin onto her shoulder, making it clear she was indulging in a view of his ass, and snickered when he adjusted his stance, which simply gave her a better view of his groin. "Vampires pick their servants for suitability of service and submission, but also for beauty. How could it not be a pleasure to enjoy that?"

All around him he saw vampires taking advantage of the humans available to them, as well as each other. Imagining Lyssa indulging in the same pleasures, he knew he'd rather subject himself to the most humiliating sexual act this corner of the ocean had to offer than to suffer seeing another man touch her.

You are far too possessive for a servant. He remembered her words, but he couldn't deny them, couldn't even say that continued exposure to her would meliorate it one bit. In fact, it was more likely to make it worse.

Seanna took him into another section of hedge garden that was more animated. The servants here were openly, frenetically copulating, a macabre orgy. One servant stood to the side, holding a bronze disk with a spinning needle, which he periodically stopped. When he did that, the servants had to switch partners and assume a different position.

"The servant with the disk is judged for his ability to have them switch right before they can climax," Seanna explained, a twinkle in her eye. "The servant who can leave the greatest number sexually frustrated is then allowed to pick one of them to fuck."

There were more vampires here, sitting on scattered stone benches. Their response to the display was obvious, and more than one had called a servant over to service them orally while they watched. Jacob tried not to think that somewhere on the grounds the gentle Debra was being forced into such a position.

"It's actually not all about sex." Seanna turned him toward the ocean and gestured. "Some of the vampires like to see gladiator sports, what battle skills their servants possess. Of course, since they're fighting naked, it's still very . . . stimulating." She ran a tongue over her teeth. "Let's go over there and I'll show you."

With another playful look, she took him toward the ocean. A field had been marked out just above where the sandy beach led to the tide edge. As they walked down the slope, he saw a group of servants engaged in mock battles on the open green. Sword fighting, wrestling, javelin throwing and footraces, as if revisiting the times of the early Olympians. If he participated here, he would be on display, but there'd be no demands on him sexually that might discomfort him.

I thought you'd find that area rather quickly.

He was pleased to hear her voice, to detect in it that the meeting was going tentatively well. They were taking a break to socialize before resuming the agenda. While he couldn't say for sure, he thought he even sensed she was pleased with his desire to avoid the sex games.

When he was inside her, he felt her desire to own him, body and soul. It was all consuming. He wondered if her purported indifference to his monogamy at other times was one of her games to prove to herself that he didn't have a similar hold on her.

Don't anger me, Jacob. I'm busy. Go play boy games.

"You're talking to her." Seanna withdrew her hand. "You can tell when you're doing it. That night, I could tell you were defying her over something. And now . . ." Her expression softened. "It's good for you to love your Mistress. Wouldn't it please her to see us . . . feel us . . ."

Jacob shook his head, but managed to make it look regretful. Taking her hand, he kissed it. Diplomacy. Richard was one of Lyssa's overlords, after all. Truth be told, after spending this time with Seanna, he didn't find her nearly as offensive as he had during the night of the dinner. Arrogant she might be, but she was entirely committed to the lifestyle she'd chosen. He was the one who didn't fit, as he'd been told often enough. "Not right now. But thank you for your kind offer."

Her hand rested in his as she studied him. Behind the cultured facade, Jacob caught a hint of the young girl from the New Orleans brothel who'd decided to follow Richard into a better life for herself. "You're different, Jacob," she said at last. "But then, so is your Mistress. Be careful here. Differences in servants are tolerated only as long as they amuse or arouse. When they disturb, your days will be numbered. Know your boundaries."

Not a threat, but a warning, similar in tone to what Debra had told him. Though it rankled, he could tell it was sincerely offered. When he nodded, she moved away, her provocative saunter suggesting she was going in search of company more receptive to her urges to play.

Monogamous he was. Dead he wasn't. He couldn't help watching that generous ass swivel from side to side, the cleft tantalizingly revealed by her movements, the long legs.

Intuition as well as countless hours of training with Gideon had him spinning around, ducking his head and throwing up an arm. The long end of the swinging javelin he caught would have smacked smartly into his back or ass, a successful attempt to humiliate him. The man who held the other end had an olive Mediterranean complexion and dark hair cropped short, emphasizing patrician features. Jacob tightened his grip, hauling forward, but his opponent let go at the same moment, overbalancing him. Jacob took the roll backward across the soft turf and came to a half-crouch defensive position, the javelin tucked under his arm and firmly in his grip.

The man's face darkened as several of the other men who had paused to watch expressed appreciation of the recovery.

"He might just be quick enough for you, Malachi," one of them suggested with a chuckle. He had a broad Australian accent, unruly red hair to his shoulders, and an open affability to his features. On his chest was a tattoo of a raven with wings spread over each pectoral. While Jacob wasn't in the habit of ogling men's genitals, the Aussie's were hard to ignore. Hung like a horse, literally. His eyes twinkled. "Like staring at your granny's face tumor, isn't it? Can't hardly look away. Have to have my pants specially tailored, which is more than these blokes can say."

At the wave of jeering responses, he grinned. "Anyhow, Lord knows, we're all tired of getting thrashed." He inclined his head to Jacob. "Knock this bastard on his arse just once, mate, and I'll shout you your first beer in Sodom and Gomorrah."

"You're Lyssa's new Irish whelp, then?" The observation was made by a muscular Viking with tied-back blond hair and clear blue eyes. His cock, while not as sizeable, was pierced with multiple gold rings. He towered over Malachi but stood at his back, making it clear he was the Mediterranean man's ally, if needed. The Aussie stood off to the side, his body language neutral, though Jacob sensed a level of concern under that amiable expression. Though he seemed nonconfrontational, he was all lean muscle and therefore a potential threat until he proved himself otherwise. Jacob kept his eyes on all three.

"That's Lady Lyssa to you." His tone stayed cool as Malachi took up another javelin and paced forward, making it clear he intended to engage. Jacob fell into rhythm, pacing a half circle around him as the others dropped back, giving them their space. Malachi had a muscular, compact physique. He'd be quick and powerful, and wouldn't tire easily.

"If you want a fighter, call a Roman. If you want a ballad, call an Irishman. Can I make you sing, Irishman?"

He switched direction to pace out another half circle, moving the javelin in a comfortable rotor twirl, apparently to impress Jacob with his grasp of the weapon. Jacob stopped in place, choosing a closed grip on the shaft and a ready stance. He cocked his head.

"Are ye goin' t'ask me t'dance then, or should we be proceeding with yer arse whippin'?"

A burst of laughter emitted from the outside circle. Even Malachi curled his lip back in a fuck-you grin, telling Jacob his opponent had been gauging his capacity to be goaded.

"My lord Belizar feels you need a lesson in humility."

Jacob flashed his own teeth. "Then see if you're the man to teach it to me."

Malachi inclined his head and sprang.

There was precise skill and speed involved in using a double weapon, where both ends could be brought into play. There were opportunities for displays of raw power when the opponents held toe-to-toe, testing strength until one would get clever and shear off the wood, trying to come under and rap the shins or, better, sweep the feet.

He and Malachi were well matched physically. Comparable heights and builds, almost equal training, though he suspected this was not Malachi's preferred weapon. He was trying to pull the sharp end into play more often than not, quickly telling Jacob the man meant to do him some damage as part of his Master's bidding, not just beat him.

He was equally aware of a gathering crowd. The singularity of the sound of wood hitting wood told him other sports, both the sensual and physical, were coming to a halt to watch theirs. Which likely meant they had the attention of the upper verandah as well.

Of course. They wanted to see what this new servant of Lyssa's could do.

Malachi's javelin rolled, jerked back and turned faster than Jacob expected, rapping his knuckles hard enough to knock his hand off the upper part of the staff. Jacob dropped to one knee, took the brunt of the next strike along his weapon one-armed. The impact sang down the length of it and reverberated in his shoulder joint. When Malachi flipped the javelin to thrust with the point, Jacob dove into his legs, taking them both down. He didn't agonize over the mixing of weapons practice with hand-to-hand. This wasn't a match. Malachi was spoiling for an out-and-out fight.

They rolled over the ground. The sudden wetness of soft sand told him they'd made it to the shoreline. Malachi drove his elbow in hard under his rib cage, and Jacob retaliated by getting a leg under him and connecting to his face with a yell and a strong uppercut that knocked his opponent back from him, making him stumble in the wet sand.

Both men scrambled for their staffs, and Jacob spun in time to knock away the spear point that would have gone through his face below his left eye.

Not a fight then. Something deadlier. With a snarl, he rammed Malachi full body now, taking him into the water and rolling him, bringing the weapon into play to hold him under. After a satisfying moment on top of the struggling man, he shoved away, flipped and came back up in the same crouch as before. Only this time he had both spears, one balanced in each hand.

Malachi got to his feet, his lip cut and bleeding. "You've fought to the death before." He spat.

Jacob raised a brow. "You want to push this that far?"

Malachi's gaze flickered, just enough. Jacob spun in time to be struck a glancing blow on the temple by the Viking's javelin staff, instead of taking the full swing that could have compromised his skull. Malachi lunged forward, seized his spear and yanked, recovering it, though Jacob managed to hold on to his own weapon. He fell backward, bringing the two of them into his range, creating a melee of arms, legs, thrown punches. When a point grazed his thigh, he heard Malachi's curse as he missed the penetration angle.

Jacob propelled himself to his feet with a roar and used his bare fist to strike Malachi as the man rushed him. Spinning, he engaged the Viking behind him, ducking under his guard and thrusting upward to deliver a sharp blow into his throat, again with his fist. The man stumbled back, wheezing. One out, back to one-on-one.

Jacob, do not engage further. Back off and surrender. Malachi will cease. He is only seeking for you to concede dominance to placate his Master.

He can wait for that until Hell freezes over.

Jacob, obey me. This is important, for reasons more than your ego.

Jacob gauged his opponent. *I don't think that's going to do the trick, my lady.*

I know what Belizar seeks in this. I know my opponent.

As he knew his.

Jacob.

He bit off a snarl. Knowing it was a mistake, and one galling to the point he thought it might choke him, he spread his arms, an open gesture. Reluctantly he tossed the spear to the watching Aussie, whom he'd noted had not been one of the ones who'd tried to unbalance the struggle.

"Your match." He gave a slight bow, though he didn't take his eyes off Malachi. "My lady sends her high regards for your skill."

Malachi nodded, wiped his brow with the back of his hand and turned to offer his gasping mate a hand out of the water.

Diplomacy. Jacob managed to create a mask of it as he turned to the Australian, though from the man's look he suspected he wasn't concealing his expression of murderous fury well enough. "So, this drink—"

"Watch out!" The man shouted it a mere second after Jacob sensed it and spun. The movement kept the spear from going through his kidney. Instead, it tore into the meat of his thigh, the blade end as razor sharp as a sword.

He had time to see the red spurt of blood, telling him Malachi had hit a vital artery. But that thought was immediately consumed by a surge of bloodlust so strong, he knew it didn't come all from him. Perhaps most of it didn't.

Malachi and the Viking charged, slammed into his body and took him down into the water. Struggling for control of emotions not his own, plus the male fury that was, he reached out to her. *My lady?*

Kill him.

Every man had a reservoir of primal rage. He'd learned that in fighting at Gideon's side. When opened, fear disappeared, and there was only blood. Propelled by the force of his lady's reaction, it consumed everything but instinct now. The solid spike of fury in her response confirmed the source of the nuclear rage boiling through his blood. It made him understand why she commanded so much fear and respect. If she turned even a tenth of what was rushing through him on her enemies, none of them would survive it.

Surging up, he seized the neck of the staff and twisted it decisively. Malachi had no opportunity to let go, crying out as Jacob broke his wrist and followed it up with a jab that shattered his nose.

His vision was graying, his leg going numb. *Oh, no you don't,* Jacob silently snarled to his weakening body. *Not until we do our lady's bidding.*

He dispatched the Viking as an afterthought with a second precisely aimed blow to the windpipe that crushed his airway completely, if the sudden look of panic and clutching of the throat were any indication. Jacob flipped the spear as Malachi stumbled back to a fighting stance and raised his own, but Jacob's point was already against his chest, inside his guard.

"Two against one . . . some code of honor," Jacob spat, noting that the knee-deep water in which he was standing was swirling with his blood. His leg was slick with it.

"We have no honor other than what our Masters permit us to have." Malachi dropped his weapon and went to his knees. Jacob had to give him points for bravado. His expression was cool and indifferent, though his chest was laboring, a tremor running through his hands. "My Master concedes the match. On his honor and mine, which serves his will, may his life be forfeit to your lady if he lies."

It was a mouthful to get out while facing the fatal end of a spear. Jacob forced himself to still his forward motion while keeping enough pressure to create a trickle of blood down the man's stomach. He was getting dizzier and didn't dare grip it harder or he'd betray himself by impaling the man.

My lady?

"Let him go, Jacob." She spoke just behind him. When he tilted his head, he saw she was in the water with him. The surf made her skirts float in rippling waves around her calves and bare feet.

Jacob managed five steps toward her before the spear fell from his fingertips. He barely felt it. His knees gave way, mortifying him, but she caught him, easing him to his back. The hands of the Australian were on him as well, taking him to the wet sand, his friendly face and concerned hazel green eyes just to the left of his lady as he stepped back and gave Lyssa a respectful distance. His hands were red with blood. So were hers.

Looking down at himself hazily, Jacob saw as fast as the water was washing it away, the blood was still spurting. Then her hand was over it. "Femoral," he said. "Going to be dead."

"No. It's already healing as we speak. Your third mark gives you a remarkable ability to knit wounds, though you'll need some of my blood. After you drink, you'll be as good as new in less than half an hour." Her green eyes still held the glimmer of red fire he'd felt racing through his whole body when Lord Belizar had apparently ordered his servant to spear him through the back. "You won't be able to get out of your duties here that easily, Sir Vagabond."

Bringing her hand to her throat, she extended one finger, pressed into the artery in a practiced move that immediately welled with blood. Jacob blinked. His fuzzy brain slowly processed the fact she'd fitted an ornamental metal tip over her forefinger, allowing her to make the clean and fast puncture.

"Other women carry lipstick. Breath mints . . ."

"Sssh." She bent over him, pulling her hair over to the opposite shoulder so it fell forward and curtained him as she brought her throat within reach of his mouth. "I command you to drink. Your ability to heal *is* phenomenal with the third mark, but you've not matured in it long enough for us to delay."

As she felt his lips close over the wound, drawing in her life force, Lyssa closed her eyes. The wound under her hand was slowing even now, but his blood loss had been great. At one time, she supposed she'd understood these power games that sated her kind's bloodlust, their need to prove domination. She'd drawn back from that in the past two years, after Rex and Thomas.

As recently as the last Council Gathering, she would have admired Lord Belizar's canny test to determine the suitability of her servant and the test of her own mettle. Power was always shifting, and a vampire was a vampire. Such challenges confirmed that those in leadership positions deserved to be there. She understood all that, had even helped tailor those dual strengths and failings into the present structure they had that kept the more brutal practices to a minimum, but it didn't make her feel any less furious, imagining that spear coming at Jacob's back.

She'd worried so much about him not being prepared for this

event, she'd overlooked her own need for a refresher course in vampire politics. She was angry at herself. Just because she was weary of always being on her guard was no excuse for allowing herself not to be. Jacob had handled himself more than capably, winning the respect of the spectators. Servants would report back to their overlords, Region Masters and Council members what they had seen, that Lady Lyssa had chosen her servant wisely.

Instead of being glad, triumphant, it made her head hurt. Earlier he'd defied her as a male was wont to do in the face of another man's challenge, but when it came to the value of his own life, his obedience to her had been more important to him. He'd *waited* for her permission to defend himself.

What have I done to deserve you? What horrible thing did you do to deserve me? She didn't let him hear such thoughts, of course. She was aware of the others retreating. Malachi. Devlin, with a short bow. His Australian Mistress, Lady Daniela, was known and liked by Lyssa, for all that she ran a small territory and was not considered of much consequence among this Gathering. She was here, however, because she was a full-blood, born vampire. Lyssa would not soon forget her servant's aid to Jacob, which likely had saved him from an even more grievous injury.

She also noticed he was regaining his lucidity, on several levels. His tongue had gone from a functional press against the wound to a swirling pattern, his lips pressing against her skin with remarkable sensual intent. He knew exactly how sensitive her throat was, having been a quick study from the first. Over their short time together he'd taken every opportunity to practice.

It brought to mind one night in her rose garden, when he'd somehow managed to talk her into lying naked under the stars with him. He'd started at her toes, exploring every part of her with his mouth, asking with a combination of husky spoken words and thoughts how each contact felt. If she liked this better . . . or that. By the time he reached her hip bone, words were no longer articulated. He was simply reading the swirl of her responses as an answer.

Drinking a vampire's blood could arouse a human, for usually the vampire ensured the servant was ingesting the proper chemicals to spur that reaction. With the second mark, Jacob had asked her never to use the pheromones on him again. Except for the night with his brother to override his objections, she had honored that request. It always moved her how aroused he got despite the pain. Or because of it. His choice not to explore that dark part of himself analytically might amuse her, but when he allowed it free rein, its power was overwhelming to her senses.

His response could be explained in a variety of ways. But since he didn't have any pheromones to release, she found it difficult to explain why the touch of his lips in this very public place caused an immediate flow of heat through her body, into fingers chilled from the lack of movement during her meeting with the other Council members. She had her arm diagonally across his hips, low, where she'd placed her palm on his thigh wound to gauge the rate of healing, the stemming of the blood loss. Now his cock was hardening, pressing up against her forearm, making it an irresistible compulsion to shift her grip and close over him. Because they were still within the tide line, a gentle surge of water lapped over his body, across his belly, over her folded legs and bare feet. The water rushed over her fingers, gave her knuckles a lick of cool foam while the heat of him increased, as well as the thickness which filled her so well.

Since vampires expected sexual interaction between servants and their Masters and Mistresses, particularly here, there was nothing technically inappropriate about her indulging the moment. Except she had been with Thomas for some time, and she'd not made the monk break his vows of chastity except once. Even before that she tended to be more private in her personal, direct indulgences. Straddling Jacob, letting her wet skirts cling to his bare body as she rode him to sate the longing he stoked inside her would be a bit shocking, particularly for what they knew of Lady Wentworth. But God, how she wanted him. It never seemed to stop for either of them, no matter what they faced. Worry, anger, passion, joy, danger . . . everything they felt together or about one another seemed to lead to this need to join, to reaffirm the inseparable bond the marks gave them. Or something more.

A soft whisper of air escaped her lips when his large hand came up to cradle her face. He increased his fervency at her throat, the soft trim of his beard stroking her collarbone and the top of her sternum.

Jacob. Stop, before you embarrass me before this mob.

Your taste is sweet, my lady. I must have you to regain my full strength. I'm sure of it.

With an effort comparable to the removal of a vital organ, though she knew it only appeared as if she calmly extricated herself, she pulled back. As she rose and stood over him, he propped himself on his elbows and stared up at her face, raw hunger in his expression. She had to stifle a groan. His lean body lay in the shallow surf completely naked, the blood washed away and wound almost completely healed, such that all she saw was an expanse of muscle slick with the water's passage over him in waves and moon-illuminated drops. The brace of his shoulders and elbows bearing his weight made his biceps round, his broad chest taut. Every curve emphasized, as well as his long, proud cock, the weight of his testicles.

All of it hers to do with as she wished, when she wished. On her terms. The reminder as well as her surroundings helped her rein in her response.

"I will have you when I say it's time, Jacob. Rise now." At his ironic look, she bit the inside of her cheek. "Don't test me, Sir Vagabond."

A twinkle sparkled through his beautiful blue eyes as he got to his feet. The effort cost him, for she knew it would be a couple of hours before he was restored to full strength, but he made it into a smooth, lithe move, giving her a slight bow as he rose. He was so much taller than she that the moon haloed him, disturbing her. She couldn't help reaching up and threading her hands through the wet hair that brushed the tops of his shoulders, letting her fingers play along the ridge of bone and muscle there. She drew her hand away before he could take it as an invitation. His hungry cock was still erect and too temptingly close.

Damn it, why the hell shouldn't she have him? Why did appearances have to matter so much? She didn't care about any of this. His blue eyes were so bright, their color somehow getting more brilliant by the moment, more blue than she'd ever recalled before. Calling to her. Taking a step forward, the ground didn't seem to be where she thought it was.

Jacob caught her hand when she stumbled, making it appear as a hitch in her stride caused by the weight of her clothes. "Be careful of your skirt, my lady. I apologize for making your clothes wet. Would you like me to carry you from the water, take you back to our rooms so you can change?"

She wasn't sure if she nodded. She hoped she did, so it wouldn't look incongruous, her servant gathering her in his arms and lifting her to stride off the shore. She had to fight not to close her eyes. The colors were getting blinding. Nausea was surging forth at a rate that brought a flood of panic with it.

Hold on, my lady. It's all right. Jacob's voice, soothing, helping her balance the desperation. She'd fought things in the course of her life that would have given an archangel nightmares. So this emotional panic attack—no other term for it—was a new symptom, something else out of her control. Everything was starting to be out of her control. She had to go . . . fly . . . She couldn't . . . Why was the world so bright? It was like the sun, the threat of burning. The consumption of fire . . .

"A good match, as I said. Tomorrow evening perhaps I can think of a suitable way for Malachi and Jacob to make up. Something we'll all enjoy."

Lord Belizar's voice. Where?

To your left, my lady. Turn your head no more than an inch or two. Give him a smile with that touch of disdain you do so well. Let him worry whether he's displeased you.

A good tactic. Hoping she did it successfully, she turned her face back to Jacob. She needed to give him an order, something that would make sense, of course. Dispel any suspicion. Her clothes were wet.

None of this was adequate. She couldn't do this anymore. Her skin felt on fire. Jacob's hands were like hot brands. Oh, God . . . it was not close to dawn, but she could feel the sun as if her skin was anticipating its eruption from the earth. She was responding to it. Suffering for it.

I can't . . . Jacob. Where . . . ?

I'm here, my lady. Sssh . . . Somehow they were in her rooms. It seemed only a few seconds had passed, but it would have taken him at least five or ten minutes to get her there. She could only hear roaring in her head. Her limbs were shuddering and she was overwhelmed by a fear so strong she didn't know how to control it. She was afraid. She'd never been this afraid.

Jacob . . . I'm frightened. So frightened and no reason for it. Help me . . .

He'd put her down and stepped back, and she was sinking. Just sinking.

No. He had her. Stripping off her clothes. Leaving her naked and damp, shivering in his arms as he lifted her, took her to the cool touch of the sheets. She clung to his back, seeking him, his life, his presence. Her legs lifted, locked around his hips.

He hesitated. Then in one gentle move he lay down upon her. Sliding his cock deep, he caused her to rise up to him and cry out as the fear and emptiness were severed inside her soul, like a two-headed monster he'd just cleaved with his decisive penetration, driving out everything wrong.

He settled in and stayed there. Pressing his forehead to hers, he framed her throbbing head with his hands, holding her body down, giving her a certain anchor.

She didn't need to be afraid. He was here. Her words or his? It didn't matter. Only this mattered. This sensation of reassurance, his large body covering hers, his cock firmly seated, his arms around her.

"Sssh . . . my lady. You're fine. I'm here. Hold on."

Her mind was completely open to him, telling Jacob she was unaware or wholly unable to keep herself shielded from him. Her body now was sweating, her skin so hot it almost burned, but she gripped him to her as if she didn't want a fraction of space between them. A jumble of frightening images of her past and present filled his head, her fears for the future . . .

Those she protected hunted down. Everything she'd built with the Council destroyed by Carnal and his type of vampire, those who wanted savagery and chaos to rule the world. She thought they were up to something. They needed to be on guard, all of them, because she had no idea from which direction the threat would come, but one was coming. She might be able to protect her fugitives with a Council decision, but how could the Council hold together if she was gone . . .

It was the first time she'd acknowledged what he suspected. She was perhaps the one vampire capable of keeping order all on her own. Not just with her royal lineage and wisdom, but the enormous power that was hers to command. She was their shield. She was the army that gave them the time to grow in wisdom and strength. While she understood she would not be around forever, she knew her death might be too soon. Far too soon.

Then those images slid away and he was falling into the well of her soul. As he spiraled down into her unconscious, it reared up to meet him, blasted him with the desolation of her most personal fears.

A storm of them, no order or reason. The nightmare stories of vampires being damned and soulless, facing Hell . . . Ruthless hands on her, Carnal and Rex hurting her, taking everything, leaving her nothing. Her voice cried out to him like a child's in the night with a trembling vulnerability.

The image struck him like a fist, filling his mind so he couldn't deny it had the shape of a memory.

Those beautiful green eyes in a little girl's face, silky dark hair wisping around her delicate features. She'd woken in tears, screaming of her stepfather's death. He'd held her, her favorite samurai guard. Sung her back to safer dreams. While he'd had very different feelings about her then, one thing had been the same. He'd known the small girl child in his lap was the most important thing in his life. The beginning and the end of it.

Jacob was glad she had no ability to read his thoughts right now, for it tore his heart to pieces to feel her fear and pain. But he could and would stand between her and any threat, even this one. Tightening his grip on her, he began to stroke, slow and powerful, reaching deep into her mind in a way he'd never tried before. He'd stumbled into it one time by mistake, and she'd reacted violently. This time he wasn't prying. He was seeking her in that darkness.

'Tis bullshit, my lady. The light of your soul is so strong the sun dims before it. Your heart is so good . . . There's nothing to fear. We'll protect what is yours with all that we are, and what we cannot do, we must leave to a Power higher than ourselves. I'm here, and I bear your third mark. Wherever you go, I'll be right with you. You are never alone in this. In anything. I love you, my lady. So much I am nothing without you. You have become everything.

She clutched his shoulders, her breath quickening. He slayed her dragons with the sharp edge of his words, giving her truth, not sentiment. Increasing the strength of his thrusts, he encircled her hips with one arm, pressing his palm against one buttock to raise her for a deeper penetration.

The whirl of her thoughts was slowing, focusing, replaced by an undulating red wave of response, clearing the debris of the storm her sickness had brought crashing down on her. It left space for the rippling tide he built within her. When her muscles convulsed on him, he bent his head, covered her breast with his mouth, tasted salt water and sand. Closing his eyes, he let his own tears fall where they'd merge with the dampness of her skin. Her hand touched his head, fingers tangling into his wet hair, her body beginning to match the cadence of his.

Nothing you do shall take me from your side, my lady. You can't hurt me enough to make me leave you.

As she began to climax, her nails pierced his flesh as he knew was her way, drawing blood she would lap from his skin before a drop was wasted. He shuddered in reaction to her body releasing beneath his, allowing him to give her pleasure and peace, restore her and send her flying at once. Even as he felt that miracle, he prayed for another one.

"Jacob . . ."

He quivered, muscles rippling through his arms and across his back at that soft whisper. He hadn't asked, but she'd known he was waiting. Waiting for his Mistress's command in the way she'd taught him. The way he knew would help her regain her sense of herself.

"Give me your seed. Come inside me."

It exploded from him, raw and aching as if he had a vise tight around his heart. As it pumped furiously, keeping pace with his release, it was like a heart attack, heralding the agony of impending loss.

15

S HE slept deeply after that. Jacob slept some with her, but when the sun came, he was up and taking a morning run around the castle grounds. It was a different place in its peaceful early daylight solitude and even more beautiful, if that was possible. By happenstance, Devlin was also out and joined him. The Aussie said little, simply keeping Jacob company while he sweated out his demons. As they made their circuit, Jacob noted that with the exception of Devlin, it was primarily the servants of the more highly ranked overlords, Region Masters and Council members moving around this early in the morning, confirming old ties and establishing new ones. Networking. Since that was his purpose as well, with Devlin's help he identified several servants of vampires who had received vital communications from Lyssa in the past few months. He took the opportunity to confirm those communications had been received and understood.

None of those communications revealed his lady's illness, of course, but she was officially verifying the commitment of those vampires to the Council's purpose, as well as unofficially laying the tracks of an underground railroad for her fugitives and even her legitimate vampires if they ended up needing it. Since Lady Danny was loyal to Lyssa's cause, even if she didn't have a lot of influence to lend to it,

Devlin was exceptionally helpful, providing Jacob insights and pointing out other servants of newer, younger overlords his lady might want to approach while she was here.

For personal as well as other reasons Jacob had hoped to see Debra, or even Lord Brian, but apparently Seanna was correct. Brian was likely sequestered in his temporary lab. Debra was probably burning both ends of the candle to do his lab work when she wasn't required to serve as entertainment. Had Brian made a breakthrough in the Delilah virus? Or would his news at the Court be about something else entirely, crushing the narrow window of hope Jacob was grimly holding open?

The Australian stayed respectfully silent during the interchanges, but when they made it at last to the back side of the grounds where there was just the stretch of ocean, he slowed to an in-place jog and raised a brow. "Done with wanking now? Or you got anything left?" With a shove to throw Jacob off balance, he was off and running, throwing insults over his shoulder as Jacob raced after him. When he caught up, he found he had to stretch himself to the limits of his body to stay even with the man's powerful stride. They completed the last mile of their run dead out, taking the stairs to the verandah three at a time, lungs burning.

"You're no wuss, are you, mate?" Devlin gasped, his hands on his knees. Straightening, he winked. "I'm off to play fairy godmother on my lady's dress for tonight's doings. She's heard rumors about some of the other outfits and thinks it needs some fussing up. Bloody sheilas. Come find me tonight if you have time and I'll shout you that drink. Hell, since they're all free, I can afford a slab."

Jacob waved a hand in assent. Although he was fighting to regain his breath as well, the festering ache he'd been carrying had dissipated to a manageable anxiety. When Devlin left him with a slap on the shoulder and a "She'll be right, mate," Jacob found himself grateful for a friend.

Uneasiness had been simmering in his gut since they'd driven away from her Atlanta home and she'd watched Bran in the rear window until she could no longer see him. While at first he thought he was just anticipating his proximity to so many vampires or the many possible public ways he might be compelled to perform sexual acts for his lady's stimulation, after last night's episode on the beach, he knew it wasn't that.

As the day progressed, he stayed busy with an odd mixture of the political and domestic. The evening's event was an early dinner and entertainments rumored to be as elaborate as an erotic three-ring circus. Normally it would cause him trepidation, but she was his focus tonight.

As it got close to dusk, he prepared her bath, chose the oils he thought would suit her mood best. Ironed the ribbons to dress her hair and selected her lingerie, one of his favorite tasks. A silver-gray bra that was sheer except for a delicate embroidered pattern of swirls that would stretch along the sides and lower portion of her breasts, leaving the nipple delightfully in view beneath the shimmering net of the cup. A matching lace thong, which gave him the welcome distraction of imagining sliding the garment onto her, his thumb caught under the straps curving over her hip bones.

Everything was ready, the sun starting to sink. Sitting by her bed, he watched her continue to sleep, her internal alarm silenced by her body's fight to keep up its strength. He didn't want to wake her.

The need of a lover to protect warred with his duty as her servant, making it difficult to wake her from a sleep he knew might give her the strength to live just a bit longer. When he at last bent over her, he hesitated. Usually he spoke or touched her shoulder to wake her. Sometimes the curve of her cheek.

Instead, he placed his mouth over hers, a kiss he drew out and deepened, coaxing her lips to part, his tongue touching hers. Giving in to desire, he curled his arms around her slim body, heated it with his own. He registered that her skin felt its normal, slightly cooler temperature, though he detected she needed to eat. As she began to rouse, his third mark also registered her strength and vitality had returned. He held on, wanting to savor it.

She needed to be home. But his lady would never shirk her duty. Had her soul been in the body of Guinevere, Camelot would never have fallen. She'd been less than a couple of centuries old when he'd come to her as a knight during one of the Crusades. Yet he saw little difference in her self-possession and confidence between that time and this one. Since she was born, she'd been groomed to be a queen. As far as he knew, she'd never harbored any resentment over that. Scornful of those who eschewed their responsibilities in her own Region of territories, she punished them swiftly and decisively. In a correspondence to one of her young overlords, she'd stated it baldly. "There are those who spend their whole lives wishing they had power, leadership. If you are given it, you live up to it. It's a gift Fate believes you can handle. If you are wise, you don't disappoint Fate."

Now, in the present, his queen and liege lady indicated by light pressure she wanted him to draw back. He did so reluctantly, but only a few inches as she cupped his face and ran her thumb over his lips, moist from her own mouth.

Lyssa had been in a half doze, enjoying the awareness of him moving around the room. When he sat down, she expected the touch on her face or the quiet murmur of his voice. His brief hesitation had been her only warning before he'd leaned forward and given her the touch of his lips. A wake-up kiss. Something a lover or husband would do.

"It's almost time to join the others for dinner, my lady. I've laid out your clothing."

He also had hot water and a cloth for her face as usual. Taking her hand, he gave her his strength to lift her into a sitting position so she had to use none of her own. Sliding his arm behind her, he offered her the brace of his shoulder as she got her bearings. She yawned.

"I never used to wake up groggy. Is this what you humans face each day? I wonder that you get up at all."

His gaze was on her face, registering her skin tone. "You need blood, my lady. May I offer you something?"

She shook her head. She didn't want anything, though she knew she should. Her limbs felt heavy. When he opened his mouth to press the issue, she gave him a quelling look, as effective as a verbal snap. She didn't reach out to his mind, too raw to deal with the worry she knew would be there, and that made her irritable. Merging with Jacob's mind first thing was something she anticipated almost as much as seeing him upon rising.

Turning away from him, she brought one knee onto the bed.

"Do you want your hair up or down today, my lady? Or somewhere in between?"

Closing her eyes to enjoy the sensation of brushing, she didn't respond, but knew he wouldn't repeat himself. He was used to her long pauses, particularly in her "morning" phase. The brush stroked firmly, pulling out the tangles without yanking, massaging her scalp. His hand passed before it to run fingers through the strands. When he'd first begun the ritual, it had been to feel for tangles, but now she knew he did it to touch. She liked it as much as he seemed to, so she never skipped the brushing unless he'd angered her. A smile touched her lips. He did that about one third of the time.

"Tell me how you'd like me to wear it . . . and call me by my name."

She'd not made that request ever, even in their most physically intimate moments. His hand stilled on her hair, the brush pausing in midstroke.

Call me familiar. I command it.

"I want you to leave it down, Lyssa. With just a piece here. And here." He took a lock from either side of her temples. "To hold it back."

When his fingertips drifted down, she turned her cheek into his hand, holding it there between her shoulder and jaw. "When it's all the way down, like this," he said quietly, "it reminds me of when you're riding me, all your glorious hair falling around your face. If you wear it that way, I'll think of you that way, all evening long."

Say it again. She wanted to hear it.

Rising to one knee behind her, he wrapped his arms around her body, dropping the brush to the covers. He was wearing slacks and a tailored cotton shirt, his hair brushed and gleaming, queued back.

He smelled fresh, bathed. She detected the provocatively light blending of the cologne scent of his deodorant and aftershave. His well-groomed beard pressed against her temple now. She curled her fingers around the forearm he pressed across her bosom as his hand clasped her shoulder, holding her back against his solid chest.

"Lyssa." He murmured it against her ear. "My heart. My soul. My lady."

She closed her eyes, nodded. She could be what she needed to be. Cruel when she had to be. He would stand behind her.

Always, my lady. I will be whatever you need me to be.

She hadn't meant for her thoughts to be open to him, but she knew her control of that was slipping. She found she could even accept it, at least at this moment. At length, he released her and began to tend her hair again. Reaching back, she put her hand high on his thigh. "Any tenderness?"

"None. I could have used this healing ability when I was a kid, as frequently as Gideon tried to kill me."

"You fought that much?"

He chuckled. "No, my lady. We did fight, but we were most likely to kill each other during play." He tugged her around, the brushing done, and guided her touch to a bump on his head just under his hairline. "We couldn't find our baseball one day, so we decided to pitch rocks. Gideon was first at bat. He insists if my head hadn't been in the way, he would have hit a line drive clear out of the field. Since he fractured my skull, our aunt was inclined to agree with him."

Jacob was glad to see a smile on his lady's lips again. He was having difficulty turning his thoughts from his concerns, and he knew she was likely staying a safe distance from them as a result. Though her strength had returned, he could sense her fragility, an impression he'd never been able to detect this long after an episode.

Do you think I don't know I'm getting worse, Jacob? The disease had to start progressing at a certain point, and of course it's Murphy's law that it would do so here, where it's so important that I appear healthy and well.

"I think I better take that breakfast you say I need, Sir Vagabond," she said before he could respond to that. "Are you up for it? No weakness from yesterday at all? Before you lie to me, recall I can still hear your thoughts." Her eyes glinted. "There are many punishments available to me here."

Yesterday Lady Helga showed me a thick metal collar she'd had made by a jeweler who is displaying her wares at this Gathering. It's nearly three inches in width. I could lock it around your throat and keep the key on a chain around my neck, dangling between my breasts where it would tease you.

"You think you need a key to tease me with that sight, my lady?" He raised a brow, struggling to maintain a mild expression and hammer down the lust her words provoked so easily.

She continued, that sultry half whisper weaving itself among the rational centers of his brain, fogging his ability to think. *There are two tiny spikes on the inside that press against the throat, irritating the skin and reminding the servant of his bond to his Mistress. Their location is marked on the outside with a pair of bloodred rubies. Whenever she wishes, the vampire places her fingers on those two rubies and presses. After the spikes puncture the side of the throat, the lady may partake of the blood by holding a lovely matching goblet against her servant's flesh to catch the flow. But I wouldn't use it. I'd wait until the stream of blood reached your nipple and start there, lapping it up all the way back to your throat.*

He closed his hand over hers. She'd effectively driven any thought out of his head but the images she'd created, and he had to bite back a smile at the satisfied gleam in her eyes.

"I can serve your needs, my lady, whatever they may be. Your blood nourished me well. Let me offer the same gift to you."

She studied him another moment before she nodded. Leaning forward, she bit into his throat, into the area that had begun to show a dual puncture scar because of her repeated use of it. Though she preferred the throat, when her hand brushed high on his thigh, his mind immediately turned back to one night when she'd chosen the femoral artery. His cock had stood hard and heavy as her cheek brushed his testicles, her throat working against the muscle of his thigh as she swallowed the alarming rush of blood that came from the area. When she was done, she'd put her mouth over his cock, and he'd immediately exploded against the back of her throat. She'd tied his hands to the bed rails that night so he was at her mercy. He'd looked down to see traces of his own blood on his genitals, markings from her mouth upon his length.

Now he settled his arm around her back, holding her close to him, her body cradled between his knees. Her hand curled loosely around his hip, letting him hold her weight in his one arm as she drank.

Despite her pleasurably distracting thoughts, holding her this way made his mind turn back to his primary concern. He wished she'd let him take her home, care for her. With every passing hour, a dread was growing in his belly. He wanted her to be where she was happiest. With her roses and her dogs.

Devlin wants to buy you a drink. Why don't you plan on joining him after you get me ready? You can meet me at the outdoor pavilion for the dinner. I won't need you there until around nine. I have some things to do. Some acquaintances to meet.

She pulled away, taking his hand and placing it against the bite, a reminder to hold pressure. Rising and moving toward the bathing area, she slid off the straps of her nightgown, letting it pool at her feet. She stepped out of it, continued toward the tub. "He's a good man. I'd like you to honor him with your company. It will send a message to his Mistress that she has my favor."

He cursed his overprotectiveness, which often provoked this need in her to push him away, force him to acknowledge his first responsibility to her as her servant. Her tone was indifferent, her attitude as imperious as ever as she left the gown for him to pick up. Gliding into the bathing area, a small, raven-haired goddess with skin like cream, she closed the door, sending a ripple of annoyance through him. As he was sure she knew it would.

There was nothing, no emotion she couldn't wrest from him. He supposed that was the way loving someone was. Adventure, exhilaration. Quiet contentment. The desire to strangle her.

Or maybe that was just the way being in love with Lady Lyssa was. He'd never been in love with anyone else. Not in this life, and perhaps not in any other.

~

"You know, in the central courtyard they're offering drinks served on the bellies of women. The women lie on a marble slab, tip the wine onto their stomachs and men suck it off their skin, drinking from their navels."

"You saying you'd rather be doing that than drinking a beer with me?"

Devlin gave Jacob a sardonic look. "It's a privilege offered to the vamps. Or I'd ditch your arse, no worries."

"I'd have beaten you there."

Devlin chuckled, touching his beer to Jacob's as they sat companionably on the lower verandah wall, feet dangling over the twenty-foot drop as they faced the ocean view. "Bullshit. You're gone over that Mistress of yours. Plus, you run like a one-legged girl."

"That's a long fall there," Jacob noted.

"Yes. Yes, it is." Devlin grinned. "Anytime you feel lucky, Irish."

Jacob would have retorted, but his eyes had narrowed.

Carnal.

He knew Carnal was here, but it was the first time he'd seen him. The tall vampire wore a tuxedo and cape—a pretentious affectation in Jacob's opinion—and had his dark hair pulled back from his face, emphasizing the angular, cruel planes. He strode over the lower lawn, meeting two other vampires who were obviously waiting for him. He had no servant with him, but Jacob didn't dare to hope that meant he hadn't picked another victim to replace Melinda.

"Friend of yours?"

"Hardly. Who's he meeting there?"

"Different versions of the same brand of wanker," Devlin observed frankly. "That's Lords Hollenbeck and Martingale. They fancy themselves rebels against the establishment, but they're thugs. To my way of thinking, Council's gone soft on their kind. They think they can reason with them, give them bones to keep them in line when anyone with eyes can see all they're out for is the wholesale destruction of the

Council so they can set themselves up as supreme tyrants. And God help humans—not just the servants—if they succeed."

"You think they're up to something?" Jacob watched Carnal move away with the other two, taking wine from a passing servant with barely a glance at her.

"Rumor is they're planning some political coup at the big meeting tomorrow." Devlin took another swallow from the beer as if trying to clean the taste from his mouth. "That they're going to introduce a motion on the floor to overthrow the policies they find so irritating. Like not being able to tear open a human's throat in broad moonlight on busy city street corners every other day."

"They make motions." Jacob tried to get his mind around that.

"Abso-fucking-lutely. They're fanatical about their Roberts' Rules of Order." But Devlin looked uneasy. "Sometimes I think our world is about to change, Irish. And with vampires, it was already a pretty unstable world to begin with. They could try to oust the Council. If they get enough votes, they could do it. All hell will break loose."

They drank in silence for another few moments. There was no answer to it. Jacob knew it, just as he suspected Devlin did. They just had to be prepared for what would come.

"Psychopathic poser," Devlin muttered, watching Carnal disappear through one of the castle archways.

Jacob bit back a smile. "That's a Yank term."

"And a good one. Malachi's impressed with your skills, by the way." Devlin shifted to a lighter tone. "It's not easy to spar with him, let alone a real fight like that."

"Particularly when he called in reinforcements."

"Ah." Devlin waved his beer dismissively. "Malachi's actually not a bad sort when it comes to most things. He was following his Master's orders. Belizar wanted you taken down a notch and tested.

"Malachi *is* a sexist asshole, though. He's got that whole cultural, men-should-hold-all-the-power thing going. He's been a servant for ninety years; you'd think he'd get past it. But he got powerfully ticked off the other night when Lord Brian's servant showed he didn't know what the hell he was talking about when they got into a debate on global warming."

"Debra?"

"Yeah, that was her name. Soon after that, she got drafted into being one of the entertainments. Malachi probably ratted her out, told Belizar there was a midlevel new servant who wasn't doing her time in the trenches."

"I should have speared him through his balls. Why would Belizar feel I need to be tested specifically?"

Devlin gave him a sidelong glance. "I keep forgetting how new you are. Male–female vampire dynamics have some very old-world prejudices. Male vamps think the females are at risk for getting overly attached to their male servants. Something happened a few years back and a male servant was executed. It struck a spark on the fertilizer pile of the theory."

"Executed?"

"I was at the Gathering where it happened." A shadow crossed Devlin's face as he looked out at the ocean. "A female vamp in the higher ranks was acting all moony over her servant, openly favoring him in situations where servants are supposed to take a backseat. And he was getting full of himself over it. He mouthed off to a Council member, and was stupid enough to throw a punch. The female vamp didn't call him to task. Instead, she tried to protect him. Even offered her own life as forfeit. Bam, it was all over then. He was executed on the spot, and she was imprisoned in a coffin for a month. She was forced to marry a vampire lord senior in age and chosen by the Council. She chose to meet the sun."

As Jacob looked down pensively, Devlin shook his head. "It was bad before then, but in a low-level way. Now the male vamps are positively rabid on the issue of female vamps and their servants. My lady thinks it's just a typical power-play issue. Male vamps are possessive, but they also like power. They don't necessarily like sharing it with the females, and they're looking for ways to relegate them to second string."

He sighed. "When it comes down to it, no matter how much we love our ladies, we love them best by remembering our place. You won't find me stepping out of line, not if it means I'd endanger my Danny." He smiled sheepishly at Jacob's ironic glance. "Lady Daniela,

I mean." He tapped his beer against Jacob's. "Your Mistress is under the microscope these days in particular."

Jacob's head rose. "What do you mean?"

"This can't be a surprise to you." Devlin gave him an even look. "How did the most powerful vampire on earth let her husband get murdered by a mere human? How did a mere human kill the second most powerful vampire on earth without help? The only thing that has kept those questions to a dull roar is that Lyssa killed her servant for his transgression, and a select few in power knew Lord Rex was succumbing big time to the Ennui, which is basically the vampire brand of Alzheimer's."

Jacob turned and brought his feet back to the Mexican tile floor of the verandah, leaning his hip against the wall.

"Did you know Rex?"

Devlin shook his head. "Not much. My lady knew him . . . before he changed." He glanced cautiously at Jacob. "She said he was powerful, intelligent. Not a warm, nurturing sort, very competitive. But he loved your lady. Lady Danny said his love was so strong for Lady Lyssa it almost made up for his weaknesses. Until they caught up with him." He turned and leaned back on the wall, mirroring Jacob. "Lady Lyssa is considered a fucking force of nature. No one really knows the full extent of her strength. The only one who might be able to stand toe-to-toe with her is Lord Mason. Like her, he has more secrets and mysteries than the rumormongers can keep up with."

"And that's bad?"

"Not bad. Just peculiar. Vamps like a mystery. If they don't understand it, they do their best to pick it apart. But it's more than that with her. Lady Lyssa is very important to all the Council supporters for what she symbolizes, as well as what she knows and can do. Danny doesn't make any bones about it. Lyssa isn't just queen. She's the Council's champion."

"Their muscle." Jacob recalled his earlier thought.

"You got it. Whereas Carnal and his crowd would build their kingdom on the illusion of power, and use blood to keep it painted as reality. Watch your lady's back, mate. Part of the reason I wanted a beer with you is to let you know folks like me will help watch yours while you do." He grinned. "You're okay. I like the way you handle yourself, and some of these buggers can get awfully stodgy and hoity-toity. We can help keep their reality a little bit more real. That's what mates are for."

He straightened, checking his watch. "Time to go. If you can, come back here around noon tomorrow. There's a gathering of servants, sort of a tradesman meeting. It's a chance for those like you who haven't been in it as long to ask questions, the insider tips on things to make our jobs easier. Then, after that, we get pissed on drink and tell stories." He winked, then sobered somewhat. "It's a good way to loosen up some before the Ball and the Court after that. If something intense is going to happen, it's going to happen at one of those. Just between you and me, I always wish we could go home after the second day."

16

THE courtyard where the evening's entertainments were being held was in the center of the castle. The area was cobblestoned and embedded with elaborate fountains that sparkled with lights under a sky filled with stars. Tall maypoles with fluttering, colorful ribbons marked out areas for groupings of lords and ladies and the various entertainments. Jugglers moved in and out of these boundaries, handling flame torches whose arcing paths and rush of sound gave the night a mystical flavor.

Servants of both genders in various harem wear performed graceful, sinuous belly dances and acrobatic feats for their intently watching vampire audience. Musicians and bards played flutes and steel drums in different corners. There were even carnival tricks Jacob recognized, like the eating of fire. On the outskirts of these areas were small tents for the jewelers and craftsmen his Mistress had mentioned. He saw the blacksmith in one corner doing a busy trade with his branding irons. It reminded him of a cross between the Faire they'd attended and a medical convention with pharmaceutical vendors waiting patiently on the outskirts.

He found his Mistress easily enough. In the center of the courtyard the largest marked-out area was for the Council. Divans for the members and his lady had been provided, as well as cushions for those they invited to join them around the most dramatic of the entertainment displays.

The snug silver wraparound dress she wore had a fan train in the back, the point of which drew attention to the top point of her buttocks. The back of the dress was low enough to drive a man to distraction wondering if he'd get a glimpse of that provocative dip at the tailbone. Her hair was done as he'd dressed it, though they'd agreed on a twist over her shoulder that complemented the onyx stone necklace she wore and matching onyx and diamond earrings. The way she reclined on her hip, the dress hugged her body and created a pleasing, curvy terrain from her shoulder to her slender ankles, one of which was adorned with a thin diamond anklet. She wore silver ankle-strap sandals. With one hand lying loosely on her hip, she could have been Cleopatra. More than one man was eyeing her appreciatively, even though there was of course no shortage of beautiful women. She simply stood out.

He looked at her and saw the vampire queen, a warrioress. A cruel tyrant, a gentle nurse. A girl. A cold, haughty bitch, a generous and loving woman. A woman who loved fiercely. She'd stayed by a husband who'd been lost to violent madness. She'd shielded Thomas with her own life and risked all the power she was now trying to protect, all for the benefit of others.

Nothing ever just for herself. Except perhaps for the one time she'd reached out a hand into the fiery desert sun to draw a knight back into her embrace.

He shifted his attention to the central entertainment. Twelve female servants, all naked and kneeling in a circle. To enhance the impression of a flower in the best Isadora Duncan tradition, they were curled forward, their elbows and arms stretched out, foreheads pressed to the stones. Since they all had long hair in various colors, the hair was fanned out in a perfect shape, trimmed to form scalloping around the outer edge of the circle. Real flower petals in different hues were scattered over their backs. In the center of the circle formed by their bodies stood twelve black men of extremely dark complexion, also naked. They had their heads bowed and arms around each other's shoulders so the overall effect was of a white-petaled flower with a brown center, like a daisy scattered with color from those strewn petals.

He'd found Debra at last. She was one of the prostrate women. He recognized the others as equally midlevel-ranked servants. It was too much to hope the purpose of the artistic arrangement was just for aesthetic enjoyment.

Noting that the servants of the Council members who had arrived were kneeling at the feet of their respective Masters and Mistresses, he eased into the circle of divans and did the same at the feet of his Mistress. His palm itched to run along the silk-clad line of her hip and feel her bottom through the thin material. His lady had an exceptional ass. While he was all too aware after his conversation with Devlin what wasn't advisable, he wanted to give her some kind of tactile awareness of his presence.

You think I don't feel your heat the moment you come into a room, Sir Vagabond?

In answer, he did ease his hand onto her foot. He braced his thumb on the thin heel, his fingers lightly curled over her ankle.

Sitting there as regal as the queen she was, so beautiful most men would never dream that they'd have a right to touch her, he couldn't help but think of her sleep-rumpled in his arms, soft and yielding, her fangs in his throat, her slim hand resting on his chest. As beautiful as she was now, he thought she was perhaps even more beautiful like that.

You are stroking my ego. The ego of an old, old woman.

He stifled a smile, maintaining the solemn mien expected, though he wondered if the others were conducting similarly entertaining dialogues with their Masters or Mistresses. *You are ancient, my lady. As a goddess is ancient. You are why the word* timeless *exists.*

Charmer. Stop preying on me with your distracting thoughts and behave.

He turned his attention to observation. Lyssa had one invited guest. Sitting on the cushions next to her divan was Lady Daniela. Devlin had arrived, though he stood at attention to her at the outside of the circle. Daniela was leaned forward, the ladies head-to-head, sharing murmured confidences. Because he picked up a rare easiness in his lady's manner toward Devlin's Mistress, the way most women might treat a friend, Jacob studied the woman with interest.

Daniela was gold to Lyssa's raven. Her hair was like the spun gold of fairy tales, dressed in beads and ribbons. She wore a Roman-type garb, soft white silk, the fabric defined by a crisscrossing of silken cord with tassels of gemstones made to complement the beaten gold collar around her throat and pendants at her lobes. Her eyes were deep blue, enhancing the soft beauty of her face. There was a good-naturedness there that seemed unusually revealing for a vampire. He knew enough not to underestimate any vampire, however. Even one who looked as if she should have a flock of bluebirds chattering over her head. He suspected each vampire tailored his or her strengths to enhance their allure. For Lyssa, it was her dark mystery. For Lady Danny, it was disarming goodness.

Looking at the blond vampire, Jacob suspected she could convince a man that he'd found a treasure to take to his bed as well as home to meet his parents. Whom she could easily drink for lunch.

Lord Uthe had arrived, filling the last empty divan. When he gave a slight bow to Lyssa, she nodded in return. Jacob had exchanged many correspondences with Uthe's servant over the past couple of months, so Jacob knew Lyssa rightly recognized him as the strongest force for stability on the Council.

Lord Belizar rose, drawing the attention of the gathered circle and those beyond it. The courtyard began to quiet down. The individual entertainers withdrew to the outskirts, making the dual ring of servants, the "flower," the center of attention.

"Now that all Council members, servants and their guests are here, we have a special entertainment planned." His gaze flickered over Jacob. "Many of you witnessed the fine display of weaponry this afternoon. Lady Lyssa's new servant is indeed a credit to her, a worthy opponent. As such, we are going to pay him a special honor. He will be the main focus of our event this evening."

Oh, holy Christ on buttered toast.

At Belizar's gesture, the black men moved forward and knelt, one man behind each woman. A motor engaged, eliciting a murmur from the assembled, because the men had been concealing a sculpture anchored on the mirrored center of a dais that now rose to form a new center within the flower arrangement. The sculpture was a smooth, stylized version of a reclined nude male body, with all the dips necessary to drape a woman over it in a variety of provocative poses. The nude body also had an erect, angled phallus.

"Lady Lyssa's servant is commanded to choose any petal among this flower of slaves and bring her onto the dais to service him to climax with her mouth."

Belizar did not even deign to look toward Jacob as he delivered the edict. "As Lyssa's servant is serviced, the lower tier of men will stoke their lust in the succulent fruit kneeling before them. When they prepare to climax, they will do so simultaneously. An impressive display, if they manage it."

He bowed in Lyssa's direction. "As with all of our games, my lady, I offer you a wild card you may utilize at any point. To give your servant an inspired and prolonged performance, we now offer him an aphrodisiac, in case he has the common human fear of performing in public."

Laughter swept the crowd. Jacob glanced toward Lyssa, but her expression was neutral, her mind silent, telling him she expected him to do what was being asked of him.

Christ.

A masked servant was allowed inside the circle of divans. She stepped to Jacob's side with a deep curtsy of deference to Lyssa. It was not an easy maneuver since she was having to keep her back ramrod straight. Around her throat was a silken garrote attached to a silver cup. The cup floated on top of a bowl of crimson fluid held in her cleavage by way of a rigid parallel harness that squeezed the generous breasts and distended the nipples. Jacob noticed that when he lifted the cup, he would have to either bring her close enough to press her breasts and the rest of her against him, or the garrote would choke her.

"The restraint is designed by our own Lady Marquet from the Canadian provinces," Belizar explained. "It is available for order through her servant if you like it. There are those who of course choose to make our water girl stand her ground while they drink, testing her fortitude and trust as they cut off her air. Others prefer to bring her very close and allow her hands to wander as they will."

The masked slave had brown eyes and carefully trimmed nails. A birthmark on her right breast. A gasp swept through the crowd as Jacob drew the knife he carried beneath the back waistband of his slacks. The torchlight flashed off the blade as he sliced through the garrote strap. With anger, he noted the deep marks on her throat caused by those who'd done as Belizar described.

Feel her pussy, Jacob. Lyssa's voice echoed in his head. *Obey me. Reach between her legs and feel her.*

Reluctantly, he did. The girl watched him with heavy-lidded eyes that suggested prolonged exposure to inhaling the libation beneath her nose might be as effective as drinking it. She was soaked. At his faintest touch she shuddered, parting her lips.

"Your servant is still young enough to be affected by puritanical qualms, Lady Lyssa." While Belizar's voice suggested he was simply amused by Jacob's reaction, the hard look in his eyes when Jacob turned his attention to him did not.

"But there is a pleasure in that as well," Lady Helga, another Council member, pointed out. "It's intriguing to watch them learn and lose such inhibitions."

Jacob decided that all that was missing was a set of bars dividing the humans from the vampires. And one of those gumball machines which, for a quarter, would provide a small handful of food to feed the zoo animals, or in this case, the zoo humans.

With vicious satisfaction, Jacob tipped the bowl, watched the red fluid rush down the girl's stomach, over her shaved mons and down her thighs to her bare feet. Turning away, he bowed deeply to Lyssa. "I need no such aid," he said. "Just the pleasure of my lady's attention and command will keep me hard more than long enough."

At the appreciative reaction from his audience, Belizar's jaw tightened. But he inclined his head. "Very well. Choose the woman you desire, Irishman."

He'd been a showman most of his adult life. He'd learned enough about vampires to know what they appreciated, though it was a dangerous line to walk. Jacob raised a brow and pivoted more fully toward Lyssa, giving her a deliberate look. A smatter of amusement and applause passed through the group.

"Every man's choice," Lord Uthe called out. "But not an option, servant. Choose from the flower."

Others from outside the canopy had gathered to watch the entertainment, reminding him of his time in the circus, though the performances offered had been nothing like this. Jacob suspected Carnal was out there, but he didn't look for him. He really didn't want to know if the bastard would be watching this.

My lady, would you choose?

She shook her head and surprised him by speaking. "I want to see your choice."

Quelling an uneasy feeling at the lightness of her response, the faint smile on her lips that seemed stiff to him, he began a slow walk around the outer perimeter of the "petals." As he considered each one, he kept in mind the entertainment of his audience. He paused, considered, moved on, increasing tension and speculation. There were some bets being placed.

All the women were beautiful. Their raised haunches had been oiled to a high polish, same as the bodies of the dark-skinned men behind them who had set their fingers against the white flesh of the hips, preparing to drive deep. Either these men were specifically selected for their equipment or the stereotype about black men was exponentially true. It was not going to be an easy entry for most of the women.

Even worse, Belizar was now explaining that the men would be fucking the asses of the women displayed before them. Because of that, each woman selected was a virgin to anal sex, which would add a dose of pain and some anticipatory fear to the mix.

Part of him abhorred it. Part of him was grudgingly fascinated. He himself had been repeatedly aroused by all the games vampires devised to plumb the depths of human sensuality. He couldn't deny the mores of a lifetime had been challenged considerably in his lady's service. Seanna had stated it as much less than a day ago. *"It makes you hot, doesn't it?"*

What he was being commanded to do was an empty, purely physical performance of his cock. It couldn't compare with the deep fulfillment, the perfect solitude of being deep inside his lady while next to the fire blazing in her bedroom or lying in her bed together. But even as he thought it, he knew he couldn't rationalize this moment to the purely physical. Being commanded to perform for his lady's pleasure did have an emotional component to it. It roused a primal fury and lust in him he was incapable of explaining. With her eyes on him, he could get erect, could perform almost any sexual act required of him in public. Lord knew she'd tested him enough to know that.

The most recent memory of it was less than two weeks ago. She'd been at home, for it was daylight, but it was getting near twilight. He'd taken Bran with him on errands and had given him a break in a public park. They'd been running. Stripping off his T-shirt to play tug-of-war with the garment, Jacob had tussled with the dog. When he finally stopped, collapsing onto the grass in a shady group of trees on the edge of the mowed green, he'd felt her wake, reaching out with a mental touch to confirm awareness of his whereabouts.

There'd been a pair of women nearby, having a picnic. He hadn't really noticed them until Lyssa saw them through his eyes. She registered what he had been oblivious to, their surreptitious, appreciative glances. His Mistress had commanded him to lie back on the grass. He'd been covered by distance and the shadow of the tree's canopy so that no one else could see him but them. She'd commanded him to open his jeans, under which he wore nothing, lie there with one hand behind his head and stroke himself with the other as if he thought no one was watching.

Despite his discomfort, his lady had made it a command, her purring voice spurring him on, telling him how wet he was making those avidly watching women who were pretending not to notice so he wouldn't stop. In the end, they were openly staring, and he was staring back, watching all the subtle, lovely signs of arousal. Peaked nipples, hands absently pressing to their throats, touching their own lips. The shift of their bodies, the tightening of thighs.

When he told his lady later he'd expected them to run screaming for the cops about a man exposing himself in the park, Lyssa had merely smiled. "Timing and presentation are everything to a woman, Sir Vagabond. And to vampires."

So now as he strolled with apparent casualness along the diameter of the circle, he let his fingertips graze the bare backs of his petals, his touch whispering along their napes, catching the actual petals scattered there. They were on a slightly raised platform as well to put them at a better angle for being fucked by the waiting black men, so they were right at the level of his hand. Round and round the merry-go-round, slowly. Blond hair, silky brown, deep black. He paused once more by a redhead, then kept going.

Now as he walked, he unbuttoned his shirt, pulled it loose. Stripped off his belt as he removed his trousers and shoes, letting the strap swing from his hand. As he shrugged off the shirt, he held on to it, along with the belt.

When he reached Debra, he was naked. Bending, he took her hands. With his heightened third-mark senses, he knew she was cold, though mainly from nerves. So he brought her to her feet before him and threaded her arms through the sleeves. He looped the belt around her wrists, knotted it so he could place his hand on the joining point to walk through the space she'd just vacated and use the offered shoulder of the man behind her to step onto the dais. By the time they'd done that, another woman took her place as a petal to close the circle again.

The shirt came down to Debra's bare thighs, the open front making a delectable display of the crescents of her breasts, her shaved and oiled mons. He heard some murmuring, sensed the vampires' surprise at his choice to restrain her hands, play Dominant to her.

It was all for show. You intended to choose her all along.

Yes. He answered his lady, picked up on something dark in her thoughts, but couldn't investigate it further as Belizar's voice cut through the silent conversation.

"I'm certain Lord Brian will appreciate your interest in increasing his servant's experience, since he has so little time to do so."

Get on with it, you old bastard, Jacob thought.

So eager, are we?

He glanced toward Lyssa when he heard his lady's acid thought, but she was not looking at him. She was studying Debra intently, somewhat like a cat examining a quivering mouse. She seemed particularly absorbed in the way his shirt hem grazed her thighs.

Debra wasn't cut out for this, and no matter what Seanna said, no amount of training was going to do it. His precognitive ability told him she was one step away from a full-scale panic attack. She would shame her Master, and that terrified her even more. Her hands were shaking under his.

Maybe this was part and parcel of learning to be a servant in the vampire world, but he wasn't sure if he could have done any of it from the beginning if his lady's mind wasn't inside his own, helping him get through it . . .

She is not going to be harmed, Jacob. She's just learning to overcome her inhibitions to serve the pleasure of her Master. What about you, in that park, doing what you thought you couldn't do? You got hard and came solely because of my voice in your mind. Goaded by those women's eyes on your cock, the way they stayed glued to the way your hand was rubbing yourself.

Exactly. I could do that because you were there. It makes a difference. And Debra was a woman. Where the hell was Lord Brian to help steady her? Protect her.

She has a different type of Master. One I'm sure that makes her appreciate you all the more.

My lady?

Tend to your task and stop whining. You're irritating me.

Frowning, he nevertheless had to do as she bid, for Belizar chose to add another element to the mix.

"Over the course of a century or two, Lady Lyssa has taught us all manner of ways to get along with one another, how to mend fences." Belizar flashed Lyssa a smile that made Jacob want to roll his eyes. "There is some animosity between our two servants as a result of their conflict, Lady Lyssa. To get them to shake hands and be in accord again, Malachi will join your servant on the dais. While the lovely Debra takes your servant in her mouth, Malachi will take the other end. As it is obvious she needs some tutelage to understand total surrender, he will apply his sizeable cock to her far too tightly clenched ass. A virgin hole because our esteemed Lord Brian wishes only to fondle the sphincter of his microscope."

More laughter from the Council members. From what Jacob had seen of Brian, he suspected the man would have stood up well to the razzing, perhaps even expected it. Debra, however, was another matter. Her shaking was growing by leaps and bounds.

Jacob managed to keep his reaction passive even as he suppressed the desire to snarl. When Lord Belizar gestured, Malachi moved from his side. The platform started to rise again, taking them up several more feet to increase the sense of being on a stage before the entire courtyard gathering. What little color remained in Debra's cheeks drained out. Her eyes, fastened with intent desperation on Jacob's chest, were getting glassy. He tightened his hold on her.

"Don't you dare faint," he ordered gruffly.

As Malachi came toward the dais, her head began to turn toward him. Jacob took a firmer grip on her bound hands, placing the other hand behind her neck to bring her up against the warmth of his body. Roughly he covered her mouth, demanding the kiss. He put all the seductive charm he had into it, coaxing her lips apart, moving his tongue inside, his fingers playing over the pulse on her wrists. He knew she was a true submissive, because most of the female servants were. So he used that knowledge, administering romantic, tiny caresses of her nape with his fingers, overwhelming her with the sweep of his tongue in her mouth, nibbling on her lips with his teeth. His thumb passed over the place on her throat he suspected was Brian's preferred area because of the faint depressions there. Pressing her body against him, he gave her his heat, let her hear his heartbeat.

"Easy," he murmured onto her lips. "Obey me as you obey your Master and it will be all right. I'll take care of you."

Her eyes sought his, no longer reflecting the self-possession of the scholar but the fear of the woman, grasping at his reassurance.

"Lie down," he said with quiet authority, guiding her so she was on her stomach, lying on the body of the sculpture. Reaching between her thighs, he dragged his fingers through her pussy lips to find her wet despite herself. She rocked against his hand, a soft gasp coming from her. He guided her onto the sculpted erect cock, easing her down onto it as she gave a moan. It stirred the crowd, for Jacob felt the collective energy rising with her arousal. When fully seated on it, her hips were tilted up. The sculpture's knee was bent, splitting the seam of her legs so they had to be braced on either side, positioning her for a perfect anal penetration and allowing her no way to resist the invasion. The statue had a raised hand. Into its palm, he guided her chin so she could take his cock in her mouth at a straight angle. Her breasts hung down, just the tips of her nipples grazing the face of the sculpture, stimulating her further.

The scent from her cunt was getting stronger, even as nervous tears started to trickle down her face. Reluctantly, it reminded him of Seanna's words. She could be tearful and aroused at once, the situation stoking her need to be dominated. She'd allowed Jacob to step into the surrogate role, obviously realizing she needed something to anchor her so she didn't embarrass Brian.

As Malachi was given a hand onto the dais, Jacob spoke in a mutter. "You hurt her, and I swear I will shove that spear up your ass."

Malachi's teeth bared in answer. Jacob noted his nose was almost healed, revealing how long he'd been a third-mark servant. The Mediterranean man's hands immediately went to Debra's buttocks, opening her up and using his thumbs to prod at his destination. He leaned down, putting his lips to her spine as she quivered.

To distract her, Jacob caught his hand in her hair, easing his length between her parted lips. She suckled him instantly, almost too roughly as Malachi apparently probed with his fingers and earned a jerk of response. He sent Jacob an unrepentant grin when Jacob flinched. Amusement swept through the watching vampires.

"An oral bit, if you please," Belizar called out.

"No. She doesn't—"

Jacob's protest was overwhelmed by the supporting calls of the crowd. One of the black men was handed the metal contraption. He gestured Jacob back and Jacob reluctantly complied, forced to watch as the large dark fingers put it around Debra's head, easily quelling her attempts to pull back. The circular metal ring was inserted past the upper and lower bridge of her teeth and buckled to her head so her mouth was kept open wide, allowing a man to slide himself in and out as rapidly and deeply as he wished.

Malachi raised the fingers of his other hand, which he'd swept over her cunt lips, taking them away glistening. "Her tears may be protesting, but her pussy's not," he observed loudly. "New slaves are the sweetest. So afraid of their own responses, so overwhelmed by them. Feed her your cock, Jacob. Let's make her scream together. I want to feel her ripple around me, even as she gags on your big dick."

Jacob registered the shuddering of her body, the quick jerks of her hips. While he abhorred the man's attitude about it, Debra was powerfully stimulated. *By the time she leaves here, she'll have been brought to climax so many times, she'll start internalizing the intense pleasure of being a submissive.* Now he hoped Seanna was right, because he couldn't deny his own response to the situation. He was hard as granite.

He slid his cock back in, felt her lips strain to close over him around the bit. The ease of going unencumbered past her teeth was too tempting. He slid along the wet flat edge of her tongue where it rubbed against the underside of his cock with perfect friction in its restrained state.

He knew the moment Malachi began to enter even without looking, for Debra tensed.

"Tight little dry ass," Belizar's servant said silkily. His voice dropped down low, ensuring his words, like the sudden malevolence in his eyes, were only registered by Jacob. "I'm going to ram you hard, tear that virgin hole so you never forget my cock, never forget that a woman was made to submit. Think you're so smart . . . Well you're not so smart about this, are you?"

Damn the niceties, Jacob was going to tie the man's dick in a knot, after he broke his fucking neck. Debra's voice vibrated against his cock, a sound of pain and fear. He wasn't going to stand by and see a woman brutally raped. No matter his conflicting feelings about the games of Domination and submission and the wavering lines they painted between consent and force, he knew where the line was at this moment. Clear and dark in the sand.

"A pause to the game, please." Lyssa spoke abruptly, halting Malachi's forward progress and Jacob's murderous intentions. "Lord Belizar, I believe you offered me a wild card on this little game of yours."

"I did, Lady Lyssa. What would you suggest to enhance our pleasure?"

"A fourth participant. Of my choosing."

When Belizar inclined his head, Lyssa crooked her finger to someone outside the Council circle, nodding as a silent question was apparently asked and answered. She made the gesture more imperious. The murmuring intensified as Devlin stepped to her side.

"Strip and join Jacob on the dais," she ordered. "He'll tell you what he wishes you to do. Then you all may proceed with Lord Belizar's desire."

Devlin stepped back a respectful distance from Lady Lyssa's divan and bowed. When he stripped off his clothing, he revealed his impressive organ, reminding Jacob of how monstrous the thing was.

At the smatter of applause, Devlin grinned, turned in a dramatic circle to display himself. "They grow 'em big Down Under. When I crack a fat, the ladies run screaming." He winced in the middle of a wink. "Ah, my lady doesn't appreciate my demonstrative nature. She says if I know what's good for me I'll get my arse up on that platform."

Lyssa had given Jacob a tool to use, no pun intended. He had no idea what she wanted him to do with it, or if she just had that perverse vampire curiosity to see *how* he would use it to change the game. Her mind was closed to him. And when she shut down, he was all too aware that usually meant he was in some kind of trouble.

Without any clues to solve that, he focused on the issue at hand. Keeping his cock firmly seated in Debra's mouth, he grimly reflected it was serving as a pacifier of sorts. She was trying to suckle and lick at it as best she could with the bit, such that he had to grit his teeth to focus. Moving his hand over her hair in a part-tender, part-rough caress, he reminded her he was still in charge, her well-being as firmly in his hands as her body was.

Malachi began to step back, his irritated look conveying his displeasure at being replaced and made to perform some lesser role, but Jacob shook his head. "Stay where you are. But don't move yet. You're going to fuck her." God knew he wasn't going to break Debra into anal sex on Devlin's cock.

Jacob met the man's dark eyes. Like a pet who'd been too long with the same Master, Malachi had adopted his lord Belizar's contemptuous stare. Jacob took private, vicious satisfaction in watching it vanish from his face with his next words.

"After you're inside of her, Devlin is going to ram that cock of his up your ass. Then you can fuck Debra to climax. You do anything I even think crosses the line, causes her any pain, I'll tell Devlin to dish you out three times the same until your ass bleeds so thick everyone here could dine on it."

He'd never demanded one man fuck another, but he wasn't allowed to put Malachi's head through the wall.

Perhaps he was not so different from Malachi. The longer he spent in the company of vampires, the more he found himself adapting to the different mores and violent rules of their world. When under the orders of their respective Mistresses, Devlin's rank was far below Jacob's. Jacob had the right to make demands on him in this setting, so he had.

It affected his liking of Devlin not one bit. He anticipated sharing another "stubbie" with him later. Hell, probably a whole "slab" after this. He wanted to know Debra's position on global warming. But right now a whole different set of rules applied.

Devlin seemed to have no difficulty accepting the direction. The affability was gone, and he looked far more dangerous than Jacob had yet seen him. His eyes glittered, the red- and brown-streaked hair falling around the planes of his strong face. Perhaps through Lyssa's communication with Danny, he'd picked up what was going on.

"I like that idea fine," he said, moving a step closer and pressing a bare thigh to the back of Malachi's leg. "Haven't had me a good prison rape in a long time. You're the pretty poster boy of my dreams." Rising on his toes, he put his mouth close to Malachi's ear. "You know the best way to reeducate a dickhead who thinks violence is the proper way to treat a woman? Fuck him until he cries like a little girl."

Malachi trembled with fury and dared a glance at his Master. Jacob saw that Belizar and Lyssa had locked gazes. His lady had that same faint smile on her face, but it did not detract from the coldness of her eyes. If Belizar pulled Malachi out of the game, he was as much as admitting it wasn't a game. Not that anyone here appeared to be under the delusion that their games were ever in fact simply games. Make Malachi stay up here, and he'd get ass fucked by a much lower-ranking servant, a passive insult that Jacob had a feeling was Lyssa's payback for Belizar's earlier affront of Malachi trying to kill him. He wondered if that was the true reason Devlin was up here. Not to ward off harm from Debra, but to settle the unresolved nature of the power play between the two vampires. As he'd been told, the Gathering was an opportunity for new slaves to be taught what it meant to truly submit. Perhaps, like the other vampires, she'd not seen anything wrong with Debra's rough initiation. Perhaps there was no wavering line for Lady Lyssa and the other vampires on the Dominance and submission issue. Maybe there was no line at all.

No. There was a line. He thought of the servant he'd seen being branded earlier. The arousal, the lack of fear. He also remembered his lady's words about Carnal and Melinda. *If I'd known what he was going to do, I'd have stopped him* . . . He let the image and words bolster his belief.

Belizar cut his glance back to Malachi. When Malachi's jaw flexed, Jacob felt a surge of cruel triumph, knew the man had been given the order to stay on the dais. Jacob inclined his head to Devlin.

"I believe"—Devlin took his sizeable cock in one hand and put his other on Malachi's back, pushing him so he had to bend forward, taking him inch by resisting inch to a curve over Debra's body—"you have some lubricating to do, hmm?"

Malachi reluctantly lifted the crystal bottle that had been provided. He uncorked it, drizzled the oil between Debra's buttocks.

"Work it into her now. Easy. Very easy. There's a pleasure to initiating a lady to a proper arse fucking. She'll come like she's never come before, eh, darling?"

Jacob blessed the sexy, soothing cadence of Devlin's accent as he felt Debra's lips convulse on him, her hips lift in an unmistakable welcoming move. Her eyes lifted and locked on Jacob's face, however, as if the contact was giving her the courage to believe he would do as he said. Take care of her.

He began to work himself in her mouth again, dividing her attention between the two stimuli of taking him into one opening while they prepared the other. The straining movement of her hips indicated her pussy was busy milking the sculpture's shaft. Her toes flexed on the dais, pushing herself up and down in involuntary response.

"There you go." As Malachi began to ease into her opening, Devlin put his hands on the man's hips, a warning. "All the way in, one slow inch at a time."

Debra groaned, vibrating against Jacob, making it difficult to focus. The undulation of her tongue became more frenetic, despite the fact it was restricted somewhat by the hold of the bit.

When Malachi made it past Debra's inner muscles, moving carefully, gently, Devlin took a more secure grip on the side of the man's throat and waist and shoved his own now-oiled cock between Malachi's cheeks. Malachi gasped, his powerful thighs trembling, his eyes tearing. A curse slipped between his lips.

"Oh, there we are, balls deep now. Good thing your Master's stretched you before or we might have had some messiness then. Bet that burns like a son of a bitch, don't it?"

Malachi grunted and Devlin started crowding him, putting his thighs in tight behind the other man, applying pressure as Malachi began to sink, slowly, gradually into Debra's rectum. As Devlin rocked, Debra writhed. Jacob gripped her hair hard, stroking in and out of her, trying to control his own reaction at the feel of her wet mouth forced to take him in deep. Her hips rose to meet Malachi's as he did his task as it was meant to be done, kept focused by Devlin's slow pumping in and out of him.

Debra made a strangled sound. "Not until I come," Jacob ordered. "Your Master trained you. You know the rules. Don't shame him."

She made a noise, half assent, half sob, in her throat. As Malachi fucked her ass, her wobbling breasts were rubbed in a ruthless friction against the face of the statue, the ridges of its brow and nose. Her nipples were erect and hard, such that Jacob indulged himself by reaching down and pinching one. Her hot breath expelled, gusting against his balls. He increased the power of his strokes, matching Devlin. As Devlin had gotten well seated, Malachi had adjusted and now they were moving in sync, Malachi losing some of his fury to the power of forcibly provoked lust.

Jacob's control slipped another notch as his Mistress fed him the sight of it through her eyes. He didn't know if she wanted him to see them as she was seeing them, or if she was too aroused to guard her thoughts, but the effect was the same.

The torchlight had been angled to focus on the dais, making the musculature of the three men gleam. Devlin had a broad, rippling back, tight, hard buttocks that were rhythmically clenching as he fucked Malachi. Malachi's arm muscles stood out in cords as he neared climax and gripped Debra's ass even harder. His body curved over her, his chest rubbing against her lower back, his face almost pressed into her nape. Debra's mouth was held open, restrained by the metal bit, her body draped and spread over the statue, her pussy impaled on the alabaster white cock so her juices were running down it like a fountain against the sleek marble. Malachi's big cock moved in and out of her, her thighs spread so wide the attendees could see her stretched pink openings.

And then there was Jacob, his cock glistening as he pulled it out of Debra's mouth almost to the head and then shoved back in again, distending her cheeks, making her throat work, her helpless fingers curling against the restraint of his belt.

As if this wasn't enough to make him spurt, the black men, their oiled bodies gleaming, had taken hold of the "petals" and lifted their hips so they were straight legged. Each woman's ankle crossed over the woman next to her, an organic binding that would make the vibration of their movements ripple throughout the whole circle. The men drove their cocks in as the women's voices, aroused by what was going on above them, cried out in unison. The noise rose and connected them, creating an aphrodisiac Jacob suspected was far stronger than what had been around the slave girl's neck.

The women threw their heads back at the same time, the flow of hair like the toss of a sheet of silk in the air, a rippling wave of multiple colors. The men wrapped their big hands in it like reins, holding them at painful, revealing angles, breasts hanging down loosely and quivering from the shock as the men's cocks pounded into them.

The dais was turning—when had that happened? His gaze was full of the tableau from every angle, thanks to his lady and his own eyes. A dozen pale female asses, bobbing up. Dark, tightly packed ass muscles clenching as the men beat their cocks into the tight rosebud channels. Devlin's head dropped back on his powerful shoulders as he shot his load into Malachi. Malachi cried out as it pushed him over. Debra's gasp, her desperate look, got through to Jacob as she worked herself furiously on that stone cock.

"Please . . ." the word was garbled with her mouth full of him.

"Come," Jacob snapped, and she screamed as her body instantly released, a flush sweeping over her skin as Malachi continued to fuck her, drawing out the sensation. Jacob came against the back of her hoarsely crying throat, reveling in the vibration he felt against the sensitive head. He kept going, stretching her jaws, knowing they must be aching, but knowing that, too, was part of the pleasure of being a sub. Pushing you past the point where you thought you could go.

After all, his Mistress had done it to him. Again. The long, continuous shot of his semen down Debra's throat told him he hadn't failed her.

As one, the men in the circle below pulled out and took their organs in hand for one, two quick strokes. The women spun around on their knees, their arms braced behind them, knees spread wide, bodies rising in an arch, heads tipped back. The men's release shot against their breasts, so much like a fountain it couldn't help but impress the assembled gathering.

The viscous white fluids spilled down the women's flat bellies, pooled in their navels and slowed like molasses, drawing the eyes down to the smooth mounds. Jacob's cock convulsed once more and Debra moaned, taking him to the last drop. Brian didn't know what a lucky bastard he was.

"Jesus," Devlin gasped, propping an elbow in between Malachi's shoulder blades. Reaching down, he stroked the side of Debra's hair and then even rubbed the back of Belizar's servant's neck with an absent affection, as if they'd just been two squabbling siblings. He was studying the aftermath of the "petals" and black men below them. "Can you imagine how awful it was to practice that? My woman would have had to wear protective goggles. My cock's got no sense of direction at all."

Malachi pressed his forehead to the center of Debra's back. Jacob heard a grim chuckle from him. "I suppose the only way you're going to beat my ass in a sport is by fucking it. Get that mutation out of me, you great fucking horse."

"Well, you asked for it by being a right fucking arsehole, didn't you? When she can think straight again, I think you better offer the lady an apology and a drink."

When Devlin removed himself and helped Malachi straighten so he could pull out, the conversation continuing between them, Jacob knelt before Debra. Unbuckling the bit, he eased it out of her mouth, soothing her jaws with his fingers as he did so. Her nose was running, her eyes tearing. He took a section of his shirt and dabbed at her. "All right, then?"

She nodded, her eyes full of wonder and exhaustion. He doubted she could even rise from the sculpture.

"You were beautiful. Outstanding. Where's your Master?" he asked. Worthless piece of shit that he was.

"Makeshift lab. He's still testing some things."

Devlin looked down at himself in disgust. "Men," he muttered. "Vile creatures that we are. I'm going to go clean up. Now my lady's lovely arse is clean as—"

"Devlin." Lady Daniela had risen from her cushions. Her eyes were alight with rebuke, as well as bright lust, a promise that partially explained why Jacob's new friend was suddenly in a hurry to excuse himself.

In that regard, Jacob noted that their verbal exchange had gone largely unnoticed. After raising their glasses in tribute to the performance, the Council—in fact most of the attendees—had been impatient to find an outlet for the overwhelming wave of lust that had saturated the courtyard. He was surrounded by an out-and-out orgy, much less aesthetic than what had been orchestrated for their entertainment, but no less stimulating. Many vampires were taking their servants outright, or allowing themselves to be serviced the way Jacob had been. There were groupings of three and four, even five, and the sight couldn't help but begin to stir him to life again.

His gaze found his lady, still reclining on her divan, watching him, her dark eyes glittering. A still point in the storm. There was empty space around her, for no vampire would dare to approach her uninvited, no matter how strong his lust.

Though he wanted to go to her, he was mindful of his duty to Debra. Helping her down from the platform, he freed her hands from the belt to rub her wrists. He pulled on his slacks, but when she made to take off the shirt, he shook his head, buttoning up several of the buttons, pushing away her protesting hands. Framing her face, he kissed her forehead, calling one of the masked servants to his side. "Escort this lady back to Lord Brian's quarters to await his return."

To her, he murmured, "Council's busy. Keep your head down, get out of here and you won't be missed. You've had enough for one night. Put a hand over your mouth like you're nauseous and no one will stop you. No shame to it. You've earned it. Screw 'em."

She nodded, her expression too dazed to argue. He slid her hand through the masked servant's arm. Once he made sure the man understood his orders, he sent her off with a gentle pat to her bottom, a reassurance he felt she needed right now. When she reclaimed her Mensa-shattering mind, he'd enjoy teasing her about it.

Now all he wanted was to be near his lady and hope not to attract any more attention tonight.

But as he moved toward her, she deliberately tilted her head away from him, exchanging a comment with Lord Uthe, apparently the only other vampire not engaged in carnal activity. When Jacob knelt at her feet in just the slacks and attempted to lay a hand on her foot as he had before, she drew it away without looking in his direction. Puzzled, he rested his hand on his knee, waiting. She glanced at him over her shoulder.

"Where's your shirt?"

"I let Debra keep it," he said, knowing full well she had seen Debra's departure. Was she hallucinating again?

Before he could blink, she'd sat up on the divan and had her hand on his throat in an unforgiving tight grip, restricting his air flow. Her nails dug into his flesh, bringing him nearly off his knees. "I see most things quite clearly, slave."

He had to force himself not to try and pry her loose or defend himself in any way. It was always a struggle to submit to her when she was in this mood, but apparently his attempt to do so now ratcheted up her temperament further. It swept through him like heat from a volcano blast.

~

Good. He could feel her fury. Lyssa wanted him to feel it. She *was* angry. Enraged. Not because Jacob had rammed his cock down a woman's throat in front of her. Not because he'd come as a result of her wet tongue and the overwhelming vibrations of sex all around him. Not even because he'd thought Brian a very lucky man. All of that meant nothing.

He'd championed Debra. Protected her. Of course, championing and protecting a woman were second nature to Jacob. Lyssa wasn't special in that regard, and she didn't need his protection and championing anyway, damn it. She'd expected no less than the ferocity he'd shown when Malachi threatened the girl, though the ruthlessness of how he dealt with it had surprised her as much as she'd felt it surprise him. Perhaps like Thomas, he was learning a little too much from his Mistress.

No, what bothered her was that Jacob had *chosen* Brian's servant.

Out of a dozen women, he'd chosen her, as if he had a preference for her above the others. She was cold, so he'd put his shirt on her. He'd stood there before her, before this whole assembly, as if they did not exist. As if Lyssa did not exist. He'd threaded her arms through the sleeves, freed her hair from it and took her hands, bound them in the belt in a simultaneously uncompromising and gentle way that had gotten the juices of every woman watching flowing. As Lyssa had watched them stand there, her Irishman and the shy scientist, she'd seen the potential chemistry, the type of girl he would have loved, even married if his destiny hadn't taken him to a vampire queen. Debra or someone like her could have given him children, a lifetime of quiet, domestic and enduring love. Lyssa had given him a death sentence. She hated it, hated the tender way he'd treated Debra, the regard he'd shown her . . .

It didn't matter that she knew his thoughts, his heart. There were some things that were instinct, not rational, and no amount of mind reading would convince her they were false.

"My lady." Lord Uthe's quiet voice. Not interfering, for another vampire would never interfere with a disciplining between Mistress and servant, but he was tactfully drawing her attention to the fact Jacob's breath was laboring.

She dropped him. Slapped him. It startled Jacob so much that for a moment, anger lost footing to hurt. While he bowed his head, he sensed Uthe's too shrewd regard and cursed his inability to mask his reaction more quickly.

"For having your servant such a short time, lady," Uthe observed carefully, "his confidence in your bond appears extraordinarily strong. Perhaps it's time you consider another lover, if not a husband. You know servants can get the wrong idea of their place in a vampire's household quickly."

At least Uthe had a strong enough sense of self-preservation he didn't imply that Lyssa was subject to such influences. Jacob expected she would have incinerated the other vampire in the mood he felt pouring off her. But his lady respected Uthe. He was a peer, while Jacob was the mortal apparently not worth even her attention as she turned her back on him, leaving him on his knees, trying to breathe again.

"My servant has simply been overwhelmed by all the stimuli here. I'll take care of reminding him of his place. Thank you for your advice, Lord Uthe." The frostiness of her voice seemed to reassure the man, for he moved away with a nod, giving her privacy to deal with the infraction she perceived her servant had committed.

"That was my shirt, bought with my money," she snapped.

Jacob wanted to rise, dare her to knock him back down. He didn't want to have her standing over him as she did now, rising off the divan, but he fought through the anger, knowing there were eyes on them. "A shirt? I'll be happy to pay for the shirt, my lady. If that's what's truly bothering you."

What the hell is *bothering you?*

You care for her. You chose her. You looked at her . . . the way you've looked at me.

Like he would protect her, no matter what the cost was to himself.

Lyssa turned away from him, not waiting to see his reaction to such ridiculous thoughts. He was human. Debra was human. Servants were servants. She'd never demanded a servant be wholly monogamous, damn it.

My lady. When his hand brushed her side, she didn't turn, but she didn't move away. His grip curled around her forearm, slid to her wrist, then to her hand, his fingers twining with hers. Suddenly she didn't want him on his knees, didn't want him like that, even as the tiny part of her brain that was still rational knew it was better for him to be so.

Despite the fury that had rolled through him like a wave at her contempt, Jacob had stayed on his knees, demonstrating his loyalty was greater than his pride. But it wasn't his loyalty she doubted.

She turned. His shoulders were bare, still gleaming from the perspiration he'd generated. She knew every line of that elegant body, knew how it felt pressed against her while his cock slid in and out of her pussy. She knew the many expressions of his blue eyes, the taste of his lips. She didn't want to share him with another woman like Debra. One too close to what he truly deserved.

She didn't want to share him with any woman. Ever again.

Studying her face, he slowly rose. Which put him much closer, standing before her, holding her hand, their bodies almost touching. Her breath was rapid as she tried to keep a handle on her reaction, but she knew he saw everything. During their performance, even as her anger built, so did her desire, and when Jacob had come, when Debra had screamed, she could have come simply by imagining Jacob stroking her deep, hard.

"Come with me." He altered his position so he stood beside her. Lifting her hand, he moved them into a sedate walk where she appeared to be leading, rather than him pulling her along in a spurt of physical reaction she could feel thrumming through his muscles, the wake of the emotional response rippling through him.

It reminded her of a day he'd built a rack to equally space and anchor the dogs' food bowls. The structure would catch and divert the overflow she always complained about crunching underfoot. So excited by the modifications he'd made, he'd caught her hand and tugged her through the kitchen to the side door to see it, making her laugh at his eagerness. He'd been like a six-foot-tall child who'd forced her into a trot to keep up with his long legs.

Her lover, her innocent child, her servant. Her protector.

He navigated her past the wide variety of very intimate couplings occurring and took her to the outskirts of the tents, to the canopies of the craftspeople. At first she thought he was bringing her to the jeweler whose collar she had described, but instead he stopped before the blacksmith. The man was in Lord Mason's employ and helped maintain the grounds year-round. He also cared for the two Arabians Lyssa knew Mason stabled on the property.

"My Mistress needs to punish her servant," Jacob said quietly. "Somehow he has made her doubt he lives only to serve her."

The man nodded dispassionately and gestured to the myriad irons displayed on velvet.

"The larger brands hurt more, my lady," he explained. "They of course leave no permanent mark unless you use your blood. That also intensifies the pain considerably, but it will heal to a scar on a fully marked servant in less than a night's time. You will not find your use of him hampered."

"I beg you to use your blood, my lady," Jacob said, looking into her face as if there was nothing else for him. Lyssa felt like weeping. "Set your hand on me, brand me as yours so you will have no doubts. Wherever you desire."

"When you wish to do it, my lady, each of these designs is already in the fire." The blacksmith nodded to the vat behind him. "They're sketched in the handle. Simply take your preference and hold it to his flesh as long as you like."

The man was then called to explain some of his other offerings to another vampire overlord. Jacob's hands went to his trousers and he dropped them, leaving him naked from neck to ankles before her.

If it will ease your mind and keep you from having a shred of doubt in your soul, my lady, then do as you will.

Despite her wish to appear indifferent, the vision of Debra in his shirt rose in Lyssa's mind. She knew it was pathetic. Childishly dangerous and cruel. But if she didn't hurt him, test his willingness to suffer for her, this feeling would not abate in her chest. And she didn't care for the feeling one bit. She wanted it gone.

Hands laced behind your head.

He did it without hesitation, though he certainly knew what she was capable of doing, where she might choose to place the brand. Bringing her hand to her lips, she bit into the Venus mound of her palm with one fang.

He waited. His jaw firm, his eyes steady on hers. She found herself perversely aroused as if she were on the pinnacle of climax, even as the pain radiating from her heart made it seem as if a bed of nails pierced her insides. He was aroused, too. In his thoughts she saw his memory of the branding he'd witnessed earlier, how it had intrigued him in a disquieting way he hadn't expected. Seeing him getting harder at the idea only fueled her need to mark him this way. Claim him visibly.

Lifting the closest brand from the fire, she let the blood run down her palm and drip onto the white-hot metal. Those blue eyes never wavered. Reaching up, she curled her hand on the back of his neck, under the soft hair. Locking her green eyes with his, she pressed the brand to the inside of his left hipbone, above the pubic area.

His face contorted with the effort to remain silent, his upper body going rigid. The muscles drew up tight and hard, close to the skin. His hands became fists behind his head, the biceps flexing to the consistency of smooth rock. As his fingers clenched, her hand curved on his neck was drawn in to the bond, his fingers holding hers, locking them together in a knot of reaction. It reflected the torturous snarl in her heart, the way she'd felt watching him and Debra.

His flesh was burning, tears glistening in his eyes from the effort of maintaining his stillness. Several times tonight she'd dwelled on the fact that he was *her* servant. It had served as a reassurance, something to bolster her strength and courage. With this act, he was telling her he knew he was hers as well. One hundred percent, irrevocably. As a human, man, lover, as a living, breathing being. He considered all of it *only* hers, to do with as she would.

He'd hurt her by doing what he'd been told, in that unique way that made him who he was. The man she wanted like no man or vampire she'd ever met. In return, she'd hurt him deliberately, slapped him, forced him to prove himself, punished him for making her feel this burning pain in her heart she didn't understand.

With an oath, she pulled the brand from him. She extricated her fingers from his while he gasped, holding the pose she'd demanded and managing the pain. He couldn't help but capture attention. A powerful man standing before his Mistress, his slacks a soft pool at his feet, the upper body displayed in fine detail by his subservient position with the hands locked behind the head. But that was all physical. Being a slave, subject to another's will voluntarily with all one's heart, was not defined by postures or brands. It was in everything he did, and she'd come to count on it. Until tonight, she'd never let him know how much, but he'd known just how to answer her fears. She was a fool.

Her gaze coursed down to the brand. For the next few hours until it healed, the pain of it would be fierce. She'd placed the brand at his hip because she wanted to have her hands on it when she rode him, scrape her nails over it. If she took him in her mouth, she would abrade it with her hair. She'd wanted it close to his cock so he'd always know to whom that powerful organ belonged, along with the rest of him.

"An unusual choice, my lady," the blacksmith said, returning to them. "As a permanent mark."

It was a Christian cross.

Stepping forward, she ran her fingers lightly over it. Jacob sucked in a pain-filled breath, but because he knew his pain aroused her, she didn't stop, the rising agony in her breast an odd contrast with the gentleness of her touch, the razor edge of her nails. "Perhaps I should have chosen something else." Her voice was strange to her, almost broken, and Mason's man gave her an odd look.

Jacob shook his head and lowered his hands. Brushing one along her hair, he cupped the line of her face. "A symbol of faith, my lady. You couldn't have picked a better one, for my heart is faithful only to you. You are my religion."

It was also a symbol of sacrifice. Taking on her sins. The insidious whisper from her own mind had the power to gut her.

She drew her head back from his touch, giving him a sharp look. In response, Jacob returned his hands to his head, dissipating the curiosity of the blacksmith. Taking the edges of his slacks in her hands, she brought them back up, zipped, fastened and belted them, cinching the strap in tight until she earned a grunt of pain. Smoothing her hand over his cock, she fondled his testicles. Knowing the brand was burning fire under the tight yoke of the belt even as he began to get hard again under her touch sparked other needs.

Gods, Jacob was right. She was a piece of work. She knew Jacob had wrestled with the possibility that her brief moments of vulnerability toward him might just be the progress of the disease, not real. She found she couldn't tolerate the idea of that doubt. Or the conflicting feelings he was making her feel right now.

"You're forgiven," she said abruptly. Nodding to the blacksmith, she handed him a folded bill, a tip for his service. Then she pivoted on her heel with deliberate regal indifference and moved away from her servant.

Jacob didn't know which was worse. The throb of the brand or his continued failure to make her understand. Maybe the two things were the same, one a physical manifestation of the emotional.

Everything she let him offer her was a gift to him, not a sacrifice. Her willingness to let him be with her forever was the Paradise he'd always sought. The emptiness that had followed him throughout his life had dissipated the night she'd given him the third mark, gone as if it had never haunted him. And yet she couldn't accept what that meant to them both.

She'd always been a woman whose relationships were fraught with politics and often peril. Perhaps Thomas's beliefs had gilded their memories, making them believe what they wanted to believe. However, to know his bond to her was true he only had to remember the present, the handful of weeks they'd had since he'd become her servant.

He'd expected her to be a queen, an infuriatingly arrogant female vampire, but there were many things he hadn't expected.

Her watching him when she thought he didn't know. While he was doing repairs, cooking, reading. He'd even sensed her presence sometimes when he napped, a lazy, pleasurable vision at the edges of his dreams.

Finding her fast asleep by a window. *The Secret Life of Bees* had been open in her lap as the rain trickled down the stained glass behind her, painting her pale face in translucent rainbows of color.

Hiking her dress around her knees like a young girl to squat barefoot in a rain puddle. All for the pleasure of catching a frog and holding the creature in the palm of her hand. She'd coaxed him closer to dump the hapless amphibian down the front of his shirt. Then she fished it out to spare the disgruntled animal harm. Her fingers had caressed, girlishness disappearing into a wild sensuality that had them drenched and coupling on the back lawn. He remembered rain drumming on his bare shoulders, her heels clutched over his hips, her body arched so he could suckle rainwater off her throat.

To hell with it. As she left the courtyard, he cursed under his breath and went after her.

The stone defiles that allowed exit from the courtyard were strung with fairy lights to guide the way. Jasmine flowers woven into the cords allowed vampires to be guided by their scent. In this corridor there was an alcove with a wall fountain installed. An elegant frieze had been propped behind the bowl in the hollowed-out area, depicting a medieval lady among a meadow of stone flowers.

His lady had stopped at the frieze, her fingers resting on the lip of the bowl of water. The area was narrow and dim, providing privacy, the shadows protecting them from too close a scrutiny. Good.

He didn't expect his approach to be equally camouflaged, but when he caught her slender arm by the elbow and whipped her around, her green eyes widened in startled reaction.

While she'd felt him coming up behind her, Lyssa hadn't expected this. She'd assumed he would stand quietly behind her, awaiting her cue of where she wanted to go next, what she wanted of him. She'd expected him to try to soothe the tides of her emotions stirred up by his branding, his touching of Debra. Instead, he yanked her up to her toes and took her mouth with his own, giving her a tide of passion so strong it went beyond usual response into the realm of a blood bond. Her hand clutched the edge of the stone fountain, cracked it as her grip convulsed in reaction. Catching that hand, he unerringly put it on his hip, right over where the brand was, squeezing his hand over hers so her fingers dug in, causing a ripple of response to shudder through his body. Even as the pain shot through him, he gathered her more firmly to him with an arm cinched around her waist, so close his fingers wrapped around her hip and grazed the edge of her stomach, pressing on her sensitive navel region beneath the thin silver dress. Through it, she could feel all the heat of him. Every hard, insistent curve of muscle and the press of his groin. When he raised his head at last, his eyes were blue fire, made incandescent by the lights, his mouth a hard line.

"Only you, my lady. I'm all yours." *Say it to me and mean it. How could any woman take a man away from Lady Elyssa Wentworth? Say it.*

"Mine," she whispered.

"All of it. Not just this." He increased the pressure of his pelvis against her, making her thighs tremble. "Nor this." He inclined his head, indicating his mind. "All of it. Now tell me why the hell you would ever get a daft notion otherwise, woman? Just because I chose to protect an innocent girl."

His kiss had swept away her doubts. Now the impudent comment restored her fully to herself. She pushed away from him, giving him a reproving look even as she let her fingers linger at that place just below his belt.

"I don't have to explain things to you, Sir Vagabond," she responded, tossing back her hair. "You'll do well to remember your place."

But he'd expected—no, demanded—that she mark him, place another visible sign of ownership on him. His thoughts were tangled in her mind, giving her images she couldn't ignore. He was hers. He wanted her, needed her. He cared nothing for anyone but her.

I love you, my lady.

Capturing her hand, he brought it to his lips. Then he laid her palm meaningfully over his heart.

"That's all I ask you to remember as well, my lady. My place is with you. Only you."

17

After that, the temptation to pass the evening tangled in sheets with Jacob was almost too much to resist. There was an animal edge to her lust she knew she couldn't afford to let control her tonight. But as difficult as it was to resist the need to sate the desire he'd roused, she knew it was the emotions he could evoke that had too much power over her. She had to keep herself balanced, so she made them both return to the festivities.

Even so, throughout the rest of the evening, she stayed in close communication with her servant, seeing things through his eyes, hearing his verbal responses as well as sensing his less articulated ones as they worked together as one mind. In its own way, it was as deeply pleasurable as having his body.

She was pleased to find a majority of the Council members prepared to confirm asylum for her fugitives. Not permanently, as she'd wished, but they were amenable to a twenty-five-year moratorium. The formal vote would occur at Court after the Ball tomorrow night.

She also heard snippets of conversations confirming what she already suspected: Carnal and his kind were rapidly gaining support for their belief that immortality made vampires omnipotent and beyond the laws of nature. While it had begun among the younger, made vampires, she was disturbed to hear it gaining ground in more mature ears, those who had not acquired the power or territory they felt they deserved. They believed they could rule the humans and become the dominant species.

At yesterday's Council briefing Belizar had brushed aside her and Uthe's exhortations to address the problem before it got out of control. Feeding on the same arrogance as Carnal, Belizar was too confident in the Council's power.

After tomorrow night, she would no longer be part of that battle. Perhaps it was the frustrated helplessness in that knowledge, or the dwindling sense of her own self, but she found the savage desire to link with Jacob surged up as if it had never been banked when she finally allowed him to escort her back to her rooms.

Almost as soon as the door shut, she tore off her dress, revealing the sheer gray lingerie beneath it. The lingerie he'd picked out and put on her with caressing, teasing hands hours before. When he reached for her, she shoved him down on his back on the bed, tying his hands to the rail with a strip of the dress before she took him in her hand, squeezing the hard, pulsing length of him.

He fought her, perhaps sensing her desire for that and perhaps still riding his own frustration with her earlier mood, but before he could yank against the binding to the point it cut off circulation, she removed the panties and bra and straddled him in a quick, lithe move. As she slammed herself down onto him, her thighs spreading wide to take him in hard and deep, her cunt coming in contact with his pelvis, she watched his eyes go vibrant, his mouth tighten. His muscles strained, his upper torso curving up and making it easier for her hands to touch his chest, his flat stomach. His youth, his strength and pure life. All hers, tragically and miraculously both.

She fucked him, pure and simple, growling as she did so. At one point, she could almost feel that feral part of her wanting to metamorphose, let the talons come forth and slice ribbons out of his skin. Since she'd not completely lost her control, she settled for her fingernails, but she was ruthless with them. Marking his chest, his shoulders, listening to him groan in reaction, feeling his cock harden even further inside her as she bent and licked up the smeared blood, stabbing him with her fangs. He cried out when she raked her nails across the brand. But still he urged her on, the Irish in his voice as he told her to fuck him, fuck him hard, the way she wanted. The way he wanted.

Her flesh spasmed against his rigid flesh, the climax roaring over her. Crying out like a she wolf, long and low, she pounded down on him so her breasts moved generously with her movements. When she craved the press of his fingers on her hips, she shredded the restraint, sparking off the iron headboard with her bloody nails. He was ready, rearing up to grip her hip with one hand, taking possession of her breast with the other, his mouth suctioning over her nipple. As her moan elevated to a scream, Jacob bit and came hard inside her, holding her fast on him, letting her feel the electric shock of those fluids jetting on the sensitive areas inside that only wanted more, more, more. Even as she thought she was going to die from the pleasure of it.

But when his warm, sleeping body curved behind her and she was alone with her thoughts in the dark, the disturbing revelation intruded again.

She had no more battles to fight.

Since she'd realized she had the Delilah virus, all her energy had been focused on bolstering the Council and surviving long enough to see her people and territory protected. There was nothing else she could do now that wouldn't take more time than she had.

All she had time to face was her own death.

As she considered that, over a thousand years of remarkable images pattered against her memory like a quiet summer rain. Rex, Thomas, her parents. The unnamed knight. Jun . . . So many come and gone. So much she'd seen and experienced. There were vampires here who had fought at her side during the territory wars, willing to kill to see Council rule instituted and enforced because they believed, as she did, that a harmonious balance with the human world would ensure the survival and prosperity of their species.

There'd been vampires, humans and others who captured her attention and remained in her memory because of an admirable action or a simple, witty remark that made an impression. She'd even been intimate with a handful or so of the vampires here, before Rex. Nothing that lasted, but nice memories. Tonight would be the last time she would see any of them. At least in this lifetime.

Such thoughts wafted like fog through her predusk doze and followed her into a deeper sleep where they became vivid dreams. So when Jacob woke her in the early evening to prepare for the Ball, it was perhaps no wonder she woke with a knot of anxiety in her lower stomach. She wondered if he sensed it, explaining why he watched her with such close concern as he helped her dress. He said little, dispensing his lingering caresses and quiet murmurs about mundane things that helped steady her nerves. When he finished helping her prepare her appearance, she told him she would go on to the Ball early. He could join her when he was dressed.

He simply nodded, brushing his lips alongside her throat as he made one last adjustment to her dress. "I'll be there, my lady."

Reaching up, she pressed her hand against the side of his cheek, holding him still against her neck a moment before she released him and moved quickly away before he could lift his head and she'd see his eyes in the mirror. His solitary reflection.

She sensed there was something going on in his head, but if she was too fragile to look into his eyes, she knew she was far too fragile to look into his mind.

~

So now she stood on an elevated platform where tables and chairs had been arranged so those not dancing could get a better view once the dancing started. Right now there were only monumental amounts of milling. Political positioning, seductive flirting, friendly acquaintances renewing ties . . .

As she stood there, the nostalgia she anticipated feeling gave way to that disquieting roil in her lower belly again, making for a stew of simmering emotions. She found herself wishing she'd waited for Jacob. She would have liked to feel the reassurance of his presence at her back.

What she really wanted was to be with someone with whom she

had a connection. A connection achieved without effort, words or even thought. Who understood where her mind was right now. Jacob was that person, though she knew there was no logic to why she felt that way. He certainly wasn't over a thousand years old. But when she was with him, she felt like he'd always been with her, through every step, every century.

Carnal was talking to a few of the type she'd seen too many of last night. Young, made vampire overlords impatient with things as they were, hungering for change just so they could feel important, a part of something. So much to learn, and yet they would burn down their school before the lessons could be taught. Such was the way of the world, and of youth.

If it were not Carnal standing with them, she supposed she would feel indulgent toward them instead of edgy, wary. She wondered if her uneasy feelings were like a grounded boat captain come to the edge of a river to watch the boats glide past. She'd once been a part of that flow, but those times had passed. The flow might change somewhat because of her absence, but it would still flow forward. She had to believe that. *You are not God, my lady.* Jacob had said that to her once or twice. Everything ended, even her.

"There you are." Lady Daniela's arm slipped through hers. "Everyone down there assumes you're up here making your dance partner decision, examining us all like we're insects under a microscope. I've never seen so many male vampires preening. Checking their hair, their breath . . . the fit of their trousers."

Perhaps Danny was the next best thing to Jacob. They'd met at a Gathering, Danny's first. She'd gravitated toward Lyssa despite their differences in rank as if they were two inseparable schoolgirl friends, and Lyssa had surprised herself by welcoming it.

Lyssa smiled. "Male vampires are far too arrogant to be self-conscious. Even if they could see themselves in a mirror, they'd never use one."

"Hmm . . . that's the truth. That overlord from Florence needs a better servant. He's needed to blow his nose for the past two days. Every time I talk to him I want to tell him he has a pea factory growing out of his nostrils."

"Oh, gods, that's far too graphic." Lyssa covered an undignified snort of laughter with her hand.

"But so true." Lady Daniela's gaze shifted, stilled. Her eyes sparkled appreciatively. "However, on the brighter side, it looks to me there's a human servant putting them all to shame this year. The male vampires are fair seething about it."

Lyssa rolled her eyes. "Danny, if you don't stop fawning over that cocky servant of yours, he's going to be hopelessly spoiled."

"Cocky is a way to describe Devlin, on several different levels. He's one of a kind, the cheeky bastard. But . . ." Danny adjusted her stance, and with her arm through Lyssa's, she forced her to turn toward one of the arched entranceways. "Not my servant, dearest. I'm talking about *yours*."

She hadn't known what Jacob was wearing tonight. After confirming early in their relationship he had the ability to attire himself appropriately without guidance, she'd found she liked being surprised by it, to enjoy the impact on her senses when he appeared.

He'd outdone himself.

The room was filled with vampire males who emanated otherworldly beauty. Some of it was glamour, but most was not. Generating glamour for humans was far easier than for other vampires, and for the most part, it wasn't necessary. Whatever the genetic makeup of vampirism, it was disposed to making their species exceptionally attractive. Perhaps it was evolution, a helpful mechanism for attracting their prey. It was a reassuring indication they were somehow part of the natural world, not an exception to it as legend and nightmare folklore liked to depict.

Jacob was handsome; there was no denying that. But as she'd known from their first meeting, it was more than that. Put physical human beauty against a vampire's and it could not compare. But his charisma, the quiet self-possession, the incredible intelligence and resourcefulness . . . the many talents he wielded, some of them unexpectedly dangerous and deadly, all somehow integrated into his physical appearance in a way devastating to the female senses. Put that in a tuxedo and Lyssa was sure she wasn't the only woman in the room whose breath had caught in her throat.

He was tall enough to pull off the swallowtail coat he'd chosen. Perfectly pleated dark slacks, dress shoes that shone. Black studded shirt instead of white. He'd chosen a Nehru collar with a white satin ribbon edging that left his neck unencumbered by a tie. His hair, so often tousled at home because of his charming habit of raking his hands back through it as he worked, was brushed to a silk mane that feathered across his high forehead. The trim moustache and beard gleamed copper under the chandeliers, attracting her attention to his lips as it always did, the softness contrasting with the firm manner in which he held them.

She raised a brow at Daniela's chuckle. "What?"

"Nothing." Danny made an innocent face. "I just asked if you thought Lord Belizar might do karaoke for us tonight."

Lyssa blinked. She experienced trepidation at being caught so baldly besotted until Daniela gave her a droll look, reminding her that Australian vampires were far more laid-back than their European and Eastern cousins. And that Danny was very young and irrepressible, by vampire standards. "You responded"—Danny cleared her throat and did a credible imitation of Lyssa's manner— " 'Undoubtedly.' "

"My apologies, Lady Daniela." Lyssa made the attempt. "My mind must have been on tonight's Council Court. There will be many weighty affairs discussed."

Danny shot her a look. "Undoubtedly, my lady."

Even as Lyssa elbowed her with a smile, her gaze was pulled back to Jacob.

As if she needed another reason to be captivated by him, he'd found her instantly and waited until she met his gaze to proceed into the room. While every servant in the room had a link with a Mistress or Master, he acknowledged her visibly, first and foremost, and waited for her attention to proceed, to be sure she knew he was there, available to her needs. She had the impression of it like the heat of his body curled at her back while she slept.

Now, glancing at her often, he moved through the milling group with one hand at his back, the other loose at his side. A comfortable pose that allowed him to bow cordially as he made the appropriate level of greeting to each person. His gift for recall of names and status was impeccable. When he encountered Devlin, his teeth flashed in a grin at whatever the man said, showing he'd already developed a comfortable male rapport with the Australian. That smile almost made her forget herself and curl her toes in her open sandals.

She thought of him the previous night, the way he'd closed his hand over hers on the brand at his hip. When she'd taken him back to their room, she'd feathered her lips over it more than once, teasing his cock with the fine line of her cheek before she'd ridden him to climax.

Rex had tried to control and dominate her, but in the end he'd had no ability to do so because she never trusted him enough to let him into her soul. Now she'd put her heart and soul as well as her physical well-being into the hands of a mere human. And she'd never felt safer in her life.

Around him, the ballroom somehow became fantastical with its array of characters. He was surrounded by things that were temporal, no longer her reality, but there he was in the middle of it. The soul who had bound himself to her, even through death. The lights of the chandelier sent out rays that sparkled in her vision.

It occurred to her that he, Bran and Mr. Ingram had become the most real things in her life these last couple of months. She wanted to experience only what was real from now on. She had no patience for anything else. Why had she even come here? The reason seemed to escape her.

She turned abruptly, thinking to leave. Registering the startled look on Daniela's face, she had no chance to make a vague excuse, for Lord Uthe stepped onto the platform. He reached out a hand to her as if he thought she'd turned at his approach. Apparently Danny came to the same conclusion, because her puzzled expression vanished and she respectfully withdrew.

"It's nearly nine, my lady. Are you ready?"

The dance. The male vampires checking their hair and the fit of their trousers. An unwelcome palm hot against her waist, a male body too close. His eyes speculating on thoughts so far away from who she was, had been. What she wanted.

Lyssa made herself rest her hand in Uthe's, her lips pressed together to keep from screaming. That roiling feeling suddenly expanded exponentially. She didn't have stage fright, didn't even know what this was. It wasn't the virus. That was the only reassurance she could give herself, for suddenly her throat was so tight she could barely speak.

Uthe brought her to the edge of the platform and commanded the attention of the large room with a raised hand, projecting his voice as the ballroom quieted. The lights closed in on her, his voice setting off a headache.

"My lady. As our revered queen, we always ask that you lead off the first dance of the Ball. Will you honor us and one fortunate gentleman? That is, unless you've changed your preferences this year and wish to choose a lady?"

There was some laughter, but the male vampires who thought they might be eligible were a palpable energy in the large room. Feeling it, those assembled quieted further with hushed expectancy. The candlelit chandeliers were lowered, other light sources dimming to give the main floor and herself the focus. She well understood the perceived significance of this moment. Back in Atlanta, in the far more casual atmosphere of her study, she and Jacob had reviewed a short list of candidates critically. Brian had been the easy choice. It would be clear she was honoring him for his scientific advances on behalf of their species, but no one would surmise that she had anything but respect for the far more lower-ranking vampire and his well-known father.

The last time she'd been here, she'd been with Rex and Thomas. Her monk had stood in the shadows, the lights reflecting off his spectacles. Now Rex was dead, killed by her hand. Thomas had died alone in a monastery.

No, not alone. Jacob had been with him.

The first time she'd danced with Rex here, he'd been pleased with the prestige of the honor, but more than that, he'd wanted her. He'd believed in the Council she'd built. He'd fought at her side. He hadn't been a kind man, but he'd been a strong leader, a man to respect. And he had loved her. Until he lost his mind.

The lights were dim, but they still hurt her eyes. She wanted utter darkness. Her eyes were burning, trying to fill with mortifying tears.

"My lady," Lord Uthe said gently. She turned a desperate glance toward him. "We are on par, you and I," he said. "I have no motives or designs upon you. If it would be easier this first time since your husband's death, I will be happy to . . ."

He let it drift off, a courtesy.

No. Never in her many centuries of life had she allowed her control to slip voluntarily. Though it was a savage internal struggle, one during which her mind told her she would be wise to take Uthe's offer, she shook her head. She did manage to reach out and clasp his hand in an offering of thanks for his kindness. Then she was moving off the platform, toward the center of the floor where a circle had been opened to allow her room for her dance.

She went to the center of it and let her gaze travel over the arrayed faces as the second hand on the ornate clock over the orchestra reached a minute before nine. Whoever she was looking at when that final ninth chime tolled was her chosen partner. He would come to her, meet her on the floor. Decades before, it was the decisive move that confirmed to all she intended to accept Rex as her husband.

Now she passed over overlords, ladies. Region Masters. Council members. Belizar was missing, oddly. She almost snorted as her gaze passed over Carnal, and he straightened in one self-delusional moment, thinking she might choose him. She would cut his hands off before they ever touched her again.

When she coursed fully over the room, she pivoted on her heel, began the same examination in a counterclockwise motion. Brian was not readily visible. In case of his absence, she had several neutral choices like Uthe, where she could bestow the favor with little expectations beyond the dance. She saw at least two of those choices in the crowd.

But she didn't want any of them touching her tonight. Maybe she was wrong and this tide of emotional response was attributable to the disease, but even Uthe had sensed what Jacob had pointed out to her before, in his quiet, logical way. She was a woman who'd lost her husband and human servant less than two years ago and was now facing the end of her own life.

All these rituals she'd last shared with Rex . . . It was overwhelming at times.

She wouldn't live to share Christmas with Jacob. That bothered her. She liked Christmas. Would she have made it this far these past few months without him? She doubted it. She needed to tell him that. Be damned any concerns about him getting too full of himself. They'd gone beyond that.

Her skin shivered with desire for one man's fingers to be trailing along the line of her spine in her low-backed dress, one man's thighs pressing against hers in the turn of the waltz.

The clock began to chime. One beat, two beats, three beats. She was measuring the beats of her heart rather than the counts of the clock. She let her gaze linger over the alternate choices, saw the humble appreciation for the consideration in their eyes. It was well-known she often bestowed her second and third choices with a strike or two of the clock before she settled on her final choice.

The crowd shifted as the sixth chime struck, tension and excitement gathering. A few smiles, enjoyment of the moment among those who knew they were not competing for it. Then she altered the direction of her gaze by ninety degrees, turning precisely on her heel. The murmurs died away, bitten off by indrawn breaths.

The last chime echoed in a now completely silent ballroom. The preternatural stillness of vampires had descended, even their servants frozen in the gravity of the moment.

She could tell Devlin, as he stepped back from her choice, was dismayed and not a little shocked. Though he loved his own Mistress well, perhaps he was even a little disapproving. Yes, the Aussies were more informal. But there was a baseline code that governed them all, and she'd quite deliberately decided to grind it under the point of her heel.

Jacob moved forward, the tap of his dress shoes loud on the floor of the ballroom, a beautifully arranged Rosetta pattern done in varying shades of wood. While there was no falter or hesitation to his steps, the set of his mouth was tense. As the chime's final note vibrated away on the air, he reached her, perfectly timing his approach.

Dropping to one knee, he bowed his head, perhaps trying to soften the adverse effect of what she'd just done. But she extended her hand, bade him rise. When he brushed it with his lips and rose, she dropped in a low curtsy before him.

The shocked gasps were audible this time, increasing the swell of mutters.

When she straightened, she used the pressure of his hand to draw her back up to stand before him. It was expected to be adored by one's servant, but the way her skin burned with pleasurable fire when he looked at her as he did now . . . gods. How could they not see it?

My lady . . . Brian is not here, but we had some other choices . . .

I didn't look for Brian, or any of the others.

A pause as he digested that, the light of his blue eyes fierce on her face. A light that did not hurt her eyes in the least. Concerned he might be, but she'd also reached into his soul and touched him. She knew he would deny her nothing. Hadn't he said so from the beginning?

Is this wise?

What can they do? Kill us?

His lips tugged in acknowledgment of the irony.

I will bear no man's hands on me tonight, Sir Vagabond. Only yours. Not just now, but to the end of my life.

He swallowed. When he backed up a step, he took her with him.

It was a traditional waltz, though she'd chosen one of her preferred slow and languid 1920s torch songs as the music for it. He bowed to her again as she dipped into a more shallow curtsy, the formal beginning to the dance. Taking her other hand as she straightened, he drew her into his arms.

There was no music. Lyssa glanced over her shoulder with an imperious, faintly annoyed look. The music director snapped out of his slack-jawed amazement to give the violinist his cue.

The first pure, sad note quivered in the air, joined by several other string instruments. Jacob moved into the four-step count, entirely proper spacing between them. She was having none of that. She moved into him so he had to slide his hand more fully around her waist, his hand on the small of her back and point of her hip as she wished. The dress she'd chosen for tonight was a black sheath with a transparent overlay of jet sequins. The front neckline displayed her creatively raised bosom to give an eye-catching setting for her necklace of blood rubies and diamonds. The back dipped low, the sloping side edges cut in a jagged, lightning pattern held fast by a transparent piece of black net embroidered with the image of a Chinese dragon, matching the ink tattoo of one she'd had Jacob put on her shoulder. She could feel the heat of his hand through that transparent net.

Closing her eyes, she let him turn her, his arms and the press of his body guiding her. He was a good dancer. A wonderful lover. A man she could lean on. She imagined the picture they made, like the top of a music box, the swallowtails of his coat and the fluttering edge of her skirt rippling as they turned, stepped.

She didn't try to listen to his thoughts, but she wasn't closed to him. She was just drifting deeper into him, past the level of words, feeling the mélange of emotions that was Jacob swirl through her soul as he swirled her around the floor.

Once the clock hand changed to the first minute after nine, others could join them on the floor. The Council members did first, tight-lipped and formal, choosing their vampire partners. Soon the floor was floating in multiple colors and faces she blurred out. The only thing she wanted in focus was Jacob. She was flying, the rest like a cherry tree's blossoms drifting around her in the void.

"My stepfather did that once, a long, long time ago. Do you remember? I stood under the branches and he shook them. It was pink snow. Fluttering around me, never ending."

That's what Heaven was. Cherry blossoms fluttering around her as a handsome man danced her around a wide floor. The petals landing on her eyelids, the tops of her breasts, his hair . . .

The safety of a protector, the passion of a lover . . .

When she reached up to touch the hair feathered over his brow,

Jacob gently caught her hand, tightening his grip. Pressed his lips to her knuckles. *My lady, I sense you are not yourself. Perhaps we should retire as soon as is acceptable—*

Black and white. In a blink, color became black and white, and Heaven became Hell. Burning heat exploded as rage, scattering the cool, tranquil touch of the memory. Sensual feeling became passionate, irrational anger.

Locking her fingers around his hand without care for her strength, she narrowed eyes that had become filmed in red. "I'm not your servant, Jacob. Don't propose to order me to do anything."

A muscle flexed in Jacob's jaw as he managed the steps without faltering. Another fraction of pressure and she'd break several of his fingers. That didn't concern him. It would be a welcome distraction from the tidal wave of fear that filled him. They were under the scrutiny of everyone, many of the males already eyeing him as if they'd be happy to tear out his vitals. Devlin's description of what happened to male servants perceived as having undue influence over their Mistresses was uncomfortably vivid. Would they be that aggressive toward Lady Lyssa's servant? He suddenly was all too aware that if an attack came, he was her only protection. If they took him away from her . . .

The victim's condition will begin to deteriorate quickly. The mood swings will be so sharp they can almost occur midsentence . . . When that occurs, the physical attack will come quickly on the heels of the emotional . . . The vampire has entered the final stage, and it will be far more rapid than any of the previous stages . . .

He should have made the call to Ingram. Earlier tonight, when he'd helped her dress, he knew he should have. He just hadn't wanted to believe . . . He'd been stupid. The cell phone was in his pocket.

The other dancers were giving them a wide berth. Normally, he knew they would have maneuvered to be close to her, to win the favor of a word. Instead the circle of space they left around her was filled with a buffer of hostility, suspicion.

"May I cut in?"

Jacob turned, his hand still clamped in his lady's grip, even as he kept his steadying arm about her waist. He found himself facing a vampire he'd not yet seen at the three-day Gathering. If he had, he was sure he would have remembered him.

He had several inches on Jacob in height. His skin had the smooth olive texture of the Middle East, and his eyes were piercing amber. Not brown, not gold, but a liquid amber so startling he doubted the man could have passed as mortal before color-altering contacts had been available. His hair was a burnished copper, long, bound back with ribbon to form a tail that fell just past his shoulder blades. He was dressed in a black, long-tailed coat much like Jacob's, only his shirt was white, his tie white silk and tied in a cravat style. A stick pin of a griffin done in amber and gold matched the setting for the ruby crest he wore on his left hand. Instead of slacks, he wore fitted black breeches and polished Hessian boots.

His presence was causing quite a stir, which Jacob saw with relief had distracted the assembly from his lady's unacceptable choice of dance partner.

Lyssa blinked at them both. Jacob tightened his fingers discreetly on her waist as a reassurance, waiting for her cue. But her mind was a whirl. Trying to get in tune with it, to grab a corner and slow it down, he was disorienting himself. He wasn't practiced enough at doing it yet, had only managed to get in sync with her once or twice, and that was with her cooperation.

An energy reached into him, steadying him, joining him in his Mistress's mind with effortless ease. Almost like the hand of a master painter guiding his apprentice on the canvas, it gave him the ability to circle around his lady's wildly spiraling thoughts, cushioning them from their erratic convulsions against the walls of her mind.

The only vampire who can stand toe to-toe-with her . . . who has as many secrets . . .

Jacob met Lord Mason's gaze. Somehow Mason knew what was happening here. He'd no doubt Thomas's hand was involved in that. Though he didn't have time to dissect the whys and hows, like how the hell Mason could get into his mind and Lyssa's, Jacob made the instant, gut decision to trust Mason as an ally. He was in over his head, and her life was far more important than his ego.

She needs to get out of here, soon.

"My lady?" Mason's gaze flickered in acknowledgment before he dismissed him with proper vampire indifference. Jacob turned her hand over to him, which had loosened its painful grip, even though she'd not stated her will in the matter. She was staring at Mason. Jacob could feel the wheels of her mind struggling, trying to right it with the help of the two of them.

Then, with a click, it happened. A hard tremor went through her body, so strong he felt it through his fingertips as he made himself slide them from her waist. He forced himself to step back and let Mason's hand take its place.

Lyssa blinked. Once. Twice.

"It would be my pleasure, Lord Mason," she said at last.

Thank God. A shudder of relief passed through Jacob, almost as violent as hers.

"Just Mason will do, Lyssa. We know what a farce titles are." He handed his cane to Jacob with a curt nod. "Shall your servant retire from the floor?"

"Yes." She glanced at Jacob. "Thank you for the dance, Sir Vagabond. Await my pleasure with the other servants."

Jacob gave a half bow and retreated. Though he wasn't tied into any other minds here, the shift of reaction in the room was as abrupt as her temper and far more reassuring. Appreciative laughter and amazed murmurs. It now appeared as if she'd dallied with her servant until Mason arrived, a fine bit of drama to amuse the other vampires. She'd actually duped them all into thinking she would choose a *human* . . .

"Just like Lady Lyssa . . . She knows how ridiculous it is, all this nonsense about female vampires and male servants . . . So clever, allowing Lord Mason to make such an impressive entrance . . . Fine entertainment . . ."

He should be relieved and pleased by the turn of events, the incredibly fortunate save. So why did he feel like Malachi had speared him through the chest with a javelin, after all? Why did he want to snarl at all of them as he left the floor?

When he moved past Devlin without stopping, the man gave him a look that fair screamed, "What the hell was that all about, then?"

One thing he'd learned from his lady was inscrutability. He gave Devlin the cane for safekeeping but kept going as if he were on an errand for his Mistress. He had a third mark. She could speak in his mind, after all.

As he reached the arched entrance to the ballroom, he turned to see Mason talking to her. There was a light smile on her lips. His lady appeared mysterious and in control, her usual impressive mien, but Jacob knew it would be fleeting. Like contractions coming too close together, only in this case her behavior heralded the delivery of death instead of life.

But for now her new partner had his face bent close as they danced. Her head was tilted back, their mouths tantalizingly close. Everyone was watching them. How the hell could anyone not look at them? They were perfect together. If she wasn't dying . . . Lord Mason was more than capable of protecting her. Loving her. Caring for her.

When he'd mailed correspondence for Thomas in the last month of the monk's life, Lord Mason's name had been on one of the letters. Though he hadn't known the contents then, Jacob now had the answer to an unanswered question. Thomas had known what fate awaited his lady, and made sure her strongest ally among the vampires would be present when she most needed him.

Regardless, leaving the ballroom, leaving her in the care of another man, was the hardest thing Jacob had done yet.

As he turned the corner into a wide corridor, he saw the hall was lined with heavy tapestries. They likely allowed quick trysts between lovers who had the unusual vampire quirk of preferring privacy. When he ducked behind one portraying a medieval scene of the Knights Templar, he found it thankfully unoccupied.

He'd just wanted a moment to collect his thoughts. He rethought the wisdom of that a bare second later when his body broke out in a cold sweat, his hands shaking.

He had to protect her, and yet in a blink she'd made it clear that if she lost control, there'd be little he could do to contain the most powerful vampire in the room, sick or no. Five minutes before Mason arrived, he'd been facing a situation he knew he didn't have the resources to address. He'd been counting too much on his lady being an active partner in her own protection. Debra had warned him the disease could progress rapidly once it hit a certain stage. His lady, who'd meticulously prepared for so much, had displayed a very human trait in avoiding preparations for the worst on her own condition. He was a fool. He should have planned better. He should have tried to convince her to cut her time here short.

But would it have changed anything? They had to make it to the Court session. He'd known that and had hoped, as he was sure she had, that she would make it. They'd had no choice but to keep going. They still had no other choice, racing against the clock and hedging their bets against death.

Several weeks before, she'd realized it took too much of the energy she needed to explain certain things to him. It was easier to let him ride along in her thoughts as she developed her plans and intentions. She just asked that he not interrupt her thinking or argue with her. She knew what she needed to do, and she needed his obedience to do it.

She'd told him everything he needed to know about the Gathering. He had a brain, and he would use it. If Mason hadn't come, they would have danced. She would have ripped his arms off for trying to get her off the floor and that would have been perfectly acceptable treatment of a servant. Equilibrium would have been restored.

He pressed his temple against the cold stone of the wall. When Carnal's face swam up in his mind, ironically it helped him shove the last of the panic attack away. No way that piece of shit was getting near her.

Tonight. They just had to get through tonight.

Then, God willing, he'd have time to get her home to die there.

Recalling again his nervousness before his first vampire fight, he remembered Gideon giving him a cuff on the ear, saying, "We're all going to die, bro. Either there's nothing after, in which case you won't exist to care about it, or Mom and Dad will be waiting. Mom'll say something like, 'Now why did you do a fool thing like fight a bunch of vampires and get yourself killed?' And Dad will say, 'At least you should have waited until you got laid by a pretty girl.'"

Well, he'd accomplished the latter. The privilege of being in his lady's body was more than any man could ever ask from Heaven or Earth.

Regardless of what happened, it was time to make the call they'd agreed Jacob should make to Mr. Ingram if things went downhill. Her actions tonight were the trigger. If they couldn't make it through the Court session, couldn't get the Council to pass the vote and then get back on the plane, then the only thing they could do to protect her people now would be done.

Tears burned at the back of his throat. Pulling the cell phone out of his coat pocket to start the clock on his own death seemed to occur in slow motion, as if his limbs moved through something far more resistant than air.

Since the tapestry currently protecting him depicted the Knights Templar, he obeyed a sudden compulsion from the memory of those warrior monks and dropped to one knee, bowing his head. *Dear Lord, I don't believe that her soul is damned. But I'll gladly go wherever she's going, if I'm worthy to follow. I'll know I'm in Hell only if I wake and find I'm somewhere she's not. Please help me do what I must do to protect her.*

Calmer, he rose, pressed the button and listened to it ring through. Thank God Mason had included a cell tower in the palace's modern-day upgrades; otherwise there'd be no way for him to get a connection. When Ingram answered, Jacob said quietly, "Start the clock."

A pause. "You got it, son. God bless you." Another pause. "Both of you."

Jacob nodded, unable to speak, and closed the phone.

If Ingram did not hear from them within the next twenty-four hours, he would make his own call. The one that would start the chain reaction to alert all of her fugitives and give them the information to find safe harbor in allied territories.

Jacob didn't know where his brother was now—hopefully somewhere out of trouble. But Ingram would also make sure Gideon received the letter Jacob had written to his brother before he left, saying the things he wanted to say.

Whatever awaited them after that, Jacob and Lyssa would deal with it together.

Hold on to my heart, Jacob. Keep it safe . . .

One night she'd teased him with her vampire speed, confusing him by moving the tools he'd been using to repair a fence from his left side to the right and then back again before he knew she was there. When he finally caught on, he looked up to see her sitting on top of the shed, her playful smirk touched by the gloss of moonlight. She'd shrieked indignantly when he went after her with the garden hose.

Then he remembered her peeling an orange in the darkness, eyes glowing green like a cat in the night. Smiling at him.

Whatever time we had, we used it well.

Nodding to himself, he stepped out from behind the curtain. And collided with Debra, moving at brisk clip toward the ballroom. The purposeful strides of a lab assistant, used to hurrying even when she should be walking at a pace more suited to the sequined, sleek evening dress and teetering heels she wore.

"Oh!" She yelped as he caught her arms, steadying her. When she smiled at him it was with an air of distracted excitement that fair pulsed off her skin. "Jacob. It's so good to see you."

"And you." As he studied her, he saw no self-consciousness in her face about their earlier exhibition. She was wholly absorbed in something else. "What's going on? You're wound up like a kid about to go to Disney for the first time. It can't be for this group."

She giggled, startling him. Putting her hand up to her mouth, she shook her head. "I'm sorry, Jacob. It's just . . . Oh, my God, I can't believe . . ." She made a visible effort to rein herself in. "I can't really tell anyone yet. Of course, you're her servant, and Brian certainly wouldn't deny Lady Lyssa the knowledge, since he's meeting with Lord Belizar. I'm sure . . . Lyssa has taken such good care of my lord, made sure he had what he needed . . ."

His heart began to pump more rapidly. Jacob hardly dared to say it. While not normally able to read words from people's minds, it was resonating so strongly from her he couldn't miss it. "You've found the cure. To the Delilah virus."

"Yes!" She said it in an ecstatic whisper, squeezed his arms and rocked up on her toes with ebullience. "Well"—she attempted to re-claim her objectivity—"we're ninety-nine percent sure we have. That's why Brian's been working so hard these last few days. Running and rerunning the data. We'd done a limited test on affected vampire cells, but seven of the test subjects responded to the model exactly the way we hoped. The model simulated the vampire-servant physical connection. The cure serum worked on a Canadian vampire, our first patient. There were some side effects because we haven't got the dosage percentage down yet. But it worked, Jacob. *It worked.* We got the call a little while ago from Alabama. The vampire is cured. And it's all thanks to Andrev and Helene. The servant-vampire connection was the key, just as Brian thought it was. How ironic is that? Oh, Brian is . . . I've never seen him so excited."

Jacob's grip on both her arms drew her attention to the fact he wasn't smiling, his expression battle intense. "I need to speak with them. Brian and Lord Belizar. Is Lord Uthe with them?"

"Yes, I think so. He was headed that way a few moments ago. I think we should wait for them, because he thinks they'll make an announcement at the Ball after he talks to them . . ."

"It's a matter of life and death. Of my lady." He was propelling her down the hallway even as he said it. Debra caught his arm, bringing him to a halt with firm resistance.

"Oh, my God. That's why you were asking that day . . . Oh, God. I wish . . . But of course she wouldn't have allowed you to . . . How far along is she?"

"Based on the description you gave me that day, she entered Stage Four about three or four hours ago." He hesitated. "She had an attack a few moments ago, the type of mood swing you said would come shortly before the next physical episode. Lord Mason's working on getting her out of there after her dance. This evening"—he clenched his teeth, made himself say it—"when I was dressing her, I noticed she had a small series of blemishes just at the top of her buttock. When I rubbed my fingers over them, the skin came off. She hasn't noticed any pain yet, so I didn't tell her." At Debra's incredulous look, he shook his head. "It's a long story. She had to make it to the Court meeting. Telling her wouldn't have changed her mind on that."

She paled, and now she grabbed his hand, hurrying with him. "You're right; we need to tell them now. She could have less than a few hours. We can't lose Lady Lyssa."

He cursed himself, even knowing he could have done nothing differently. "Tell me how the cure works while we're moving."

She stopped abruptly then, losing even more color on her face. When she looked up at him, her eyes reflected a pain he didn't understand. When she told him how the cure worked, he did. But he captured her hand, pulling her in motion again.

Lord Mason might be the only one capable of protecting Lyssa from other vampires. He could even love and care for her.

But Jacob now knew only her servant could save her life.

18

MASON paid court to Lyssa, ignoring any attempts by anyone else to speak to him. When the dance was over, he offered her his arm and escorted her to a quiet and secluded spot on the far end of the outside verandah. Moonlight provided a spectacular view of the ocean. When she leaned against the rail, he casually pressed against her back, looping an arm around her waist to give her body his support if she needed it.

"When did you last feed?"

"A few hours ago." She looked out over the rail, her gaze coursing over the view.

"The boy is very devoted to you."

"I've learned many things about Jacob. Enough to know he's not a boy. I was blessed to have him come into my life at this point." Lyssa laid her head back on his shoulder. "I guess we'll be fueling the gossips, you and me. Where have you been, Mason? You've been missed."

"Only by you. The rest just miss my influence and wealth."

"Well it's hard to miss you for your charming and affectionate nature."

He smiled, ran his knuckles along her cheek. "You break my heart, dearest."

She tilted her face up at the tone of his voice, and saw the pain in his eyes. "You know."

"Thanks to Thomas. And to the delicacy of this beautiful face of yours." At her alarmed look, he shook his head. "No one else would see it. I just know you. I can tell something is draining your strength."

Shaking her head, she turned her face into his large palm. "I don't know what to say. I'm grateful, Mason."

"Oh, bollocks on that," he murmured. "How will I get along in a world that doesn't contain Lady Elyssa Wentworth? The only woman who can terrify me with nothing more than the sound of her voice."

"The only woman who's ever beaten you in a fair fight."

"Now, I wouldn't say that. I was in a weakened condition. Wallowing in misery and trying to poison myself with alcohol. You knocked me around and told me to stop feeling sorry for myself."

She reached up, touched his jaw. "You didn't have to come."

"I know that. But I have very few people I love, my lady. God has made my heart extremely stingy in that regard. You are one of them. And the boy you consider a capable man is still human and very outnumbered here."

She shook her head again. "Your heart isn't stingy. If anything, it's too tender. I saw one like you less than a month ago. A mortal. Jacob's brother. Eaten up by his hatred and grief, his guilt. You men of honor. Such foolish creatures you are."

"We are. But it's unforgettable women such as yourself who destroy us with your loss." He paused. "He took the third mark, even knowing."

"He did." She looked away, out into the gardens. "He insisted and I . . . couldn't deny him."

"Good." At her surprised look, Mason shrugged. "He's yours entirely, body, heart and soul. You'd break him only if you left him behind. Trust me." His amber eyes flickered. "I know."

Tears welled in her eyes and she hastily blinked them back as Mason gallantly pretended not to see, though his hand rose and lay on her nape. His thumb stroked her there, following the strands of her hair over her shoulder.

"It's funny," she said quietly at last. "Before Jacob, I was ready to die. Had accepted it. These past two years . . . the awfulness that Rex became. Thomas's loss . . . When I found out I was sick, it didn't bother me so much, not from a personal standpoint. But then Jacob came, and he's like something I've been seeking my entire life. Now that I've found him, I just want more. More time. How greedy is that? To have been given so much time and want more?"

"When you find the right love, eternity isn't long enough."

"Lady Lyssa?"

Lyssa straightened and turned with Mason. Brian stood a respectful distance from them.

"There you are." She cleared her throat, attempting a lighter tone. "I'd intended to grace you with tonight's dance and had to settle for this scoundrel who didn't have the courtesy to arrive on time. I'm not even sure he has an invitation."

Brian looked between them, something obviously filling his mind to the point he couldn't quite comprehend the banter.

"It would have been my honor to dance with you, my lady," he said at last. "But . . . I apologize. Lord Belizar and the others have convened in the Council chambers on an important matter and need your attendance most urgently. Lord Mason, they asked if you could attend as well."

"It's a long walk to those chambers in high heels," Mason observed. "Perhaps a chair could be arranged . . ."

"I can walk," Lyssa said.

"Certainly," Brian said at the same time. He gave a low bow to her, an apology for the interruption. "We've already arranged for it."

Even now a traveling chair was being brought onto the verandah via the stairs by a quartet of the naked and masked servants. Seeing them reminded her of a group of executioners, their faces hidden. When they came to a halt, they blocked the stairs.

"I've not lived this long by being stupid, or unaware." When Mason reached out a hand to her, Lyssa stepped back to the balcony rail.

Jacob, where are you? She struggled with the effort to hold back her panic when her attempt to establish the mind link was met with a black fog of confusion. The holes in her shields were so frequent now she barely expended the effort to keep his mind out of hers except when absolutely necessary, perhaps because she didn't want to know when she completely lost the ability to do it. Like a person going deaf, wondering why everyone was mumbling.

She hadn't questioned her decision to permit him full access to her thoughts during the last several weeks. Or why more and more she preferred to hear him speak aloud in addition to thinking thoughts when he was at a distance. It had increased the strength of her reception. Now, she could hear him only like a murmur of static through a cell phone, devices she'd always disliked intensely and never needed. She strained to bring that voice in focus. Knowing he was talking to her, she nevertheless couldn't hear him clearly.

The panic that flooded her now was another wave of what she'd felt at the ocean when Jacob was hurt. Brian and Mason had moved a step forward, as if they were closing in on her like she was a wild animal. She could go over the rail, tumble to the ground, get away. If she didn't break a limb. If she did, she wouldn't have time to heal before they'd be on her.

You'd muss your dress, my lady. It's a beautiful dress, all the more so because you're in it.

She closed her eyes, her hands balling into fists at the effort of grasping that voice, holding on to it. Her temples started to pound. Nausea heaved in her stomach, and her skin was tingling along her back, a faint burn, something new in her category of symptoms.

Jacob, where are you?

There was a vocal reaction of surprise and affront in the gardens below. A breath later, Jacob finished scaling the trellis, a shorter distance from the ground than the winding stairs. He dropped lightly onto the tiles in bare feet, tux still in place. He was breathing hard, as if he'd come at a dead run from wherever he'd been.

"I am here, my lady. At your back, as always."

Lyssa closed her hand on his forearm. His hand settled over hers, warm and reassuring. She wanted into his head. Still couldn't get there. "What's going on?"

"There's nothing for you to fear at all, my lady." Jacob smiled at her, his pleasure genuine enough to make her draw a wary breath of reassurance. "Brian has good news to share with the Council. He's found the cure to the Delilah virus, and he can administer it to you here. He was testing the serum and so brought enough dosages." Despite their audience, he cradled her face, tipping it up to his. "You'll be around to enchant men for as long as you wish."

"You told them . . ." She swallowed, keeping the bile down with effort, though the headache was starting to make speech difficult.

"It was time, my lady. When I heard about the cure from Debra, I knew—"

"I can't hear you . . . inside me . . . I need . . ."

"I'm right here, my lady." Without permission, he simply bent, lifting her in his arms. He shouldered past Brian and Lord Mason to the chair, gently setting her on it.

She held on to his neck, drawing his face close. "You are telling me true?"

"I told you I would never be false to you, my lady. Let's get to Council chambers and we can get it taken care of."

"I will want to know how it works," she said as they lifted her. "I won't have"—she let go of him to press her fingers to her temple as his brow creased in concern—"it resulting in warts . . . or my hair falling out. There are . . . worse things than being dead."

"Yes, my lady," he said, a ghost of a smile crossing his face as he urged the servants forward with their precious cargo. He exchanged a glance with Mason. The Middle Eastern vampire as well as Brian fell in behind them.

They got down the stairs well enough, but as they reached the bottom and rounded the corner to traverse the gardens, Jacob stopped abruptly. "Wait. Put her down. Now."

Brian spoke the question behind him, but Jacob shouldered the vampire aside. Snatching up an ice bucket left on an outside table, he quickly dumped it and moved to his lady's side, blocking Mason and Brian's view with his broad back as she doubled over, a cry coming from her lips.

He held her hair out of the way as she vomited blood, but when she rocked forward on another spasm, her body contorted as if she'd been struck.

Pain exploded in his own body. Jacob staggered, the ability to breathe suddenly restricted, weakness overwhelming him. Mason leaped to his side as he dropped the bucket, stumbling to one knee. When his lady desperately reached out for him despite her own pain, he managed to lock his fingers around hers.

Mason was not quick enough with the bucket to keep her next expulsion from splattering the front of her dress. She vomited far more than Jacob had ever seen. When Brian eased her back, she had the pallor of a true corpse, something that would never be mistaken for a vampire despite the lore. Her limbs were shaking.

"Jacob." The light in her eyes was crimson, her fangs lengthening.

"Take her quickly," Brian snapped. The servants hesitated.

Though it felt as if he were ripping off a limb, Jacob extricated his fingers. His lady's face warred between panic and a Herculean effort to maintain her composure. The disease was taking away the control of a lifetime, both mentally and physically. It pained him as much as the symptoms to see her fighting such a battle with it.

"I'll make sure he's behind you every step of the way, my lady. Council chambers. Go." Mason snarled the command. The servants bolted forward.

The next wave of pain knocked Jacob back to his knees.

"No. Jacob—" Lyssa cried out to him, struggling to get past Brian. He was holding her fast on the chair, moving with the servants, his expression grim. "I shouldn't have done this to you. Help him. Mason. Help . . ."

"I've got him, my lady. Be easy. We'll be right behind you."

Mason knelt and got Jacob's arm over his shoulders, helping the other man to his feet.

"Hold the mind block between us as long as you can," Jacob muttered. "We need to get her to Council chambers."

"She may not want this," Mason said under his breath as they moved after the chair. They could hear Brian reassuring her, glancing back often to confirm for her that they were there.

"She's not herself right now," Jacob managed to keep an even tone, though it felt as if a baseball bat was being applied to his rib cage. He didn't want his lady feeling this kind of pain. "Let's save her life, then solicit her opinion."

"She would say that's typical male thinking."

"Lady Lyssa is a force of nature. A constellation. A guiding force. They need her. Bad things coming if she goes." How many like his brother would die if Carnal and his kind took over? What would happen to servants like Debra or Devlin?

At the tightening of Mason's mouth, Jacob knew he understood. Just being with her for a handful of months and training with Thomas, Jacob knew her influence was felt far outside of her territory. Would the Council be able to maintain control of vampires like Carnal without her? Not just her power, which was considerable, but the power of example, the ideal they sought to emulate? So inspiring that for centuries the bulk of them had been willing to control their bloodlust to be like her, and the rest had been too afraid of her power to go against the Council.

"I've been successful keeping her out of your head only because she's not yet figured out it's not the disease separating you. If the episode she's having ebbs, she'll know. And tear a strip from my brain obliterating the shielding."

"Then we need to get there quickly to preserve your sanity."

"She's not going to agree to this."

"She's not herself," Jacob repeated and grunted. Mason slid his arm around his waist, taking more of his weight.

"If you're going to throw up, do let me know so I can move out of the way."

"You . . . let my lady's blood ruin her dress. She'll consider it . . . equal payment. Christ, this hurts." If this was anything like the agony his lady was suffering, he admired her all the more for not screaming.

"You . . ." He gripped Mason's coat at the shoulder, his hold strong and desperate enough to rip the seams. "I can do this. She needs me for this. But . . . she's so . . . lonely. I'm just . . . a human. She . . . You make sure; you swear to me . . . Take care of her. She may be a goddess, but she gets so lonely. Help her . . . Tend her roses. She likes company when she does that . . . or she gets sad. Stay with her. Don't go back to the desert. She needs . . . you."

"Sssh . . . easy, boy. Come on." Mason spoke gruffly, took most of Jacob's weight on his arm and broke into a trot to keep pace with Lyssa's entourage.

They reached the chamber before Mason's prediction came to pass, thank the gods. Just as Jacob gained the threshold, the vampire's grip on him faltered and he shuddered, his jaw flexing. He looked at Jacob, then his gaze darted across the room.

"Let it go," Jacob gasped. "We're here, my lord. Do not suffer further on our account."

The pain was receding, a blissful sign the attack was passing. However, the fact it had affected him as harshly as it had his lady told him they were close. The next one could be the final one.

When Mason's expression eased, his lady burst into Jacob's mind with the force of an asteroid, knocking him to his knees once more as her energy spun around wildly. First she reassured herself of the connection, then she sought understanding of what had been blocking her. Feeling her hands on his head, he looked up as she gripped his chin, her nails biting cruelly into the skin beneath his beard, into the vulnerable throat.

The relief at the pass of the attack fled as he realized it might be far more difficult to get her to agree to the treatment when she had the ability and strength to resist it. But though strength surged back into his own limbs, a curious lassitude remained, telling him she hadn't recovered fully despite the appearance to the contrary.

Her eyes glittered with fire, her mouth tightening into a hard line. Before he could call out a warning or protest, she'd left him. Mason was slammed up against the wall, so hard the elegant, thick planking cracked. Lyssa's head whipped around as several Council members started forward. Her fangs glittered, her eyes glowing with hellfire.

When Jacob stood, he had to hold on to the edge of the table. He wondered where she was finding the reserve of strength to put on this show when he could feel her weakness in the marrow of his bones. There was a tingling, unpleasant heat in the same location, as if he was being microwaved. It was making the room warmer than it should have been.

Her eyes moved in slight, erratic motions as if she were reading small type, then her expression shifted to Brian and Debra. For the moment Mason was not fighting her hold, though his hand had closed over the wrist of her hand, holding him pinned.

There was a tray on the table with sterile pads. A cloth covered whatever else was on it. The Council members were arrayed tensely around the chamber, their faces somber. Watching her.

"No," she whispered. She released Mason. "No." More firmly.

"Lady Lyssa." Lord Uthe spoke first. "Perhaps your servant misrepresented the situation. Lord Brian has found a cure to your illness. You can walk out of this room in thirty minutes, completely healed."

"No," she said.

I'm sorry, my lady. But I will not let you die.

Lyssa turned. The Council members were moving into a semicircle around her. Brian looked torn between a scientist's overwhelming eagerness to prove his cure before the most prestigious of his sponsors, and a man's concern for her. Lyssa knew he had compassion, but it was misplaced at the moment. He should be worrying for his own well-being.

"I will not submit to this."

"With the greatest respect, my lady, our queen." Lord Uthe bowed. His expression was stern, implacable. "We believe your judgment is already too impaired to make that decision. We seek only to restore you to yourself."

She curled her lip. "Then I suggest you try to make me."

Despite the blood still spattering her dress, no one doubted she could be deadly. If anything, Jacob knew it just reminded all present of what she could do. The amount of strength she had was the only thing in question. He suspected he and Mason were the only ones who knew it was not as formidable as it appeared.

When Uthe's expression shifted to Mason as if reading Jacob's thoughts, Lyssa's did the same. "Don't even think of challenging me, Mason."

"On a good day, a fight between us might go either way. Today, I think you know I'll win." He met her furious gaze with a steady amber one, a determined light there that said he would make good on the promise. "But it would break my heart. Please don't make me prove it."

"My lady, don't—" Jacob spoke as she turned to square off with the vampire. Mason tensed.

You be still. When she flicked her attention at him like the sharp end of a knife, she was the lady he knew, even as he could feel the vibrations of dull pain. There was no separation in their symptoms now. Her body was like the shore before a tide, getting ready for the next flood of spasms to roll in.

My lady, please. We don't have time.

Her gaze shifted to Brian. "I'm understanding his thoughts correctly, am I not?"

Her voice was ice, and Jacob didn't blame Brian for the hesitancy with which he responded. They were watching her like a roomful of children trapped with a poisonous and angry snake. "Yes, my lady. We have found a cure. If we inject the serum into your servant and you drink from him, it will destroy the virus entirely. That is what our cell models and data from our test subjects tell us."

"Test subjects?" Her voice dropped, deceptively soft. "Servants you murdered."

"Servants who sacrificed themselves for the betterment of our species. Their loss regrettable but valued." Belizar spoke when Brian could not seem to find an answer, his discomfiture obvious.

"I was not speaking to you," she snapped. Her gaze never left Brian. "So the serum is injected into Jacob. What then?"

"My lady." Jacob felt his heart lurch with a different but no less potent pain as she refused to turn and acknowledge him. "You said you trust my judgment. You've said as much numerous times over these past several months."

"I was wrong."

Brian swallowed, pressed on. "It infects his blood, mixes. How much does he weigh?"

"A hundred and ninety-eight pounds," Jacob said before she sent him a searing look.

"It will take approximately eleven minutes for the integration," Brian said hastily. "We draw a sample to be sure. Then the vampire drinks." He paused. "You drain his blood, though we think someone of your size would be cured with no more than two quarts."

"But it will still kill him."

"The serum is deadly poison to a human, even a marked one." He nodded once, a quick jerk.

"He is already dead if you die, my lady," Lady Helga offered in a quiet voice. "You serve no one with your sacrifice."

And if you live, my lady . . .

Jacob interjected the thought and was rewarded with a flash of pain through his head like electric current.

Don't make me tell you again.

His jaw hardened, and he reached out, clamped a hand on her wrist, drawing her startled attention. He straightened to his full height despite the fire in his gut, meeting her fiery expression with the flared temper of his own. "You told me. Protect what is mine. No matter what, that is my first priority." *If you live, the people of your territory remain safe until you can get this Council to agree to a permanent pardon or changing the rules altogether. You can make sure that Carnal and his cronies don't take advantage of this group. This Council needs their queen awhile longer. You know they do.*

She pulled her arm away. "You bastard."

He inclined his head. "It doesn't change the truth of it, does it, then?"

She was furious, frightened, hurt and dangerous. While he knew some of it was the disease, much of it was her resistance to losing control of the situation. *Perhaps it would have been better that first night if you'd let me put you on the St. Andrew's Cross. Put the manacles on you, the ones you couldn't break. You told me, "True submission is not only the most courageous act a person can commit to another, it's an act of faith. Of trust." Like now.*

She turned a startled gaze to him, her mind on that night with him, when everything had been dark sensuality, their relationship all tempting possibilities. But was she capable of fully trusting any human, even him?

Perhaps I could have handled this better, my lady, but there was no time. The next attack will likely kill us both. Give me the gift of your trust.

He knew his thoughts were a book for her to read, though he could tell nothing yet from the angry swirl of her own.

"Will he suffer, Brian?" She pivoted. "Lie to me and I will rip your throat out."

"Yes, my lady." He swallowed again, glanced toward Jacob. "The pain is excruciating. But it's not long. After you drink from him, we may end his pain, but he will die within fifteen minutes of the serum's administration."

She turned back to Jacob. "When did you learn all of this?"

"About half an hour ago, my lady."

"And you . . ." She shifted her gaze to Mason. "You, who value your self-determination so much you're willing to leave our species rudderless to preserve it. You jumped in with both feet to take away mine. To block me from reading my own servant in order to trap me here."

Mason did not flinch from her accusatory glance. "As I told you, my lady. I have very few friends."

"I understand why much better now."

Please do not blame them, my lady. You know this disease impairs judgment. Think. Why should both of us have to die if there is an option where one of us may live? It is possible, isn't it, that your judgment is impaired? Don't you want to do what needs to be done to get it back?

Jacob stepped in front of her. Tension emanated from the others at his back as he dared what no one else in the room did. Reaching out, he closed his hand on hers again, twining his fingers in hers. She kept her arm rigid at her side, but did not withdraw it. She was staring at his mouth, refusing to meet his eyes. He extended his other hand, caressed her chin with gentle pressure, asking her by that gesture to raise her gaze.

I used the best judgment I had, my lady. I don't think I was wrong.

He couldn't stand the dispassionate stare another moment longer, the wall of silence in her mind. Only his royal-blooded Mistress would divert precious energy at such a moment to convey her disdain. His temper broke.

"Damn it, woman, you wouldn't have listened. You would have just seen in my mind that it meant my death and refused. Does that make logical sense?" He grasped her upper arms, gave her a frustrated shake as her green eyes shot fire at him, her mouth compressed in a hard line. Energy was building around her, her body quivering with nerves or fury. "For centuries, you've believed that humans are here to serve your needs. Why in the hell would you be willing to die with me when I could willingly give you your life?"

Because I don't want to lose you. The wall shattered, and he was flooded with emotions so strong they scalded his insides. She gripped the front of his shirt. As she pinned him with her gaze, she told him with her body language and her thoughts that this moment was just the two of them, consequences be damned. "Because I've lived all those centuries and never wanted anyone, anything, the way I want you. No matter what anyone in this room believes, including you, Jacob Green, that is real and true, not illusion."

His stunned gaze couldn't move from her tortured expression, the love that was there as well as the sorrow. "My lady—"

"No. No." She shook her head vehemently, stepping back from him but perversely keeping a grip on his shirt. He ran his hands up arms that had become ice cold, like her hands. "We're leaving. I want to go home."

They wouldn't make it beyond this room, but Jacob was spared the effort of pointing that out. When she turned toward the double doors, Mason shifted, blocking them. "Don't make me do this, Lady Lyssa," he exhorted her.

She moved faster than Jacob expected. He could barely follow her until she caught hold of Mason's lapels and tossed him out of her way. Yanked at the door. Just as fast, the vampire was back on her, holding her fast from behind. She shoved away from the door, trying to shake him off. Her struggles became something else, more violent and erratic.

Jacob fell to one knee again, grabbing at the edge of the table. "Mason," he rasped, "ease your—"

"She's having another attack," Debra cried out.

Fire roared through his blood. The head-splitting pain and nausea made him want to throw up his internal organs to get rid of it. Her shields had kept her pain from him for so long, but now he absorbed her every physical and emotional reaction such that it was hard to separate what belonged to whom.

Lyssa seized in Mason's arms, convulsing, her eyes rolling back. As she thrashed, dark, oblong marks appeared on the tender underside of her forearms. The smell of burned flesh filled the room. Council members gasped, shrank back.

"Do it, now," Uthe ordered Brian.

Two Council vampires moved swiftly, yanking Jacob to his feet despite the fact he was doubled over and gasping for air. They lifted and slammed him down on the conference table, each holding one side of him. He cried out in agony despite himself.

"No."

Unintelligible a blink before, Lyssa's voice rolled like thunder. The hoarse sound a demon emerging from Hell would make. Mason still held her fast, her feet barely grazing the floor. Her hair was snarled, blood running from a corner of her mouth where she'd apparently speared herself with a fang. She looked decidedly vicious.

"Let me go," she hissed at Mason, her gaze red fire. "You've made your point. This is going to happen, my will be damned, so you let me go be beside him. Now."

Mason cautiously complied, keeping between her and the door. Fast as a snake and just as venomous, she spun when he released her, raking his face with her nails, slicing deep enough to tear ribbons of flesh that caught on her nails and fluttered gruesomely there. He caught her wrist, his own gaze flaring with temper. Then he dropped his touch, apparently startled at the thinness of the skin under his hands. It started to peel back and blacken as soon as he let go, as if the abrasion had spurred the process in that area. Though her face was rigid with the pain of it, she didn't let it diminish the contempt on her face by so much as a flicker.

"You son of a bitch," she said quietly.

His eyes were gold flint. "If you live, you may choose, as we all can, to take your own life. But it will be your choice, as is our way. Not the way of humans, who must face the inevitability of their own mortality. I won't let you die, not knowing if it is your true wish or the disease speaking."

"If he is dead, nothing matters. Nothing."

"That does nothing to convince this assembly that my judgment is unsound, and if you were in your right mind, you would know that."

"You don't understand."

"Don't I?" This time there was an undercurrent of anger in his tone, of bitterness so sharp it could almost draw blood. She ignored him, focusing on the two Council vampires holding Jacob to the table.

"He has acted with honor his entire life," she said in a quiet, terrible tone. "Though he's chosen to sacrifice everything for me, you treat him as a coward. Get your hands off him. If you don't, I swear if I survive this I will stake you myself."

19

WHEN they backed off, she moved forward. She stumbled, reaching for the table, and hissed in warning as Mason stepped toward her. As Jacob watched, she worked her way around the edge until she got to him.

It all struck him as surreal. There was Brian in a tuxedo, accepting a large syringe from Debra. The cylinder appeared to contain a cup of a blue serum. It was pretty, sparkling sapphire in the dim light. A pretty potion that would kill him. Meanwhile, Uthe had been courteous enough to bring his lady a chair. Perhaps when this was over, they would all—except for him—return to the Ball. Such was the way of life for vampires. Killing and death and socializing and civility so intertwined it colored their entire world in a way that no human would ever mistake for their own.

"His shirt, my lady," Brian gestured, looking uncomfortable but determined. "The serum is delivered directly into the heart."

She made a threatening noise as Debra began to move. The woman immediately backed off. After a tense moment, Lyssa reached across Jacob. Her fingers trembled, though her face remained impassive. A lesion had appeared at her chin and was moving down her throat, a hateful serpent of disease eating away her beauty. Yet no physical blemish could mar the fierce beauty of her soul, the wild purity of it he'd had the pleasure to touch and experience.

"You choose now to flatter your Mistress, when you've disobeyed her to the point I don't know of any punishment great enough to inflict upon you."

"No, my lady." He closed his hand over hers when she rested her hand on his bare chest, the black shirt sliding free with the pull of gravity, pooling on either side of him on the table. Brian raised him enough so that Uthe could step close and slide the rest off, leaving his upper body bare. His insides felt as though they were boiling, but suddenly he was cold on the outside, feeling the surface of the table, his nerves acting up, making his jaw tremble. He was about to die. He was lying here, waiting to have his life taken from him.

He tightened his jaw fiercely and increased the grip of his hand on hers, feeling her slim fingers, the disease eating the soft skin on the top. Her nails had already blackened, and it appeared two of them had fallen off. Jesus, it was moving fast.

"I never should have given you that third mark. They couldn't have done this to you."

"Ah, my lady." He cupped her face, the fear washed away by the aching need to ease the pain he heard in her voice. "Look at me. Please." When she did, he raised his head enough to brush her lips. "I would have coaxed you into it. From the day we met, you've never been able to say no to me and you know it."

She pressed her lips together hard and managed to cut herself with a fang. She averted her face when he tried to touch the wound.

Debra approached now cautiously with stethoscope and blood pressure cuff. "To monitor the progress of the serum," she explained. She managed to wrap it around his biceps efficiently, despite being pinioned under the cold stare of those green eyes.

"Not the usual accessory for a ball gown." He coughed, catching the end of her stethoscope and tugging on it for emphasis. Debra's glance flickered toward him but she didn't smile. She pressed two fingers on his chest, marked with a swab the entry point for the needle where it apparently wouldn't strike a rib. Then she put the stethoscope to his chest.

He could have told her his breath was starting to labor, a symptom his lady wouldn't display. But she had ones that told them the same thing. The blackened skin on her wrists was creeping upward like the slow ooze of mud. The trembling of her hands had increased. There was a twitching motion to her head that he didn't know if she had noticed. Her fingers spasmed on him, revealing that she was fighting pain. The smell of burning flesh was getting stronger, and when her other hand went to her abdomen, her expression tightening, he knew it was spreading inside. He felt it intensifying in his vital organs, though it was not eating away his skin as it was hers. Sweat collected on his skin and his body jerked of its own volition, just as hers did the same. She grabbed at the edge of the table, trying to stay upright.

"Hurry," Jacob said sharply.

No. No.

"We'd do this with an IV if we could, my lady, but there's no time. I need to do it." Brian paused.

He was smart enough to wait for her word, Lyssa reflected, though she knew that wouldn't be for long. They were clustered around her like vultures. Only instead of wanting to feed on her death, they were forcing her to accept a life she didn't want.

"Did you tell her she looks beautiful?"

Brian looked at her, startled. "My lady?"

"Debra looks beautiful in her dress. Did you tell her that?"

He blinked. Debra shifted her attention to the vampire queen.

"Of course she looks beautiful." Brian seemed to recover himself, his tone one of a person dealing with a mentally unbalanced patient. He flinched as Lyssa's hand closed on his wrist over Jacob's body, her eyes glittering.

"My mind is all here, young Lord Brian." Despite the rasp in her voice, she conveyed menace enough to capture his complete attention. "That's not the question I asked."

"My lady, there is no time for this," Lord Uthe said. Lyssa followed his gaze down to her sternum where the burning pain she'd thought was only in her chest had burned through to the outside, a charred expanse of flesh visible and spreading. The fire moved with it.

Jacob caught Brian's wrist and yanked him forward, taking advantage of the man's surprise to plunge the needle into his chest at the spot Debra had marked. He cried out at the pain, screamed as Brian depressed the plunger.

"No, no . . ." It took precious seconds for Lyssa to fight free of Mason, who'd lunged forward to hold her back until Brian injected the serum fully into her servant's body. Lyssa shoved him away at last, covering Jacob with her body and knocking Brian's arm back just as he withdrew the needle. The syringe fell to the floor, the large glass vial shattering. Several vampires started forward, but Brian cut a sharp hand at them despite their seniority, warding them away from her.

"It's done. It all went in. Debra, start the timer."

A silence fell over the room, the Council retreating to a tense half circle on the other side of the conference table. The stillness was broken only by Jacob's gasping as he tried to accept the pain like fire burning him from the inside.

"It's like being . . . branded all over for you, my lady. All over, inside and out . . ."

"He does not have to be conscious for this," Debra said urgently. "Brian—Master . . ."

"No." Jacob forced the word through clenched teeth. "My lady . . . please . . . will you hold my hand . . . ?"

The way he asked, Lyssa could tell he thought she was still angry with him. She wrapped her hand around his, despite the fact she had to see the beauty of his strong fingers overlapping her hands where the skin was peeling away, exposing muscle and tissue, pink for only a moment before it, too, began to burn. She'd borne pain before, knowing it would not kill her, that it was just a period of time to bear. Now she bore it the same way. For even this was just a moment, one scant moment that might be her last with Jacob. To be part of his mind, one with his soul . . .

The serum was a pain like the tearing of the inside of his artery walls. Her own pain merged with it, taking her to a point beyond screaming, almost into the trancelike numbness inflicted upon those seeking visions through agonizing torture. She couldn't stop the moan that broke from her lips.

"My lady, break the link." Brian's voice was sharp. "If you try to share his pain, you can put your body under worse duress."

Mason's hands clamped on her shoulders. "Damn it, Lyssa. Stop it."

Lyssa tried to shrug him off, but Jacob made a noise, drawing her attention to him. His fair skin tone had gone the white of a virgin's wedding dress and sweat pooled under his body on the table. He was bleeding from his nose, his eyes bloodshot. There was something unforgivable in making something so beautiful into this, she thought dully, tumbling in the surf of her own agony.

"Break . . . it, my lady. Talk to me . . . with your beautif . . . beautiful l-lips. I'll hear you . . . You don't have to share my pain to atone . . . for Thomas. He knew. He understood. As I do."

If it was possible, the words tore into her with even sharper claws than the pain. She shook her head, clutched at his arm and watched the impressions of her fingers remain, bruise the skin instantly. "I don't want you to leave me," she said, fighting the thickness in her throat. "You've left me . . . twice before. I won't tolerate it. You've disobeyed me enough today."

His face contorted. Fire rose in her, a reflection of the fire in him. Blinding, excruciating. He was mortal. He shouldn't have to endure this.

"Please, my lady," he pleaded. "I can't bear to cause you more pain. Please . . . a last request."

With an oath, she broke the link, but only because she knew if the pain ratcheted up any further, she'd lose consciousness. As awful as this was, knowing she'd wake up on the other side of a faint and find him gone was worse.

Though his body remained rigid with physical anguish, his expression eased. Her tears burned down her cheeks.

"It never occurred to you, did it?" She spoke softly, not because she cared if they heard, but because she had no strength left to raise her voice.

His clear blue eyes found her as she stroked his cheek. His limbs were trembling, his teeth chattering as he fought to focus on her words. She suspected any other man would be screaming. Without the connection, she couldn't feel the level of his pain, could do nothing but wait to take his life force from him like a parasite.

"W-What, my lady?" His lips had dried out and now cracked so that more blood seeped from the full and sensuous bottom one she'd nipped more than once.

"That I wouldn't want to live in a world without you in it."

Her sentimental Irishman. Her words made his eyes fill with tears, but when he lifted his shaking hand to her face, his thumb found the track of wetness from her own.

"Ah, my lady . . . you know you don't mean it." Somehow he found the strength to stroke her with the reassuring, calm touch he'd always used. He even reached out an arm, drew her away from Mason and closer so she lay half on his chest and could hear his heart thundering, racing, running out of time. "Once your strength . . . is restored, you'll say it was . . . the disease. Making you talk . . . like this."

Jacob could feel her weakness. It only reinforced what he knew he had to do. He would save her. She would live.

"You bastard." She clung to him. "You know it's not that."

He tipped her face up. He tried his best to fight past his own agony, to put his heart in his eyes. There was too much pain for him to know if she was still in his mind against his wishes. "Well . . . when you're . . . all better, I'll . . . My spirit . . . We'll wait to hear you say it again, and know you mean it. I . . . regret nothing except . . . leaving you." *Getting hard to focus.*

She swallowed. "I order you not to do this."

"Too late." *This you cannot command, my lady, because my first duty is to protect you. I will serve it faithfully, always.* He touched her lips with his, despite the charred skin on her face, despite the blood still running from his nose over his lips. That didn't matter. He made her hold his gaze, his shaking thumbs tracing her tears, unable to speak anymore, but still able to give her his thoughts. *In this life and the next. There will be a next. I'll never leave you alone. Not ever.*

Lyssa pressed her forehead to Jacob's shoulder. "I will not tolerate this," she said again into his flesh.

You will, my lady. 'Twill be all right. A vampire's . . . nature is to embrace life. Live . . . to the fullest.

"Shut up," she said, a sob choking her. "I don't wish to hear such things from you now."

Debra discreetly inserted a needle in his arm, drawing out a sample. Brian took it from her, both moving at a quick step to the microscope.

There were painful flashes of color in his vision. Sharp, knifelike silver, the red of blood, the glaring yellow of a too hot sun. Gods, he'd never hurt so much. Go on; get it over with, he thought hazily. My lady needs my blood.

Jacob . . . Her sob of anguish called him back.

Sssh, my lady. He was grateful that he could still be coherent in his mind in a way he could no longer accomplish verbally. *You always hoped that your sacrifices for Rex . . . that one day it would be enough. He would become the man you wanted him to be. That's not the way it works. He has to deserve the sacrifice. My lady, you deserve the sacrifice. You deserve everything I can give you and more.*

When he turned his head, pressed his lips to her temple, something inside Lyssa's heart cracked, an audible sound. Why didn't any of them understand? This was *her* time to go. Had she not suffered enough loss over the past two years to prove it, lived enough centuries, completed enough?

Perhaps she would like to live in this world longer, but for once with no expectations of her. She'd been prepared to die because Jacob was going to die. She couldn't imagine what compass would be there to guide her on the other side of this. She could choose to meet the sun once she was restored to herself, and Mason had as much as said no one would stop her. But where would Jacob be by then? If they went together, as irrational an idea as it might be, it was in her mind that he couldn't be taken from her. She'd worried about the idea of Hell, of having no soul. Now she only worried about not having him by her side in the afterlife, whatever it might be.

Damn it all, she'd always provided her *own* compass. Why should this situation be so different? She was not helpless; she never had been. Jacob was right. A vampire's natural desire, contrary to their dark reputation, was to embrace life. How could she embrace it for both of them?

"My lady, it's time. You need to drink now."

She raised her head, feeling Brian's light touch. As she heard the terrible words, she met Jacob's eyes, inches from hers.

"No," she whispered. Her eyes filled with tears anew, thinking of life draining out of that clear gaze. She knew what death looked like there, the cloudy glassiness. She couldn't bear the idea. How had he come to mean so much in such a little time? She was sure everyone in the room thought it the distorted effect of the disease. Thomas thought it was because they shared a link that extended far beyond the past handful of months. But her head was filled with everything Jacob had said or done during the short time in this life they'd had together. From the very first he'd made an impression like a launched arrow, and the shaft of his presence had embedded itself more firmly every moment since then.

She didn't care that they saw her tears. Brian was shifting, obviously warring with the need to press her and the automatic reaction of their kind to draw back from an emotional display, give her the courtesy of privacy. She felt him exchange a glance with Mason, and Mason start to step closer to her again.

"Do not push me on this," she said. *You can lead a horse to water . . .* The menace in her voice was enough to push them back. She kept her gaze on Jacob's suffering form, those beautiful blue eyes no longer able to pay attention to what was going on in the room. He was just staring at her as if memorizing every feature in her face, just like the first time she'd seen him at the Eldar.

"I almost walked out that night," she said. "Impulsive, brash man. You know that?"

I knew you wouldn't leave. You wanted me too much.

The trace of humor that flickered through his eyes broke her heart further. His voice in her mind had become as erratic and harsh as his breathing now. She laid her hand on his chest, watched it shake with his movements. "Liar," she whispered. "You were nervous. You lie to your Mistress now, even on your . . ."

"Deathbed." He finished the sentence when she couldn't. Threading his trembling fingers in her hair, he began to apply downward pressure to her nape, even as she began to resist. "Please . . . my lady. Come let me nourish you . . . once more, give you life. It will be . . . my honor."

He sucked in an abrupt, laboring breath. His body began to ripple, the precursor to a convulsion. His hand clutched involuntarily against her throat and dug into the rotting skin there. *Hurry. Please, my lady.*

The muscles of her face were going to shatter with the force of the grief that swept her. With a cry of animal pain, she pressed her face to his throat and bit, cupping his neck to hold him, to convey her presence, her awareness of his sacrifice even as she took what he offered. His life for her own.

The serum was there, a taste that made the blood even more metallic and somewhat bitter, interfering with the taste of Jacob she loved, that she wanted uncorrupted. She remembered her first taste of him had been spoiled by the medicine that had staved off the virus for a while. The beginning was the end. Full circle. She'd seen that proven throughout her life. Now she knew it held an important key, if she could struggle through the agony of this moment. Beginnings and endings . . . Beginnings.

Her hand found his other hand, lying across his bare stomach. Their fingers intertwined once more. She gripped hard, and he gripped back. She knew she was giving herself an unwelcome barometer, for that grip would slacken as life left him.

No one lived up to expectations, most especially herself. But once the soul could find a way to swim out of that defeatist quagmire, it would reach a quieter plain. See someone as they really were, not as the artist intended him, not the interpretation of the viewer, but what he was, the simple truth of a soul . . . A still place where things were simply as they were.

There was a poignant beauty in the finding of that reality, because so much of life was seen through the mind-numbing, deafening cacophony of illusion. Hell was noise, and Hell could close in every day.

In the silence that descended upon her, the pain was just a backdrop, a roaring wall like the water at the mall that evening when she gave Jacob the second mark. It stilled everything outside of where she sat next to him. The only thing that lived was her and the man on the table.

A soul is a soul. Thomas's words.

Jacob was Jacob, whether in the body of a samurai guard, a knight or a young man carrying both mantles as his legacy. Even as he spun the tires of his bike and made Bran chase him, Bushido had been his life and his philosophy, whether he knew it or not. The way of the warrior, spiritually, physically.

Serious, amused, sometimes even shy or naive, though he would be disgruntled to hear her think of him that way. He would apologize for none of it, only challenging himself to be and do more for her well-being. No, he wasn't appropriate to be a servant. Not by the definition that existed in the vampire world. But when the expectations fell away, disappointed, there he stood inside her, everything she'd ever wanted. He also was exactly what she needed, and she wished she'd realized it sooner, so she wouldn't have made him fight so hard to earn her realization of it.

She was a queen, and a vampire. Daughter of a Fey lord. She had her compass, and it did not answer to anyone surrounding her now, only to the man whose life she was taking, who'd given it freely. To whom she'd given her heart in a way she hadn't to anyone else, not in her entire long life. As a vampire, she didn't possess the humility that mortals with their short life spans had to cultivate. She expected things to occur the way she wanted them to occur, and by God she wasn't going to accept this outcome.

"My lady—"

"Can it hurt her, to keep drinking?"

"Perhaps she needs the additional strength . . . She was so close to the end . . ."

Disparate voices, worried murmurs, irritations only. The lesion on her hand disappeared. The one on her breast closed, healing into smooth skin. She felt the burns on her face receding like their worries. Their awe and amazement vaguely reached her, as did Brian's sense of triumph.

She released the serum from her fangs, felt it speed through Jacob's body and merge with the antivirus serum as she opened herself to what was going on inside him, his body nearly drained of its blood. It caught her heart in a fist, the feel of those systems failing, the process of death she knew intimately, but she also saw the serum winding through those passages, quicksilver mixing with the blue among empty passages that had been filled with blood she'd drained from him. Just a little more . . .

The effect of Brian's potion was rocketing through her like a hallucinogenic, only in reverse. The clarity of her reality was now so sharp it was as if everyone in the room but her and Jacob were moving and speaking in extreme slow motion.

His fingers were loose. No responding pressure as she held them. Somewhere his soul was hovering, wanting to go to the place he deserved, but he would still want to see he'd done what he swore to do. Protect her to the end.

But I haven't released you. You are still my servant, and I command you to come back to me, Jacob. I won't let you go.

Silence. A void. Her soul suddenly emptied as if it had been tipped over, obscenely quick. She knew what having a servant die felt like. Thomas had been the worst of all those she'd lost, until now. A never-ending emptiness, the very definition of loss.

What she wanted didn't appear to matter. She looked, searched desperately within him for any indication, but now her serum glittered in his system like malachite on rock. Inanimate, sparkling but inert.

"He's gone." Debra's voice, soft, compassionate. The stethoscope was pressing over his heart, just above their linked hands. His hand was heavy, wanting to fall, drop away from hers. Lyssa wanted to kill Debra, silence her forever for saying those words. "Lady Lyssa, it's over."

Lyssa lifted her head, her fangs marked with the remnants of his blood. Traces of ethereal silver mixed with it.

"She . . ." Uthe's eyes widened, flicked to Jacob. "She turned him."

"She tried to turn him." Mason stepped forward before panic could sweep the room. "She was unsuccessful. The man is dead."

A pause, where she could hear her heartbeat. One, two. Thump. Thump. Something was . . . odd. The physical pain was gone, but she wasn't going to survive the tearing agony of Jacob's death. He was gone, no longer in her mind. She was alone. Completely alone. Something was dying . . . something important but she couldn't seem to care . . .

Energy exploded through her. Lyssa arched back, screaming as the transformation clamped down on her, tore her into pieces. The dress split. Her fingers, rising to untangle herself from it, lengthened with the razor-sharp claws of her talons.

It was as if by emptying her reserve of conversion fluid into Jacob's blood, there had been a reaction between Brian's serum and hers that had kicked back through her own system and overloaded it. Her Fey form was the only one strong enough to take the reaction. Like Mason and the Council, her own body had ignored her wishes and was forcing her to grasp at life.

Whenever she transformed, the exponential melding of her two forms was something she could control with careful precision, as Jacob well knew from the night she'd taken him on the forest floor. She'd transformed portions of herself between human and Fey as needed without effort.

Not now. Her other self literally exploded out of her vampire-humanoid form, tearing her flesh to ribbons, tearing screams from her throat as she inadvertently dropped Jacob's lifeless fingers. His hand flopped to the side, his blue eyes staring, glazed over. She snarled, her fangs lengthening to curve over her chin. With serpent-quick movements she lunged onto the table as Brian started forward with Uthe and Belizar. Now they stopped as she hissed, going to a crouch.

"You will not touch him."

Her wings cut from her back as if coming into the room from a different reality. Ten feet from tip to tip, she filled a good portion of the chamber with her physical presence, though the mental impact was far more considerable. The Council members were up against the wall.

"Holy Christ," Brian murmured. "My lords, I didn't take into account . . . There was no time. She isn't full vampire. This must be a mutation of the serum because of her Fey blood. My lady, stay calm. We can figure out what has happened . . ."

The wildness of her soul manifested itself, throwing off all yokes of restraints. She had nothing left to lose. She laughed, the rasping sound of a harpy's deadly hiss whispering through the trees at a soulless hour of night. "I am calmer than you can imagine, Lord Brian. I am as calm as death."

For years, she'd exercised rigid control over her words and actions to achieve her goals for her own species, to protect her servant, to try to love a husband unable to accept love. Always knowing what was expected of her, never resenting it, knowing the advantages that power gave her to live her life as she chose. Until now. They would know what it meant to try and wrest power from a queen.

Lord Belizar's eyes narrowed. "It is not a mutation, Lord Brian."

Cocking her head, she placed her claws on either side of Jacob's head, covering him completely, like an eagle guarding her young. "If you are clever enough to figure that out, Lord Belizar, you are clever enough to let me take my servant without attempting to molest me further." Her voice was a rough growl.

"Lady Lyssa," Helga said, "you cannot convert a servant. It breaks our most basic law. And there is no telling what he could be, particularly converting him with the serum in his blood."

"She's no longer Lady Lyssa. Perhaps she never was." This from Carola.

"She is your queen," Mason snapped, despite the fact his attention was riveted upon her, his expression one of fascination and amazement.

"She just abdicated." Belizar threw out an arm, gesturing angrily in her direction. "Look at her. She has deceived us, for how many years? We cannot follow one such as this. Nor will anyone follow a Council that does. As head of this Council, I order her execution for her deception. Her servant's body should be burned and so should hers."

"Over my dead body." Mason moved so he was at her side.

The Council shifted, muttering. "With all due respect, my

lord . . ." It almost made Lyssa laugh, Brian observing courtesy when the air was rife with barely suppressed violence. "A human body cannot take the serum. She has not converted him. I tell you without doubt that Jacob is dead. I could study the effect of the serum on him. If you burn him—"

Lyssa blinked. "You think I would let you dissect him?" The harsh menace of her voice in this form would have been intimidating even if she was in a mild mood, so she appreciated that he squared his shoulders and met her gaze when he began to respond.

"My lady—"

"She is not to be addressed thus." Belizar was practically frothing at the mouth. It took visible effort for him to look at her. Lyssa remembered how Jacob had looked at her the first time she'd changed. Touching her sleek, muscular gray skin with wonder. Making her shiver with longing.

"We have not voted," Lady Helga said. Over the shouts and arguments, in which she could smell the tension moving to boiling point, Lyssa met Brian's confused but not unsympathetic eyes. But they would not get Jacob's body. Would not set fire to it. Would not cut it up. None of them.

He was cold. All the steps of mortal death, followed by the slow rot of his corpse. The blue eyes would decay and disappear. How could God bear the inevitable end to one of His most beautiful sculptures? Did none of it matter? Were all the noble principles simply the fantasies of living beings who assigned them to a Divinity who didn't care? If that Divinity didn't care that Jacob's body had been destroyed, then Lyssa couldn't imagine It would care if she turned the walls in here red with the blood of the very Council she'd created.

"Kill her . . ." Belizar's command. Seconded by another Council member. And another. She'd known vampires were like this, had accepted it as a weakness even as she appreciated their strengths. What was remarkable was how humans tolerated it enough to become their servants, this superiority that, when challenged, proved itself to be no less self-serving and motivated by fear than any other form of prejudice, human, vampire or otherwise. She was weary of it all.

She was hungry for blood. Anyone's blood would do at this point. If they didn't stop their cacophony, she would impose silence in a way that would most satisfy the ache inside her.

She dropped low, readying herself. Mason was at her side, his body still, waiting. His eyes had narrowed, his lip curling back. He pulled the sword hidden in the cane he'd brought with him to the chamber and gripped the wooden shaft in his opposite hand.

Only on Belizar's face did she see complete resolve. The others were uncertain, angry and confused. Some were perhaps willing to follow Belizar's lead, but not with the odds so decisively stacked in her and Mason's favor. But just like a scene from *Gone with the Wind*, where the Southern gentlemen were so certain that all that was needed to win the war was their honor, so her Council still clung to the naivety that their "purity" made them invincible. If they charged, she knew without a doubt she and Mason would kill them all. And the vampires would be once again lawless, leaderless . . . She struggled to care, but all she felt was the weight of loss and fury.

"Take her now," Belizar thundered.

His voice was swallowed by a muted roar outside the chamber. The walls shuddered as if the structure of the west wing had been shaken on its foundation. Distant screams speared through the walls, under the door. The smell of smoke reached their heightened senses.

Several vampires had thrown themselves forward, but now came up short in confusion. Lyssa cared not for what was happening outside of this room. The second they moved, she lunged into the air. Her wide wingspan cut sharply through the air, talons reaching with deadly chaotic and unpredictable intent. Her barbed tail lashed out like a whip as she hovered over Jacob where none could get to him. Mason went to a half kneel, weapons at the ready, ducking under the movement of her wings as if he'd fought next to a Fey warrior all his life.

"Earthquake? What—"

"No," Lord Mortimer said. He stood at the wall, still uncommitted to Belizar's suit. "Explosion."

Belizar's eyes were focused inward. "Malachi says we are under attack by . . . vampire hunters," he said tersely, affront in his tone at the very idea. "A significant force in numbers, if not capability. They somehow planted explosives on the verandah and have swarmed into the castle."

Lady Helga cried out, doubling over. Lord Welles caught her by the waist, steadying her. No one in the room asked what had happened. They all knew the signs of losing a servant abruptly with no time to brace the body against the loss. Hadn't they just seen an example of it moments before? "Tristan," she whispered.

Jacob's loss was like a fire roaring through Lyssa's blood, squeezing her vital organs. She was going to go mad.

Hold, lady. Mason's voice. *Be our queen.*

"Malachi says the explosion wounded perhaps sixty, killed a dozen servants at least. They targeted the upper levels and are taking advantage of the surprise to advance. We will go to their aid," Belizar said shortly.

His gaze rose, met Lyssa's. "You have your head start, Lady Lyssa. If you do not want this Council to hunt you down and bring you to justice for your deception, then you should make certain we never see you again. We will purge the memory of your hybrid existence from our ranks."

"If you have so little value for your life," she responded, red eyes glittering, "come and find me, for I will never hide from the likes of you. It is not so difficult to defeat a mind that refuses to change."

Belizar's eyes flashed, but abruptly his expression suffused with shock. "The vampire hunters have breached the inner walls, but there is . . . another group." His attention snapped back up to Lyssa. "Vampires. There is a group of vampires apparently part of this, using the humans to attempt an overthrow of the Council. They are on their way here, led by—"

He stiffened. Though he managed his reaction better than Helga, his face still went rigid with pain. "Malachi."

"Who?" Mason stepped forward, his eyes narrowed.

"He did not . . ." Belizar shook his head, struggling to overcome the effects of the severed link. "He couldn't show me before they took his life. They must have seen him. He exposed himself to be sure of what he saw."

"We know who it is," Lyssa said flatly. "It is Carnal and his carrion eaters."

Lord Stewart snarled. "We should have known. He has been increasingly defiant."

"Joining with humans to attack us?" Mortimer scoffed. "Carnal, who despises humans far more than anyone else?"

"Perhaps Carnal was able to overcome his prejudices to use their strengths. He has a bit more adaptability than this Council. Unfortunately, he's also a sociopath," Mason observed contemptuously.

"Carnal has been traveling a great deal these days," Lyssa said. She didn't want to be involved in this, didn't want to care, but she was speaking despite herself. "Recruiting for this, I suspect, and he was wise enough to choose those who were in his camp, no chance of the secret slipping out."

"You foresaw this—" Belizar accused.

"Oh, good Christ. You all foresaw this. You fools just assumed he would use the Council floor to try to initiate his coup. In all your civility, you've forgotten that the root of a vampire's nature is violence, particularly when the end he seeks is total domination," Mason snapped. "You did nothing. You should have staked him out years ago."

So in the end, it is your cynicism that is our ultimate truth. You were right. I was the biggest fool of all.

Mason glanced at her. *No, my lady. To try to make your world a better place and fail is far nobler than to never have the faith to try.*

He turned his attention back to the Council. "If we are to stop this we need to get out there. Now."

"Where we cannot tell friend from foe?" Belizar shook his head.

Lyssa snarled. Even during this, the most horrible moment of her entire life, she refused to let someone like Carnal take control of what she'd worked so hard to build. She felt the horrid stillness of Jacob's body beneath her, remembered Carnal striking his face, remembered how close Jacob had come to staking him. If he'd been alive, she knew what he would be saying.

What are you waiting for, my lady? Go finish what I started. Kick his goddamn ass.

She registered the fleeting feral grin on Mason's face as he caught the thought and reminded herself to break his jaw later, just on general principle. It would heal, after all.

"Your opponents will be Carnal and the territory leaders who have been seeking pre-Council ways."

Where vampires could rampage unchecked in the human world, which would spell vampire extinction. She played for just a blink with the idea of letting it happen, and then let that go. All she had to do was remember Danny, Devlin, Mason . . . Thomas. Jacob.

Even more appealing, she'd have the immediate opportunity to kill someone. Many someones, and that was what she wanted more than anything. At least of the things that were within her power.

"That means he will likely have twenty percent of the overlords with him. They'll have armed their servants," Uthe spoke. "There's no time for subterfuge. Either we go out now and respond with aggression or they corner us here. Mason, it's your home. Malachi said they destroyed the verandah. What way are they likely to take to get here?"

"The west corridors are the quickest route. They might divide their forces though, bring someone around the east side to cut off escape."

"We have allies out there." Lyssa found it easier to concentrate on the problem at hand instead of the terrible reality of the still body on the table. "Any of you who have a blood link to a vampire here you trust, let them know what is happening. That was the point of Carnal's alliance with the hunters, or however he accomplished their presence here. Those loyal to Council are out there fighting human hunters. By the time they understand the real enemy is Carnal and his group, they'll have us cornered and slaughtered."

"Do it," Uthe said, since Belizar seemed at a loss for words at the moment.

Lyssa nodded, gazed into space for a moment, mirrored by other Council members. She looked for Danny. Blinking several times, she started at the click of the link, like the blast of a television turned on at high volume. Through Danny's eyes, she saw carnage. Smoke, fire, the rubble of the verandah. Bodies flung and sprawled. Limbs amputated. The chaos and noise of battle.

She and Devlin were fighting back-to-back, fending off a quartet of hunters. Praying she would not distract her to adverse effect, Lyssa fed her the information.

She heard Danny swear colorfully in acknowledgment. As she tore the head off a hunter, Lyssa appreciated not only the viciousness but the creative suggestion related to Carnal's origins. Danny kicked the body out of her way and went after another. Slamming him to his back on the ground, she ducked as Devlin launched a pike and took a man in the chest who was coming to the aid of her current victim with a crossbow.

"It's done. But how long it will be before she can act on it, I don't know. She's under siege."

The other vampires reported similar results. Mason's eyes narrowed.

"An unexpected aerial attack will slow Carnal down, confuse the hunters. It will give those we've contacted time and space to muster the other vampires. And give us cover to get out there."

Lyssa shook her head. "I won't leave Jacob here alone."

"He won't be. I'll stay here," Mason responded.

"You are as powerful as she is," Helga pointed out. "We need you to fight."

Brian stepped forward. "I will stay by him, Lady Lyssa. As I live, he will suffer no desecration, not even from me."

She pinned him with a gaze, and he bowed. "I may not be everything you want me to be, my lady, but I do not lie."

Lyssa glanced down, slid her talon along the side of Jacob's brow. She couldn't bear the dead expression of his face, but she couldn't close his eyes, not with her hands like this. She tried to make the claws retract, something that was typically easy for her, but there seemed to be no link to her human form she could trigger, the familiar path back to herself.

Debra stepped forward. Brian reached out a hand to hold her back, a protective gesture that brought her to a halt.

"Please, my lady," she said softly. "Let me help."

"There's no time for this," Uthe said. He was always sensible, logical. He didn't have Belizar's ambition, just the desire to see the world as she'd envisioned it. Nevertheless, at the moment Lyssa still wanted to destroy him with all the others.

Lyssa inclined her head. Brian did not release Debra's arm. "My lady . . ."

"I will not harm her. I may not be everything you want me to be"—she tossed his words back to him, indicating her altered form— "but I do not lie."

His jaw tightened. Nodding, he allowed his servant to move forward into the shadow of Lyssa's tensely poised body. Debra gently closed Jacob's lids. Removing her earrings, flat silver circles ironically bearing the Celtic knot symbols for love, she took out the hooks and laid the disks on his eyes. When she lifted her head, Lyssa saw no revulsion, only a sorrow that wrenched her own up several notches. It was easier to handle her grief when she knew it wasn't shared by anyone in the room. The tears in Debra's eyes could undo her.

"Jacob had more honor than any man I've ever met, Lady Lyssa. We will make sure your wishes are respected or die trying."

"How do we know she won't get out there and join them against us?"

Anger flushed Mason's expression. "Damn you, Belizar. She's given more to this Council and our way of life than anyone in this room. You—"

"Because Carnal was responsible for my husband's death. He drove Rex to complete madness, such that I had to kill him." Lyssa spoke flatly, ignoring the gasps. "I want him dead. I can assure you I would not stand with Carnal for any reason, even if it meant the destruction of this Council, or the end of the universe for that matter." There was one stuttering flame in her heart, trying to stay alight for God knew what reason. Was the desire to see Carnal dead the only thing she'd have left after this night? "However, if you do not swear to me that you and the Council will leave Jacob alone, then I will sit back and watch what happens to you."

"After all your years of dedication, you would abandon us now over this dead human," Belizar sneered, but there was desperation in his face as more screams came under the door.

My lady . . . Mason, his voice urgent.

"After all my years of dedication to this Council, you shunned me in less than a blink. Turned your back on me because my blood is not as pure as yours."

Belizar's jaw clenched. A long, tense moment commanded the chamber as they felt the rumble of further explosions, possibly grenades, bullet fire snapping. Roars of rage. Sounds of death. Getting closer.

"Done." Belizar nodded his head. A quick jerk. "He will not be touched by any in this room or anyone under our command."

Lunging aloft, she burst through the arched design of glass above the double doors, her wings pinned back like a Stealth fighter.

20

FUELED by visions of darkness and blood, Lyssa twisted and spun out of the arched walkway along the castle wall, spearing up over the east side of the castle to get a view of the ocean and garden side where most of the explosions had occurred. On the way, she saw hunters traveling close to the castle walls on the outside levels, moving in three-man teams to flush out smaller groups of vampires and servants who'd not been in the ballroom area. They were not her concern. The hunters no longer had the advantage of surprise. It was a fair fight at this juncture, and would soon swing to the vampires' favor, if it had not already.

The blast charges had turned the sweeping verandah into rubble, as Malachi had reported. They had blown out the ocean-facing walls of the ballroom, scattering glass and chunks of stone across the gardens. Bodies lay in the wreckage. More vampires than she would have expected, but she could tell they'd not been killed by the explosion, but by the hunters who'd rushed upon them before the dust cleared and took advantage of their dazed state to stake or decapitate them.

Among the ruins, the servants and vampires still standing waged battle with the hunters. Danny had spread the message, for Lyssa noted that a main force of vampires was engaging the hunters, slowly closing together to form a wall behind which a select group of Council allies could retreat into the castle, seeking to intercept Carnal and his group and come to the Council's aid.

Though she saw approximately three hundred hunters, she still wondered at the absolute foolhardiness of an attack on two hundred vampire overlords and Region Masters at night. But as she hovered at her vantage point, she saw the open verandah and ballroom area were the most vulnerable points to detonation. Tonight was the one night they were all gathered in the same place, at the same time, for the Ball and Court meeting. And somehow Carnal had fed them that information, was part of this, of why the hunters were here.

The Council's unexpected and timely departure had likely made him froth at the mouth. That alone gave her black satisfaction. He could not count on the hunters' assistance to assassinate the Council. Successful hunters were those who struck quickly and retreated. Even those three-man teams were not making incursions into the castle's interior. They were working their way along the walls and likely would disappear back into the rain forest cover once they reached the end of their assigned area.

She noted dispassionately that they were purposeful, calm, determined. As she plunged and took the turn around to the west wall, she could tell these were mostly hardened veterans, not zealous youths.

There was a leaden weight in her chest where her heart should be. She used it now to tip her into a circle, bring her into a tight, silent glide.

Carnal was moving along the walkway on the second level toward the Council chambers. He was in the lead of a cluster of vampires, almost fifty of them. So young and stupid. So vicious. Carnal bore a silver ax and a look of deadly confidence.

Enjoy your five minutes of power and fame, you bastard.

Because of the communication she and the Council had made with Danny and others like her, it was now impossible for them to slaughter the Council, claim it was the hunters and then take power by opening up a blood war on the human race. But if they did take out the Council, they would have chaos, civil war. Wholesale attacks on humans would result in the widespread realization that vampires did in fact exist. Mortals would turn all their technological resources toward wiping out vampires entirely. And since the hunters already knew about the Delilah virus, they'd simply inject it in any human willing to carry the inert virus as a deterrent against vampire bites, drying up the only food source vampires had.

That was everything that could happen in the future. For her, there was only this moment. The wind sheared over her skin and her fangs pierced her lips, goading her lust for blood with the pain. She swooped down toward Carnal. Apparently she drew the attention of the group of hunters in the courtyard below him, for an arrow struck her leg a glancing blow, creating fire in her blood. She turned her head, hissed a warning and kept on in a straight line toward her prey.

But as was the way with all creatures of pure evil, Carnal had a second sense when it came to self-preservation. At the last moment, he looked up.

His eyes widened, and he bolted. Narrowly missing him with the grip of her talons, she plunged into the wall behind him instead. As it crumbled, slabs of concrete showered around her to create a cloak of dust. She was aware of the startled group of vampires, some holding their ground, some retreating. Several were brave enough to throw themselves forward, thinking to attack her. She didn't see Carnal. Screaming in rage, she flipped backward and shot through their ranks. Saliva pooled in her mouth as she caught hold of one of them, tore him into two pieces and showered the rest with blood, sending them scattering. The predator in her rejoiced. *More.*

Run, for there shall be nowhere you can hide.

Out of the peripheral vision of her widely spaced eyes, she saw Mason and the other Council members materialize, striding down the open walkway. Mason's coat flapped around his torso, giving the impression of a hawk's dark feathers as the Council members ranged out across the expanse of the walkway just behind him in three staggered rows of six, ready to charge. Nearly five millennia of experience, and there was no fear in any of their faces, whereas Carnal's vampires were still reeling from her attack such that they'd not yet presented a real threat to her.

But the Council was still outnumbered.

She did a somersault and dropped like a stone, intending to feed the panic and her own bloodlust with another couple of corpses.

Just before she reached them, a rumble gave her warning. The upper walkway exploded, erupting in the expanse of space remaining between the Council and their adversaries, taking several of them down in the blast. Lyssa flipped back from the concussion and bounced off the castle wall, screaming in fury as hot bits of debris showered her skin. She launched herself into the smoke, out into the open courtyard.

Angry shouts came through the obscuring clouds. She heard Mason's battle roar and knew he'd recovered quickly enough to take advantage of the moment.

It gave them an unexpected advantage. The fact the walkway had blown where it could endanger Carnal and his followers told her that he hadn't been working as closely with the hunters as she'd supposed. He'd perhaps fed them information through a human plant serving him. But he hadn't gotten all the details of their attack.

Such was his arrogance, he assumed he would murder the Council and deal with the "disturbance" the humans caused afterward. He'd never considered them capable of interrupting the execution of his own plot. Based on their pattern with the previous explosions, the location of this detonation meant the hunters below were preparing to charge this level.

She needed to disrupt the hunters to give the Council time to regain control. They couldn't afford the distraction the humans would cause. The fortunate thing was they'd managed to slow the forward progress of Carnal's challengers. She had a moment or two.

Don't be greedy, Mason. Save Carnal for me. I'll be back.

His voice was a savage snarl in her mind, telling her he was engaged in combat. *I'll do my best to honor my lady's wishes. Though I'd prefer she not sully her fangs with his filth.*

She hoped when she got back, Carnal would still be on his feet. She wanted him to see her coming.

～

"Jesus Christ, Gideon. There it is again. How did it survive that blast?"

Gideon paused on the second level, staying close to the wall for cover, his eyes everywhere. The flying creature that looked like a cross between a gargoyle and a harpy swooped over the courtyard, seeking them, he assumed, since it winged in close to a pack of the rear guard behind them, sending them retreating into the shadows of the lower-level defiles for cover. The vampires just ahead of them on this level were snarling, sounding almost as if they were . . . fighting. The glimpses he was catching of them through the dust showed them grappling, a few weapons flashing. But there were no other hunters up here, just his team of a dozen, hanging back fifty feet, waiting for the go order to charge forward into the fray.

They'd managed to get up here in less than eight minutes from the original blast, but he knew every moment would swing the tide further against them. He wanted to give the command to charge in, to take those disoriented vampires out before they could rally their defenses, but the sounds of battle were throwing him. Besides which, he couldn't move forward out into the open on the remains of the walkway without dispatching that winged threat. First things first. He notched an arrow to his crossbow and took aim. "Let's hope it's some type of vampire, or something even more destructible."

This setup stank. His gut told him they'd gotten in too easy. When two of their members had disappeared almost immediately upon reaching the inner gates, he was certain they'd been sold out. But they'd forged ahead. Too much planning, too much invested. Already they'd taken out more vamps in thirty minutes than they'd managed all year. Three dozen, though of course they'd lost a third of their own people. They were supposed to be in and out in fifteen minutes. Guerrilla warfare, not toe-to-toe combat. The loss of the human servants was regrettable, but hell, who knew they'd fight so fucking viciously for the bloodsucking fiends who had enslaved them, brainwashed them into thinking being a servant was something they wanted?

Your brother went willingly.

He shoved that away. So far, everything was going as planned. Better than planned. Perhaps that was what was making him uneasy. Things never went as planned. Why did he feel as if a trap was closing around them, the deeper they forged into the resort?

Fuck it. He raised the crossbow, steadied as the creature poised in midflight, wings stretched out full, head cocked, looking. Then it turned in the air and saw him.

Gideon. No.

It reverberated through his head, locked his trigger hand, overwhelming him like he'd been caught in the electric field of a thundercloud. He fought it, even as he saw the beast dive, coming toward him with death in its eye. Oh, shit. He couldn't get his damn arms to move. Let . . . go . . . of . . . me. *You son of a bitch.*

He closed his eyes at the last moment, the pain of the final, unforgivable betrayal so sharp he almost welcomed his own death. The creature's heat encompassed him like the sharp burn of sulfur.

Tobias screamed.

Gideon's eyes snapped open, and he spun to find Toby sprawled on the ground. The creature had one set of talons on his torn throat, the other clamped on Gideon's crossbow, holding it toward the ground though he hadn't released his grasp on it.

Its head was turned to gaze directly into his face. At this level, he realized only the wings were big. Though sleekly muscular, she was definitely female. The mounds of her slim breasts were obvious, as were the folds of her bare sex. Her body was small and fine boned.

"There is a faction of vampires seeking to overthrow the Council right now, Gideon." Her voice in this form was a harsh rasp, close to a growl. "Up on that walkway. They infiltrated your ranks, used your attack. They've set up patrols all around the perimeter of the compound so when they succeed they'll have all of your hunters who survive trapped. They probably plan to torture and dine on your friends in grand celebration of the new order."

Looking down, she nudged Tobias with a toe. For the first time, he noticed the man had been taken down with a knife clutched in his hand. "This was apparently one of the spies," she said in that serpentlike hiss. "Chosen to take you out as one of the leaders, I assume. He stinks of Carnal's blood, and he was getting ready to put this between your shoulder blades."

He knew her eyes and that mocking tone, despite the mutation of her vocal cords. Gideon took a deep breath. "You."

She gave a faint smile, a disquieting gesture with her fangs longer than his fingers, and blood staining them. She glanced up at the portion of the sky from which she'd struck. "Help cometh from Heaven, no? Rally your people. If you go down to the third level belowground, accessible through the kitchens, you'll find a dungeon. It's been made into a sexual playground. Behind the iron maiden there's a loose stone. It guards a passageway underground that will take you a half mile down the road, into the jungle. You'll take no more lives today, but you'll keep your own." Her green eyes, round and spaced widely, narrowed in pure malevolence that sent a chill through his body. "Don't expect that passage to be there again. I'm not stupid, nor is the vampire who owns this place. Did you have a plan to spare your brother, or did you even care to check that he was here?"

Gideon's jaw flexed. "We both made our choices."

Lyssa stared at him. Something changed in her expression that made him wish she didn't have him trapped against a wall with no ability to lift the crossbow in defense. "I should have let him stab you in the back," she hissed.

"Why did you even come down here?" he snapped. "Jacob held me back with no effort. Why not just disarm Toby the same way? And when did you teach Jacob how to do your mind tricks? Servants can't do that kind of shit. You finally figure out how to exploit his psychic power for your own benefit?"

Lyssa blinked. "No one controlled your mind. I can't . . . I move too swiftly to be hit with one of your arrows. He's . . . dead. They . . ."

His stomach dropped at the words. With his free hand, he reached out to clamp onto her arm, demand what she meant. But she was aloft, headed back toward the second level as though she'd been launched from a cannon.

"Jesus, she's like something out of a children's nightmare."

The comment came from one of his people just behind him. He'd smartened up enough to give the man a sharp glance, make sure it was someone really covering his back instead of intending to spear him, but his mind was whirling. Jacob, dead? No, he'd *heard* him, loud and clear. But from Lyssa's face, he could tell she'd thought he was dead. Suddenly the ravages of pain he'd seen around her eyes, the ones he saw every time he forced himself to look into a mirror, made sense.

Gideon spun at the yell of warning. There was a wave of new shouts and curses and the clash of more weapons as a full legion of vampires swept down upon them.

They were dead, he thought.

Instead, the vamps swatted him and his hunters out of the way.

The faction that mowed over Gideon and his men was led by a slender woman in white with gold-blond hair. She looked like a blood-soaked version of Barbie, another disquieting image he didn't want imprinted in his head.

The Barbie's servant, sticking grimly at her side, roared at the vampire challengers and drew their attention, spinning them around. They snarled in return. Both sides accelerated into a lightning charge, coming together in a flash of gleaming fangs, snarls, weapons.

The overthrowing faction and the faction loyal to the Council, just as Lyssa said.

His people were smart enough to take advantage and shoot arrows into the mob. But Lyssa was right. They were in the wrong place at the wrong time. They needed to get going, because whatever side won, they'd obliterate his small army. The original plan needed to be followed. Strike swiftly, get out. Their fifteen minutes were up, for now.

He snatched out his radio, even as he began to shout out commands.

~

Jacob. Jacob. It was in her head, a cry in the darkness. She reached out, looking for him. Felt something. A fog of clouds, confusion. A clip of a thought. There was so much energy and death around. She knocked vampires out of her way, tossed hunters out of her path, screamed a cry like an enraged eagle when she swooped down the corridor and saw the Council room doors on their hinges. Diving inside, she spun in a circle, but in a blink she knew Jacob wasn't in the chamber. There were hunters and vampires fighting here who had worked their way down from the main battle ensuing on the walkway. Brian had put Debra in the corner, and she was crouched down as he shielded her, fighting off one of Carnal's followers, his face a mask of protective fury. Lyssa picked up his opponent, dashed him against the wall, crushing his skull. Before Brian could digest her sudden appearance before him, Debra scrambled over and staked the disabled vampire with a chair leg.

"Lady Lyssa, we didn't abandon him . . . Jacob . . ."

His expression told her, lodging her heart farther up into her throat. She tucked in her wings and shot back out, circling over the area, eyes frantically moving over the battlefield. Blood everywhere, the flash of fangs. Weapons that had been in the hands of the humans were now in the hands of other vampires, being used against Carnal's followers. There were many servants in the mix, fighting capably as so many of them could. The communication link between Masters and Mistresses and servants was turning the tide. From her vantage point she could see them getting organized, mobilized. The loyalist servants were commanded to turn their attention to the retreat of the vampire hunters. Their Masters and Mistresses focused on Carnal and his group. She briefly saw Danny smeared with blood, her hair tied back hastily with a strip of the dress she'd torn off completely so she could fight in just corset and short slip. With her bare feet, she looked like some type of petite Roman warrior, her blond hair streaked with blood, her fangs gleaming, eyes hard.

A stray arrow whizzed past Lyssa. So busy seeking Jacob, she barely avoided it and it scored her shoulder.

Where are you?

～

Gideon plunged back down into the courtyard with a set of wooden knives and the rage of a berserker. He'd watched Lyssa charge into a room and return to swoop over the courtyard, taking dives over them with the frenetic speed of an erratic bat. Something had happened to Jacob. She was looking for him. Jacob might need him.

So while he'd ordered the retreat of his own people according to Lyssa's direction and they were managing it just as they were trained to do, one group falling back as the front line held their retreat, he'd surged forward, helping with the coverage. He'd be damned if he'd leave until he knew what was going on.

Lady Lyssa didn't need to know that he'd had one of his people pose as one of the masked servants and affix a tracking beacon to Jacob's cuff earlier in the evening. He had known where his brother was at all times. Jacob's call to the chambers had been fortuitous and saved him having to figure out a way to haul his ass out of the ballroom before it blew.

The tracking beacon said Jacob was still in the Council chambers, but when she emerged and launched herself again, he knew somehow Jacob had gotten separated from his jacket.

Gideon turned, looking. Reached out with his own senses. He'd always known how to find Jacob when they were on a vampire hunt together. It was a sense, like breathing. It wasn't words, a call. It just was. An instinct.

And there he was. He stepped out of the shadows at the opposite end of the walkway. God knows how he'd gotten past that snarl of vampires. He was pale and entirely savage looking, shirtless, bloody. But there was a wandering look to his eyes, suggesting some type of disorientation as if he'd been hit in the head. Then he was gone, another cluster of struggling vamps engulfing him. He was alive and apparently okay, though he wouldn't be for long, standing there dazed and unprotected. When he pulled his mind back together he wouldn't likely forgive Gideon anytime soon for this. As if Gideon gave a damn about forgiveness anymore.

There he was again. Now he was up on the railing. He turned, looking toward the sky. No question who—or rather what—he was looking for, though his timing was lousy. *Wake up, you stupid bastard.*

Gideon broke into a run, yelling it. Carnal was bearing down on Jacob, materializing from one of the side hallways where he'd probably decided to take a coffee break while his lackeys did his blood work.

No one was taking his little brother down while Gideon lived. Even if the bastard had given his heart and loyalty to a vampire. Then Jacob leaped from the rail and was gone, retreating down another corridor into the castle, Carnal in pursuit.

Son of a bitch. He'd been drawing him, using himself as bait. Gideon cursed, took the stairs three at a time onto the landing. He stumbled over some rubble, regained his feet and charged after them.

When Gideon reached the corridor he found it was a tribute hall and practice room for different periods of ancient weaponry. Jacob had seized a nimcha blade as his first choice. Carnal unfortunately had chosen a mace.

Jesus, that third mark allowed his brother to move fast. Jacob was keeping pace with the vampire remarkably well, such that Gideon could barely follow their movements until the mace caught on the blade, wrapped it.

"Jacob!"

As the ball swung toward the guard, forcing Jacob to release the handle, Gideon ripped the closest available weapon from the wall, a flat-headed Danish battle ax. They were turned so he couldn't attack Carnal's back, and there was no time with that superhuman speed anyhow. Desperately, he tossed the heavy weapon with a grunt the few feet in Jacob's direction, hoping to give him something with which to shield himself. Gideon lunged for a sword, planning to spear Carnal from behind while Jacob held his attention.

In its heyday, the Danish battle ax was assigned only to the burliest fighters, for they were the only ones strong enough to wield it effectively. Jacob was likely to get gutted by the mace while his hands were occupied in lifting the thing for a swing.

Instead Jacob caught the ax one-handed and swung upward, faster than Gideon could follow. Carnal roared, shock coursing over his features, but it was a final act of defiance. The blade severed cleanly through his neck, his head rolling off his shoulders and thudding to the ground.

In real life, it had all the macabre look of a badly done special-effects movie. Gideon didn't like horror movies for just that reason.

Jacob drew in a shuddering breath, his blue eyes alight with a rage that made Gideon oddly hesitant to draw closer. Then Jacob's knees buckled, and it didn't matter. He was next to him, putting his brother's arm over his shoulders to help draw him to his feet. "Are you hurt?"

Jacob glanced at him, something unusually still and focused about his eyes. "That was *so* fucking satisfying. It was almost better than sex. Let's put his head back on so I can do it again."

"You've lost your mind," Gideon stated flatly, but he couldn't help the giddy relief at the humor in his brother's eyes. "Are you *hurt*, you idiot?"

Jacob chuckled, his head dropping forward as if he suddenly didn't have the strength to hold it up.

"I was dead, Gid. Absolutely dead. You know . . . what you said? About Mom being up there, saying, 'Why'd you do a fool thing like that?' I think I heard Dad for a moment . . . felt Mom's hand on my head. You remember how good that felt . . . the answer to everything . . . I need to find my lady. She's unhappy."

"You're seriously freaking me out. We've got to get you out of here."

Jacob nodded. "I feel like shit. But I'm going to live, Gid. Even if you don't want me to."

When he smiled this time, he revealed the pair of gleaming fangs that had split his lip open.

"Oh, bloody fucking hell."

21

THE private airfield was quiet in the hour before dawn. As the limo pulled in and Elijah Ingram put it in park, he focused on the small plane waiting there. He had the Beretta ready, but lately he'd realized it might as well be a BB gun. So his hand also moved over the small crossbow that Jacob had given him. Thoughtful one, that boy.

Jacob was first off the plane. Elijah's brow creased. He was moving slowly, his face down. And he needed assistance. His brother was with him, but he was on point, keeping a lookout, not helping him walk. That was being done by a tall, elegant man with copper hair whose perfect beauty, even impossible for a comfortably straight man to deny, screamed vampire. Gideon walked a few paces away, an ax hefted in one hand, a crossbow in another. He was fairly relaxed—for Gideon. It told Ingram he didn't think they were being pursued, but it was obvious from the torn clothing and the blood all over them, as well as the weary expressions, that they'd been in one hell of a fight.

Where was the lady? That boy didn't go anywhere she wasn't nearby. Almost as soon as he had the thought, a shadow passed over the windshield, a current of wind that had him touching the crossbow, craning his head to see what had just moved over the limo.

When the men were within thirty feet of the car, a creature landed behind them. Ingram jumped out of the car with the weapon before his brain registered that neither Gideon nor the pretty one appeared startled by its appearance. Her appearance, on closer examination.

Jacob dragged them to a halt, managed to straighten and turn to face her. Gideon's lips tightened in that expression that suggested he wasn't entirely happy about matters. More than usual.

The boy moved toward her unaided, the other two men standing back. When he went to his knees, it seemed a planned move, though it visibly cost him quite a bit of effort. But she was already there to catch him, her talons wrapping around the back of his vulnerable neck, drawing him into her, the wings balancing her at half-fold as she bent her smooth, hairless head over his.

"Holy Mother," Ingram breathed softly, for he knew those haughty, elegant mannerisms.

Knowing about vampires, he had room in his mind now for other creatures not part of the human experience. While she was entirely frightening, there was a fascinating beauty to the lean, feminine muscle, the long pointed ears and intimidating fangs, the graceful way she tilted her head over Jacob and focused on him with large, almond-shaped, entirely dark eyes.

Jacob's body slumped into unconsciousness. Lyssa lifted him, carrying him to the grass running alongside the tarmac. The copperhaired vampire knelt on the other side of him, and Elijah came to join them as Gideon stood off to the side, still standing guard.

"He's just passed out again," Lady Lyssa said quietly. "He shouldn't have tried to kneel. Honorable knight. Foolish man." Her voice cracked.

When the tall man lifted his gaze to study Elijah, Elijah remembered a friend of his who had raised wolves from puppies. He'd assured him they were tame. But whenever Elijah went to see his friend, the wolves looked at him the way the vampire did now. The civilized veneer was just that, and he was tolerated only because it would upset his friend if they ate his company.

"Elijah Ingram," the limo driver said at last.

A faintly ironic smile crossed the vampire's face and he inclined his head. "Mason."

Bending his attention back to Jacob, Mason reached over him and gripped Lyssa's wrist. "We need to get him belowground and give the transition time to complete, build his strength," he said in accented tones that whispered of deserts and trade caravans.

"How about we start by getting him into the limo? It's close to dawn." This from Gideon. Sharp, tense. He looked at Ingram, not at the others.

"Gideon." Lyssa drew his reluctant attention. "You need to stay with Mason awhile. Jacob will need your care and his connection to you as his brother. It helps, to keep a new vampire centered. After the first three days, newborn bloodlust will strike hard. The strongest reminder he has of his morality will be you."

She had something tied around her neck on a ribbon, and now she bent so Mason could untie it. "It's a vial of my blood," she explained at Gideon's narrow look. "The vial came from Brian's temporary lab and Debra helped me fill it. Because I'm his sire, Jacob will need a drop of it once a day for the first thirty days after the full moon to manage the pain of the transition. If he needs restraining, use a cell. Not wrist restraints."

"I can't fucking believe this." Gideon walked two paces away, turned in a circle, came back. "I can't . . ."

"You can't what?" She raised a brow, her eyes narrowing.

He closed his eyes, pinched the bridge of his nose. "I can't believe he let you in on that trick." He said it as if from a great distance. "How he gets out of wrist restraints."

"I guessed. He didn't tell me." She gazed up at him. "Gideon, do you remember the famous story of Gandhi telling a Hindu man how he could be forgiven for killing Muslims?"

"You're not seriously going to compare—"

"He told him to go find an orphaned Muslim child and raise him as his own. And that he must raise him as a Muslim. Hate isn't working for you, Gideon. Your brother is a vampire now, and he needs you. He loves you more than anything."

"No," Gideon said. The words came out thick, full of anguish.

"Not more than anything." He squatted then and laid his hand on Jacob's brow with a surprising gentleness.

At this moment, Lyssa could easily imagine Gideon many years ago, sitting on the edge of a bed, stroking the sleeping head of his eight-year-old brother, taking the place of their mother and father. She wished she could reach out to Jacob and touch his head, too, but the minute she raised her hand, saw the long claws, she remembered. Drawing back, she cleared her throat to continue, conscious of Ingram and Mason's regard.

"After that, he can drink moderately from another, but chain his throat, waist and legs when he does, standing guard so you can pull the donor away when he's reached a pint. He needs no more than that, but he won't be able to control his hunger. It takes three moon cycles before they gain that ability, but only if he has a drop of this every day. Mason knows all of this, of course."

She shifted her gaze to the limo driver. "You won't see me again, Mr. Ingram. I need you to make that phone call for me as we planned, for I don't know what the Council will do about their vote. I suspect many of the lords who would have gone after my fugitives will have other priorities for a while. Mason will explain the details. Before I left Atlanta, I had Jacob make one last transfer to your account, enough to keep you comfortable a long while. I don't tell you that to obligate you. But if you would help Gideon with Jacob, I would be grateful." Her voice broke a little as she brushed her knuckles along Jacob's brow again. "And don't tell him I carried him. You know how you men are about those things."

Mr. Ingram hesitated a moment, then he extended his hand. When she indicated the status of her own, he shook his head, reached out and circled her wrist. She watched, nonplussed as he bent and kissed the top of her mutated hand.

"Ma'am, I don't know a man who hasn't been carried by a good woman at least once or twice in his life." He paused, apparently thinking before he took something from his pocket. Folding it in his handkerchief, he handed it to her. "This is something that belonged to my wife. I gave it to her to keep her safe and blessed when we fell in love, short though that was. I know you can't wear or touch it, but—"

Lyssa felt the metal through the cloth. She took a corner and shook the contents free of the fabric into the cup of her clawed hand. When she saw the silver cross, despite herself her gaze strayed down Jacob's bare chest, down to the waistband of the torn and blood-stained slacks, under which she knew the same symbol rested.

It had a long chain fortunately, which made it easier to manage with the talons. Looping the chain around her neck, she let the talisman drop between her bare breasts.

"A final lesson for you," she said at Elijah's surprised look, extending the kerchief back to him. "A vampire with faith may embrace relics as much as anyone. I've never lost my soul."

She'd come close with Rex and the loss of Thomas, but Jacob had saved it. Carried it for her. Kept it safe. A good man was known to do that occasionally for a woman as well. In fact, he carried it now.

My heart, and my soul. Everything that matters.

"If you will all take care of him, I will owe you a debt I can never repay." She gave an arch look to Mason. "And you perhaps will have absolved yourself of one or two of your many sins."

Then her gaze lowered. Looking at her servant, the trace of humor fled. Bending, she pressed her lips to Jacob's brow. *I shall miss you, Irishman. Sir Vagabond. Sir Lancelot of the purest heart. My life will be empty without your laughter, so be happy. When the sun shines more brightly, I will know you are still out there, laughing and smiling for me.*

She moved her mouth down to his, a featherlight touch. She couldn't bear more than that, because it reminded her too much of the size of her fangs. But suddenly, she didn't have a choice. A hand curved around her nape, his knowledgeable fingers teasing the sensitive skin there. His mouth was kissing her back, lips parting, tongue seeking hers, drawing her down more closely so her breasts pressed against his chest. The nipples drew up in aroused reaction, making her ravenous to lie upon him, press her sex to his, feel that searing connection, the affirmation that he was alive. Alive.

She couldn't do that. For several reasons. But she couldn't find it in herself to immediately draw back either. Her tears spilled over her lashes, baptizing his face, and he murmured softly into her mouth, caressing her face, the three tight folds of skin molded beneath each of her eyes. One hand slid down her shoulder to take a grip on the clawed elbow of one wing. Her tail curled around his calf, the barbed tip resting just inside the thigh.

When at last she did draw back, her mouth was soft and wet as the expression in his eyes.

Mason cleared his throat and rose. "We'll wait over there and give you a moment to say good-bye. Mr. Ingram, are there any spirits in your car?"

Ingram frowned. "Not certain. Haven't felt any."

The vampire chuckled, and even Gideon's lips twitched. Both gestures went a long way to easing some of Elijah's tension about the odd band, their postbattle appearance. And the lady's unexpected metamorphosis. "You've been keeping too much paranormal company, my friend."

"Booze, Ingram. He's wanting to know if you've got a drink." Gideon grumbled it, shouldered the crossbow. "I could use a hit of the strongest thing you've got myself."

Ingram nodded. When he saw Mason exchange a significant look with Gideon, he reluctantly joined them in the walk back to the car, giving the man on the ground and his Mistress their privacy.

Jacob watched Lyssa gracefully lower herself from her haunches to her knees next to him, the wings at half-spread to balance herself. *So, you want to explain how Lord Mason can read your mind so well, my lady?*

The depths of her entirely dark eyes in this form were so deep he could lose himself in them. *I don't answer to you, Sir Vagabond. And you once told me if I knew all of your secrets, I would tire of you in no time . . .*

Christ, his arms weighed a bloody ton. Regardless, he brought her down to him again and was even rougher this time, holding her fast, hands moving to her shoulders to grip. He could feel her struggling against the desire to curl her claws into him. When he growled at her she capitulated, biting into his skin, drawing blood. Her body was shaking. He splayed out his fingers, touching her throat, the ear. He wanted to hold her more tightly, but the moment felt fragile. As if their brush with death was still too close, and moving too quickly or wanting too much might shatter the fantasy and take them back to a horrible reality.

He let her ease back only because the grayness around his vision from the intensity of the embrace made him worry he'd pass out again.

"I thought I'd lost you," she said.

"You very nearly did. I saw tunnels, white light. Relatives."

Her face grew still. "Should I have let you go?"

He shook his head. "You weren't there. It isn't Heaven if you're not there. Plus, I think I saw my uncle Wilhelm, which means it must have been Purgatory at best. I can't imagine God wanting to put up with him on a daily basis."

She closed her eyes and lowered her head farther. His touch slid to the back of the small skull, fingering the pointed tip of one ear.

There were no shields between their minds now, probably because of the emotion of the moment. Since she was cured of the virus to all appearances, he was sure she'd regained the ability to block him at will. However, he was too tired to focus on the whirl going through her mind. He could sense she'd compressed emotions so strong inside her they were ready to detonate.

"I've never seen you hold this form so long," he said.

As soon as he had the thought, the answer flashed through her mind, despite a tightening of her lips that told him she tried to block it.

She wasn't choosing to not raise her shields. She *couldn't.*

The significance of what Mason had said struck him then. Why did they need a moment now, when they could have all the moments they wanted somewhere protected—a hotel, her house in Atlanta, anywhere but in an open airfield?

Must say good-bye . . .

Though she tried to obscure it with other thoughts, she was too used to relying on her shields, and he had a whole new level of psychic clarity in addition to his own to defrost the window of her mind. Pushing his weariness aside, he concentrated and got it all dumped on him in one flood that hit him low in the gut.

She couldn't change back. Whether it was the effect of the serum on her Fey blood that Brian had not factored in, or the stress of turning him when he was already well on the other side of the Veil, she'd lost her ability to return to the form she knew he loved so much.

"Don't be daft, my lady." He processed her thoughts and his own, separating them instantly. The shot of adrenaline at being alive had carried him far enough to dispatch Carnal, but no further. He cursed how weary his body was, how he could do little more than touch her face, grip her hand, but he marveled at this new hyperclarity of his mind, as if he could process a hundred thoughts at once. He wondered if it was that way for all of them and wryly reflected there might be some truth to the vampire sense of mental superiority. "I love you in any form. All of them are beautiful. I remember a night in a forest when I gladly would have taken you like this. You denied me."

"I would have killed you. This form is not gentle when roused."

"I think I can handle it now. I'm invincible."

"You look ready to conquer the world." Despite the dry tone, she hesitated, her long talons hovering. He captured her closed hand, took it to his face and turned into it, kissing her palm while her lethal claws curled into his hair.

"You'll regain your strength in three days," she said unsteadily. "Or rather, a fledgling vampire's strength. Right now your body is regenerating for a vampire's unique physical attributes. Once you get that strength, Mason will teach you how to make the most of it, manage it. How to feed, how often. How to use the mind link, though as a servant you already have the basics of that. But I think, because you already had psychic ability, that Mason will be a good teacher of how to take greater advantage of that. Gideon is going to help, too."

Jacob shoved past the muzziness that was hatefully trying to draw him into a doze. "How? By pushing me into a murderous rage to test my control?"

She wasn't able to keep the humor from her eyes this time. "I've rarely seen you in a murderous rage. That seems more his area than yours."

"And what are you talking about? Where are you going?" He

circled her wrist with both of his hands, as if he could hold her there, when he knew she could shake him off like a clumsy infant. Which at the moment he was.

"I don't know yet." Her lips twisted ironically. "Which is good, since I no longer have the ability to keep you out of my head. But I can't stay among you like this. Whether or not the Council comes after me, Belizar is right. They won't accept me like this, not as their queen. Even if times change, it will take time. Right now, in their minds, the line is ended. No more royalty in the vampire ranks. I'll go where I'm safe, never fear."

"I'll go with you."

"No." She shook her head. "You need time to think. This is a whole new world for you, Jacob, and the punishment for making a vampire out of a servant is only against the maker. With Mason's backing, you'll be accepted. He'll find you a place in the Middle East, or you could even go to Lady Daniela's territory. You need time to figure out your place in your new world."

"I've always known my place." He said it with heat. "It's with you."

The blaze of anger in his blue eyes shot longing through her. He was *alive*. So alive. She wanted to devour him. Hold him to her breast forever. "You stand a better chance with Mason."

If they did hunt her, she couldn't bear seeing him harmed, isolated, ostracized. If she was killed, she didn't want him seeing it. The anguish he would feel . . . She would feel it. Making it that much worse as she was shot from the sky like a poached eagle. Them trussing her lifeless body, hauling it back to Brian's lab to be cut up like a piece of meat.

"No." He sat up then, seized both of her wrists.

She closed her eyes. Despite the seriousness of the moment, she teased him softly with his own words, from what seemed a long time ago, when he had thoughts he didn't want her to hear. "I forgot you could do that."

"You won't leave without me, my lady." Jacob glanced behind him at a quiet step. Mason approaching again, his eyes locked on his lady's.

"He can't stop me forever. There's nowhere you can go that I won't follow."

"Think, Jacob. Please, for my sake"—*for one breath, just one heartbeat*—"don't think of me. Think of yourself. Learn from Mason. If you don't, you'll not live long as a vampire. I need to know you're alive and well. That's all I want."

"Like hell." Did she think he couldn't feel the ache of her loneliness already? She'd never needed many around her, but those she chose, she chose carefully, loved fiercely. In less than two years, they'd all been taken from her. She would shut down, retreat from the world, let the animal part take her over as she lived in some cave. She'd willingly forget what it was to be humanoid because reverting to animal instinct would be easier. That way when they hunted her down and killed her, she would only have an animal's confusion about what was happening. She wouldn't be tortured by the anguished remembrance of why.

"Yang-Sun, my old teacher, told me a person who loses everything is being given a new beginning by the gods. This is what's best." She freed one hand to trace his lips, then realized she couldn't without cutting him. Her face crumpled.

That doesn't matter. Kiss me, my lady. Please.

"I can't." She couldn't stay another moment or her heart would disintegrate into pieces. She had to let him go. *Good-bye, Jacob.*

"No!" Though he tried to hold on, she wrested away, tears gathering in her eyes again, and launched herself.

"My lady . . ." He tried to struggle up, staggered. When Mason came to his aid, he threw him off with a snarl, managing it himself. As he watched her wing away, a dark shadow against the predawn sky, he swallowed over jagged glass.

"My lady."

I release you from my service. Be happy.

"Son of a bitch," he swore, glaring at Mason as the man drew close again. The amber eyes were sympathetic, but implacable.

"Come. We need to get you inside."

It hadn't occurred to him, but now Jacob realized he was getting warmer. A great deal warmer. Uncomfortably so, warning him of the dawn. He would never feel a sunrise again, but knowing he could never feel his lady's touch eclipsed that loss, made it insignificant.

No, he *would* see her again. He would learn the damn lessons, learn everything he needed to protect her, use his new strengths to do that, and to find her again. He had to. Not just because he loved her so much life wasn't worth living without her, but because she needed him in a way she'd never needed anyone since she'd matured into her adult vampire abilities.

She'd not only lost the ability to shapeshift into human form. She'd sacrificed her vampire blood to save his life. When the dawn came, she wouldn't have to go to ground. Jacob had become a vampire, and she'd transformed fully into a Fey creature.

Because of their link, or his new abilities mixed with his own natural ones, he'd picked it up from those last subconscious thoughts. While she was still immortal, she only possessed the strength and quickness commensurate to the musculature she bore. The way a lion or tiger had power. She was fast, but not so fast she couldn't be followed with the eye. If the vampire world learned that, she'd be as vulnerable to them as . . . a human. She was not strong enough to stand against even one of the lower echelon. It was possible even a human's tranquilizer dart could take her down.

She might or might not have her unknown scope of magical Fey abilities to aid her, but in her mind she'd doubted it. Without that, Jacob knew even among the Fey she'd be considered little better than their lowest caste. An untouchable.

She was his lady, his to protect. His to love. He was not going to lose her.

22

Four Months Later

HE'D been in the Appalachians for two weeks now, hiking deeper and deeper beyond the touch of human civilization. The last evidence of human existence had been twenty miles ago, the remains of a camp for recreational hikers. By day he pitched his tent, made with special fiber to screen out light. By night he moved with silent, deadly grace through the wood, not even detected by the forest creatures until he was right upon them. He could place a hand on a deer's flank, feel the soft coarseness of her hair, smell her scent before she darted away, startled, crashing through the night. One evening he'd emerged from a creek where he'd been bathing to find a wolf pack surveying his small camp. He'd snarled, baring fangs. They'd snarled back. But then they turned and loped on.

Tonight, he'd been traveling for several hours before the moon managed to rise above the cloud cover. As he squatted by a stream, he dropped his head on his shoulders, enjoying the feel of the darkness, the way the breeze lifted his hair. The sounds of the night. The stars.

He'd noticed them before of course, but until his lady, he'd always been more of a daylight person. Now he knew the constellations, the phases of the moon, and studied with interest the way shadows moved over the silver face of the symbol of feminine power and mystery. He'd realized the night wind was actually silent. It was what it passed through that gave it a voice.

After months of nearly being driven mad by his own burning impatience, a calm had finally settled over him. She was near.

Do you really think you can hide from me, my lady? I know you've been close for several days now. Staying just out of my sight.

During the time he'd had to endure his full transition to a vampire form, sometimes they'd had to chain him to hold him. Chains that no fledgling should be able to break he shattered within three nights. So they doubled them, strengthened them. As he fought the bloodlust, he knew what was tearing at his vitals was not a hunger for blood, but for her. Knowing she had no one to protect her. Robbed of the great strength she had.

Handicapped. Like him, she would be adapting to her new form, its capabilities. Only he was adapting to a strength and quickness far beyond a mortal's. She was adjusting to far less of those qualities than what she'd always known. Alone.

He'd had the company of Mason, Gideon, Mr. Ingram and all the resources at their disposal. She was a fugitive.

He did everything Mason told him he needed to learn and more. But there were things he could not rush. The ability to control the bloodlust only came with the full transformation and maturing of the systems in his body. Gideon made it clear he'd stake him if he tried to leave before then. Mason, while a little less vitriolic, had also made it clear he wouldn't be permitted to leave until he wasn't a danger to innocents.

"Once the transformation is complete, it will not completely rule you," Mason had said. "But even during the first decade it's tempting at times of great stress or anger to let it take control. You must fight it whenever it arises until you are certain you can control it. You need that discipline even more than a normal fledgling, for your power is exponentially greater than one."

That anomaly had disturbed Mason enough that he talked Jacob into allowing Brian to study him to help them understand what had happened. Brian was amazed to discover that somehow Lyssa had given Jacob over a thousand years of matured vampire powers when she converted him. Strength, quickness, compulsion.

He would have traded some of that strength for his lady's experience at reading minds over a great distance. While the ability to communicate with a human or vampire whose blood he'd taken was a common vampire skill, the ability to maintain the clarity of that communication over great distances was apparently something a vampire acquired with practice, not as part of conversion. A week after her departure, Jacob had panicked upon rising, for he could no longer discern her thoughts in his mind. While his precognitive ability had helped him adapt to the skill quickly as a servant, he hadn't realized how much of it was guided by Lyssa's own abilities.

He could feel her. Locate her generally. But he couldn't hear her thoughts. Only a jumble, a puzzle of words, as if the signal was scrambled. Mason and Gideon both thought that was for the best. That it would make the passage of time easier. Instead, he kept waking from nightmares in which she was locked in a coffin, screaming his name while he was unable to hear her.

He had no interest in vampire politics or finding a place in vampire society. He knew where his place was. To help him elasticize the frayed wire of his patience, waiting for the damnable transformation to complete so he wouldn't be tempted to drain innocent Girl Scouts, he made the decision to let Brian study him to his heart's content, in return for a vital favor.

As a result, in addition to his carefully rationed store of blood packed in his cooler backpack, he carried something even more important. All he needed to use it was his lady.

When he tracked her to the Appalachians with Mason's help and had Elijah drive him there, he began to read her thoughts again, once he was close enough. But she was elusive, so that he only heard snippets. Sharp, brittle pieces of thoughts, quick syllables cut off. Sometimes there was a stillness to her mind, so full of nothingness it was like she had found a way to compress it and make it tangible, keeping everything else crowded out of her brain.

During one part of the drive, he'd felt her fear. A blast of fury followed by physical exertion. As if she was running . . . being chased.

Knowing he was too far away to do anything to help her, he'd only been able to sit there in the second seat, frozen with rage, wanting to rend, to tear . . . fighting for control as the sound of Elijah's blood pumping through his heart nearly drove him to madness.

Now that he was in the forest, narrowing the distance between them, he still sometimes broke into a swift run on his treks at night, trying to get even closer. He felt her restlessness. Aching want. Sometimes tiredness. Once or twice even illness, when it seemed she tried a food that wasn't the best source of prey.

He began to feel her physical reactions. The way water moved smoothly down her throat as she swallowed it from a flowing creek. Leaves fluttering against her skin as she curled up in the most dense part of a tree to sleep.

She was so close. She'd been watching him for several days now. He could have tried to see her, find her, but he had to be patient. The humanoid part of her kept her staying close. The instinctual part, the creature, was mistrustful, uncertain whether he was friend or foe. As he'd feared, she'd allowed that part of her to take over a significant part of her reasoning functions.

Because she was close, he could wait, be still and silent. The nature of a vampire was not to rush. He understood it now. He could be patient, not only because he had time, but because there was nothing beyond his reach to acquire. The gift he wanted was her trust.

Tonight would be the night. He was sure of it. There was a stillness in him that was far from empty. It was filled with everything.

"You seek the aberration among us."

Jacob's head snapped around. He came to his feet in a lithe, quick move as the man stepped out of the shadows of the forest on the other side of the creek.

Not a man. Not exactly. A Fey male.

Jacob had never seen a member of the Fey other than his lady and the depictions in the books given to her by her mother centuries before.

All of them were associated with an element. Like his lady, this one was a creature of the earth. His wings reminded Jacob of the brown leaves that drifted to the ground in fall, the edges curled. The delicate inner web of veins was like gold thread against the smooth silk of the brown. His long black hair did not completely cover the point of his right ear, which was curved back. He was tall and lean, his face elegant and chiseled, reminding Jacob somewhat of Mason. The aura of magical power told Jacob not only was he facing a man of some class distinction, but a Fey who had nothing to fear from Jacob's speed, quickness and power.

"The Fey can completely kick our asses any day of the week," Brian had told him. "They consider us beneath their notice most of the time. An irritant. However, what's odd is your lady's Fey form is unknown to us and possibly to the Fey themselves. Quite frankly the two species, vampire and Fey, have never been able to procreate, before or since Lady Lyssa's parents."

Irritant or not, Jacob wasn't going to let the insult pass. "I seek my lady. The Lady Elyssa Amaterasu Yamato Wentworth, Queen of the Far East Clan. Daughter of a Fey lord and a vampire princess. I seek no aberration."

The man cocked his head, his eyes gleaming like almond-shaped moonstones.

"She has wandered this area for a week or so now. I have chosen not to drive her out as my kind have in other territories she's passed through."

Jacob took a step forward, anger flashing through him. *Feelings of fear, pursuit* . . . "She should be welcome anywhere."

The Fey ignored that. "She is liked by our little ones. Our pixie fairies are our more simple brethren, but their hearts are pure and playful. They will not tolerate proximity to anything that is not good. Well, except chocolate." A faint smile touched his lips. "I do not suppose you brought any with you."

Jacob shook his head, nonplussed. "Pity," the Fey male said. "They will likely wreak mischief with your belongings as a result. If they had not championed her, I would have killed her."

Then he was gone into the forest again, just like that. As if he'd never been, his words hanging in the air like a warning.

Jacob stood silently, watching the movement of the trees where he'd disappeared. He wondered how many Fey lands he'd passed over unmolested the past two weeks. Lands his lady had been driven out of as if she were unwelcome vermin. A queen.

Control, Jacob. He remembered Mason's admonishment, though he didn't think the vampire lord would argue with his desire to go back through those same areas and pluck wings off the Fey as if they were oversized flies.

Moments of great emotion will be the worst . . .

Then the anger was gone. Everything was gone except his awareness of what was in this clearing. She was behind him.

He knew it, because her proximity was like the brush of hands on his mind, moving outward onto his nape, his back. How he'd missed that touch. Even her touch as a Mistress. The mark of her nails, her hands restraining him. The vulnerable woman lying beneath him, her body open to him.

She would not vanish on him this time. She would be there.

Please, God.

As he completed the turn, he stopped and gazed upon the one thing he'd wanted and needed to see more than anything else over the past four months.

She sat in a tree, her wings at half-mast, gazing at him out of her luminescent dark eyes tinged with red, her fangs curving under her chin. She blinked at him. The tail curled once around the branch, the excess flicking slowly from side to side.

The desire to touch her was so strong he had to fight it down like the bloodlust. He stood there, his hands clenched, counting, waiting, regaining control. She watched him curiously. Wary.

"My lady? Are you there?"

Her brow winged up and she cocked her head. A questioning croon came to her mouth. Rasping. The noise seemed to puzzle her, as if she'd meant to form words.

"My lady." Jacob controlled the compulsion to leap on her then and there and hold her fast. He wanted her to trust him. He didn't want to have to overpower her, even though he knew he might be being a fool. He'd missed her so much. There was no way to describe how much in words. It was all about feeling, and he was nearly choked with it now.

Mason had been surprised the serpentine mark on his back had not disappeared, for in the past the third mark had disappeared on the small handful of servants who had been illegally turned. Jacob's had simply turned more silver. It hadn't surprised him in the least.

"Are you hungry?"

Squatting carefully, he removed three of the strips of meat from his pack and laid them on the ground. When he looked up at her, she was studying them. As she raised her gaze to him, he felt her reaction. Contempt.

Not a scavenger.

His lady was definitely in there. While he bit back a smile, it drew tears to his eyes.

"I've dreamed of you, my lady. Have you dreamed of me? Do you dream of your servant, or have you forgotten me? Tried to forget me?"

Her eyes shifted back and forth. She was blinking, shaking her head, and she put a talon to her forehead, scraped. "Buzzing," she rasped. "Music. Sweet."

Her voice was so rusty from disuse, it made his own throat close up in pain.

"My lady." She stayed in her tree though she tensed as Jacob rose, came to the trunk and put his hand on the bark, splaying his fingers. Her eyes rested on his hand, moved up his arm to his face. Lingered on his lips.

Not . . . serve me. No longer. Not call . . . my lady.

"I couldn't imagine anyone who has seen you daring to call you anything else, my lady. And I am your servant." His voice took on an edge of possessive command. "As you are my lady."

His eyes marked the shudder that ran through her as she responded to it. Oh, she was definitely in there. It made him remember the night she'd allowed him to master her. Wanted him to master her.

Jacob had thought waiting for four months would drive him to insanity. Suddenly four more minutes seemed more than he could bear.

As if she sensed his mood, she shifted, got her haunches under her. Was he mistaken, or was that the light of challenge in her eyes?

"Come down here." His eyes glinted. "Or I'll show off and come up."

She launched herself from the tree, taking flight, moving to the next clearing on the other side of the stream. And found him waiting for her there, crouched just below the branch she was on. He sprang and she took off again, but he anticipated her, caught her ankle.

She turned on him, hissing, and they spun through the air. While she was able to dislodge herself and soar free again, he managed to right himself and land on his feet half-crouched, as sinuous as a cat.

~

It was an impressive move, and Lyssa's heart stuttered in her chest confusingly. She leaped away again.

But with each jump, things that had been nonspecific swirls of images were becoming clearer. Words and thoughts exploded in her mind, hurting her head because she'd denied herself thought. She hadn't wanted to think anymore, didn't want to be anything more than a creature of the forest, living by reaction and defense from day to day.

The first day she'd allowed herself to get close enough to see him, not just feel him, she'd sat in the trees and yearned.

A handsome man as a mortal, that handsomeness was now enhanced by his otherworldly quality, the comfortable power of a man who'd fully embraced all the things he was, all the energy that was his to command. When he spoke out loud as he often had these past few days, sensing her near, his voice had been smooth, melodious. Words caressed her body as if they were kisses from his mouth, intimate touches of his tongue.

It perhaps had been a sin beyond measure to turn him into a vampire. He'd already been devastating to female senses as a mortal.

In the end, she didn't know if she was really trying to escape him, or make him prove himself to her. She led him on the chase for several miles, and he wasn't even winded. From tree to tree, path to path. Over water, up steep grades.

As she evaded and he followed, the more he stayed with her, the more the wordless desire burning in her heart expanded through her body, kindling hot and steady in her loins until it almost became too difficult to maneuver, the rubbing of her thighs too much of a distraction because of the way they compressed swollen tissue.

When she came face-to-face with him on the next embankment, she perched precariously on the edge. He studied her from the other side of a dry gully.

He could close the distance at any time. He'd proven it. He was letting her run, letting her know he was chasing only as an indulgence, knowing he would have her in the end. He somehow knew letting that thought sink in slowly and sinuously, like a lover's tongue teasing her folds, would affect her this way.

But he apparently realized she was ready for a change in the game. Or perhaps he was intending to change it regardless. Opening the shirt without care for the buttons, he yanked off the hiking shoes and stripped off his jeans to face her gloriously naked, one of the most potent weapons he could use against her. She couldn't take her eyes from him. All the rippling muscle, the hard and long cock stretching up toward his belly, the firm sac of his testicles. While she missed the thatch of hair that had been on his chest, the ability to touch the hard, smooth curves of him was tempting her fingertips. As her thighs trembled, his eyes registered it. He knew everything that was going through her mind, every reaction of her body.

He sprang, making it across the wide gully without a running leap. Just as his foot landed on the opposite side, she took flight again.

When she landed in the crotch of a live oak, she shrieked to find he'd used the mind link to anticipate where she would land. He was right above her. He dropped and seized her from behind, pinioning her wings against her, holding his wrist with a closed fist across her breasts, an effective lock. She could struggle but not gain a purchase with her taloned elbows.

His vampire strength was fully developed, and she might as well have been a child struggling against a parent. Or a human against a vampire . . . The sly whisper inserted itself in her mind.

You must have hated me, the way I reminded you of this, all the time.

"No, my lady. Sssh . . . calm down. Hush."

Her breath was sobbing in her throat, or perhaps she was just sobbing, weeping at the way it felt to have his arms around her. His warm bare body pressed behind her, his erection against her buttocks, fitting aggressively into the channel, making her want to rub herself up and down his length.

Brushing his knuckles along the firm gray skin of her cheek, he traced the outline of her prominent brow, the bone of the eye socket and curve of the pointed ear. She twisted her head. "I know how much you love my touch, my lady. Need it. Don't deny yourself the pleasure I can give you."

"You're not my servant anymore."

"I am always your servant. Your lover. Your mate. I want no other."

Trust me, my lady. Please don't run. I've wanted to touch you for so long as well. God, you don't know how much . . . I hated you for leaving me, but I would forgive you anything. Don't you know that?

She wanted to clutch at his wrists, but she would hurt him.

Do it. I've missed the way you like to draw my blood. The way you like to watch me react to the pain you inflict. Feel how hard I am, just from remembering it.

She gasped as he pressed against her back, lowering his hand to her abdomen, holding her there to feel his erection. She got wetter, her body slippery, begging for him. She couldn't hide her thoughts, any more than he'd been able to do when she'd given him the second mark. Every desire was his to tease and pluck, like the petals of a flower. His fingers descended, finding her. She arched up against him, crying out, the soft birdsong she made when aroused or distressed in this form.

"How I've dreamed of your cunt. I've had dreams that are all about it. Me fucking it, tasting it, putting my fingers deep into it, watching you do this . . ."

His voice was rich music in her ears as her body bucked. He held her so easily. Almost violently, he yanked her around, easily balancing them both on the oak's thick limb. Pulling her legs around him, latching his hands on her hips and staring into her eyes, he thrust into her, hard and deep, no foreplay, nothing but a rough, pleasurable claiming. A reconnection that had a cry wrenching from her throat. His eyes were priceless gems, mesmerizing, capturing her.

Her pussy spasmed on him as she wrapped her tail around one of his legs, the barbed tip digging into his thigh. She had her arms around him, spearing him with her hooked talons. She felt the raised abrasion of his third mark beneath her palms.

It didn't go away.

"No, my lady," he said hoarsely. "The powers that put it there know I am always yours, no matter what I am. *I told you the only safe thing to tattoo on the outside of a body is what's branded on the soul. This is branded on my soul and will never change. I am marked as yours forever.* "Mark me some more."

She hadn't talked in over six months, and so thinking was easier than speaking, but she wanted something from his lips.

"Please . . . call me . . ."

"Lyssa. My lady. Mine."

When he tightened his arms around her, held her close, she clung this time, just absorbing his scent, his strength. Her warrior, her knight. Her lover. Her servant. The man she loved.

In her Fey form, a climax could take minutes to be over, a pleasurable torment beyond description that took all control beyond the reach of the senses. As it swept over her with just the first few strokes of his cock inside her, she arched back, screaming, her talons ripping upward, tearing his flesh, muscle. She'd feared taking him in this form for just that reason. But she wasn't taking him. He was taking her.

He held on, his cock getting even harder inside her, thrusting, his arms pounding her down on him, over and over, making the climax even more intense. His head dipped, his mouth capturing her nipple. He bit, drawing her blood from that excruciatingly sensitive area as she'd once bitten him to give him the second mark. The thought as well as the sensation pushed her even higher. No matter how she fought him in the throes of ecstasy, he held her easily, his face fierce with his own desire, his cock spurting inside her, claiming her again.

I'm here, my lady. You're mine, as I'm yours. I don't want you ever to forget it. My Mistress. My slave. My lover. My mate. My lady. Mine.

With a sudden fierceness, he lifted her off him and turned her again, only this time he thrust his cock hard into her ass, collaring her, bringing her back against him and holding her still, making her suffer the ecstatic torment of shooting up the roller coaster again, taking as long as it needed, his hand coming forward to sink three fingers into her pussy as her heels hooked the outside of his knees, keeping herself open, wanting to take him deep.

And when we're done with this, I will come in your mouth, my lady. You will take me in every orifice, so I feel I've come home to you . . . marked you in every possible way. And I will eat your cunt until you come, and fuck you all over again, until you know you can never leave me, not for any reason . . .

He was still her knight, her samurai warrior, her vagabond. But now he was also vampire. The natural dominance, combined with the alpha nature he'd always carried, had blended in a way that made her feel helpless to resist him . . . and she didn't want to resist. She wanted to trust, to not worry, to believe she could love him and not have to give him up . . . that he could be hers, and she could be his . . .

Everything she'd wanted from Rex, but he'd been unable to give her. Jacob could now give her all of it.

Believe it, my lady. You are a queen, but for once, believe that you can have someone for your own . . . forever.

She came again, the sensation almost too much to bear as he spurted again as well, shifting his grip to hold her breasts in his palms, the nipples hard against his touch. He went for a while, thrusting even past the point when she was lying against him, exhausted. He pressed a hand to the side of her face, a gentle lover's touch. It should have seemed at odds with the fierceness of the past few moments, but it was all part of the same.

The emptiness was starting to fill. The hopeless wandering of the past few months, where she'd thought of nothing and didn't allow herself to want anything, proved itself a lie. She'd just numbed herself against the pain of being without him in the only way she knew how, short of dying. *Jacob. Jacob.*

He turned her face slowly, inexorably, away from him, pressing her cheekbone into the firm muscle of his shoulder. She went completely still as his thumb swept her delicate jaw.

When Jacob brought his lips down to her throat, the whirl of thoughts she was having were not intelligible, but her emotions were like a storm building in force. Loneliness, wonder, need, all keeping her still as if she knew he had in his touch the answer to all of those things.

Her thoughts made him close his eyes, overwhelmed. He sank his fangs into her bared throat, holding her. When he released the serums needed to give her all three marks, it was heaven. Heaven to feel her shudder with the knowledge of his claiming. There were no words for the feeling, this taking and marking of the woman he considered his heart, his life, his . . . and at the same time, giving her back herself.

Lyssa heard his thoughts, knowing they were interwoven with her own reaction as she allowed herself simply to be immersed in feeling, giving up thought with no regrets, no worries. Jacob was here. She knew something was wrong with it, that she should be sending him away to protect him, but here in this minute it felt as if she were the protected one . . . and she didn't have the strength to let that feeling go.

Jacob had placed the false fang back behind his real one as Brian had instructed. He'd done it on one of the last jumps, right before he'd caught her. Now as he pressed down, it sent the elixir Brian had crafted from the remains of her vial of blood into her system with the marking serum.

He had his face pressed against her throat, so he felt her stiffen, convulse in his arms. He held on, hoping Brian was as brilliant as Lyssa had believed him to be. The sharp bite of talons receded and abruptly there was the press of a woman's fingertips, the brush of her hair along his cheek. Reminding him of his first night with her when she'd curtained him with her hair.

No . . . no . . .

He had just a second to realize he should have warned her, prepared her for the transformation. The wildness that had been with her so many months took over, panic and animal flight reaction shutting down rational thought. The jumble of her thoughts gave him some startling images, which he had no time to digest as she shoved away from him and tumbled from the tree, rolling and getting to her feet to run naked across the forest floor, a primal thing reacting to him as if he were a threat.

Her disorientation boiled something up from the deepest level of her subconscious where she'd managed to bury the most important thing of all. The revelation stunned him, such that she managed to make it twenty steps before he caught her.

He held her when she struggled, but he didn't know what to say as he bore her to the forest floor and lay upon her. His body between her thighs, arms hard around her, face buried in her neck. His heart was fair choking him.

When he thought he couldn't bear her fighting him any longer, she broke into tears. *Afraid . . . missed you . . . needed you . . . love you.*

The words were magic, a chant in her mind. Her tears wouldn't stop even as he tried to catch every one of them with his lips.

I missed you so much . . . Her voice, so soft, no longer holding any defenses against him. *I died inside . . . I wanted to die, to just fade away. But you wouldn't let me.*

She laid her head back on the earth, and managed to move one of his hands between them, rest his palm on the slight round of her belly. Her eyes closed, and he felt the searing sweetness of her reaction reverberate through him. "You wouldn't let me."

Not only had she had to protect herself alone, she'd had to protect their child. He should have told Mason and Gideon to go to Hell and go after her. What was the world with a few less Girl Scouts, anyway?

"Oh, my lady. My sweet lady." He pressed his lips to her temple, held it there as it all washed over him. "How could you do it? You gave me everything."

"You were worth everything."

~

As the night waned, they sat by a creek, and he let her find her voice again. Find herself again. He managed to coax a smile out of her and had the bliss of holding her and their unborn baby in his lap. His family. He couldn't stop touching her, wanting her. It was easy to move her to straddle him, take them back up again until her cries shattered the forest's quiet.

When they lay twined together, he felt her worries that they would be hunted, that she would face losing him.

He rose to one elbow and pushed her to her back, leaning over her to cup her face, touch her lips.

"My lady, I swore an oath to protect you. Thanks to you, I now find myself tremendously gifted to do just that. There are some vampires who tried to track you, other than me." Before she could suffer a moment of worry, he pressed on. "I taught them the penalty for disloyalty to their queen."

"You've"—she wet her lips—"you've learned quickly to defend a territory."

"With great help from Mason. Even from Gideon. We had some squabbles." He smiled and it took her breath. That smile always had, from the first time she'd seen it flash from a knight's dusty and blood-streaked face. "He goaded me into putting his head into a wall when I hadn't quite mastered my temper. I had a terrible moment thinking I'd killed him. I'd forgotten there's little you can do to break a head made of solid rock. He stabbed me in the thigh with a poison arrow and covered me in boils for three very miserable days. No one would ever accuse Gideon of having a nurturing soul."

"And is Mr. Ingram all right?"

He was pleased to give her good news, and the warmth of it spread through her, reassuring her before he even voiced the thoughts. "Mr. Ingram is the majordomo of your estates now. Bran and his pack are entertaining his grandson regularly. Brian and his father spoke on your behalf before the Council," he added. "As well as Mason and some others. As a result, your properties remain in your name, and I am a fascinating scientific subject. Brian is actively courting my favor."

His voice teased her. She couldn't tease back, not yet.

"Mason spoke quite eloquently on your behalf. You *are* going to tell me what kind of friends you are one day."

She closed her eyes, overwhelmed by the knowledge of it all. "So . . ." She didn't dare hope, or believe, but as he coaxed her to look into his mind, she saw the truth there. "They won't be coming after us."

"No, my lady. There is just you and me. And there are several territories in which we will be welcomed. We can find a home, and you can be or do whatever you wish." He traced a hand down her throat, making her open her eyes again.

Her lower abdomen still quivered with the shock of having him here, of being in this form again. Physically and emotionally exhausted by their rough lovemaking, which she had yearned to experience for so long, she'd let her tears wash so much out of her soul she'd been carrying these many months. And while she was no longer vampire, only Fey, her mate was vampire. It was too much to digest in one night.

However, despite her postcoital exhaustion, an aroused growl rose in her throat again, inciting a matching red glint in his eyes. When he passed a hand over her rib cage, the lean flank as she quivered under his touch, his fingers played at her still slippery cunt. "You haven't been eating, my lady. I think we'll have to punish you for that, make you eager to claim life again." She shuddered.

Abruptly, however, he tightened his grip on her there, making her arch up at the aggressiveness of the hold. "There is nothing you can do to hurt me, my lady, except leave me," he said, his blue eyes intense, determined. "Don't tear a hole in my universe again. I need you to be with me. You're not alone anymore."

The words he'd said to her at the beginning. The words he imprinted on her soul as an eternal promise she'd never doubt again. This was the life that was theirs at last.

"The day I lost my parents," he said slowly, "Gideon and I were playing in the water, wrestling. We'd rolled out of the surf and into the wet sand. He was much bigger at the time, so he was trying to push my face in the sand and I was yelling at him. The sun was warm, and we weren't at school. You don't think of it consciously, but it was all perfect, all good. We were starting to get hungry and I was thinking of the sandwiches Mom had packed for us. Sometimes I think, well, if they had to leave, I'm glad it was then, when they were laughing, treading water, watching us, and we all were together as a family, feeling good about that."

Leaning closer, he brought his lips to hers, grazing her with his fangs to make her part her lips. The heat shimmered between them such that she felt mesmerized by his proximity, wanting to stay in that warm enclosure forever. Give him herself; take everything he was offering.

"If we ever are parted in such a terrible way," she said softly, "we'll make sure it's that way. On a very good day we can carry into eternity forever."

"We'll carry each other into eternity, my lady. I shall never leave you."

Epilogue

THERE were caverns she'd been using for refuge. At times, before she realized she was pregnant, she hadn't emerged for days until hunger and thirst and the cursed desire to live that overrode the pain in her heart had brought her forth.

She knew hearing that in her mind offended him anew. He made love to her often in those next few days, even waking during daylight hours to take her to the pinnacle of ecstasy, arousing not only her body, but resurrecting her heart and soul from the deep well in which she'd buried it. Soon she was responding with just as much desire. She shrugged off the dangerous lassitude of the past few months to embrace him fully.

While she could transform easily in and out of her winged form again, Brian had confirmed that her blood held enough humanoid properties to nourish Jacob as only a fully marked servant could. Full circle once again.

To rebuild strength, their games of cat and mouse became a nightly occurrence. As her endurance and agility improved, she explored the full range of both and tested his as well, as was her nature. As of yet, he hadn't failed to catch her, though she was able to lead him on some merry chases that sent him cursing into briar patches and into a comical tussle with a displeased bear one night. When he caught her, he took out his revenge in ways that were searingly sweet, ways that sometimes made her wonder if she'd died and this was the illusion of Heaven, the real Jacob somewhere on Earth without her. It didn't take long in their primal couplings for that thought to slide away in the face of erotic fires much too hot to be blazing among the clouds of Heaven.

When she was in her winged form for hunting, he finally got to see the pixies who often followed her. It amused him how they perched on her shoulders and completely ignored her. They'd sit, feet dangling, heels tattooing her breasts as they chatted with each other in their odd birdlike language. She ignored them as well as she went about her business, though she was always careful not to dislodge them.

"They're like spectators at the Elephant Man tent," she scoffed. "Gauche creatures." But Jacob sensed her affection for them. Since they were the only ones who had accepted her no matter her form, he always treated them as honored guests.

By day Lyssa hunted for herself, though he preferred her to wait. She knew at first he'd been reluctant to have her more than a few feet from him for obvious reasons, and she couldn't say she disagreed or wanted anything differently. But her prey was easier to find during the day. As the link between them strengthened in frequent use again, he could always find her once he woke, if she wasn't already back at the cave by then. Oddly enough, Lyssa thought she'd never been so happy and content in her life. A tranquility filled her that she'd never had before, a sense of completion so absolute there were times she just sat in the sun on a branch outside the caves and did nothing but absorb the treasures of sun and wind, the aromas of earth and the nearby creek waters, anticipating the evening with Jacob.

"What would you think about staying here for a while? Is it terrible for you?"

He sat with her on the edge of their favored embankment one night, she curled against his side, they watching the moon together.

"Anywhere with you is not terrible, my lady." He bent, brushed his lips over her ear. "'I went to the woods because I wished to live deliberately, to front only the essential facts of life, and see if I could not learn what it had to teach, and not, when I came to die, discover that I had not lived. I did not wish to live what was not life, living is so dear.'"

"Thoreau," she murmured, touched. "'I wanted to live deep and suck out all the marrow of life . . .'"

"Indeed," he said quietly, putting his lips to her throat.

Before she could arch back to give him better access for his dinner, he was on his feet, taking a defensive posture in front of her so quickly it amazed Lyssa. While she knew he had all of her abilities, it still took her by surprise, how formidable and dangerous he could be. He used his powers as a vampire with a skill that should have taken much longer to acquire. But then he'd been a warrior in every life, and he adapted any resource he had at his fingertips, particularly to protect her and their baby.

She stiffened when she saw it was the Fey lord. The one she'd seen several times before Jacob came, who'd discovered her while she was with the pixies. She'd sensed the threat of him, had been prepared to run as she'd had to do before, but he had merely moved on with his bow to do his hunting.

When she'd discerned the disdain in his expression, she'd summoned enough of herself to eye him just as scornfully. She'd dealt with vampires with an overinflated sense of themselves for too long to be intimidated by him, his ability to drive her out of his territory notwithstanding. A grudging smile had pulled at his lips at her reaction, and he'd surprised her with a nod before he disappeared into the wood.

Now he gave a slight bow, and extended his hand. "I have something for you."

It took Lyssa a moment to realize what he was offering. Aware of Jacob's still watchfulness, she took a couple of steps toward the Fey lord.

It was a rose bloom, which shimmered when he turned his long-fingered hand and carefully rolled it into her smaller one. The petals were fresh, soft, wet with dew.

"What you are holding is centuries old, preserved by old magic. As long as your love for your father lives, it will never dissolve."

She drew in a breath. "My father."

"It was plucked from the branches of his bush before the desert was allowed to turn him to dust. Those who felt the punishment to be too harsh wove the spell, with the intent of one day giving it to the daughter. Time passes fast or slow to the Fey folk, Lady Lyssa." The moonlit eyes gleamed. "It is all the same. A gift. You are welcome here, both of you, as long as you wish."

With a nod, he turned and vanished into the wood.

"Oh, Jacob . . ." She touched the petals with one finger.

"I think he recognizes a queen when he sees one." Jacob stroked her hair, gazed after the man. "I'd planned my own surprise for you tonight, but I think he just stole my thunder."

Lyssa turned her attention to him. "No, I want to see it. I can't have too many surprises in one night."

"Eager for gifts, are you? Just like a woman." He took off and let her chase him, staying just out of reach, letting himself be caught a couple of times to give him the opportunity to kiss, to bury his hands in her hair, to spin with her under a moonlit sky, where there were no Masters or Mistresses, just two souls too much in love to deny one another anything.

He came to a stop abruptly. "Stay right here, my lady."

He disappeared. Lyssa spun around, looking. She started as feathers brushed against her skin, and then she realized they weren't feathers, but small disks of silken white. She looked up in time to be baptized by a shower of them, floating down on her with the fragrant smell of cherry blossom petals. "You found a tree . . ."

"Every once in a long while, you find a volunteer sapling determined to survive the odds, even if it's not in its known environment." He smiled, joining her back on the ground now. "It's spring, my lady. Time for new beginnings."

She closed her eyes, leaning into the circle of his arms, feeling his palm over her stomach as he brought his lips to her throat, scraped her neck with his fangs, giving her a shiver of desire as the petals flowed down on her. As she cupped the rose bloom in her palm.

In the end it was a blessing.

My lady?

"I knew from the very beginning you wouldn't be able to accept your place as a human servant."

"My lady, I know my place. I've always known it." He drew her chin up so he could meet her gaze with an intent one of his own, a look that pulled her in and was like that swirling cloud of petals . . . a handsome man dancing with her . . . Heaven.

"My place is by your side. In front of you, behind you, wherever you most need me to be. That will always be my place, now and forever."

Look for Joey W. Hill's next book in November 2008

A Mermaid's Kiss

An enchanting, beautifully written romance
about a mermaid who doesn't believe in herself and
a heroic angel who believes in no one but her.

And don't miss the next book in the Vampire Queen
series coming Spring 2009.